THE BONE FIELD

Simon Kernick

B**THE**ONE
FIELD

CENTURY

1 3 5 7 9 10 8 6 4 2

Century
20 Vauxhall Bridge Road
London SW1V 2SA

Century is part of the Penguin Random House group of companies
whose addresses can be found at global.penguinrandomhouse.com.

Penguin
Random House
UK

First published in Great Britain by Century in 2017

www.penguin.co.uk

A CIP catalogue record for this book is available from the British Library.

ISBN 9781780894539 (Hardback)
ISBN 9781780894546 (Trade Paperback)

Set in 11.75/17.25 pt Times New Roman
Typeset by Jouve (UK), Milton Keynes
Printed and bound by Clays Ltd, St Ives plc

Penguin Random House is committed to a sustainable future
for our business, our readers and our planet. This book is made
from Forest Stewardship Council® certified paper.

MIX
Paper from
responsible sources
FSC
www.fsc.org   FSC® C018179

Day One
Tuesday

One

The whole thing started when a young man took his girlfriend of a few months on a trip to Thailand.

This was way back in 1990, in the days when Thailand was still in the process of being 'discovered' by backpackers, and mass tourism, with its big hotels, and stag and hen parties, and five-star yogic spas, was pretty much unheard of. The young man's name was Henry Forbes. He was twenty-five years old and a lecturer in Humanities (whatever that is) at Brighton Polytechnic, as the University of Brighton was called in those days. His girlfriend, who had just finished her last year at the same place, was called Katherine Sinn, but I remember from reading about the case at the time that everyone referred to her as Kitty.

Kitty Sinn. I always thought it was a nice name.

Anyway, the trip was to last two months, beginning just over a month after the end of Kitty's final exams. We know for a fact that they arrived in Bangkok on the afternoon of Sunday, 29 July 1990 because they were recorded entering the country by Thai immigration, and their passports were stamped. They stayed two nights in Bangkok before taking the overnight train down to the resort of Phuket, where they spent four days at the Club Med on Kata Beach. They were remembered by the staff as a polite, quiet couple who kept themselves to themselves and who seemed very much in love. From Phuket they took a taxi to the Khao Sok National Park, site of Thailand's oldest rainforest, a two-and-a-half-hour drive north, hoping to see some wildlife as well as the spectacular limestone karsts for which the area is famous. They stayed at what at the time was the park's only guesthouse, arriving there on Sunday, 5 August.

There were only four other guests there that night: an Australian couple in their sixties and two young Dutch backpackers. All the guests remembered Kitty and Henry having dinner in the restaurant before retiring to their bedroom, where later that night they had a blazing row that was so loud that the guesthouse owner, a local man called Mr Watanna, had to intervene and threaten them with eviction if they didn't quieten down. According to Henry's later statement, the row had been over a former girlfriend of his and had got out of control, culminating in him slapping Kitty, something he claimed was totally out of character.

The following morning the row clearly hadn't been resolved because Kitty asked Mr Watanna to drive her to the coastal town of Khao Lak, offering him five hundred baht in payment as long as he didn't tell Henry where she was going. She said she needed time to think. Henry tried to stop her leaving, apologizing profusely, at one point getting down on his knees and literally begging her to stay. But, by all accounts, Kitty was adamant and she left with Mr Watanna.

According to Mr Watanna, he dropped her off outside the Gerd and Noi Bungalows near the main beach at Khao Lak, where she intended to get a couple of nights' accommodation while she pondered her next move. He then drove straight back to the guesthouse, arriving approximately four hours after he'd left.

For the next three days, Henry remained at the guesthouse, hardly venturing outside his room as he waited for Kitty to return. These were the days before mobile phones and the internet, so when someone was out of contact, they were definitely out of contact. When she didn't come back, Henry persuaded Mr Watanna to tell him where he'd taken her.

Henry then called the Gerd and Noi Bungalows, only to be told Kitty hadn't been staying there. Worried now, he paid Mr Watanna to take him to Khao Lak, and spent the day searching the town and its handful of hostelries for Kitty, which was when he discovered that she hadn't been staying anywhere else round there either. Finally he called Kitty's mother but she hadn't seen or heard anything from her daughter. That was when Henry contacted the Thai police to officially report her missing, while her mother contacted the police in England.

An alert was put out to police stations across the southern Thai peninsula to look out for her, but still she didn't show up.

Kitty was a very pretty girl, petite and dark, with a sweet, almost childlike face. According to both staff and students at the poly she was a lovely person who even volunteered for the Samaritans in her spare time, and she came from a wealthy, respectable family. In other words, she was a newspaper's dream, and her disappearance in what was then considered an exotic and far-flung country where a lot of British youngsters were heading attracted a huge amount of media attention both in the UK and beyond.

Suspicion quickly fell on Mr Watanna who was the last person known to have seen Kitty alive. He was arrested and interrogated by Thai police. There were even claims by his lawyer that he'd been beaten and tortured. The police were under huge diplomatic and media pressure to get a result and doubtless they in turn put pressure on Mr Watanna, who was held in custody without charge for more than two weeks. But with nothing linking him to any foul play, and no sign of a body, he was eventually released.

Finally, with Kitty missing close to a month without any confirmed sightings, and having been interrogated several times himself by the Thai authorities, Henry returned home, where he was questioned at length by officers from Sussex CID. But, because of the circumstances of the disappearance, he was never considered a real suspect. He took an extended leave of absence from the poly citing emotional stress, and didn't return to his job until the following year.

In the meantime the investigation had steadily faded into the background as other stories muscled their way on to the news pages, and there were no new confirmed sightings. People just lost interest. But the mystery element remained – the fact that no trace of Kitty was ever found, nor any record of her leaving Thailand. It was as if she'd disappeared into thin air. Many people – and I have to admit I count myself among their number – assumed that Mr Watanna was responsible. He may have been happily married with no criminal record, and there may have been no evidence linking him to the murder, nor any changes in behaviour to suggest he might be carrying the emotional burden of having killed someone, but even so, he was the most obvious culprit. He died in 1997, at the comparatively young age of forty-six, having never managed to rid himself of the black cloak of suspicion. If he'd had any knowledge of what actually happened to Kitty, he took it with him to the grave.

And so life moved on and, I'll be honest, I hadn't read, heard or even thought anything about the strange disappearance of Katherine 'Kitty' Sinn for years until, more than a quarter of a century after she went missing, I got a phone call out of the blue from a lawyer called Maurice Reedman saying he represented *the* Henry Forbes – his emphasis, not mine – and telling me that he had information that might be of interest to the police.

And so here we were in the dining room of Reedman's grand period house just outside London, Henry and him on one side of a big wooden table, me alone on the other.

Henry Forbes had the look of a man weighed down by the world. His face was pale and sagging round the edges, the lines deep and unforgiving, the black hair I remembered from those old photographs now grey and thinning. He looked every inch his fifty-one years. His eyes were narrow and suspicious, and a thin sheen of sweat clung to his forehead. He also couldn't seem to sit still. Reedman, on the other hand, must have been at the wrong end of his sixties, and looked every inch the plump, well-fed lawyer with his expensive three-piece pinstripe suit, its waistcoat straining against his ample girth, and small, perfectly manicured hands. His grey hair was thick and lustrous. All told, he was far too dapper for a man called Maurice.

I kicked off proceedings. 'You asked to see me, Mr Forbes?'

'I did. I've read about you, DS Mason, and I trust you. So does Mr Reedman.'

I didn't say anything. It was 8.30 p.m. and I hadn't eaten.

Henry sighed. 'What I've got to say . . .' He paused, placing his hands on the table and staring down at them. One finger began to drum a nervous beat on the wood. 'I have a secret.' He glanced at his lawyer, who nodded. 'It concerns a possible murder.'

I opened my notebook. 'Well, you'd better tell me then.'

It was the lawyer, Reedman, who spoke next. 'I asked for this meeting in my home because I'd like it to be off the record. Now I'm aware that this is an unusual request but hear me out. I've spoken at length to my client and I firmly believe he has information that will be of great relevance to you. However, his information will incriminate a number of very powerful individuals, and may, to a lesser extent, incriminate himself. So, in essence, he's not willing to make an official statement until he and I have assurances that he will receive the full protection of the law, including a new identity, and immunity from prosecution.'

'You know as well as I do that I can't offer immunity from prosecution, Mr Reedman,' I told him.

'Exactly. Which is why I want this conversation off the record. Then you can go back to your superiors, tell them what we tell you, and they can decide whether they want to help my client. If they don't, he will say nothing and there will, I promise you, be nothing you can do about it.'

I frowned, not liking the threat in Reedman's tone but curious about what Henry Forbes knew.

'I explained to you on the phone earlier about who my client is, didn't I?' continued Reedman. 'He was Katherine Sinn's boyfriend, the man who reported her missing in Thailand in 1990.'

'And is this about Kitty Sinn's disappearance?'

'Is this off the record?'

'Effectively this conversation's off the record anyway, you know that. We're not in a police station, and your client's not under caution, so nothing said here is admissible in a court of law.'

'Can I ask you not to take notes?'

I sighed and closed the notebook. 'OK, but as long as we get to the point of this meeting. I'm hungry.'

Reedman sat back in his chair, putting his manicured hands together and steepling his fingers. 'This meeting is about Katherine Sinn, yes. As you may or may not be aware, unidentified human remains have been dug up in the grounds of a private school in Buckinghamshire.'

I'd seen something on the news about the story the previous week. The school, running low on funds, had sold a parcel of land to developers to build houses on, and when the first bulldozers had broken ground they'd turned up human bones belonging to a young woman. It was currently Thames Valley's case and, as far as I was aware, they hadn't ID'd the woman yet, or released details about how or when she'd died.

'My client believes those bones belong to Katherine Sinn,' said Reedman.

This, as you can imagine, was something of a shock to hear, since the last time she was seen – and it seemed from the records that there'd been a number of witnesses who'd seen her – Kitty had been more than six thousand miles away from Buckinghamshire.

I looked at Henry. 'Is that right, Mr Forbes? Are they Kitty's bones?'

Henry swallowed, his Adam's apple bobbing up and down. 'Yes,' he said. 'It's her.'

'So how did she get there?'

'She was murdered.'

'By you?'

'I want immunity before I say anything else.'

'I told you, I can't offer immunity for murder. If you were responsible, it's in your best interests to tell me now.'

'I didn't kill her. I promise. I'm not a killer.'

He took a deep breath, a thin bead of sweat running down his forehead, and Reedman cut in. 'But my client is in a position to identify the individuals who did kill Ms Sinn.'

Henry looked at me. 'These are very powerful people. They have friends. They can get to me. And they would kill me if they knew I was here talking to you. I need immunity, a new identity. Protection for the rest of my life. If I get that then I'll give you something huge, I swear it.'

'That's why we need to make a deal that suits everyone,' said Reedman.

Henry seemed genuinely terrified, but then in my experience a lot of people scare easily, particularly when they know they're in trouble. At the time I doubted the powerful people he was talking about were really all that powerful, or capable of doing Henry any harm.

Which turned out to be a very big mistake on my part.

'It doesn't work like that,' I said. 'We need to know what Mr Forbes knows before we even start talking about deals.'

'I'm afraid not, DS Mason,' said Reedman, putting a hand on Henry's arm – a clear gesture for him to stop talking.

I kept looking at Henry. 'I could arrest you right now for obstruction of justice.'

Reedman shook his head decisively. 'On what grounds exactly? You agreed to have this conversation entirely off the record. Now, you have some bones that will inevitably turn out to belong to Katherine Sinn, but that's all you'll have. It won't actually change a thing regarding my client. At the time of Katherine's disappearance there were a number of witnesses who said that he couldn't have killed her. His story has always held up under the scrutiny of both the Thai and the British authorities, and will continue to hold up. There will be no evidence connecting him with the bones. And, after twenty-six years, almost no chance that there will be any evidence connecting anyone else to them either. You'll be at square one, and that's where you'll remain. Unless . . .' He held up a finger and eyed me closely. 'Unless you can make a deal that will protect my client, allow him to be treated leniently by the courts, and give him a completely new identity under the witness protection programme. Then he will tell you all he knows. Now, we need to move fast on this, DS Mason. I strongly believe that Mr Forbes is in real danger. So, please, why don't you call your boss and see what he, or indeed she, has to say?'

'Give me something I can use,' I countered. 'Something that will make it easier to sell a deal.'

'This deal sells itself,' said Reedman firmly.

'It doesn't,' I said.

Henry stood up, walked to the window and took a couple of deep breaths, then walked back. 'I think there'll be another body buried in the same place as Kitty,' he said. 'There may even be more than one.'

'Henry,' snapped Reedman, 'sit down and stop talking now.'

'I know they'd killed before Kitty and it wouldn't surprise me if they'd carried on killing afterwards.'

'Henry!' Reedman shouted.

I glared at Henry, tempted to reach over the table and wring the truth out of him. 'How the hell do you know that? Because this isn't some little game. We're talking about murder victims. If you know something and you don't tell us, we will dig up every last aspect of your past and we will find out what you did, and you'll be locked up for a very, very long time.'

Henry looked like he was about to burst into tears. 'I didn't kill anyone, I swear it.'

Reedman reached across and pulled his client back down into his chair. 'Just make the call, DS Mason,' he said. 'Please.'

I got up, wondering what I was getting into here. 'I'll be five minutes,' I said, and went out through the front door, leaving it on the latch.

The night was chilly – it was still only mid-April – and clear. Reedman's large detached home was set in a narrow stretch of greenbelt land just inside the M25 between RAF Northolt and Gerrards Cross, with fields to the back and front of the property. You could hear the drone of the traffic on the M25 and the stars were obscured by the wall of light to the east, but there was still something comfortably rural about the place. The house itself was set in about an acre of grounds with a long driveway leading down to wrought-iron gates, and was probably worth the best part of £3 million. But then you rarely come across a poor lawyer.

I walked slowly round the side of the house and pulled out my phone, dialling my boss at Homicide and Serious Crime Command, DCI Eddie Olafsson, or Olaf as he was universally known behind his back. For the last six months I'd been working for one of the Metropolitan Police's Murder Investigation Teams, based out of Ealing, having moved across from Counter Terrorism Command where I'd spent much of the previous fifteen years. Things had ended badly for me in CT and I'd been suspended for close to four months before finally being given a second chance as a detective sergeant in Olaf's team, having been told in no uncertain terms that he was one of the very few DCIs who'd have me. When I'd told Olaf earlier about Reedman's call asking me to meet up with him and Henry Forbes, he hadn't been keen for me to go, given that we already had a big enough caseload, but he'd agreed because he was old enough to remember the Kitty Sinn case.

As luck would have it our team were on twenty-four-hour

callout all week so I wasn't disturbing Olaf on a night of galli-vanting, and he answered on the third ring.

'So, did Henry Forbes have anything interesting to say?' he asked me.

I told him that he had claimed the remains found in the school in Buckinghamshire the previous week were Kitty Sinn's, and that he could name several people involved in her murder. 'And there's something else too. He says there may be other bodies in there.'

'Are you sure he's not yanking your chain, Ray?' boomed Olaf, who had a very loud voice.

'No. He's telling the truth. And he's scared too. He says the people responsible will kill him.'

'And he didn't give you any details about how Kitty Sinn got all the way back from Thailand without being spotted, even though her face was all over the papers, and ended up buried in the grounds of a boarding school?'

'No, nothing. His lawyer's keeping him on a tight leash. He doesn't want Forbes to say anything until he's got him round-the-clock protection and a new identity, plus a deal which means he won't serve any prison time for perverting the course of justice or anything like that. But the thing is, he must have been heavily involved in her murder otherwise there's no way he'd know where she was buried.'

Olaf made a low growling sound that I'd learned was his version of a sigh. He was a man who could do nothing quietly. 'That's what I'm thinking too,' he said. 'Well, the good thing is, it's not our problem. It belongs to Thames Valley. I know the SIO running the case. I'll give him a call now and tell him what you've just told me, and they can take it from there.'

'Aren't you intrigued as to what happened to Kitty Sinn?'

'Sure I am. But not so much that I want it added to our case-load. I'd rather read about it in the Sunday papers.'

I was about to ask how best to handle the immunity issue when I heard Maurice Reedman's front gates open with a loud metallic whine. A black 4×4 drove through them, moving very slowly, with its headlights off.

Straight away my alarm bells rang. You only drive like that when you don't want to be heard or seen.

I was a good thirty yards away, round the side of the house, so I stepped into the shadow of an apple tree and watched as the car, a BMW X5, made its way down the driveway. The rear windows were blacked out but there were two men in the front. I couldn't make out their faces from where I was standing. Then I realized they were wearing ski masks.

'Oh shit,' I hissed into the phone. 'I think we may have a problem. Unidentified car just drove in with no headlights and men with ski masks inside. Can you send backup straight away. And make sure it's armed.' I rattled off Reedman's address.

'Don't do anything stupid, Ray,' said Olaf, still booming. 'Help's on the way.'

I ended the call and flicked the phone on to silent, knowing I had to act fast. As the car pulled up in front of the house, I ran out from behind the apple tree, keeping close to the hedge at the rear of the property so I was out of sight, making for the conservatory doors. I had maybe thirty seconds to get Forbes and his lawyer out the back before the men in the ski masks came through the front. The rear garden was only about fifteen yards long and ended at a low back fence with open fields beyond. It was a possible escape route.

My heart was beating hard as I reached the conservatory doors. I heard the BMW doors closing round the front of the house and remembered that I'd left the front door on the latch. These guys, whoever they were, could just walk in.

I slipped inside, moving fast through the conservatory and the kitchen, not wanting to shout out in case the men in ski masks heard me. As I emerged into the hallway, I could hear Henry Forbes and Maurice Reedman talking animatedly. It sounded like they were arguing but I couldn't hear what was being said.

And then, when I was only a few yards away from the dining room, I heard the front door handle being turned.

I darted into the nearest room as the door opened, knowing I was too late. I could still hear Henry and his lawyer talking, seemingly oblivious to what was about to happen.

I cursed the fact that I was unarmed. For two years after an earlier attempt on my life I'd been one of the few police officers in the UK authorized to carry a firearm at all times, but this right had been taken away from me after my last major case for CT. Now all I had was my warrant card and some stern words, and somehow I didn't think that was going to do either me or anyone else much good right now.

I heard footsteps coming down the hallway, only a few yards away from where I was hiding. The room I'd darted into looked like a library with bookshelves lining two of the walls, and aside from a heavy glass ashtray on a coffee table next to a reading chair there was nothing I could use as a weapon. I stayed still, barely a foot from the door, prepared to ambush anyone who came through it, knowing there was really no more I could do.

I could hear the intruders talking in hushed tones out in the hallway, their voices barely a mumble.

Then I heard the dining-room door open and cries of shock and surprise coming from Henry and Reedman.

'Hands in the air, now!' yelled a voice.

Loud. North London accent. Potentially an IC3. I slipped the phone from my pocket, opened up the microphone app, and pressed record.

Very slowly, I put my head round the door. My view of the dining room was partly obscured by the staircase banister, but I could just about make out part of a masked man through the thin crack in the doorway. Muffled voices came from inside and questions were being barked by the gunman I'd just heard speak. His voice was deep and resonant and I was pretty certain I'd recognize it again, but I was too far away to hear what he, or anyone else, was saying.

I needed to get closer if I was going to record them, but I knew I'd be an obvious target if I came out into the hallway, especially with the front door wide open. There might be other gunmen outside, although I was probably a target in here too. For all I knew, either Reedman or Henry might have already told them I was here.

I felt a powerful urge to run back the way I'd just come, leap the fence, and wait in the adjoining field for reinforcements to arrive, but I stopped myself. It felt like the coward's way out and, whatever else my faults, I'm no coward.

I took a step into the hallway and held the phone at arm's length, hoping to pick up the gunmen's voices.

For a few seconds, I didn't move.

And then two shots rang out, loud in the confines of the dining room, and Reedman cried out in pain.

I knew it was him because the next second I heard Henry crying and begging for mercy, his voice becoming increasingly hysterical. My whole body tensed. They were going to kill him too. I've been a police officer a long time. Before that, I was a soldier. I'm used to standing up for the little guy. And now I was going to have to stand by while a man with a secret over a quarter of a century old took it to the grave with him.

The gunman who was giving the orders yelled at Henry to shut up, and he immediately did. There was a long pause, then I heard more muffled talking.

I took another step into the hallway.

The first gunman said something to Henry. It sounded like 'last chance to live' but I couldn't be sure. And then he said something else too, but his voice was quieter now and I couldn't make out any of it.

Henry stammered something in reply, which turned into a pleading wail at the end, and I knew that this was it, he was about to die, and that he knew it too. He started to speak again but his words were cut off by another three gunshots, a double tap followed a couple of seconds later by the coup de grâce.

It was over.

And that was when I heard it. The first haunting wail of a siren in the far distance.

I could hear the two killers moving about in the dining room and it occurred to me that I should try to tackle them as they left the room. It was possible I could get hold of one of the weapons. I've been in firefights before and come out on top. But self-preservation stopped me. It was too risky.

And yet I was tempted. God, I was tempted. To hit the first of those cowardly bastards as he left the room, give him a taste of his own medicine.

I heard the whump of a fire starting within the dining room, and almost immediately smelled smoke.

The siren was getting louder now, and it had been joined by a second. The idiots were going to get themselves caught without my help if they hung around much longer.

'Go, go, go!' I heard the main gunman shout as smoke began to billow out of the room.

I retreated a couple of steps and was just about to dart back behind the library door when a third man in a mask appeared on the front doorstep, only a few yards away from me.

'Oi!' he yelled, just as a man with a shotgun came running out of the dining room.

Adrenalin burst through me as I ran back inside the library, having the presence of mind to shove the phone in my pocket. I heard the one on the doorstep tell the other gunmen where I was and to hurry up, that the cops were coming. They were in a rush now. I had to hope they'd make mistakes.

I grabbed the ashtray from the table and swung round as the

guy with the shotgun appeared in the doorway. I threw the ashtray straight at his head and dived out of the way as he pulled the trigger.

The ashtray hit him in the face and he stumbled backwards, putting a hand up to his nose and giving me a split second to charge him. I grabbed the shotgun with both hands, shoving it to one side as he pulled the trigger a second time, sending shock-waves up my arms. At the same time I drove my body into him, sending us both crashing out of the door and into the side of the staircase. I tried to headbutt him but he moved his head to one side, and I caught a glimpse of a thin white scar at the base of his neck running towards the collarbone. His skin was golden brown – mixed race or Asian – but I hardly computed this fact as I tried to stop him from tripping me up.

Out of the corner of my eye I could see a taller gunman, the one who'd been questioning Reedman and Henry, pointing a semi-automatic pistol at me, but it was clear he couldn't get a good shot in without risking hitting his friend, and I was hanging on to the shotgun like grim death. I think the third gunman was shouting something but I'd been temporarily deafened by the shotgun blast so I had no idea what it was.

My assailant was strong and wiry and he gave me a hard shove, sending us both stumbling back into the library. I hit the book-shelves with a bang and a couple of books fell on my head. He shoved the length of the barrel against my neck, using it to throt-tle me. It felt burning hot from the discharge of shot but I ignored the pain, lashing out wildly, knowing I was fighting for my life.

I managed to push him back and we struggled wildly in the

middle of the floor. The shotgun went off again and this time the force of the discharge knocked me backwards. One hand slipped from the weapon, and the next second my assailant had slammed the stock against my jaw.

This time I lost my grip entirely and fell to the floor, hitting the shelves en route.

I lay on my back, looking up.

The gunman in the ski mask looked back down at me. I noticed then that his jacket had ridden up above the gloved hand revealing the edge of a black, sleeve-like tattoo on his left forearm. I didn't really look at it though. I was too busy looking at him. He stared back down at me, breathing heavily, his eyes very big, very dark and very cold. The end of the barrel was only a few feet from my face.

I was filled with a leaden feeling of resignation. Death has never been too far away from me, right from my earliest days, so it came as only the smallest of surprises that it had come for me now.

He smiled beneath the ski mask and pulled the trigger.

Nothing happened.

He looked momentarily confused, and for a second neither of us moved. Then my survival instinct and training kicked back in. Using my hands to push myself up, I lashed out with my foot, kicking him in the shin, and tried to scramble to my feet.

This time he wasn't hanging about. He kicked me in the gut, sending me sprawling again, then turned and ran out of the door.

The smell of smoke was getting stronger. It reminded me of a time long ago when I'd been trapped in a house fire, and the terror I'd felt then. I had to get out.

Feeling battered and bruised, I got to my feet and stumbled

out into the hallway, the buzzing in my ears beginning to subside enough that I could hear more sirens, closer now.

The front door was wide open, and as I watched, the black BMW made a rapid three-point turn on the front lawn before roaring off up the driveway and out of view.

I felt a desperate urge to run straight out into the fresh air but the need to gather evidence, or at least preserve it, stopped me and instead I ran back into the dining room, pulling up my shirt to shield my face from the worst of the acrid black smoke.

Maurice Reedman was propped up against a glass cabinet on the other side of the table, his eyes closed. He'd been shot twice in the face. Henry Forbes was lying on his back on the floor on the opposite side of the table to where he'd been sitting earlier. His upper torso was on fire where accelerant had been poured over him, yet there was no fire anywhere else in the room, meaning he'd been targeted specifically. The flames were already beginning to die down – the human body doesn't burn especially well and it was clear that Henry's assassins hadn't used much fuel – so I ran into the downstairs toilet, grabbed the hand towel and placed it under the cold tap. When it was wet enough, I went back in and threw it over Henry's upper body, crouching down and using my hands to pat out the fire, conscious that there was a slight chance he was still alive.

But as the fire died and I felt for a pulse, there was nothing. Henry's blackened face was expressionless and his eyes were closed. There was a hole in his forehead, and two more in his chest. He was gone.

And so was his secret.

Wrinkling my nose against the stench of burned flesh, I stood back up and looked down at his corpse. It seemed the fire had been concentrated on the right side of his upper body. His shirt was partially burned away and the skin beneath was charred and blistered, but something caught my eye. It was a marking on the underside of his upper arm that appeared to be part of a tattoo. Half of it had been burned away, but I could see that at one point it had been a black star-like shape, with three curved lines inside it.

Two things immediately struck me as a little odd. One, the tattoo was in a place on his arm where it would almost certainly never have been seen, even by him. And two, he just hadn't seemed like the kind of guy who'd have tattoos.

I pulled out my phone and crouched down to take a quick photo of it before getting back to my feet and walking out of there, needing to get away from the sight and smell of the bodies.

Which was when I heard frantic shouts of 'Armed police!' coming from the doorstep.

The cavalry might have arrived but, not for the first time in history, they were a few minutes too late.

Two

Half an hour later I was sitting on the bonnet of my car in Maurice Reedman's driveway when Olaf pulled up in his Audi estate, parked on the lawn, and got out, looking pissed off.

The place was already crawling with uniformed cops and ambulance crew and Olaf moved among them, his phone to his ear, barking out orders and trying to bring some order to the situation with his own unique brand of charm.

After a few minutes of letting everyone know who was boss, and organizing a perimeter, he spotted me and marched over, shoving the phone in the pocket of his coat.

Olaf claimed to be descended from Viking stock on his father's side, but to be honest, he didn't look much like a Viking. He was a short, burly guy, completely bald, with hairy ears and a head that was almost a perfect square. He looked like a retired wrestler. At one time he'd been very fat, thanks to his dietary regime of booze and crap food, coupled with long hours at a desk and no exercise, but after breaking a chair by sitting on it during a meeting with the commissioner at Scotland Yard he'd lost four stone, and any mention of the chair-breaking incident, in jest or otherwise, was strictly forbidden in his presence.

I liked Olaf. He was a street cop through and through and had cut his teeth in the Flying Squad, the Met's armed robbery division, where he'd developed his taste for pies, beer, colourful language, and strong-arming suspects. With thirty-two years' service, and seemingly no desire to retire, he was one of the last of a dying breed of old-school coppers. He even wore a sheepskin jacket that looked older than he did.

'What the fuck happened?' he demanded, stopping in front of me. 'Can't you go anywhere without someone getting killed?'

I gave him the kind of look that told him I wasn't interested in banter, and he met it with a smile. Olaf didn't smile that much but when he did, he meant it.

'Seriously,' he said. 'How are you?'

'I've been better,' I told him, dabbing a wet handkerchief against my jaw where the gunman I'd grappled with had hit me with the shotgun stock. It hurt like hell but I didn't think there was anything broken.

'What happened in there?'

'When I got back in the house after talking to you, the gunmen were already inside. I hid while they killed Forbes and his lawyer. I didn't intervene.' I had a feeling this was going to bother me for a long time.

'Well you managed to have a fight with one of them.'

'Only because I was spotted trying to record what was happening on my phone.'

'Did you get anything?'

I shook my head. 'Nothing useful. I was too far away.'

He looked disappointed. 'That's a pity. Did you get much of a look at the one you were fighting with?'

'I think he was mixed race, possibly Asian. He had a scar on his neck here. And a sleeve tattoo on his left forearm.'

Olaf nodded. 'That's a good start, Ray. It's going to help.'

'This was a targeted, professional hit, boss. They were a three-man team. A driver and two gunmen, in a black BMW X5. The security gates were closed when I went outside, and I'm certain they weren't let in, so they must have opened the gates themselves. They knew exactly who they were looking for and where they were going. They walked straight into the dining room where Henry Forbes and his lawyer were. They questioned both men. It had to be about the Kitty Sinn case.'

Olaf looked over towards the house, a thoughtful expression on his face, then back at me. 'You said Henry Forbes told you there might be more bodies buried alongside the one they dug up last week in Buckinghamshire.'

'That's right. It was pretty much the last thing he said to me. I don't know if he was talking out of his arse or not.'

'He wasn't. I've just spoken to the SIO over at Thames Valley to let him know that his body might be Kitty Sinn's.' He sighed. 'It turns out they dug up more remains this afternoon. They think they're of a teenage girl, but no ID as yet.'

I shook my head, thinking how close I'd been to finding out what had happened to Kitty, and now to this other girl. 'Oh shit.'

'There's more. They've found a clear mark on one of the neck vertebrae that indicates the girl's throat was violently cut. Whoever we're dealing with here is one sick bastard.' He put a hand on my shoulder. 'You did a good job, Ray, and we'll use what you've learned to find these people.'

With that he turned and walked into the house, leaving me sitting there with the whiff of failure hanging over my head like a noxious cloud.

Three

Charlotte Curtis lay in her bath wondering if she was finally getting over the death of her husband.

Theirs had been a happy marriage. They'd never wanted children which, because she was a school teacher, was considered ironic by some people, including members of her own family. But Charlotte had always got her fill of children through teaching and had never been particularly maternal. This meant that she and Jacques had concentrated all their love on each other. They'd formed a bond that had seemed unbreakable, and certainly neither of them would have broken it themselves; but fate, as cold and emotionless as ever, had had other ideas. In 2011, at the age of only forty-four, Jacques had been diagnosed with cancer of the oesophagus. The prognosis was poor, and within six months it had spread to his stomach and lungs. After that he'd gone downhill fast, almost as if he was willing himself to reach the end – Jacques was too proud a man to let himself wither away to nothing – and he'd died on a cold January day in 2012 in a local hospice with Charlotte holding him in her arms.

That had been four years, three months and ten days ago now, and not a day had gone by when she hadn't thought of him. At first she'd wanted to die herself, the pain had been that terrible, but gradually, step by tiny step, and with the help of friends, she'd emerged from the blackness, and the pain had slowly eased to a dull, constant ache. It had only been in the past year that she'd finally felt she could live again, and three months earlier she'd actually met someone. Lucien was ten years younger, rakishly handsome, totally inappropriate, and exactly what she needed. She knew it wouldn't last, and wasn't even sure she wanted it to. But his presence had made her feel like a woman again, and for that she was thankful.

She submerged her head in the hot water thinking that Jacques would probably have liked Lucien, and she knew he'd be pleased that she'd found someone. When he knew that he was dying, that there was absolutely no way back, Jacques had taken her hand, looked her in the eyes and told her with the utmost seriousness that he would never forgive her if she allowed her mourning for him to get in the way of her life. 'The greatest gift you can give me is to live again,' he'd said. 'To find a man who will love you like I do, and to love him just the same.'

Thinking about those words now, Charlotte felt herself welling up again. Jesus. Over four years and he can still do that to me. She sat up in the bath, took a deep breath – and something caught her eye.

One of the spotlights in the ceiling didn't look quite right. She frowned, wondering if she was imagining it. But she wasn't. The spotlight in the far corner of the bathroom had a tiny black hole on the edge of its metal attachment that Charlotte was sure hadn't been there before. She was observant like that. She hoped it wasn't some kind of rot in the ceiling. She'd always been awful with DIY, relying first on Jacques and then on various handymen to maintain her house. She wasn't exactly flush with cash either, so if it was serious, she was in trouble.

For a few seconds she stared at the offending spotlight, reluctant to get out of the bath and take a closer look. The water was warm and soothing, while the air in the bathroom had a distinct chill to it. Eventually, though, she relented and, wrapping herself in a towel, she grabbed a chair from the bedroom and placed it under the light. She was only five feet four and the ceilings in the house were high, so she had to stand on her tiptoes and stretch towards it. Placing one hand on the ceiling to balance herself, she squinted against the light's brightness, her face only a foot from the offending hole, which couldn't have been more than half a centimetre across.

And that was when she saw that the hole was perfectly round, as if it had been created by a drill, and that it had a tiny, barely noticeable lens poking out of it at a forty-five-degree angle. The lens's casing was white, making it difficult to pick out against the colour of the ceiling.

At first she was simply confused by what she was looking at, and it took a couple of seconds for her brain to tell her that this was a hidden camera, and that it had been positioned at a perfect angle to watch her while she was in the bath.

Charlotte felt her skin crawl and she began to shake as the full ramifications of what she'd just discovered came home to her. Someone had come into her home – the home she'd loved since the day she and Jacques had first driven up to it eighteen years ago, the home they'd turned from an old wreck of a barn into a beautiful three-bedroom family home through years of hard work and dedication . . . someone had come in here, drilled a hole in the ceiling and was spying on her while she was naked and vulnerable. Charlotte loved her baths. They were her nightly ritual. A time for relaxation and reflection. Now that time, so precious these past few years, had been utterly defiled. God, for all she knew someone could even be watching her now.

With an angry grunt, she grabbed the camera casing between her thumbnail and forefinger and tugged hard. The casing came loose with a crack, dislodging plaster dust, then came free altogether as she pulled again, leaving behind a hole in the ceiling the size of a penny. She moved her finger round inside the hole but there was nothing else in there.

Charlotte got down off the chair and inspected the camera. There were no wires attached, but that wasn't necessarily a surprise. Everything was wireless these days. She didn't know a thing about spy cameras but this piece of kit looked expensive.

Which begged a nasty question. Who had put it there?

She hadn't been burgled, and no workmen had been inside the house for months, so her first thought was that it must have been Lucien. After all, she didn't know him that well, and he wasn't friends with anyone she knew. He lived thirty kilometres away in Villeneuves, and they'd met online, so it was possible he was some kind of pervert, and he was just good at hiding it. But she quickly dismissed the theory. Lucien might have been handsome and macho but he was as cackhanded at DIY as she was. Also, he'd never been unattended in the house long enough to install it, and it wasn't as if he needed to see her naked either. He'd done so plenty of times.

Then who was it?

And that was the thing. There was no obvious answer to that question. Charlotte was a normal, popular woman, respected by both the locals and the ex-pat community for her work at the local school who, as far as she knew, had no enemies, and who'd lived unmolested and unthreatened in this house for eighteen years.

But someone was watching her, and his handiwork was recent. The camera hadn't been there a week ago, she was sure of it. It might not even have been there yesterday.

The bathroom felt tainted so she dried herself quickly in the bedroom and flung on a gown and slippers. It struck her that the person who'd planted the camera might actually still be in the house. It was highly unlikely, of course, but she wasn't going to take any chances. Conscious of the silence, she went downstairs to the kitchen and pulled a carving knife from the knife rack. Kado, her little black Affenpinscher, was resting in his basket. He raised his head when he heard her then slipped back into sleep. He was far too small to be a guard dog but Charlotte knew that he'd have made a serious fuss if a stranger had come into the house. The problem was, out here, a mile and a half from the nearest village and a hundred metres at least from her nearest neighbour, Monsieur Dalon, who was half deaf anyway, Kado could make as much noise as he wanted and no one was going to hear. Charlotte had always perceived her isolation to be an advantage, a bulwark against the outside world, but no longer. Now it made her feel terribly vulnerable.

She looked out of the kitchen window into the pitch-black night and felt very exposed. Maybe the person wasn't inside at all. He could be out there in the darkness watching her right now and she wouldn't know it.

Clutching the knife tightly in her hand, she went from room to room, checking that the house was empty, before pulling down all the blinds and bolting the doors. No one was getting in here now.

But they've already been in, whispered an unwelcome voice in her head.

Picking up a reluctant Kado from his basket, Charlotte retreated to her bedroom and lay down on the bed with the dog next to her and the knife on the bedside table. Kado immediately fell asleep again, nuzzled up against her. This made her feel better, not because she liked having him on the bed with her – she didn't – but because she was confident that it meant there was no one else in the house, otherwise he'd be making a lot of noise. Kado wasn't a big fan of strangers.

Charlotte sighed and looked at the knife, wondering if she could ever stab someone, then told herself to calm down. Yes, someone had invaded her home and installed a camera to film her in the bath, but it was probably some pathetic pervert from the village, someone who didn't have the balls to ask her out. Not some evil serial killer planning to do her in. And when she found out who this person was – and she *would* find out – she'd report him to the police immediately.

'This is my home,' she whispered. 'I am safe here.'

But somehow she didn't quite believe it.

Four

The boy from the burning house. That's what the media had dubbed me back in the day.

When I was seven years old, my father, a lazy drunk from a wealthy background, murdered my mother and two brothers in a fit of booze-induced rage. He would have killed me too if he'd been able to catch me, but I'd hidden in an upstairs cupboard of our rambling old country home while he'd roamed from room to room hunting me down. He'd even opened the cupboard where I was hiding, but I'd covered myself in a pile of old coats and somehow remained undiscovered. I will always remember those long, terrifying seconds that seemed to stretch for minutes as my father poked the blade of his knife into the coats, and I felt its tip against my skin, and I had to hold my breath and dared not move.

In the end, the bastard had set fire to the house in a bid to smoke me out. My own father was that intent on killing me. Even now, sometimes, the thought makes me shudder.

I'd had no choice but to break cover, and he'd spotted me. Then, with his clothes alight and a bloodied knife in his hand, he'd chased after me, screaming obscenities. To escape him, I'd had to jump from an upstairs window, landing in a flowerbed from where I'd been rescued, shivering and in shock, by fire-fighters shortly afterwards, somehow having avoided serious physical injury.

Mentally, though, it was a different story. That night has haunted me all the way down the years, and no amount of therapy – and believe me, I've had a lot – has ever managed to consign it entirely to the past where it belongs. It's also made people treat me differently, especially colleagues in the force. Everyone knows who I am. The boy from the burning house whose family was wiped out in a single act of extreme violence, who joined the army, and then the police; a man who's been stalked by violence and controversy throughout his career.

Someone you can't quite trust.

It was no real surprise, therefore, to find myself in an interview room at Ealing nick, dressed in police-issue overalls while my clothes were tested for DNA, having already had my hands tested for firearms residue, while opposite me sat two particularly grim-looking colleagues of mine from Ealing MIT. It was close to one a.m. and all I'd eaten that night was a forlorn-looking cheese and onion slice from the canteen that tasted like sawdust, so I wasn't in the best of moods as I faced down my two inquisitors.

DI Glenda Gardner, Olaf's second in command, was one of

the sternest, most humourless people I'd ever met. Everything about her was severe from her haircut to her trouser suits, but she was great at scaring the hell out of suspects just by sitting in a room and fixing them with one of her glares. Although I couldn't stick her – and she couldn't stick me – I rated her as a copper.

Next to her sat DS 'Taliban' Tom Tucker, so-called because of the immense full-face beard he sported. He was only thirty-one, but the facial hair made him look like a ginger Father Christmas, and I was fairly certain that one day he'd look back at photos of himself from this era and wonder what the hell he'd been thinking. He was a pleasant enough guy but, like a lot of the graduate cops, he was a bit of a yes man with an eye on promotion.

I'd just finished going through exactly what had happened that night in excruciating detail, and for the first time I was beginning to understand how the crims felt when they were sat in here.

Except usually they were guilty of something.

'So,' said DI Glenda, fixing me with one of her trademark glares, 'let me get this absolutely right. You get a call out of the blue from Maurice Reedman because, in his words, you're the only man his client trusts, even though you've never actually met him before. You drive over there alone to see the two of them. They try to set up an immunity deal for Mr Forbes and when you go out to discuss this with DCI Olafsson, leaving the front door on the latch, three men turn up in a car, open the security gates, even though presumably they don't have the code, then drive inside. They don't see you but just go straight in the house through the open front door and kill both Mr Forbes and Mr Reedman. You try to make an audio recording of what's going on, not a video recording, but the quality's too poor to be of any use. Then, as the gunmen make their escape, they see you, there's a struggle, shots are fired, but you're unhurt.'

'Well, I got a blow to the jaw.'

'But you weren't shot,' said Taliban.

'No, Tom,' I said, 'I wasn't shot. He was going to shoot me, and he pulled the trigger, at point-blank range, but he'd run out of shells. They were in a hurry by then. They could hear the sirens. So they left.'

'You seem remarkably unfazed considering all you've been through,' said Glenda.

It was true. I did come across as unfazed, but not because I hadn't been shaken up by what happened. I had been. I just did a good job of holding my emotions in. But then I'd been holding them in my whole life.

'I am fazed,' I told her wearily. 'But, as you know, it's not the first time I've been in that kind of situation.' I shrugged. 'I'm sure it'll hit me soon enough.'

And it would. It always did. But not in here, not in front of them.

'Is what I've just said about the events of tonight a fair summary of what happened?' said Glenda.

I sighed. 'I guess so.'

'Well, is it or isn't it?'

You see what I mean about Glenda? Sympathy tends to be in short supply in her neck of the woods. She was glaring at me again.

I glared back. 'Yeah, it is. But what I don't understand is why you're implying that I somehow had something to do with these murders.'

'No one's implying that, DS Mason,' said Taliban, using my formal title for the benefit of the tape.

'Well, you know, Tom, I think they are. But you can check my phone records. I received an incoming call this evening from Maurice Reedman's home phone. I didn't call him. He called me.'

'We've checked,' said Glenda.

'So why are you giving me all this grief?' I asked her.

'We're just trying to ascertain what happened,' said Taliban.

But they weren't. I'd given them a full and frank witness statement. I'd described the gunman I'd fought with as best I could. I'd been through my whole conversation with Henry Forbes and his lawyer. And yet none of it seemed to be enough.

I sat back in my chair and spread my arms wide. 'What more do you want from me?' I asked them both.

'You've been very cooperative,' Taliban responded with what I think was a supportive smile from somewhere underneath the beard.

Glenda nodded slowly, putting on a pretence of looking very thoughtful. 'It's just the timings seem very coincidental. You get the call to go to the house at 19.11, and within a matter of minutes of you turning up, so do the three attackers. But somehow you manage to be outside talking when they do, having left the front door on the latch. It raises questions.'

'What sort of questions?'

'You have history, DS Mason. Last year you were found in a

house with four dead police officers and two dead suspects, having grappled with a mystery killer, who subsequently escaped. You were also involved in an unauthorized operation on the same day that got your colleague killed.'

'That's got nothing to do with any of this. And the mystery killer you're referring to has a name, and no one's denying she was responsible for the deaths of those police officers.'

'It's just you always seem to be in the wrong place at the wrong time.'

'We just have to make sure we go through everything with a fine-tooth comb,' added Taliban diplomatically.

'Well you have done,' I told him. 'We've been in here close to two hours now. I've told you everything I know. Yes, the timings are coincidental but there's nothing I can do about that. Before tonight I hadn't heard anything about Henry Forbes since I was thirteen years old. So what motive would I have for being involved in his murder?'

'No one's saying you have one,' Taliban said.

'But you're not saying I haven't. You're treating me as a suspect, and I've had enough of it. I went to Reedman's house in good faith and it almost cost me my life. Now, if there's nothing else, I need to go home and get some sleep.'

The two of them looked at each other, then Glenda said, 'There's nothing else for now. Thank you for your time.'

I stood up and glared at both of them. 'And if you find a motive for my involvement, let me know. I'd love to hear what it is.'

Glenda smiled for the first time in the interview. 'Don't worry,' she said, 'we will.'

Five

It was almost two a.m. when I finally walked, exhausted, through my front door.

I live in a modern six-storey block of apartments in fashionable Fulham. The building's not pretty. It's all glass and strange angles, and ordinarily I wouldn't have even thought about buying a place somewhere like this, but it has something I covet. Security. There was an attempt on my life three years back outside my old place in King's Cross and ever since then I've been paranoid. Only the most determined and clued-up intruder's going to get into my place now. There are two entrances – one from the street, and one from the underground garage – both protected by hi-tech, heavily fortified security doors. Access is by fingerprint only, so only residents and carefully vetted staff can get in. For most of the residents the security is probably overkill. Fulham's a comparatively low-crime area and it's not even as if the people who own the apartments are multi-millionaires. For the most part they're city workers and other high-paid professionals.

But for me the security isn't overkill. As well as the attempt on my life, there's also an outstanding contract on my head. Over a decade ago, while I was still in military intelligence, I was involved in a sting operation against a Saudi Arabian radical looking to buy nerve gas for al-Qaeda, which had ended with the radical and his brother being killed. Fast forward to last year, and the radical's brother, a very successful businessman, hired a female assassin known as The Wraith to kill everyone involved in that sting. She'd done a good job too, taking them out one by one. And then on a single bloody day last year, she'd killed two of my colleagues, including one who was my oldest friend, and come very close to killing me as well. That was what DI Glenda Gardner had been referring to when she'd talked about the house full of dead bodies I'd been discovered in.

It seemed I was a man very long on enemies and very short on friends.

My earlier hunger had gone now. I just felt empty. And in need of a drink. I grabbed an open bottle of red wine from the fridge and poured myself a big glass. My hands were shaking as I raised it to my lips and drank greedily. The shock of staring down a gun barrel, thinking I was about to die, was beginning to kick in, the earlier adrenalin now a distant memory. It was a pity, I thought ruefully, that I hadn't developed the shakes earlier, in the interview room.

My mobile rang. It was Olaf.

'I heard it got a bit heated with Glenda,' he said. 'I know what she can be like.'

'Yeah, but tell me I'm not a suspect, boss. As soon as I got the call from Forbes's lawyer last night I called you.'

'You're not a suspect, Ray. But this is a big case. We've got two bodies here, and two more over in Thames Valley, and it looks like they're connected. Plus, there's a potential conflict of interest with your involvement, so I've got to get clearance from above that you can still work on it.'

'You need every man you've got on this, boss. And one thing you can say about me is I'm a good detective.'

'I know you are, Ray, and I want you on it. But take a lie-in tomorrow morning, OK? And wait for me to sort everything out my end.'

I sighed. 'Don't push me out. Please.' I almost added that it was personal now, to nick the guy who'd tried to kill me, but I figured saying that wasn't going to help.

'Leave it with me. Sleep well, and don't have nightmares.' He ended the call with a loud chuckle, and I put down the phone, thinking that, right now, things couldn't get much worse for me.

But in that I was very, very wrong.

Day Two
Wednesday

Six

The world looked a lot better for Charlotte Curtis in the daylight. The southern French sky was a watery blue and the sun was already shining brightly across the valley. Charlotte stood on the back patio with a mug of strong coffee in her hand, looking out past the swimming pool and across the narrow valley to the wooded hills beyond. It was a view she never tired of and she was determined not to allow the shock of last night to get the better of her.

She'd already been online this morning to order a bug finder from Amazon. The one she'd got could apparently locate any kind of spy camera or listening device so if the pervert who'd been filming her had planted anything else in her house she was going to find it. She'd also bought up-to-date anti-virus software for her PC. She'd read somewhere that criminals could install viruses on your computers, sometimes remotely, which allowed them to access all your files and see exactly what you were looking at while online. She'd run a check and so far, thankfully, nothing unusual had shown up.

But the fact remained that someone had broken into her house, drilled a hole in her bathroom ceiling, and placed a spy camera inside. Even standing out here in the sunshine, the thought still made her skin crawl.

Kado was running round her feet, eager for a decent walk. She always took him out for at least half an hour before school come rain or shine, and now that she was in the Easter holidays, he usually got an hour down in the valley before Charlotte got on with her day. But the valley was quiet and isolated and people rarely walked down there, and this morning Charlotte hadn't wanted to go. Someone was watching her. He might have been watching her down there every day as she and Kado walked. The thought both terrified and angered her. It was the violation of her privacy, of her space, and the worst part was that she had absolutely no idea who it was, and until she knew, every man around here would be under suspicion.

Charlotte knew she needed to get out of the house and experience some normality. She needed to talk to someone about her discovery as well. The police, obviously, but also her friends in the village. They might know what to do. But she was a private person. She didn't like the idea of involving other people in something like this. In the end, she wasn't close enough to any of them, even though she knew they all cared about her. Jacques would have known what to do, she thought ruefully; he would have protected me. She allowed herself a moment of maudlin reflection before deciding that she'd call the police later. In the meantime, she'd take a drive into the village for some supplies.

Charlotte had fallen in love with this area of France, a beautiful stretch of country roughly halfway between Bordeaux and Toulouse, as soon as Jacques had brought her here to meet his family. At the time they'd only known each other a few months but they were very much in love and Charlotte had known deep down that he was the man for her. The thought of an idyllic, romantic life in rural France appealed to her far more than it did to Jacques, though, who'd grown up there and found it far too peaceful for his liking. He liked the life they'd carved out for themselves in swinging Brighton where he ran his own small building company and they had a wide circle of friends. Eventually, though, Charlotte had persuaded him to return with her to the land of his childhood. She'd learned French, found a job at a village school about twenty miles south of his parents' place, and they'd never looked back.

Sometimes Charlotte liked to ride her bike into nearby Roquecor but today she took the car, parking in the shade of a cypress tree at the edge of the village. She bought bread, cheese and fresh milk from the village shop before settling down for a coffee at Roquecor's one and only bar/restaurant. The sun was pleasantly warm so she sat at one of the outside tables with her cup and a pastry, watching the world go by. Late morning in the village, especially outside the tourist season, was extremely quiet. The odd car came past, a couple of kids played with a tennis ball at the end of the street, and an old lady Charlotte recognized as

Madame Mennalle sat on a chair outside her house, basking in the sunshine.

Who was spying on her? It was a question she found impossible to get out of her head. It had to be someone local. Could it possibly be Lucien? You heard about those internet dates that went terribly wrong, and, really, how well did she know him? Even so, she couldn't quite believe it. As she sat with her coffee she tried her best to work out whether he'd ever had a chance to steal her keys during their time together, and concluded that he almost certainly hadn't.

With a sigh, she paid for her coffee and pastry and got back in the car, deciding that she'd drive into Agen this afternoon with the offending camera and file a report with the police. At least then she would feel like she was doing something.

As she pulled away from the kerb, the news came on the English-speaking radio station she was tuned into. She wasn't really paying much attention to it until she heard the newsreader mention the name of Henry Forbes, describing him as one of two men shot dead in London in a gun attack the previous night.

Charlotte turned up the volume but the newsreader was already on to another story. Surely, she thought, it couldn't be *the* Henry Forbes, the man she'd known so well a long time ago? After all, it wasn't that uncommon a name, and she couldn't imagine anyone wanting to shoot dead the Henry Forbes she knew. He might have been a pain in the backside and an egotistical, narcissistic arsehole – at least when she'd known him – but he wasn't the sort to get involved in anything that might lead to his murder.

Charlotte drove home quickly and immediately went online,

googling the words *Henry Forbes shooting*. There were at least a dozen stories outlining the previous night's killings. Two of them mentioned the fact that Forbes's body had been set on fire by his killers after he'd been shot. Charlotte shuddered. What kind of animals would do something like that?

There were no pictures of either of the murder victims but one of them was apparently Henry Forbes's lawyer, a Maurice Reedman.

Reedman. The name rang a bell.

She tried to remember where she knew it from, then the answer hit her. Reedman had been the name of Henry's family lawyer.

'Oh Jesus Christ,' she whispered. It *was* him.

Seven

At the time Kitty Sinn went missing in 1990, the media had one particular photo of her they liked to use. It was an upper body shot, taken outside on a summer's day. Kitty was wearing a simple white dress and her dark hair fell down around her shoulders. She had slim features and a very small button nose, giving her the appearance of a young Audrey Hepburn. In the photo she was wearing a wide smile and her brown eyes were alive and bright. She looked like the kind of girl other girls would like because they wouldn't feel threatened by her, and men would rush to protect. Looking back on the case now it was no wonder that it had garnered as much media attention as it had done. Kitty Sinn was the classic girl next door, someone who even those who'd never met her would warm to immediately.

And yet it looked like a young Henry Forbes and an unknown

number of co-conspirators had murdered her along with, it seemed, a younger girl – a girl who, according to Olaf, had had her throat cut.

Why?

It's the burning question that lies at the heart of any murder investigation. Motive. And whatever the motive for these murders was, it appeared anything but straightforward.

I was pondering this as I sat in DCI Olafsson's office at 10.30 a.m. on day two of the Henry Forbes murder inquiry, looking at that old photo of Kitty on my mobile phone. Apparently, for the moment at least, I was allowed to continue working on the case, although Olaf had suggested when he'd called me an hour earlier that certain (so far unspecified) rules would apply, and when I'd walked through the open-plan incident room the reaction from the rest of the team had been muted to say the least. A few hellos and how-you-doings from the DCs; a stern nod of recognition from Taliban Tom, who always liked to keep his options open; and a predictable blanking from DI Glenda, who clearly didn't think I should be there.

Don't get me wrong. I hadn't expected a hero's welcome. I'm a loner at the best of times, and I'm not close to any of them. But even so, given the fact that I'd almost been shot the previous night, and I was officially not a suspect, I was hoping for a little bit more of a welcome from my fellow officers.

But there you go. At least Olaf seemed pleased to see me. It was just me and him in the office with the door closed, drinking decent-quality coffee from the percolator on his desk, while outside the hunt for evidence against the perpetrators of last night's double murder had begun in earnest. It was almost certain that the murders were linked to Kitty Sinn's, but right now the emphasis was on the far more mundane task of checking CCTV footage, phone records and the profiles of known offenders in an effort to come up with hard evidence as opposed to vague theories.

Olaf sighed and picked up an old file from his desk. 'I've just been on to Thames Valley. They've now confirmed that the first remains found at the school belong to Kitty Sinn. So, as we suspected, Forbes was telling the truth. As for the other body, they've said it's a girl called Dana Brennan. Dana went missing from a village called Frampton in Hampshire in July 1989. She lived with her parents and sister about three quarters of a mile outside the village limits and she was on her way back from the village shop on her bike when she disappeared. Her bike was found in bushes only a few hundred metres from home.' Olaf took a deep breath and stared hard at me, and I could tell that the details of the case had got to him. 'She was thirteen years old.'

The details of the case got to me too. I may not be emotionally involved in many things but violence against children has always been something I've found hard to take, perhaps because of what happened to me all those years ago. One of the reasons I'd concentrated on counter terrorism and organized crime during my career was that it meant I could avoid having to deal with child abusers and, God forbid, child killers, the lowest of the low.

'Do you remember the Dana Brennan case?' asked Olaf.

I shook my head. 'Only very vaguely. The name rings a bell but I was only twelve in 1989.'

He sipped his coffee thoughtfully. 'Fuck, I remember it. Her parents were always on TV appealing for whoever had taken her just to bring her home. And as the weeks passed you could see them getting thinner and more exhausted. It was almost like they were fading away. And then the news coverage faded away as well. Like it always does.' He paused. 'But I've never forgotten their desperation. The sheer pain they were in. It broke my heart, it really did.'

I knew that Olaf had three kids from two different marriages, the youngest a boy of just five he doted on, so it didn't surprise me he felt that way. I could imagine that losing a child would be any parent's worst nightmare. It's one of the reasons I never had kids. So I could protect myself from the pain before it happened. If you don't get too involved with people, their suffering can't hurt you.

I asked him if the investigating officers had come up with any leads at the time.

Olaf shook his head. 'No. They had loads of people on it too, but they never turned up a thing.'

'But we're officially linking the murders of Dana Brennan and Kitty Sinn to the double murder last night?'

'We are, but for the moment we're still keeping the inquiries separate, with the chief super overseeing everything. Thames Valley are going to continue with the excavation at the school and remain in charge of the forensics gathering, but they're going to liaise with us, and I want you to be the main point of contact. I think we both know that the key to this lies in the past. I've got a lot of good workers on this team but you're one of the few really good detectives.'

I didn't say anything. In my experience compliments delivered in the workplace are often followed by a whole load of work.

'I want you to dig up everything you can on the Dana Brennan and Kitty Sinn murder cases, look for connections to Henry Forbes or anyone else. And look for anything that might lead us back to what happened last night.'

'That's a big job, sir. These are both major historic unsolved cases. I'm going to need help.'

'You can borrow Julia Hutchings from other duties to help you. I'll clear it with Glenda. I don't mind how you go about it but make sure you give me daily briefings of where you are with it. OK?'

I didn't have much of a choice but to accept the role. Even so, I liked the idea of digging up the past, seeing if I could find what other people might have missed. It was a challenge, even if it was a hell of a lot of work. I told Olaf I'd get on to it right away.

'Good. The first thing I want you to do is go down to Hampshire and talk to Dana Brennan's parents. They're still together and they still live in the house where Dana was brought up. They've already been told by local liaison officers that the remains are those of their daughter, and I want them to know that we're taking this investigation very seriously. And you never know, they might be able to provide something that will help.' He didn't add 'God knows what' but he might as well have done. The subtext was that there was little chance of anything new coming from the visit but, like him, I recognized it had to be done, because you never know.

The task of facing the parents, even after all this time, wasn't going to be easy, and I didn't relish it. But I wasn't going to shirk it either.

'What about Kitty Sinn's next of kin? Now that she's been ID'd, we're going to need to talk to them.'

Olaf shrugged. 'There aren't any. No immediate ones anyway. She was an only child. Her father died in 1988 and her mother in 1992. There are cousins and an uncle, I think. I'll look them up and then we'll get liaison down to them, but for the moment, let's concentrate on the Brennans. On the way back you might want to stop at the school where they found the bodies – Medmenham College, it's called. I'll tell the SIO you're coming. His name's Jerry Chesterman and he's a good guy.' He picked up two heavy-looking files from his desk. 'These are all the inquiry notes on the two girls. You're going to have to go through them, but there are abbreviated reports covering the salient facts at the beginning.'

I picked them up, opened the first one, and saw a blown-up black and white photo of a young girl with blonde hair and a round face smiling at the camera. I guessed this was Dana Brennan. She looked younger than thirteen and the image made me angry. Someone had evaded justice for her murder for far too long.

'Don't tell the parents that the killer cut her throat. I want that kept quiet.'

'I wouldn't even think of it,' I said, still staring at the photo and wishing I'd throttled the secret out of that piece of shit Henry Forbes when I'd had the chance.

'But I don't want *you* to forget that's what happened to her, Ray. That some bastard who's still out there pretty much cut that little girl's head off. I don't care what you have to do. Just find out who did it.'

I looked at him. As police officers, we're always told to avoid getting too emotional for obvious reasons, that we must concentrate on the facts. But I think that lesson had been lost on Olaf. He wore his heart on his sleeve in a way that was frowned on these days, and there was a simmering anger in his eyes.

'I'll do everything I can, boss,' I told him. 'But make sure you watch my back.'

Eight

The man who walked into the arrivals hall at Bordeaux Airport looked ordinary enough. He was somewhere in his sixties with iron-grey hair, lined skin that might have been olive once but was Celtic-pale now, and a very good posture for one his age. He was dressed in a black coat and trousers with an open-necked white shirt and he was wearing dark prescription glasses and an old-fashioned black fedora hat. Closer inspection, though, would have picked up a few strange characteristics. The nails on both of his ring fingers were unusually long, and the little finger on his left hand was missing, while beneath the dark glasses his eyes were a yellow, almost jaundiced colour round the pupils. And there was a smell about him that wasn't quite right. Like damp, manure-fed earth.

His real name was Mergim Nushi, but those few who knew

him addressed him as Mr Bone, which was a name he'd given himself when he first arrived in England back in the early seventies. To everyone else he was simply The Dark Man. For decades now he'd been called upon to clear up the mess made by others. He was a fixer of problems; a granter of wishes; the guardian of an underground empire; and for many people the last face they ever saw. But none of that was decipherable from the vaguely benign expression on his face, or the half-smile that lifted his lips at the edges.

There were a couple of dozen people hanging around the barriers, mainly taxi drivers waiting to collect passengers from the London flight, but The Dark Man walked past them and nodded at a man in a suit who was leaning against a pillar holding a sign that said 'Mr Picard', the name on the passport he'd used for this trip.

The driver peeled away from the pillar and the two of them walked out of the terminal building, without speaking. It was only when they were inside the car, a silver Mercedes C-Class, that he introduced himself to The Dark Man.

'Monsieur Picard, I am Monsieur Laroux. I am happy to be of service to you and your employers. I have organized a hotel for you in Villeneuves, and in the back seat you will find the goods you requested.'

The Dark Man nodded and, as the Mercedes pulled out of the car park, he reached behind him and picked up the small black case from the back seat. He flicked it open and looked down at the brand-new Walther PPK pistol in its casing, along with a separate suppressor and two spare magazines. Wrapped in a piece of cloth was a black K-Bar neck knife with a four-inch blade, secured in its sheath, as well as a cheap Nokia mobile phone.

'The phone is untraceable to you, as are the gun and the knife,' explained Laroux.

The Dark Man replaced everything in the case and slipped it under the front seat.

Laroux, the man next to him, was a French underworld contact of The Dark Man's boss, and it was a measure of his boss's standing that a man as senior as Laroux had come to him. His organization's specialities were high-end people-smuggling and heroin, and Laroux himself had a reputation for reliability.

'Is everything to your satisfaction?' asked Laroux.

He was a big gruff man but, even so, The Dark Man could smell anxiety on him.

'Everything is perfect,' The Dark Man replied. 'And our target? Is there any news on her?'

Laroux hesitated. 'As requested, we have a number of cameras set up in her house. But she has found one of them.'

This was the problem when you used subcontractors. Even ones with a reputation for reliability. You didn't have control over the situation. 'That isn't good,' said The Dark Man, removing his glasses and staring at Laroux.

Laroux quickly looked away. 'She hasn't been to the police yet, or looked for any of the other cameras, but she has been online.'

'What's she been looking at?'

'Bug finders. That kind of thing. Also, articles from a shooting in London last night. Two men were killed.'

The Dark Man nodded. He knew about the killings Laroux was referring to. He'd set them up himself, although he hadn't actually been there in person. If he had been, there wouldn't have been any witnesses to the crime. One of the most important lessons he'd learned about killing in his long career was that you should always eliminate the witnesses. If The Dark Man had had his way, Henry Forbes would have been eliminated many years ago. He'd been overruled at the time, and the result was that they now had a situation where a police detective had survived the attack last night. It was a problem The Dark Man knew he'd have to fix before too long.

In the meantime he had the problem of Charlotte Curtis to deal with, and this was going to be a far more subtle operation. Whether she lived or died depended on her actions over the next few hours.

'Where is she now?' he asked.

'When I checked an hour ago, she was at home. She's a teacher and it's the Easter vacation so she's not working this week.'

The Dark Man nodded slowly. 'I need you to supply me with a car and her address.'

It was time to pay her a visit.

Nine

I've only been in love once in my life. That was with the woman who became my wife. Her name was Jo and we were together from beginning to end for just under two years. It was without doubt the happiest time of my life although, to be fair, the competition's been pretty scarce on that front.

We met on the job. Before the onset of Tinder that was pretty much the only way I met anyone of the opposite sex. Jo had come into our offices to demonstrate a new facial recognition software package to my team. I remember the first time I saw her, I knew straight away she was something special. It wasn't the looks so much, it was her zest for life. She was only a little thing but she had a big smile and an infectious laugh, and she bantered easily with my colleagues. She even got me laughing, which is no easy feat.

Afterwards I took her business card on the pretext of talking to her more about the package. It took me a week of thinking about it before I finally phoned the number on it. Thankfully, she remembered me well enough, and after a couple of minutes of small talk I asked her out for a drink. When she said yes, it was as if I suddenly understood what all those songs had been about. I was delirious with excitement, even though I kept telling myself to calm down, and that it almost certainly wouldn't come to anything.

But it did come to something. Our first date in a bar in Surrey close to where she lived was fun and relaxed. It led to a second, then a third, and soon we were in a proper relationship. We didn't get to spend too much time together. We both had demanding jobs, and Jo also had twin seven-year-old daughters from another relationship, so there were plenty of obstacles in our way. Even so, I knew within weeks that she was the one for me. I met her daughters, Chloe and Louise, and they were both so polite and sweet that they won me over immediately, and deep down I began to see them as the family I'd never had. I would have proposed there and then but forced myself to be patient.

I finally popped the question after eight months. I didn't do it publicly. I'm not that kind of man. I did it while we were lying in bed at her house early one evening drinking red wine, the girls having gone to their dad for the weekend. She was sitting propped up against the pillows with a big smile on her face. I took her in my arms, kissed her forehead, and the words just came tumbling out of my mouth before I could stop myself.

There was a three-second pause while Jo stared at me open-mouthed; then, just as I was beginning to think I'd made a huge and totally avoidable mistake, her face lit up and she said yes.

The Bone Field

It should have been a fairytale. For a while it was. She was the love of my life, and I'd developed a strong bond with her girls. We moved in together in Surrey, and I was even thinking about leaving the force altogether. Life was good. In fact, it was better than I could ever have imagined it to be. We would have been together for decades, I'm convinced of it.

But then one night I saw a news report on TV, and something awoke within me. Something dark and terrible. And from that day on it was the beginning of the end for me and Jo, and our fairytale.

I was thinking about that, and the fragility of family life, as I drove down to Hampshire to see the parents of Dana Brennan. How a perfect life can be shattered by events over which you have no control.

The village of Frampton lay in a quintessentially English stretch of countryside a couple of miles west of the A33 between Reading and Basingstoke at the northern edge of the county, one of a dozen villages and hamlets connected by quiet country lanes. Frampton itself was little more than a collection of pretty cottages and a pub surrounding a minor crossroads and, as I drove into it, I stopped the car outside a row of three terraced cottages next to a well-tended graveyard. The middle cottage had an old Hovis bread sign above the front door. This had once been the village shop which Dana had visited minutes before she disappeared for ever.

On a sunny day like this one, Frampton looked a peaceful, idyllic place, and as I sat there in the silence I imagined a similar day twenty-seven years earlier: a pretty young girl coming out of the shop, jumping on her bike with her bag of shopping and riding off without a care in the world. To her death.

I thought of the twins then, Chloe and Louise. I hadn't seen them in five years. I missed them. I really did. They'd be fourteen now. A year older than Dana when she'd been snatched.

A burst of emotion rose up in me and I forced it back down, pulling away from the kerb and turning right at the crossroads. The houses quickly gave way to high, impenetrable hedges on either side of the road, before giving way again to woodland on the left side and bright yellow rapeseed fields on the right. A car came past the other way but otherwise the road was empty. It would have been even quieter back in 1989.

A small copse of trees appeared ahead on my left and I slowed down. This was the place where Dana had been taken. The file from the original investigation was on the seat next to me, and I flicked it open now and pulled out an old blown-up photo of a child's bike lying in the undergrowth, a plain white bag with its contents spilling out a couple of yards away, all barely a yard from the road and surrounded by scene-of-crime tape. It was a forlorn sight.

Straight away, I knew the killer must have known these back roads. They were too far from the beaten track for him to have stumbled on them randomly. According to the file, every male living within a five-mile radius had been questioned, and none of them had been considered a suspect. And yet a stranger would have stood out.

The case was as much a mystery now as it had been then, possibly even more so given the fact that Dana's remains had been found alongside Kitty Sinn's, and once again I was reminded of the fact that I'd come so close to getting answers from Henry Forbes, but hadn't.

The Bone Field

It was a failure on my part, one I knew I was going to have to rectify.

The Brennans lived in a small whitewashed cottage with ivy creeping up the walls, on a lane directly off the road where Dana had disappeared. An old-style Land Rover Freelander was parked in the driveway and I pulled up beside it.

I'm not used to doing these kinds of visits, and I was feeling tense as I knocked on the door.

A few moments later, a fit-looking woman in her early sixties answered the door. Her eyes looked tired, and it was clear she'd been crying recently, but she smiled when she saw me. I introduced myself and she invited me inside.

The cottage was more cramped than it had looked from the outside, and the ceilings were low and criss-crossed with old oak beams. I had to duck down to avoid getting whacked as she led us through a narrow hallway into the sitting room where Mr Brennan sat.

He got up from his chair when he saw us but it was clearly a major effort for him. Olaf had told me he was sixty-four but he looked a lot older than that. His face was ghostly pale and so gaunt the skin was stretched taut over the bones, and his hair hung in thin grey wisps over a wrinkled scalp. Even so, his grip was surprisingly strong as he shook my hand.

'Steve Brennan,' he said, looking me in the eye. 'Pleased to meet you, and thank you for coming out all this way. You've met my wife, Karen.'

We shook hands and I introduced myself.

'Not *the* Ray Mason?' he said when I told him who I was. 'Oh yes, you are, aren't you? I thought you looked familiar. I recognize you from the papers.'

The attempt on my life three years back had caused quite a media furore, not least because it involved 'the boy from the burning house'. A gang of three men had tried to abduct me at gunpoint from outside my home. Their plan, it seemed, was to film my murder, probably by beheading, then post it on the internet. At the time I was a DI in the Met's Counter Terrorism Command with a couple of successful ops under my belt, and therefore a potential target for terrorists looking to make a big news splash. The gang were acting alone, just a bunch of home-grown young men radicalized on the internet, and thankfully they were amateurs. I disarmed one of them and used his gun to shoot him dead, along with the second gunman. The driver had tried to escape but I'd shot out his tyres and nicked him. He was now serving eighteen years for conspiracy to murder.

The police had managed to keep my name out of the papers. I was questioned at length by investigating officers so that they could be satisfied I'd acted lawfully by using the minimum force necessary to protect my life, but, although they'd concluded I had, the families of the two dead men had persisted with a private prosecution against me for murder. At about the same time I'd been involved in another case where I'd shot dead several terror suspects, and my name and photo had ended up being leaked to the media. Other aspects of my past, things I wanted kept secret, had come out too, and as a consequence I was now probably the most famous detective in the land – a situation I hated.

There was no point denying it, so I told Mr Brennan that yes, I was *the* Ray Mason.

'You've had a very hard time,' he told me, a new respect in his voice.

'So have you,' I said.

'I'm glad that private prosecution failed. It would have been a travesty of justice if you'd been found liable for those killings.'

'I know, but I never let it bother me too much.' Which wasn't entirely true. There'd been times when I'd let the fear that I might lose the case get the better of me.

Mrs Brennan offered me a drink but I declined. These kinds of interviews are hard enough as it is, so it's best to get straight on with them. I took the sofa facing the Brennans, who sat next to each other in matching chairs holding hands. I could feel the underlying well of tension in the room.

'I understand you were given the news that Dana's body was found by the local police last night,' I said. 'How much did they tell you?'

It was Mr Brennan who answered, his voice quiet. 'Not much. Just that her remains had been discovered in Buckinghamshire.' He paused. 'And that it was definitely her.'

'How did Dana die?' asked Mrs Brennan, her voice tight.

'We know that she was murdered,' I said, 'but at the moment we're not sure how, and it may be that we never know.' I'd agreed with Olaf not to tell them that her throat had been cut, and I made a mental note to make sure that the Thames Valley SIO did every-thing he could to keep this information out of the media.

69

'Do you know how long she was alive for after she was taken?' asked Mr Brennan.

I shook my head. 'It's impossible to tell for sure because of the length of time she's been gone, but usually in these kinds of cases the victim is killed within hours of the abduction.' I wanted to add that it was unlikely she'd suffered too much, but I didn't know that, so I said nothing. Instead I told them that there was a second body buried close to Dana's, and that it had now been formally identified as Kitty Sinn. They were both familiar with Kitty's disappearance and were as shocked as everyone else to learn that her remains had turned up in England when she'd been reported missing in Thailand. 'Obviously it's no coincidence that they were buried near each other,' I said, 'so we believe they were killed by the same person, or persons. I know this is a long shot, but can either of you think of any connection between your family and Kitty Sinn?'

I wasn't surprised when they both shook their heads and said no, but you have to ask these things, because you never know.

'Do you have any suspects at all?' asked Mr Brennan.

'Not yet, I'm afraid. But I'm going to tell you something in confidence, and I would ask you not to repeat this to anyone. You may have heard on the news this morning that a man called Henry Forbes was murdered last night along with his lawyer. This is the same Henry Forbes who reported Kitty Sinn missing back in 1990, and who was her boyfriend at the time.' I gave them some basic details of what had happened, knowing that they'd be able to get more out of the newspapers over the next couple of days, but didn't mention anything about my meeting with Henry and his claims of information about who Kitty's killer was. 'We've got a number of active lines of inquiry going because if we find who killed Mr Forbes, it may well lead us to whoever murdered your daughter.'

The Brennans had a number of questions about these new developments and I answered them as best I could before asking questions of my own about Dana's abduction: was anyone seen acting suspiciously in the area in the days or weeks prior to the attacks (no); had Dana ever been approached by strangers before (no); et cetera, et cetera. Unfortunately, they stirred up painful memories, and Mrs Brennan became increasingly upset as the interview progressed until eventually she burst into tears.

'I don't know what else we can tell you,' she said, dabbing the tears away with a tightly clutched tissue. 'There was nothing to make me suspicious. Our life was good. We were happy. I didn't see it coming. I just didn't. And I should have done. I bloody should have done. Then maybe Dana would still be alive.'

'It's OK, love,' said Mr Brennan, putting his arm around her. He held her for a while, then turned to me, and I could see that he too was fighting back the tears. 'You finding Dana has brought the whole thing back to us. Since it happened, we've got on with our lives, as far as you ever can when something like this has happened. I suppose we never lost hope that she would be found alive one day, that she'd turn up all these years later and we could start again.' He paused, fought hard to compose himself, and a single tear ran slowly down his cheek. 'It's strange, but I can still picture her smile and hear her voice perfectly in my mind. That never fades. Never.'

'She was such a lovely girl,' said Mrs Brennan, no longer making any effort to fight back her tears. 'She was so kind and thoughtful. Do you know what they said on her last school report? I'll show it to you. I want you to see it.'

Mr Brennan tried to put a hand on his wife's forearm as she moved out of his embrace. 'I'm sure DS Mason hasn't got time for this, love.'

'No, it's OK,' I said. 'I'd like to see it.' I could see how much it meant to her that the police tried to understand Dana as a living, breathing human rather than a statistic.

Mrs Brennan hurried out of the room and returned a minute later with a worn-looking report book in her hand. Her tears had stopped now and she was actually smiling. 'Look at this from her form teacher, Mrs Eagle.' She opened up a page, held it in front of me, and started reading. ' "Dana is a real shining star and a lovely, hard-working girl. She is popular with her classmates and always ready to help out. In short, a real pleasure to teach and to be around." That's what my Dana was like, DS Mason. It's not an exaggeration. She was such a good, sweet girl. And her little sister Katie doted on her. Can you imagine what it was like for her when Dana went? Katie was only ten. She was absolutely lost. You know, she blamed herself because it was her idea to do the baking that day.'

I remembered reading the twins' school reports. How proud I'd been. How close I'd come to asking Jo if we could have a child of our own. It could all have been so different. A life. A family.

But I'd fucked it all up.

'I've got something else to show you,' said Mrs Brennan. 'This.' She produced a photo from behind the report book and handed it to me with an imploring look. 'I keep this picture with me all the time. It was taken when Dana was eleven. It was my favourite one of her because it showed all the joy that was in her soul.'

I looked at it. Saw a young girl down on one knee hugging a cocker spaniel and giving the camera a huge gap-toothed smile.

'It's beautiful,' I said, and I realized my voice was cracking with emotion. I couldn't bring myself to say anything more, I just kept staring at this innocent little girl whose life had been ended by a killer who'd got away with his crime.

'How could someone do this to my little angel? She was riding to the shop to get some ingredients for a cake because Katie wanted to do some baking. I was going to drive down there but Dana said, "No mum, I'll do it for you." Why did I let her go? Why?' All the pain came hurtling out of Karen Brennan now and she burst into great howling sobs.

Once again Mr Brennan took her in his arms and led her back to her chair, the photo and the report book still clutched tightly in her hand like precious stones.

He turned back to me, frail yet composed, and I saw a strength in him I hadn't noticed before. 'Thank you so much for coming but I don't think we can help you any more. We just want the chance to bury our daughter in peace.'

I didn't know what to say, but in that moment I felt that these people had to hear more than simple platitudes. Every police officer knows you should never promise anything you can't guarantee to crime victims or their relatives because it can so easily come back to haunt you, but the fact was I couldn't help myself. The need to see justice done in this case was so overwhelming that it no longer mattered to me what it cost to get it.

So I stood up, my hands no longer shaking, the tension fading as a renewed purpose took hold of me, and looked at them both in turn.

Mr and Mrs Brennan looked back at me, and Mrs Brennan's sobbing subsided.

I took a deep breath. 'I promise you both, here and now, that I will find who killed your daughter. It may well have been more than one person, we don't know yet, but I'll find whoever was involved and whatever it takes – *whatever* it takes – I will bring them to justice and make sure they spend the rest of their miserable lives behind bars. You both know who I am. You know my history, and what happened to me as a child. And you know that I mean it when I give you my word that I won't give up. Because I won't.'

Mr Brennan came forward and embraced me. 'Thank you,' he whispered in my ear, before letting go.

Mrs Brennan put the picture of her daughter into my hand. She looked up at me and her eyes were alive with passion. 'Take this, so it'll always remind you of your promise.'

I could have objected, but it was too late for that. I took the photo and placed it carefully in my wallet. Because she was right: it would always remind me of my promise.

A promise that would take me all the way to hell.

Ten

Henry Forbes. Before she'd heard his name on the radio that morning, Charlotte Curtis hadn't thought about him for a long, long time. They'd been lovers once, back in the early nineties in Brighton. Henry was an ex-public schoolboy from a wealthy Home Counties family who lectured in Humanities at Brighton Polytechnic, as it was then. He'd had little ambition and seemed content just to drift through life, taking what he could from it. When she'd thought of him, which was extremely rarely, Charlotte was always reminded of the phrase 'there was less to him than met the eye'. He'd only had one claim to any sort of fame and that was that in 1990 his girlfriend had gone missing without trace while they'd been travelling together in Thailand.

Kitty Sinn, the girlfriend in question, had been one of Charlotte's closest friends. They were the same age and they'd been on the same teaching degree course, both graduating just before Kitty went missing. Kitty had been a lovely girl – fun, vivacious, but most of all kind and loyal. Charlotte had no doubt they'd have stayed in touch if she hadn't gone missing like that.

Strangely enough, it was Henry's link with Kitty that accounted for the fact that he and Charlotte had ended up together. After he'd come back alone from Thailand, Henry had had a nervous breakdown, taken a leave of absence from his job, and disappeared for a year to a beach in Indonesia – which was typical of the Henry she remembered: he'd never actually go and do something worthwhile like help build an orphanage in Africa or put his teaching skills to good use, he'd prefer to sit in the sunshine feeling sorry for himself. Charlotte, meanwhile, had got herself a teaching job at a primary school in Brighton, and she and Henry had run into each other after his return from Indonesia. It was the first time she'd seen him since before the Thailand trip and they'd got talking. Kitty was still missing and Henry had the haunted, spaced-out look of a man who'd been on the wrong end of far too much unwanted attention. Charlotte had felt sorry for him and, if she was honest with herself, she was intrigued to spend more time with the man who'd been one of the last people to see her best friend before she'd disappeared. She and Henry had gone for a drink and somehow they'd ended up in bed, which wasn't what she'd been planning at all.

The relationship, if you could call it that, had lasted eighteen months. The sex had been good but everything else had been dull and superficial, and she'd found Henry hard work, like a child who wants his own way the whole time. She hadn't even found out anything insightful about what had happened to Kitty. Henry hadn't wanted to talk about it, and that was that. Very occasionally she'd catch him staring into space and it had made her wonder what there was more going on back there than he liked to let on. In the end, though, she hadn't been prepared to hang around to find out.

When she'd broken up with him, Henry had been mortified. He'd tried to win her back with constant phone calls, and turned up on her doorstep at all hours, often drunk, declaring his undying love for her. She'd tried to be as patient and as nice about it as she could, but when that hadn't worked, she'd started ignoring him. Unfortunately, that hadn't worked either. He'd bombarded her with more phone calls and letters; he'd threatened suicide and blamed Charlotte for everything that wasn't right with their relationship. Finally, she'd opened her back door one morning to find a human turd on the doorstep. Whether Henry had been responsible or not she didn't know but it was the final straw. She'd contacted the police, they'd spoken to Henry, clearly given him a real scare – he'd always struck her as a coward – and that was it. She'd never heard from him again. They'd never even crossed paths on the street in Brighton, which wasn't the biggest town in the world. A few months later she'd met Jacques, a big man who she felt sure could have protected her against anything and anyone, and the memory of her time with Henry, and the unpleasant aftermath, faded into the past.

Now, almost a quarter of a century later, two gunmen had shot him dead at his family lawyer's home. His family lawyer! Only someone as pretentious as Henry Forbes could have a family lawyer. She wondered if Reedman had in fact been the target and Henry was simply in the wrong place at the wrong time – although, now she thought of it, there was something weirdly coincidental about his murder happening at just about the same time she'd discovered the camera in her bathroom.

It was a gorgeous spring afternoon as she returned home from walking Kado. She knew she still needed to talk to the police about the camera she'd found, but was certain they wouldn't do anything about it, so decided to put it off until later.

Kado still had plenty of energy so she let him stay outside in the garden where he ran about the place, sniffing in bushes and generally acting as if he'd been fed amphetamines. She watched him play while she made herself a cup of green tea in the kitchen and then, leaving the back door slightly ajar so that he could come back in when he was ready, she settled herself in her favourite armchair by the fireplace and picked up the book she was currently reading, the new one by one of her favourite authors, Peter James.

For a while all the stress of the last twenty-four hours disappeared as Charlotte turned the pages, immersing herself in the story. She loved reading. She always had. It relaxed her completely, even during times of stress. It was only when the clock dinged to announce it was three o'clock that she put the book down, wondering vaguely why Kado hadn't come back into the house.

Getting up from her seat, she made her way back towards the kitchen and saw him asleep on the floor, basking in the sun's rays just inside the back door. She smiled and walked past him, contemplating making another cup of green tea.

It was only as she was rinsing her cup did she see it, out of the corner of her eye.

The patch of red on the floor next to Kado.

Slowly, and with a growing sense of dread, she looked down.

Kado lay completely still on his side facing her, a deep wound in his throat where it had been cut almost from ear to ear. The blood was still oozing out and clinging to his fur before dripping down on to the tiles and forming a small but growing pool.

The cup fell from Charlotte's hand, shattering into dozens of pieces, but she hardly noticed. With a wail of raw emotion, she rushed over and crouched down beside him, placing her hand against the wound, desperate to stop the bleeding even though she knew immediately that he was already dead.

And then she heard movement round the corner in the entrance hall and, as she looked up, a man wearing a black fedora, with a scarf pulled up over his face, strode into view, a bloodied knife in one gloved hand.

The sheer terror Charlotte experienced then didn't exactly root her to the spot but it slowed down her reactions so much that she moved like an old woman as she got to her feet, her bare knee slipping in Kado's blood.

The man moved purposefully but unhurriedly, as if he'd done this kind of thing many times before, grabbing her by the hair with his free hand and pulling her towards him. His grip was strong, and when she felt the sharpness of the knife's blade against her throat, she suddenly realized she was about to die. Her one hope was that it would be quick.

But the death blow never came. Instead, the man wrapped an arm around her midriff so there was no possibility of escape, and put his mouth close to her ear. 'No struggling,' he whispered, 'or the knife will drink your blood.' His accent was foreign. Eastern European, or maybe Middle Eastern, it was hard to tell. And he smelled strange too, almost musty, as if he'd been lying in a cellar for a long time in the clothes he was wearing.

'What do you want?' she managed to whisper.

'Some time soon, people will come to see you,' he continued, his voice a low hiss. 'Police officers. It may be a day, it may be a week, but they will come. They will ask you questions. You will tell them you know nothing. Do you understand?'

'Questions about what?'

'About your old friend Kitty Sinn.'

Charlotte couldn't believe what she was hearing. 'Kitty? She disappeared years ago. I haven't seen her in . . .' God, how long had it been? 'Twenty-five years, maybe more. I don't know anything about her.'

'Good. When the police and the media come knocking on your door, you say you hardly remember her. Because if you tell them anything, anything at all, it won't matter what protection you are given, I will find you and I will kill you. Just as I killed your dog. Now, do you understand what I'm saying?'

She had no idea why this man was so interested in her or Kitty, but he had a knife to her throat and it was obvious after what he'd done to Kado that he was ruthless enough to use it. 'Yes,' said Charlotte. 'I won't say anything. To anyone.'

'And do not try to find any more of the cameras either. We are going to be watching you these next few days and weeks. You will go about your life just as before, but you will not leave the house for more than three hours at a time, unless it's to go to work, and unless you receive permission from me. If you fail to abide by these rules, I will hurt you. Badly.' His mouth caressed her ear as he spoke this last word, and she felt the coldness of his tongue on her skin.

'I won't do anything, I promise.' More than anything else in the world right now, she just wanted him out of there. Then she'd go straight to the police and tell them everything.

'I know what you're thinking, Charlotte Curtis,' the man hissed. 'But no one can protect you from me, least of all some backwoods gendarmes. Look at your dog. Go on, look what I've done to it.'

Charlotte lowered her eyes, her throat tightening as once again she saw Kado lying there, his blood still spreading across the tiled floor.

'Now, bury it, tell anyone who asks that he died of natural causes, then go on with your life as before. That way you live for a few more years.'

He moved the knife away from her throat and ran the tip gently up one cheek and into the folds of skin only millimetres from the corner of her right eye, then slowly slid it down again, running it over her breast, touching the nipple through the fabric of her dress, deliberately violating her.

Charlotte remained absolutely still, sick with fear and unable to speak.

Finally, he removed the knife, released her from his grip, and walked back round the corner into the entrance hall.

Only when she heard the front door shut did she run over to the sink and vomit profusely, knowing that for a reason she couldn't even begin to fathom her life had suddenly changed for ever.

Eleven

It was mid-afternoon by the time I reached Medmenham College, an all-boys public school for both day pupils and boarders which thankfully, given the circumstances of its new-found fame, was closed for the Easter holidays.

The gates to the school were open and two uniforms stood guard to prevent any members of the public getting inside. They moved aside for me after I showed them my warrant card and I drove down a long, perfectly straight driveway which led to the main building, a grand redbrick mansion, four storeys high, with turrets on either end and a clock tower in the centre. This, I thought as I surveyed the perfectly manicured lawns, was how the rich lived, and I wondered how much it cost to send a child to this place.

A large number of news vehicles and camera crews were

penned off to one side behind lines of police tape. Word was now out that the remains found the previous day belonged to Dana Brennan, and, although the case was an old one, it was still etched on the consciousness of those of a certain age, and therefore newsworthy. It's also true that the media love the idea of a serial killer, and two bodies dug up with the prospect of more to come was enough to get them here in serious numbers. When they found out that the other body was Kitty Sinn, I suspected their numbers would quadruple, which was going to be a serious headache for us.

I followed the road round the side of the main building and parked outside a maintenance block alongside the dozen or so police vehicles already there. Another uniform stood guard, blocking access to the path that led down behind the main building. Security was important at an ongoing crime scene like this. There was a temptation for the media and civilian rubberneckers to try to get a closer look at what was going on and, even after all these years, we didn't need them contaminating anything.

I told him who I was and he called the SIO to let him know I was on my way. Olaf had described DCI Jerry Chesterman as a good guy, but that didn't necessarily mean he was competent. Olaf knew a lot of good guys, and I had the feeling that most of them were drinking buddies and vague acquaintances he'd made down the years.

I followed the footpath as it ran alongside another well-kept lawn with playing fields beyond that led down to a quiet, pretty stretch of the River Thames, the view partially shaded by a row of well-spaced mature oak trees. On a sunny day like today, with the air largely still, the scene was peaceful and bucolic, the kind that reminds a person of everything that's good about England.

Twenty yards from the river the path forked off to the right through thick woodland and heavy tangled undergrowth, turning into little more than a dirt track. Walking along the track towards me was a bald man in a suit carrying a hard hat in his hand who, though he was better dressed, reminded me a lot of Olaf himself. Chesterman was young for an SIO, no more than mid-thirties, with a round, unblemished face, chubby cheeks, and not much in the way of what you'd call gravitas.

After we'd done the intros, I got him to fill me in on the details of the crime scene as we walked through the woodland to the place where they'd recovered the two bodies.

'They were found in a parcel of woodland right at the south-east corner of the school's grounds,' he said, 'directly adjacent to the river. The school sold it off to developers eighteen months ago to raise funds. The plan was to build a single luxury property with river frontage, and the builders broke ground here two weeks back. They'd dug about half the foundations when, last Monday, they discovered the first skeleton. It was still largely intact but broken in half by, we think, the digger's bucket. And that was Katherine Sinn. Obviously the builders called us in immediately and we dug round the area where the body was found in a twenty-foot radius, didn't find anything else, and were on the verge of finishing up when we unearthed the other skeleton yesterday. Dana Brennan's.'

'I heard her throat was cut.'

'That's right. There was one fairly even groove in her C4

vertebra that suggested a single, very deep knife wound. There was a similar injury on Katherine Sinn's vertebra as well.'

I looked at him. 'Can we do everything possible to keep that information out of the papers? For the sake of the families.'

'I'll see what I can do, but you've seen it round here. The media are crawling all over the place, and there's a lot of scope for leaks.'

I knew what he meant. Police officers don't get paid huge salaries and the temptation to feed titbits to newspapers in return for cash can be one they don't all resist. I'd never done it myself but then I'd never needed to. It's easy to take the moral high ground when you've got money.

We stopped at a large clearing in the trees that was largely taken up by a hole in the ground about seven feet deep and fifty feet across. Two diggers sat idle on the far side, while a few yards beyond, lined up in another break in the trees, was a cluster of police vehicles and a mobile incident room. Thick mud covered the bottom of the hole, which had been divided into eight equal-sized sectors using tape, and a dozen or so scene-of-crime officers, clad in their white overalls, were busy trawling through the mud. Two yellow flags sticking up some distance apart marked the spots where the remains of Dana and Kitty had been found.

I didn't feel any emotion staring into the hole. I'd used it all up earlier when I'd visited Dana's parents and now I was back in business mode. In front of me, the river was just visible through the trees about twenty-five yards away. I pointed at the track carved out of the woodland down which the diggers and police vehicles had come from the main road.

'Has that access road always been there?' I asked.

DCI Chesterman shook his head. 'No. It was put in by the developers. Eventually it's going to be the new house's driveway.'

I looked round. 'So when these two young women were buried here, this was all woodland that you could only reach on foot?'

Chesterman nodded. 'Exactly. The killer or killers could have driven as far as the maintenance block, which is forty-five metres from the nearest body, then they'd have had to carry the bodies down here. I've got maps and aerial photos of the area in the incident room. Do you want to have a look?'

I followed him into the incident room, a large campervan-style vehicle with a row of windows down each side where a couple of people sat tapping away on keyboards. In an inquiry like this, where it was all about the recovery of bodies that had been in the ground for a long time, and where any evidence was likely to be down there with them, there wasn't much need for a big team of detectives at the scene.

One of the desks had been cleared and a laminated Ordnance Survey map taped to it, along with two poster-sized aerial photos of the area, one taken a good few years ago, the other taken very recently.

'Here we are on the map,' said Chesterman, tapping it with his forefinger.

I leaned in close to where he was pointing and saw the school grounds next to a major bend in the river, where the Thames curved south to north. We were in a fairly rural area for south-east England, at the southern end of the Chiltern Hills between the two river towns of Henley and Marlow. On either side of the school grounds, narrow manmade water channels ran up from the river creating a makeshift moat protecting the school from intruders on either side. To the north of the grounds, a succession of fields ran adjacent to the river for more than a mile before coming to the nearest riverside property. To the south was an adjoining property consisting of a large house with grounds that ran down to the river, and included part of the same woodland that we were now in. There were no other immediate neighbours.

'Who lives here?' I asked, pointing at the house next door.

'A Russian businessman called Dimitri Valkov. He bought the property two years ago. He's obviously got deep pockets because he offered to buy the school as well for forty million pounds but they turned him down.'

'What's his history?'

'He made his money in natural gas, moved his operations to London in 2006, and he's been UK-based ever since. He never visited England before 2000 though, so he's not a suspect.'

I inspected the two aerial shots of the school and the surrounding area. Aside from the addition of the access road and the fact that in the old shot the area round where the bodies were discovered was much more overgrown, both photos looked remarkably similar.

I pointed to the old one. 'When was this taken?'

'June 1988, so that's what it would have looked like when the girls went missing.'

'Who owned the house next door back then?'

'A couple called the Butlers. They owned it between 1954 and 1992. Mr Butler died in 1983 and Mrs Butler in 1991. It was then sold nearly a year later to an American divorcee who owned it until it was sold to Mr Valkov.'

I looked at him. 'Jesus. How do you remember all that?'

He shrugged. 'I've got a good memory.'

'So, the big question. Have you got any potential suspects?'

Chesterman shook his head. 'No one. I was hoping you might have something.'

I told him what Henry Forbes had told me before he'd been killed: that there were a number of people involved in Kitty Sinn's murder. 'I think Henry was involved too, otherwise there's no way he'd have known that Kitty was buried here. And I think at least one of the killers must have direct links to this school, either as a staff member or pupil, because there's no way you'd bury bodies here unless you were very familiar with this place.'

Chesterman looked at me. 'But why bury the bodies here in the first place? I know both girls went missing in the summer holidays so it's unlikely the killers would be disturbed, but it would have been a real effort to transport them here, carry them down to the river and then bury them deep in the ground. Because these weren't shallow graves. Both girls were buried six feet down.'

'Unless they were killed nearby,' I said.

'But where? The school was locked up for the summer.'

'Was there a caretaker here at the time?'

'Yes. His name's Bill Morris. He worked here until he retired in 2010. He lived in the caretaker's cottage next to the maintenance block – here.' Chesterman pointed at a spot on the 1988 aerial photo.

I looked at the photo. A service entrance to the school, thirty metres down from the main entrance, led to the caretaker's cottage and the maintenance block behind it where I'd parked earlier. Both entrances were protected by high gates, and the water channels running up from the river protected the school's boundaries. Even the next-door property had a high boundary wall facing the road and entrance gates as well. In other words, the school was pretty much impregnable.

I frowned. 'What I can't work out is how the killers got into the school to bury the bodies. I'm assuming both sets of gates were locked in the summer holidays. Did anyone else have access to the keys other than the caretaker?'

'I don't think so,' Chesterman answered uncertainly, 'but I'll find out.'

'The killer, or killers, would have had to bring the victims here in a car, so the only way they could do it is to get the gates open, then park round the maintenance block somewhere, and carry the bodies down from there. I can't see how they could do it without the caretaker knowing. Have you spoken to him?'

'We have. He lives up the road in Hambleden. In fact we've interviewed him twice now.'

'Why? Has he got a record?'

'He's had two police cautions for separate offences. The first was for domestic violence back in 1997. He assaulted his wife and she called the police on two occasions but wouldn't press charges, so he got a caution instead. The second time was in 2007. He was caught accessing a child porn site in the US through his credit card details, one of about fifteen hundred people in this country. Because of the sheer numbers of people involved, and the fact that the images on his PC weren't as bad as those on some of the others, he wasn't charged. He did lose his job, though.'

I shook my head, unable to understand how anyone could possibly get off on child porn, even though I knew far too many people did. 'Jesus. And what did he say in the interviews?'

'He confirmed that he was living on site both summers but was adamant he saw and heard nothing.'

'Do you believe him?'

'He's a miserable old bastard, and when we interviewed him the second time this morning, after the discovery of Dana Brennan's body, he brought a lawyer along, and was acting more worried, but I think that was just because of the child porn connection. He swore blind he'd only ever looked at child porn once and, whether that's true or not, he had no connection to either of the two girls. He also worked at the school for twenty-six years without any problem, so ultimately, there's no reason not to believe him.'

I stared at the photos again. This case was already beginning to frustrate me. A huge amount of planning must have gone into Kitty's murder, and yet Dana's appeared to have been a random abduction. Nothing linked them except the geographical proximity of the remains and the fact that they both happened in the middle of summer. But if the killers had murdered them elsewhere, why bring them here? There were plenty of other burial sites where they wouldn't be found. And even if the girls were still alive when they were brought here, there was still the problem of getting them past the caretaker's cottage without making a noise.

None of it made sense.

And that was when I spotted it on the map. A small round building partly obscured by trees, hidden away in woodland on the neighbour's grounds, no more than fifty metres as the crow flies from where we were standing now.

I asked DCI Chesterman what it was.

He looked down to where I was pointing. 'It's a folly,' he said. 'The reason I know is I spoke to Mr Valkov's estate manager last week and he told me. Apparently it was built in the eighteenth century.'

'Forgive my ignorance,' I said, 'but what's a folly?'

'It's a building that's just for decoration,' replied Chesterman, who truly was a fount of knowledge. 'It doesn't actually serve any practical purpose. A lot of them were built by the rich over the last couple of hundred years. According to the manager, this one's in pretty poor condition and the owner's applied to get it knocked down.'

'I'd like to take a look at it if I can.'

He looked puzzled. 'Why?'

'These girls died somewhere. It might well have been there.'

'Mrs Butler lived in that house at the time so it's unlikely they were murdered in her garden.'

I nodded. 'Yes, but the folly's a hundred metres from the main house and it's only a few metres from the boundary with the school.' I studied the photo again. 'It looks like you might be able to get across to it from the rear of the caretaker's house, where the channel ends here.' I tapped the spot with my finger.

'I can't see what you're going to find there after all this time,' said Chesterman.

'Neither can I,' I said. 'But I'm here now, and I don't think it'll do any harm to have a look.'

'It's private property so I'll have to speak to the estate manager and get his permission.' Chesterman pulled out his phone and dialled the number while I waited. 'There's no answer,' he said eventually. 'I'll try him again later.'

I looked at my watch. It was a quarter to four and the traffic back into London would be getting heavy soon. 'I can't really wait around,' I said. 'Maybe another time. Could you email me copies of the photos and maps of the school?'

He said he would, and we walked back outside.

'How long do you think you'll be digging for?' I asked as we passed the hole a second time.

'Now that we've found a second body we're going to have to extend the dig. At least another week, I'd think.'

'If you find anything of note, can you let me know?'

Chesterman said he would, we shook hands, and I walked away.

But I didn't head directly back to the car. Instead, as soon as I was out of sight, I cut away from the path and walked through the woods until I came back to the newly dug access road. The channel, which was about three metres wide and filled with black, stagnant water, ran alongside the road. Woods lined the bank on the opposite side and, as I walked in the direction of the caretaker's cottage and the maintenance block, I saw the outline of the folly poking through the undergrowth.

The channel was too wide to jump across and the water looked deep so I kept walking until eventually it came to a halt and the boundary was replaced by a high hedge.

I stopped. There was a gap a couple of metres wide between the spot where the channel ended and the hedge began, and someone had put in a fence topped with barbed wire to prevent anyone getting through. The fence looked new and it was clear that at one time this had been an access point between the two properties. Up ahead I could see the maintenance block fifteen metres away, where the old road ended. I tried to picture the scene of the killers arriving in their car with Dana Brennan. I hoped that by then she was dead, but I had a horrible feeling that she was still alive.

Being led to her death.

I imagined a warm summer's night, and the killers taking her past where I was standing now.

The thought made me shudder.

I wasn't going to get past the fence. It was designed to keep out bored schoolboys and the way it splayed out at an angle over the end of the channel meant there was no way round or over.

I could of course simply have driven round next door, found the estate manager myself, and got him to take me down to the folly, but that seemed like a lot of hassle.

I'm pretty tall at six feet two, and back at school I'd been in the athletics team. I wasn't the greatest long jumper in the world, I wasn't even the greatest in my year, but I reckoned I had a chance of leaping the channel. So that's what I did. Ignoring the fact that I was dressed in my favourite suit and the kind of shoes you turn up to official functions in, I took a ten-metre run-up and leaped into the air.

I hit the bank on the other side, winding myself in the process, and just managed to get my arms over the top to stop myself falling back into the water. Even so, I got my shoes wet and had to half clamber, half roll up until I was able to get to my feet on the other side. I brushed the dirt off my jacket and shirt and clambered through the undergrowth in the direction of the folly, hoping there weren't any cameras installed round here otherwise I'd have a lot of explaining to do.

The woodland was darker and more overgrown than it was on the school side, and it took me a few minutes of hunting around before eventually the folly loomed up at me out of the gloom, a dome-shaped building made of flint and stone covered in snake-like ropes of ivy and encroaching tree branches that looked like some ancient ruin. A faded, partially covered carving of a snarling gargoyle's head glared down at me from just above the folly's single arched entrance, as if warning intruders to stay away.

I ignored the gargoyle's warning and stepped inside.

The interior of the folly was a single round room about five metres square with a floor made out of a mosaic of cracked tiles. It was almost pitch black inside and smelled musty and old. There was something unpleasant about it too. An oppressive, airless atmosphere, as if all life had been sucked out of the place.

I hadn't brought a torch with me so I pulled out my mobile, found the torch app and turned it on, partially dispelling the gloom. I looked up and saw the ceiling disappearing up into the hollowed-out dome amid a cluster of cobwebs, plaster dust and tendrils of browning ivy. A fat black spider sat in the middle of one of the webs surrounded by half a dozen dead, cocooned flies. The spider didn't move as my light ran across it, taking in the rest of this empty chamber.

And that was when I saw it. A sign scratched into the brick-work at head height, probably by a knife. It was the size of a large dinner plate and, though faded with age and partly obscured by dust, it was still possible to see that it was of a pentacle with the letter 'M' carved inside in a high, narrow font, with the legs of the letter curling at the bottom.

I flicked through the photos on my phone until I came to the one of Henry Forbes's partially burned tattoo, the tattoo his killers had tried to get rid of. I put the phone up against the carving on the wall. The patterns on both seemed identical. They were the same signs.

I smiled. I had a lead.

Twelve

The Dark Man watched through binoculars from the other side of the valley as Charlotte Curtis buried the dog in her garden.

Even from this distance he could see the pain in her expression, and the wetness on her face from the tears. But he didn't want to see pain. He wanted to see fear. It was essential that this woman was too scared to say anything to anyone. In many ways it would have been safer simply to kill her, and The Dark Man had discussed this possibility with his boss several times this past week. In the end they'd decided against it on the basis that it might arouse too much suspicion. Looking at the woman now, though, The Dark Man wasn't entirely convinced that leaving her alive was such a good idea. It was something he needed to consider further.

He breathed in the warm country air, enjoying the anonymous embrace of the trees. The Dark Man loved forests. They reminded him of a long-ago childhood far away from here, and of freedom. He always felt safe when he was among trees. Here, he was part of a much older, more natural world. The Dark Man hated people. He always had. He longed for a world where they were gone altogether, where there was just him left, free to walk alone through the mountains and forests, never to be bothered by anyone again. He gained no joy from money, nor luxury goods. He had never married, nor been with a woman for anything other than basic needs. Those few who knew him thought him cold and humourless, but in that they were wrong. His heart was full of rage and darkness. He had only two true pleasures in life. One was the forest at night. The other was killing.

The Dark Man had been only twelve years old when he committed his first murder. Since then, he'd killed many times. Sometimes it had been for business. Other times it had been for enjoyment. Every one had been pleasurable, although the slower kills when the victims' screams filled the room and he could properly breathe in their pain were by far the most satisfying. He could still remember the faces of every one of his victims, and often at night they would come to him in dreams and he would kill them all over again – young, old, male, female. They were his conquests. His trophies.

The Dark Man smiled to himself, looked back through the binoculars as Charlotte Curtis walked slowly across her patio, the dirt-covered shovel in her hand, and wondered if she too would become another of his trophies.

Thirteen

Ealing cop shop, my current place of work, is a prime example of everything that's wrong with 1970s architecture. A grim five-storey structure done out in competing shades of drab, it stands out like a cheap Soviet-era hostel between two much flashier buildings on the Uxbridge Road, and after spending time in the bucolic setting of Medmenham College, the sight of it at six p.m. in the middle of a typical west London rush hour didn't exactly fill my heart with joy.

The incident room was heaving when I walked in. As well as the rest of the team, there were a dozen or so civilian staff taking up all the available desk space. No one took any notice of my arrival. They were all too busy beavering away on their PCs, and the place was as silent as a library.

I went over to where DC Julia 'Jools' Hutchings was working

at the desk next to mine, in the corner by the window. Jools was one of the few members of the team who actually seemed to like me, and I think that was mainly down to the fact that I'd given her £300 sponsorship money to run the London Marathon on behalf of a breast cancer charity. Still, you take what you can get, and I liked her too. I also felt strangely protective of her. She was a petite little thing, barely five feet four, who looked a lot younger than her thirty-two years. She was also a happily married mum of two sons under five who kept photos of her family all over her desk, and I often wondered why she did such a stressful, unsociable and frequently unpleasant job when there were a million other things she could be doing. I never said any of that to her, though. She'd have killed me.

Before I'd left to see the Brennans earlier, I'd given Jools a whole heap of research to do, so I pulled up a chair and asked how she'd got on.

'Right,' she said, stretching in her seat. 'I've been through both case files, and there's nothing that stands out. Obviously the Kitty Sinn file's a lot thinner because the Thai police were in charge of the investigation. But Sussex police did send two detectives to Thailand at the invitation of the authorities there ten days after Kitty went missing, and they interviewed Henry Forbes, the guesthouse owner who was the last to see Kitty alive, and a few of the guests at the places she and Henry stayed. According to the file, nothing they found contradicted Forbes's story.'

'Are either of those detectives still working?'

She shook her head. 'No. The most senior of the two, DCI Greg Fairbairn, died in 2010, and his colleague, DC Roger

Powell, retired in 2005. I'm trying to track him down at the moment.'

'Thanks, Jools, I appreciate it. Anything in the Dana Brennan file?'

'Nothing we don't already know. There was a huge inquiry at the time that turned up nothing. No suspects. No witnesses. Then a major cold case review in 2001 with the same result. How did it go with her parents today?'

'Tough. Finding Dana's body brought it all back for them.' I didn't tell her about the promise I'd made to her parents. That was between them and me. 'How about Henry Forbes? What have you got on him?'

'Plenty,' she said, picking up a piece of printed A4 paper. 'Born in 1965. His father was a high-ranking civil servant in the Home Office; his mother comes from family money. He was brought up in London where he attended Westminster School and left with OK but not spectacular A Levels. He went to Goldsmiths, studied Politics, Philosophy and Economics, got a 2:1, and stayed on to do an MA then joined the teaching staff. In 1989 he moved to Brighton where he joined the staff at the polytechnic and, apart from a year's break after Kitty Sinn went missing, he's been there ever since, working for the same department, even living in the same house. He never married, never had any children, and his only long-term relationship was with a former student by the name of Roz Smith who he lived with between 1998 and 2007. He's always received an annual allowance of £35,000 through a family trust fund so he's never been short of money. No criminal record and, aside from the Kitty Sinn case, it doesn't look like he's been involved in anything remotely controversial.'

I sighed. 'Great. So he didn't have any connection with Medmenham College?'

'I can't find one.'

My earlier good mood at finding the carved symbol in the folly had faded now. 'Oh well. Thanks for that.'

I started to get up but Jools leaned forward in the seat and dropped her voice to a whisper. 'Are you going to take me along with you next time you go out for the day? Because I'm dying of boredom in here.'

I knew how she felt. The incident room at Ealing nick had all the atmosphere of a graveyard, but without the fresh air.

'I promise,' I said with a smile. 'Hand on heart.'

Olaf was on the phone in his office but he waved me in when he saw me outside his door, and by the time I'd shut it behind me and sat down, he'd finished the call.

I asked him if the team had generated any leads.

He scrunched forward in his chair, elbows on the desk, his head almost disappearing into his shoulders as he stared across at me, looking less than happy. 'Absolutely fuck all. We've got CCTV footage of the killers at the main gates of Reedman's property in a black BMW X5 with their faces covered, but that's it. They open the gates remotely somehow, probably with a cloned key, so they don't even get out of the car. We've got them driving away too, but the plates on the BMW are fake, and they obviously change them nearby, because none of the ANPR cameras pick them up again.' He sighed. 'I've got a feeling finding the shooters is going to take a while. How about you? How's your day gone?'

I gave him a brief rundown then told him what I'd learned. 'I'm certain Henry Forbes was involved in the murder of Kitty Sinn. I don't think he was a part of Dana's murder, though, but I think he might have been told about it by the people who were.'

'Why do you think other people were involved?'

'Because that's what Henry told me. I also think both murders were committed in the school grounds during summer holidays.'

'There's only one problem with that, Ray,' said Olaf. 'Everyone knows Kitty went missing in Thailand, and there's no record of her leaving the country. So how did she end up back here?'

I shrugged. 'God knows. All I do know is that somehow Kitty came back here from Thailand incognito, and that Henry and his friends killed her at some point after that.'

'Problem with that is the timings don't match up. Henry remained in Thailand for almost a month after Kitty went missing. There's no way Kitty came back to the UK and stayed under the radar with all the publicity that surrounded her disappearance until Henry turned up again and killed her.'

'Well, maybe Henry wasn't there then, but he knew about it. Either way, I'm certain she died at the school, and that at least one of her killers was either a pupil or staff member there. I also found out something else. There's a folly, an old ruined building, on land directly next to the school. It's got an occult symbol on the wall inside that looks like this.' I pulled out my phone, found the photo I'd taken, and showed it to Olaf.

He didn't look particularly impressed.

'I'm guessing you don't recognize it?'

'You're guessing right, Ray.'

I scrolled through the photos until I came to the one of the tattoo on Henry Forbes's underarm. 'It's called a pentacle, essentially a five-pointed star. Look at the markings on Henry's arm, then compare them to the symbol. They're identical. Henry's killers definitely wanted to burn off his tattoo.'

'Are you sure? They might just have wanted to burn down the house to get rid of evidence.'

'Then why not set fire to the curtains? Or something that's actually going to spread the flames? No, they set fire to Henry, because they wanted rid of that tattoo.'

Olaf gave me the kind of look usually reserved for blathering idiots. 'Blimey, Ray, this is all a bit thin, isn't it? You're not telling me you think this whole thing's down to devil worship, are you?'

'I don't know,' I said. 'But right now leads aren't exactly flying out at me.'

'Nor me. But I might have something for you to follow up on. The person I was just on the phone to was Tina Boyd.'

'*The* Tina Boyd?' That made me sit up. If you were looking for truly controversial figures in the Met's recent history, there were only two who automatically sprang to mind. One was me. The other was Tina Boyd. Shot twice; kidnapped once; held hostage; involved in at least three killings that had somehow just about held up as self-defence; suspended more times than I could remember; and now a private detective, having either been jumped or been pushed out of the Met, I can't remember which. I raised my eyebrows. 'Really? What did she want?'

'She was contacted by Henry Forbes last Monday, 11 April 2016. That's the day the first remains were discovered at the school, but the day before the discovery was made public in the media. Forbes wanted Tina to find a woman he knew from the past. And he wanted it done urgently. He even paid her two grand up front to do it.'

'Who's the woman?'

'Her name's Charlotte Curtis. Tina's got an office in Paddington. Would you mind going down there and getting all the details from her?'

'Of course not. But why are you using me for this?'

'I've got a lot of good coppers on this team, but not many good detectives. You'll know which questions to ask.' He winked at me. 'Unlike some people, I trust you, Ray. That's why I've been fighting your corner. Here's her address.' He pushed a slip of paper across the desk. 'She's there now. Find out what you can and let me know.'

I got up and left his office, not bothering to ask who it was who didn't trust me. The way most of the team avoided my gaze as I walked back through the incident room gave me my answer.

Fourteen

Tina Boyd's office was on a residential street in one of the less salubrious areas of Paddington with views towards the railway tracks and the giant A40 flyover beyond. It was just before seven and the sun was dropping off to the west as I found a parking spot about fifty metres down from her front door.

I have to admit I was intrigued to meet her. Tina Boyd was probably the most famous female police officer of her generation. Like me, she'd been involved in her fair share of famous cases and had a knack for being in the wrong (or right, I suppose) place at the wrong time. A tough yet attractive brunette with plenty of baggage, she was a survivor, and I admired that. On a dating website we'd have been a perfect match.

I pressed the buzzer, and a few seconds later she appeared behind the glass, giving me a coolly appraising look before opening the door. She was dressed in jeans and a tight-fitting white shirt with a jacket over the top. A simple look, yet there was something surprisingly elegant about the way she carried herself.

Her face broke into a welcoming smile as she put out a hand. '*The* Ray Mason. Pleased to meet you.'

'*The* Tina Boyd. Pleased to meet you too.'

She was a good-looking woman of about forty, with the lean, angular face of a runner, and shoulder-length black hair. She wore her years well, but her eyes were hard, and there was a natural mistrust in them that I guessed came from seeing too much of the dark side of life, and which was probably matched by the look in mine.

She led me through a narrow hallway that smelled of cleaning products and into her office, which smelled of cigarettes. It was a small room dominated by a big desk with a chair on either side. The window behind her was open and looked out on to a car park with a rusty skip in it. It wasn't the prettiest view I'd ever seen.

Tina offered me a drink but I declined and took a seat while she poured herself water from a cooler in the corner.

'Do you mind if I record the conversation?' I asked her, putting a tape recorder on the desk.

'Only if you don't mind me smoking,' she said, taking a seat on the other side of the desk.

I did. I can't stand the smell of smoke, even though years back I'd been a smoker. 'Go ahead,' I said. 'It's your office.'

She lit a cigarette and blew a line of smoke towards the ceiling. 'I called the SIO as soon as I saw Henry Forbes's name on the news today.'

'I understand he hired you to find a woman called Charlotte Curtis.'

'That's right. He called me last week and tried to hire me over the phone but I insisted he come in for an appointment. I always insist on seeing prospective clients face to face so I can decide whether I want to work for them or not. Mr Forbes was reluctant to come in, he said he was very busy. In fact he made all sorts of excuses, but eventually, when it became clear that I wasn't going to make an exception, he agreed to come here.'

'When was that?'

'He called me last Monday, the eleventh, and he finally came in on Thursday morning, the fourteenth.'

'So why did he say he was looking for Charlotte Curtis?'

'He said that she was a former girlfriend of his, that they'd been together back in the early nineties, but she'd emigrated to France and he wanted to get back in touch with her. He said he had something he needed to tell her, that it was very important and confidential. I told him I wouldn't give him Ms Curtis's contact details unless she gave me permission to, and he said that was fine, but he asked me to give her a message so she'd know what it was about.'

'And what was the message?'

'"It's urgent. And it's about Kitty." That's what he said. I wrote it down in here.' She tapped a notebook on the desk. 'At the time I didn't know anything about Mr Forbes's background so I didn't see any real significance in it, but obviously that's all changed now that I know about him being Kitty Sinn's boyfriend when she went missing.'

This really piqued my interest. Forbes wanted to talk to Char-lotte Curtis about Kitty. 'And he didn't tell you anything else?'

She blew more smoke up at the ceiling. 'No. But he did want me to make contact with her urgently. He even paid me two thou-sand in cash up front and gave me a number I could reach him on, although he made me promise I wouldn't divulge it to anyone. Here's the number.' She passed me a post-it note and I slipped it into the notebook. 'Anyway,' she continued, 'it was all very cloak and dagger, and I remember thinking that either he had a screw loose or he was under a huge amount of stress. In the light of recent events, it sounds like it was the latter.'

'And have you found Charlotte Curtis?'

'Yes. I finally located her yesterday. She'd changed her last name to Hollande, like the president, so it took longer than I'd hoped. I sent an email yesterday afternoon explaining who I was and giving her Forbes's message. I haven't heard back.'

'Have you got a number for her?'

'I've just managed to get hold of her mobile number. I called a landline registered in her name this morning but there was no answer.'

'And where's she living?'

'A village called Roquecor in the south-west of France, between Bordeaux and Toulouse. She's been there since 1998. Before that she lived in Brighton for eleven years, which is appar-ently where she met and had a relationship with Mr Forbes. She's a widow now, teaching in the local primary school out there.' Tina looked at me closely. 'Given what happened to Forbes, is she in any danger?'

'I don't think so but I'm going to need to speak to her. Can I take the numbers and the email?'

She wrote down the details and handed them to me. 'How's the investigation going? Have you got any suspects yet?'

I shook my head. 'It's early days.' I debated telling her that Kitty's remains had been discovered the day that Henry called her, but I held back. 'Was there anything in Ms Curtis's background, or your conversations with Mr Forbes, that stood out as a reason why he might have wanted to talk to her so urgently?'

She shook her head. 'I didn't look into Ms Curtis's background too deeply, but she seems like an ordinary woman to me. She's got no police record here or in France. I assume that at one point she was friends with Kitty Sinn otherwise Henry wouldn't have left the message he did, but that's all I know. Do you think Henry killed Kitty? It must have crossed your mind. It was always a mystery what happened to her.'

'Can I trust you, Miss Boyd?'

'Tina, please. And yes, you can.'

'I don't know if you've heard, but Thames Valley police have been digging up remains at a school in Buckinghamshire. They've found two skeletons so far, and one of them's just been ID'd as belonging to Kitty Sinn.'

Tina looked as surprised as anyone who'd heard that news. 'Well, that makes the case a lot more interesting. Every conspiracy theorist in a thousand miles is going to have a field day with that. Any idea how Kitty got there from Thailand?'

I shook my head emphatically. 'Right now, absolutely none. But I'm hoping Charlotte Curtis might be able to throw some light on things.' I looked at my watch. Twenty past eight in France. 'Let me try her mobile number now,' I said, punching it into my phone, curiously reluctant to leave this little office with its view over a car park.

The phone rang about half a dozen times before it was picked up at the other end. 'Bonjour?' The word was delivered with a degree of uncertainty as if she wasn't sure whether it was a *bon jour* or not.

'Mrs Hollande?'

'Yes.' Again, uncertain.

'This is Detective Sergeant Ray Mason of the Metropolitan Police in the UK, I wonder if I might speak to you about a Mr Henry Forbes.'

There was a pause. 'What do you want to know?'

'Last week he hired a private detective to find you. Apparently he wanted to give you a message.'

'To be honest, I hardly knew him. We had a very short relationship a long, long time ago. More than twenty years. I can't think why he'd want to get hold of me.'

'He wanted to talk to you about Katherine Sinn.'

'The girl who went missing all those years ago? She was a friend of mine back at poly, but again that was a long, long time back. I'm sorry, I can't help you any more than that, I'm afraid.'

'Mr Forbes told the private detective that it was very urgent. Do you have any idea what it could have been about?'

'Absolutely none. I'm sorry. Now, if you'll excuse me, I need to go out.'

'Henry Forbes is dead, Mrs Hollande. He was murdered last night along with his family lawyer.'

'Oh my goodness, I'm sorry to hear that. I wish I could be of more help, I really do.'

She ended the call before I could say anything else, leaving me staring at the phone.

'So she didn't want to talk?' said Tina.

'No,' I said, putting the phone away. 'She really didn't. And do you know what? She didn't even ask how Forbes died. She couldn't wait to get me off the phone.'

'You think she might be hiding something?'

I looked at her. 'Yeah, I do. And she also sounded scared. I'm going to need to talk to her, but we've got no jurisdiction in France, so I'm going to have to go through the authorities there.'

'Listen,' said Tina. 'Why don't I go out there and see her? Henry Forbes paid me two thousand in cash for the job and I've probably spent a tenth of that looking for her. He's not going to be asking for his money back now, and I haven't got a lot else on at the moment.'

'Are you sure?' I asked. 'It's a long way to go.'

She shrugged. 'It'll be an adventure. Don't you ever just feel like jumping on a plane and heading off into the wild blue yonder?'

'Yeah,' I said, picturing Ealing nick incident room and its occupants. 'All the time.'

'There you go then. It'll also be a good way of me helping on a case without stepping on anyone's toes. I miss proper detective work. You don't get a lot of it in my line, unfortunately. As soon as I've spoken to Charlotte, I'll get back to you.'

To be honest, it sounded like a good idea, and saved me a lot of trouble. Plus, it would also give me the opportunity to stay in touch with Tina, which I have to admit was quite a pleasant thought.

'Sure,' I said, without dwelling too much on Tina's well-deserved reputation for always seeming to find trouble. 'Why not?'

Fifteen

Charlotte shook with fear as she came off the phone and for a few seconds she had to hold on to the dining-room table for support.

She knew she hadn't done a very good acting job with the detective. She'd come across as flustered and possibly with something to hide, but that was only because of how scared she was. She knew that the man who'd killed Kado would do exactly the same to her if she didn't do exactly as she was told. She'd looked in his eyes and had seen an evil there that she'd never encountered before.

And now she was trapped. Being watched the whole time in her own home. She couldn't even go out for more than a few hours without incurring punishment. It was as if overnight she'd been turned from a reasonably happy, healthy woman with a good job and the possibility of a rosy future into someone's slave.

She didn't even have any means of getting help. If she went to the police and they didn't take her fears seriously – which was entirely possible: she was a widow living alone after all and her story was outlandish to say the least – she'd be killed. It was as simple as that. This man wasn't local. No one knew where to find him. He could just fade into the background and then reappear when it suited him.

Like a ghost.

For a long time after the man had left today, she hadn't been able to move. Finally, she'd got up and run to the bedroom where she'd sobbed her eyes out. Sobbed for Kado; sobbed for Jacques; sobbed for her dead parents, and for the girl who'd been her best friend, Kitty Sinn. Charlotte considered herself a tough woman but lying on her bed earlier, she'd felt totally alone. After about an hour she'd dragged herself back up and forced herself to bury Kado, a task that hadn't been as hard as she'd thought it would be. She'd dug a hole at the foot of the garden, with a view over the valley he'd loved so much. Finally, wrapping him in his blanket, she'd placed him gently inside, said a small prayer, and covered him with earth.

Standing at the lounge window now, watching the sun set over the wooded hills beyond the valley, Charlotte thought of Kitty Sinn, a woman she'd last seen nearly half a lifetime ago. They'd been great friends at poly, and had had a lot of fun together. Parties; nightclubs; live bands; drink; sex; the occasional spliff.

Although they'd been on the same course, they'd bonded in the first year through the poly hockey club, and had become part of a big gang of about a dozen students, an equal mix of male and female, who hung out together. In the third year she, Kitty and two of the other girls had shared a house, and Charlotte remembered that Kitty had been there for her when her dad died suddenly only weeks before their final exams began. Charlotte could still recall hearing the news, the tearful call from her mum telling her to come back home, that dad had had an accident, then her mum dissolving into floods of tears as she'd told Charlotte he was dead – that word, so utterly final and cold – ending in a keening wail down the phone. As Charlotte had put down the phone, her hands shaking, Kitty had taken her in her arms and held her close, letting Charlotte cry into her shoulder until she could cry no more.

That was Kitty. She was loyal and she was kind. Then one day, barely three months later, she'd left for Thailand and had never been seen again.

But was there anything about their friendship that stood out as being relevant to what was happening right now? A secret she might have divulged to Charlotte?

Something stirred in the back of her mind. A memory. As vague and ethereal as to be almost a dream. It lingered there a moment, just out of reach.

Charlotte sighed. 'Best just to leave the past in the past,' she said to herself and turned away from the window as the sun finally disappeared behind the trees and the shadows lengthened.

Sixteen

When I got back to my car and pulled out my phone I saw I had a message from Jerry Chesterman, Thames Valley's SIO at Medmenham College, telling me that he'd spoken to the headmaster and that the only person with access to the keys to the school gates were the caretaker and the headmaster. He added that the headmaster at the time of the girls' disappearances had had no criminal record, and had died of cancer in 1998, so he wasn't going to be answering either of our questions.

It was gone 7.30 and I was hungry. All I'd eaten today was a sandwich I'd picked up from a petrol station en route to the school, so as soon as I'd finished with Tina I drove back to Fulham, picking up takeaway sushi at a place I know on the New King's Road.

On the way, I called Olaf. He wasn't answering so I left a

message telling him how the meeting had gone with Tina, and adding that she'd volunteered to fly down to France to have an unofficial chat with Charlotte Curtis. I wasn't sure how Olaf would feel about a private detective doing our interviews for us – or the French police for that matter – but right now I didn't much care, and it seemed as good an idea as any of the alternatives.

I ate the sushi standing up in the kitchen at home with a cold beer to wash it down, and the map and aerial photographs of Medmenham College laid out in front of me. I was sure Kitty and Dana had been murdered at the school and reckoned it was more likely than not that it had happened in the ruined folly. It was far enough away from any nearby building not to attract attention, and the occult sign on the wall similar to the tattoo on Forbes's arm made it seem an even more likely location.

Of course, I could have been completely wrong, but in my experience it's always best to come up with a hypothesis that fits the available evidence, and run with it until something better comes along.

The problem was, I didn't have a shred of evidence to back up my theory. I needed some help, and I had an idea where I might be able to get it.

I figured there was at least a very good chance the college caretaker Bill Morris had information relevant to the murders of Dana and Kitty because, in the end, I couldn't see how the killers could have gained access to the grounds without him knowing about it. It was possible he'd also been involved in the killings, but I didn't think so. Kitty's murder had been elaborately planned by, to quote Henry Forbes, very powerful people. I didn't think they included Bill Morris. I reckoned it was more likely he'd turned a blind eye to the killers in return for something – probably money.

Of course, there was also a very good chance that he was entirely innocent, but the way I looked at it, any man who looks at child porn and knocks his wife about isn't entirely innocent of anything.

I deliberately hadn't taken Morris's address from DCI Chesterman because I didn't want anything linking him to me. For the same reason, I didn't look it up on the PNC. Instead, I logged on to the electoral roll, looked up the names William Morris and Hambleden, and quickly found what I was looking for.

I took a quick shower, changed into jeans and a dark jacket, and gathered together the things I was going to need.

Then I was out of the door and into the night.

Seventeen

Believe it or not, what destroyed my marriage was an item on the local news.

A thirty-seven-year-old Surrey man had just been convicted of dangerous driving after causing an accident during a fit of road rage. He'd rammed a female driver with his 4×4 after she'd apparently upset him. The woman's car had mounted the pavement, narrowly missing a number of pedestrians including children, and the woman herself had received minor injuries. The driver, described on the news as a nightclub promoter, was given a twelve-month suspended prison sentence and banned from driving for seven years. The footage showed him leaving the court in dark glasses, looking very angry as he pushed a photographer out of the way, before disappearing in a car driven by someone else.

It wasn't this that got me. I'm used to the arrogance of some people, and their lack of humility. It was the fact that, according to the report, this man, Kevin Wallcott, had a previous conviction from eight years earlier when, in another fit of road rage, he'd been chasing the occupants of a car and overtaking them on a blind bend when he hit a car coming the other way as it tried to avoid him. Because of the speed he was driving and the fact that he was in a Range Rover, Wallcott was unhurt. The driver of the other car was seriously injured. Worse still, his six-year-old daughter, who was in the back seat, was paralysed for life as the Range Rover slammed into the car's side.

Paralysed.

For life.

They showed a photo of the little girl on the TV screen and I remember a crescendo of rage building in me. Jo was sitting on the sofa next to me. She was upset by the report too, but it wasn't affecting her anything like as much as it was me. She asked me if I was OK, and I said I was fine.

But I wasn't. I wasn't fine at all.

Two days later I looked up Kevin Wallcott's home address on the PNC. I found out that he was divorced and lived alone, and that he had two further convictions not mentioned in the news report, both for assault.

I took to driving past his house in daylight and at night. I don't know why exactly, but I became completely obsessed. One time I watched him come out of his front door and take a taxi to a local gym. In the flesh he was even bigger than he looked on TV, and it was clear he worked out. He held his head high too, as if he

hadn't done a thing wrong. I thought of the little girl he'd paralysed for life, and I remember literally shaking with rage behind
the steering wheel as I watched him, wanting to tear him into
little pieces with my bare hands.

There were plenty of things I could have done to mess up
Kevin Wallcott's life. I could have broken into his house and
planted drugs, or stolen property. Or even child porn. I could
have got hold of his credit card details and stolen his identity. But
none of these things was personal for me. I had to actually *see*
him pay.

So one night I told Jo I was working late and I paid him a visit.

I knew he was at home because the lights were on, and I briefly
saw him in one of the windows. He lived on a street of terraced
houses with access through an alleyway at the back. I waited
until after midnight then slipped from my car, climbed the fence
into his garden, and picked the lock on his back door. I felt
nervous, but excited too, the adrenalin kicking through my system
as I crept through his house, slipping on a ski mask and taking out
a replica Walther PPK pistol from under my jacket. I knew plenty
could go wrong; that I was risking my job, my marriage and my
liberty for the sake of a little girl I would never know. But that
didn't seem to matter. I was dispensing justice.

I found him in the bedroom. He was lying naked on the bed
texting on his mobile, an idiot grin on his face that died the second
he saw me. He opened his mouth to say something but I told him
to shut the fuck up, my voice hard and calm, as I walked towards
him, pointing the gun at his head with a steady hand. It might
have been a replica but it looked exactly like the real thing.

Straight away he could see I was serious and, big guy or not, the way he was staring at me told me he wasn't going to cause me any trouble. I stopped five feet away and told him to drop the phone. He did. I told him to get on his knees on the floor with his back to me. He started talking fast, telling me I could take his money but not to hurt him, but I cut him off, telling him that if I wanted him dead he'd be dead already. He looked sceptical, as if he was sure this was some kind of trick, but he did as he was told. I ordered him to thread his hands together behind his back and, pushing the barrel of the gun against the back of his head, I cuffed his hands together, making sure the metal bit into his skin. He asked me what I was going to do with him. His whole body was shaking, he was that scared. I didn't answer him. Instead, I took a step back and kicked him in the balls from behind as hard as I could. He cried out and crumpled to the floor, rolling over on to his back.

I looked down at him as he writhed in pain and I felt a momentary pang of doubt about what I was doing. Then I pictured the little girl in her wheelchair where she'd remain for the rest of her life, and I stamped hard on Wallcott's groin before jumping on him, my knees pinning down his shoulders. 'This is for Jodie Parrish,' I said, and slammed the metal stock of the gun into his face. The first blow opened up a huge cut above his eye, the second and third spread his nose all over his face, and the fourth sliced open his forehead. Each one felt like an incredible release.

I leaned back and raised the gun high above my head, the darkness upon me, my whole body alive with fury, ready to deliver an even bigger blow to his head. Wallcott's face was a mask of blood and he was hardly moving. It would have been so easy to finish him off.

But I didn't. Something stopped me. A knowledge that I couldn't be his executioner. Not here. Not like this.

I stayed in that position for a good few seconds, with the gun above my head, before finally I lowered it and got to my feet. Wallcott rolled over on to his side, spitting out blood. I thought of taking the cuffs off, but why make it easy for him? I'd bought them with cash from an army surplus shop weeks earlier so they couldn't be traced back to me. Instead, I crushed his phone underfoot then turned and left him there, knowing I'd crossed a line.

And that's the thing. When you've crossed the line once, it's a lot easier to do it a second time. I was thinking that as I pulled my car up on a quiet side road just outside the village of Hambleden and cut the engine. Like the last time, I wasn't entirely convinced I was doing the right thing and I sat in the darkness of the car and took the picture of Dana Brennan her mum had given me out of my wallet. I stared at it for a few moments, thinking about the way Dana's life had been snatched away from her, and the fear she must have experienced in her final moments, and within seconds the anger was there like an old friend.

If Bill Morris knew anything about her murder, I was going to get it out of him.

I got out of the car and quietly shut the door. It was nearly ten o'clock and the night was silent out here in the rolling English countryside. On the other side of the valley was Medmenham College where even now they continued to dig for more bodies, and it made me wonder what was going through Morris's mind right now. Fear. Guilt. Or nothing.

Morris lived in a tiny cottage that guidebooks would have called quaint, the end one of a row of five up on a hill overlooking a field that led to the village church about fifty metres away, down a narrow tree-lined lane. A downstairs light was on, as was a single upstairs one, and an ancient Ford Fiesta was parked outside the gate, so I guessed he was in.

Slipping on a pair of clear plastic gloves, I opened the gate and mounted the steps to Morris's front door. I opened the letterbox and listened. I could hear the TV blaring loudly inside. It sounded like the news. There was no doorbell, just an old brass door-knocker. I considered using it and announcing my presence the old-fashioned way but decided against it. If he didn't cooperate with Thames Valley he wasn't going to cooperate with me.

I took a step back and looked up. There didn't seem to be any movement coming from upstairs either so I headed round the back into a small, neglected garden overgrown with weeds.

The cottage's back door was unlocked and led straight into a kitchen and dining area. Plates were piled up in the sink but the room and the hallway beyond were empty.

I walked through the kitchen and into the narrow hallway, keeping my head down to avoid the overhead beams. The only sound was the blare of the TV. I pulled on a ski mask like the kind the gunmen had worn the previous night, and the kind I'd worn when I'd visited Kevin Wallcott, and pushed open the living-room door.

It was dark inside, the TV providing the only light. The thread-bare sofa opposite it was empty but there was a half-full pint glass of lager balanced on one arm, along with a well-used ashtray, a packet of cheap brand cigarettes, and a lighter. The lager had gone flat.

It looked like Bill Morris had been settled in for the night, yet there was no sign of him now. I doubted if he'd gone for a walk without taking his smokes.

I stopped at the bottom of the staircase, listening for any movement upstairs. It was hard to hear anything above the TV, but I thought I heard something bang up there.

I'd brought a small leather cosh with me in case Morris proved a bit of a handful and I took it from my jacket now and started up the stairs.

That was when I heard another noise, like something being kicked. I caught something else too. The faint but unmistakable smell of shit.

I felt the hairs rise on the back of my neck and waited a few seconds, not moving. Then, when there was no repeat of the noise, I continued up the staircase, step by step, conscious of the loud groans they made under my weight.

The door directly opposite the top of the stairs was ajar a couple of inches and the light inside was on. The smell was worse here and I felt a clear sense of dread as dark memories surfaced inside me. Memories of being alone and terrified in an old rambling house while all around me murder was committed. I shuddered, felt the fear rise, and fought it down. I had no choice. I had to go inside.

With my grip tightening on the cosh, I kicked open the door and stepped over the threshold.

Morris was hanging from an old air vent in the ceiling at the foot of an unmade bed, his face puce, his eyes bugged open, his tongue hanging from his mouth. He was dressed in a grimy white vest and grey tracksuit bottoms, and his feet were swollen and bare, the yellowing, talon-like toenails only centimetres from the floor. A chair lay on its side nearby and next to it was an empty bottle of whisky sitting on top of a sheet of A4 printer paper.

As I stood there, momentarily frozen to the spot, Morris's leg twitched violently and a stain spread across the crutch of his tracksuit bottoms as his bladder evacuated. That was when I knew he'd only died in the last few seconds.

I heard movement behind me.

Before I had time to turn round I felt a powerful blow across my shoulder blades and I fell forward into a pile of junk boxes against the bedroom wall, just managing to put out a hand to break my fall. I wriggled round and caught a glimpse of two figures in dark clothing in the room with me before one of them sprayed something in my face.

I rolled away, shutting my eyes, but it was too late. The spray had invaded my nostrils, eyes and throat, burning them up. I broke into a coughing fit and tried to get to my feet, but a kick from nowhere sent me sprawling again, and this time I banged my head against the wall. I felt a surge of panic, knowing I was helpless, wondering what the hell they'd sprayed me with.

I felt one of them come in close and lashed out blindly at him, missing completely. The next second the ski mask was wrenched from my head and I felt rather than saw a camera flash. A boot caught me in the gut but I hardly felt it. All I could think about was the burning effects of the spray. I had to get fresh air.

The attack stopped, and I heard the sound of footsteps rapidly descending the stairs. Still blinded, I felt my way over to the bedroom window and shoved it open, pushing my head out and gasping for breath.

I hung out there for a good thirty seconds until finally the effects of the spray, which was almost certainly CS gas, began to become more tolerable. Then, knowing that I was hugely conspicuous with my head stuck out of a murder victim's window just minutes after he'd been killed, I staggered out on to the landing, found the bathroom, and splashed water over my face until the burning faded.

I needed to get out, and fast, but I also knew I couldn't leave evidence behind, so I ran back into the bedroom, barely glancing at Morris's now still corpse, and looked around for the ski mask.

But it wasn't there. The men who'd ambushed me had taken it. Why?

There was no time to answer that question, so I turned and ran down the stairs, going out the way I'd come in, through the back door.

Almost immediately I heard an angry shout coming from one of the neighbour's windows: 'Stop thief! I've called the police!'

I had my back to the neighbour so he couldn't see my face and, with my eyes still streaming from the gas, I clambered over Morris's back fence, fell down the other side, and took off through the trees, trying to navigate my way back to the road I was parked in.

By the time I reached the car, I could hear the first siren

somewhere in the distance. I was pointed in the direction of the village and there was no way I was going to risk driving past Morris's house in case someone got my number plate, so I did a rapid three-point turn, not entirely sure where I was going, and drove away into the darkness.

Twenty minutes and a lot of winding back roads later I was back on the M40 heading into London and wondering how the killers always seemed to be one step ahead of me.

Because that was the thing. They were.

Eighteen

Life had dealt some pretty poor cards to Ramon Thomas, starting from even before he'd been born. A few months before she became pregnant, his mum had discovered the brand-new drug that was sweeping London's sprawling council estates, and she'd continued smoking crack the whole time she was carrying Ramon. He'd ended up being born a month early when his mum was rushed to hospital with major complications. The doctors had been forced to deliver him using forceps and, as far as Ramon was concerned, they hadn't done all that good a job of it. He'd been left with a deep scar on his cheek and a lazy eye that had got worse as he'd grown older, making him look like some kind of retard.

With a crack addict for a mum, and a dad who was always in and out of jail, Ramon and his little sister Keesha ended up living with their granddad, who tried his best to bring them up with some semblance of normality. But then Granddad had died when Ramon was nine and Keesha only five. At the same time Ramon's old man had just finished his latest sentence and he made Ramon and Keesha move back in with him and their mum. Supposedly, they were going to be a family and everything was going to turn out OK. At least that's what his old man said. The reality was a whole lot different. His mum and dad argued and fought like a pair of stray dogs, and when the old man got in one of his moods, he'd beat Ramon with anything he could lay his hands on. Ramon could handle it as long as he didn't hurt Keesha, and usually he didn't. The old man loved Keesha. A lot more than he loved Ramon.

One day when Ramon was at school, someone left the flat's front door open and Keesha wandered outside. Something must have caught her attention on the other side of the road because she ran right across it. A car had been coming, driven too fast by a couple of kids, and they'd hit Keesha head on. The Feds said she'd died quick, which Ramon supposed was something to cling to, but the death had hit him hard. Keesha was the only person in the world who'd ever shown him real love. She'd had this way of looking into his eyes like she truly needed him, and it had always filled him with a weird kind of pride. He was her protector.

Except he hadn't been there when she'd needed him.

His old man had blamed his mum, and after the Feds had caught him beating the shit out of her, he'd gone back to jail. The social workers had wanted to put Ramon into care but he'd told them his mum was looking after him properly and they'd let him stay with her. She didn't look after him – she couldn't even look after herself – but Ramon didn't want to have to leave the estate where he'd spent his whole life.

One day, when he was about thirteen, he was walking down Tottenham High Road when a gang of older boys surrounded him. They laughed at his lazy eye and called him freak, demanding to know which postcode he lived in. Ramon recognized one of the boys and knew he was from the Man Dem Crew from an estate in Wood Green. Ramon knew the Man Dem Crew had a beef with some of the boys from his estate so he lied and made up a postcode. But they'd heard his hesitation and knew he was lying, so they dragged him into a side street and started beating him. That was what it was like in those days. You could get hurt just because you lived in the wrong place. He'd fought back, and fought back hard, but that just made them beat him more, and he was never going to win one against six.

When he got out of hospital a few days later, Ramon knew it was time to join a gang so he could protect himself. On his estate, the main crew were the N17 Murder Boys and Ramon knew one of their Youngers, a kid who lived a few doors down, so he approached him. Even at thirteen, Ramon was a big guy – his mum's crack addiction during pregnancy didn't seem to have left him with any growth issues – and the scar on his face made him look pretty scary. More importantly, he was fearless. The only thing he cared about in life – his little sister – had been taken away from him, and now that she'd gone he had nothing to live for, which made him perfect gang fodder.

And Ramon loved being part of a gang. It gave him the sense of belonging and stability he'd been missing his whole life, and it was exciting. Jesus, it was exciting. He started dealing. First skunk, then crack, and even brown when the crew could get hold of it. The crew's Elders took a big cut of the profits but still left him with more cash than a thirteen-year-old could dream of. He earned even more by robbing kids at knifepoint round near the High Road with a couple of other crew members, and found that he loved the buzz of imposing his dominance on them, and seeing the fear in their eyes as they begged him not to hurt them. He didn't. But he always took everything they had.

His mum, crack-addled ho that she was, knew what he was up to, and she tried to muscle in, saying that if he wanted to stay in *her* flat – like it actually belonged to her – then he was going to have to pay, either in money or rocks. But Ramon had soon put her right, giving her the kind of beating that made her know not to fool with him again.

Ramon knew that what he was doing in his life was wrong. He was no fool. His granddad had been a churchgoing Christian who'd recited the Ten Commandments to him plenty of times, and told him that God was always watching what he did. 'He's taking notes, boy,' was what Granddad had always said, 'and if you don't do right, you're not going to his place at the end.' But Granddad had died so poor they couldn't even afford a funeral, so how much had God really helped him?

And so Ramon had gone further and further off the rails. It was an easy journey. Once you'd robbed someone once, it was a lot easier doing it again. Once you'd punched a man in the face, it wasn't that much of a step to kicking him while he lay helpless on the ground, or smacking him round the head with a bottle.

Violence became a release for him. All his pent-up rage at the injustices of the world came pouring out. The high was better than any crack hit, or even sex. When he was fighting, it was like he was king of the world: fistproof; knifeproof; bulletproof. He built up a formidable reputation. No one laughed at him any more. No one called him a freak. He was respected. And it felt good.

He rose up the ranks of the gang, became one of its Elders so he had dealers working for him, even moved into his own flat away from his ho of a mother. And because he was a face now he bought himself a gun, and not one of those converted starter pistols either. His was a Browning nine-mill semi-automatic. It cost him two grand in cash, which was a hell of a lot of green, but now he had a real status symbol. Ramon had never handled a gun before, let alone fired one, and the white guy who sold it to him had to show him how everything worked.

He carried that gun with him everywhere, tucked into the waistband of his jeans, waiting for someone, anyone, to try it on with him.

And then one day someone did.

One of his dealers, a skinny Younger called Clyde, got held up at knifepoint by three gangbangers from the Clifton Road Shooter Posse, who forced him to hand over his drugs and money. Then, because he didn't have enough stuff on him, or maybe just for fun, Ramon wasn't sure, they'd shanked Clyde in the leg and left him on the ground bleeding. The three attackers hadn't even bothered covering their faces. It was a blatant act of disrespect and it demanded retribution.

The one who'd done the shanking was quickly ID'd as Marlon 'Raver' Jones, and he was the one who was going to have to pay.

Three nights later Ramon had gone to Raver's ground-floor flat in the middle of the Clifton Estate. This was pure enemy territory but, even so, Ramon had turned up alone. He wanted to show the world that he didn't need anyone else to help settle his business. He'd been scared though, he remembered that, and he'd had to force down his fear, knowing from long, bitter experience that the moment you show weakness, you're dead. So he banged on Raver's door, demanding that he come out and face him. Ramon knew he was in there. He could hear Raver's mum yelling at him, wanting to know what was going on. When no one answered, Ramon began kicking the door, trying to smash it off its hinges, but someone bolted it from the inside and the door held.

By this time a crowd was arriving. There were probably a dozen of them, mainly Shooter Posse Youngers on their bikes, a couple of Elders in there too. They started yelling abuse at him, then pulled up their hoods and moved towards him, their numbers making them brave as they tried to cut off his escape. One of them pulled a shank from inside his jacket and held it up in the air, a grin on his face. The others howled and whooped. They thought they had him.

Which was when Ramon took the gun from the waistband of his jeans and pointed it at the crowd. The look on his face beneath his own hoodie must have told them he was serious about using it because they stopped dead. All of them. At the same time.

Ramon could have left it at that. There was no way they'd challenge him with a gun in his hand. He could have ridden out of there, having made his point by disrespecting Raver in his own ends, thereby increasing his own rep.

But he didn't. Instead he pulled the trigger, shooting wildly into the crowd, not bothered about who he hit, rage and excitement exploding within him with such force that he didn't even have time to think what he was doing. One of them went down, rolling over in the dirt, and as the rest of them fled in all directions, abandoning their bikes where they fell, Ramon turned and fired the remaining bullets into Raver's front door. Then he got on his own bike and rode past the kid lying on the ground without even stopping to look at him.

Three days later the Feds came crashing through Ramon's front door and arrested him at gunpoint for the murder of fifteen-year-old Terrell Wright. Ramon hadn't been expecting them. He knew the kid had died and he felt bad about that, but he'd assumed that people would be too scared to talk to the Feds and finger him for the shooting, and as it happened, no one actually had. Unfortunately for Ramon, the estate's recently installed network of CCTV cameras had captured the whole thing, and he'd been ID'd from the footage.

In the face of the overwhelming video evidence, and on the advice of his brief, Ramon had pleaded guilty to manslaughter, claiming he'd been terrified of the mob approaching him, and had only fired warning shots. The jury didn't buy it though and convicted him of murder, and the judge sentenced him to life imprisonment with a minimum tariff of fourteen years.

He was sixteen years old.

That had been a lifetime ago, but he still often thought about that night when he pulled the trigger and killed Terrell Wright and the fourteen years of his life it had cost him for maybe ten seconds of true power. It was a price that hadn't been worth paying, and now, as he sat in the van listening to Junior ramble on in the driver's seat, he felt the regret washing over him again. What a waste of a life. He couldn't go back inside again. He'd rather die than that, which made him wonder what the hell he was doing here, sitting in a van on a freezing headland overlooking a black sea, miles away from home. But then Ramon had always had a knack for attracting trouble.

Junior was talking about money, which he did a lot of the time. 'If I could just save up a hundred grand – that's all, just a hundred – that's me sorted. Then I'm done. All them other boys, the younger ones, they just want to live large. They're not thinking about the future. You've always got to think about the future, Ramon. You get what I'm saying?'

Ramon looked at him and saw a pasty-faced white man with a nose that had been busted so many times it actually changed direction as it came out of his face. Junior was thirty-eight but looked older. He was an ex-boxer who'd spent a long time in the army, and had served in Iraq and Afghanistan. According to Junior himself, he'd killed a total of ten men in battle, but Ramon reckoned he was bullshitting. He was a hard man, there was no doubt about that, but somehow he didn't have the eyes of a killer. Still, he was high up in the crew and right now he was Ramon's boss.

'So when am I going to get a chance to run with the big boys, Junior?' Ramon asked him.

Junior grinned, showing teeth that looked like he was wearing them in for a dog. His breath smelled like blocked drains. 'Soon, mate. You've been doing well.'

This was true. Ramon had worked hard these past six months. He'd been involved in some rough stuff since joining the bottom rung of the Kalaman outfit. Most of the work had been debt collecting. A lot of people owed the outfit money and some of them couldn't pay (no one ever chose not to pay, that would have been suicidal). Usually a visit from Junior and Ramon was enough to motivate the debtor to somehow find the money, but occasionally a more forceful approach was needed. One time, Ramon had had to hold on to a guy while Junior held a knife to his girlfriend's face and threatened to slash her. Another time he'd held a man down while Junior broke three of his fingers with a hammer. It wasn't nice work but Ramon had done it without complaint. Just like when he'd been a kid strutting round the block with a gun in his waistband, he knew what he was doing was wrong, but he justified it by telling himself these people weren't innocents, they were idiots who'd fucked over the wrong people. And he had a firm rule: he wouldn't hurt kids. Whatever people might think, Ramon had morals.

'The thing is, Ramon, you've got to be patient,' continued Junior. 'Shit, you spent enough time inside, it can't be that hard.'

'I didn't join to shake down debtors. I joined to be a soldier.'

'And you'll get your chance,' said Junior. 'I'm going to put in a recommendation.'

Ramon grinned. 'Seriously? Thanks, man.'

But Junior was already looking away. 'Hold on, what's that?' He picked up a pair of binoculars and stared out of the windscreen. 'That's them. They're here.'

Ramon looked out to sea and immediately spotted the approaching lights. Their cargo was coming in.

Nineteen

'Tango here, we're in place,' said Junior, producing a satellite phone from beneath his seat and sounding like something out of a cop show.

A tinny voice gabbled something down the other end of the line, and Junior ended the call and turned to Ramon. 'You ready? We take them off the boat and put them straight in the back. No messing about. Understand?'

'Sure,' said Ramon, and got out of the van. He wasn't particularly nervous. Although it was his first time dealing with the smuggling side of the business, there was no reason to expect any trouble. Junior had done this run at least a dozen times before and every time it had gone smoothly. The beach they were on was in the middle of nowhere so they weren't going to be spotted and, according to Junior, the only coastguard boat patrolling this stretch of coast would be somewhere else tonight.

It was a clear night and cold as they climbed down the sand dune on to the beach and walked towards the sea. Ramon, who'd only ever been outside London on a handful of occasions, found it hard to believe there were places in England with this much space. The beach seemed to stretch for ever and there wasn't a single light on it in either direction for what seemed like miles.

Junior caught him staring upwards as they walked. 'What the fuck are you looking at?' he demanded.

'The stars. I've never seen this many before. There's millions of them.'

Junior made a noise like a fart, which he often did when he was annoyed. 'Jesus, Ramon, they're just lights in the sky. Watch where you're going. This ain't a school trip.' He switched on the torch he was carrying and pointed it out to sea, waving it from side to side as he walked.

The beam was narrow but intense and Ramon could see a dark shape with no lights on it out at sea and a smaller shape coming towards them. From the low thrum of the engine and the shapes sticking out of it he judged it was a dinghy with quite a few people in it. Someone on the dinghy flashed a light back and then straight away put it out.

They stopped near the sea's edge, and Junior switched off the torch.

Ramon was thankful the water was calm. He'd never learned to swim and didn't like the idea of wading out to sea unless he absolutely had to.

He could now see there were at least ten people on the dinghy, all crowded together. The driver, a middle-aged white guy in a beanie hat, cut the engine and the dinghy drifted in the rest of the way, coming to a halt just a few yards from shore. The driver chucked a rope and Junior caught it, telling Ramon to give him a hand getting the boat in.

Ramon grabbed the rope and pulled hard. He was a big man and strong too from all the weights he'd done in prison, and between the two of them they quickly got the boat aground.

That was when Ramon got a good look at who was in it. Apart from the driver, the rest were all young girls shivering in skimpy clothes with packs on their backs. They were barefooted and carrying their shoes and they looked scared. Ramon wasn't very good with ages, but he reckoned these girls were all about seventeen, eighteen, and they were all really hot-looking. Fresh meat, Junior had called them, and both he and Ramon knew exactly where they were going.

The driver glared at the girls and made an impatient gesture for them to get out of the boat. 'Go, go, go,' he said in a foreign accent. 'Hurry, hurry.'

The first girl stood up unsteadily and almost fell over but Ramon put out a hand to help her. She grabbed hold of it, but the moment she looked at his face, her expression changed. She looked like she'd just seen a monster. Ramon had seen that look on people's faces plenty of times before, but something about the way the girl's lips curled, like she was disgusted too, made him want to hit her. But he was a professional so he helped her ashore, then put his hand out to a second girl, who kept her head down and didn't even look at him.

It was the third girl who caught his attention. She had darker skin than the others and was much more pretty. And, as he grabbed hold of her arm to steady her and helped her out, she actually smiled at him too. Not just any old smile either. It was a real one that reached right the way up to her big brown eyes, eyes that instantly reminded him of his little sister, Keesha. In that moment, something awoke in Ramon that he hadn't felt in years and years.

Protectiveness.

'Come on, move it, we need to get out of here,' snapped Junior and, reluctantly, Ramon let the girl go and reached out his hand for the next one.

When all the girls were huddled together on the beach, looking cold and nervous, Junior told Ramon to grab the large black holdall on the floor of the dinghy, then push it back out to sea.

Ramon was used to being ordered around by Junior. He didn't like it but he accepted it because he knew the rules in the outfit. You obeyed your boss without question. The moment you didn't, you were out. And Ramon couldn't afford to be out. He leaned in and grabbed the holdall, hearing the clank of metal knocking against metal inside as he threw it over his massive shoulder. Then he bent down, grabbed the dinghy with both hands and pushed, watching as it slid back into the water, before turning away as the guy inside started the engine and it disappeared into the gloom.

Junior was herding the girls up the beach, like a Nazi guard from one of the documentaries Ramon used to watch in jail, making them run, and pushing the stragglers so they kept up, while Ramon followed behind. Now that they had their cargo, it was important they get out of here fast without attracting attention.

When they returned to the van, Junior threw open the double doors at the back and pushed the girls in one at a time, telling them to be quick. Ramon took up a position on the other side, and he was gentler as he helped the girls in. He tried to catch the pretty girl's eye again, but he didn't manage to before Junior grabbed her and got her inside.

They were a sorry sight, Ramon thought as Junior asked who among them spoke English. Five of the girls put their hands up, which Ramon thought was pretty impressive. One of the hands belonged to the pretty girl. Again he tried to smile at her but she was staring at Junior who was speaking now.

'OK,' he said, 'you all keep quiet in here. Tell the others. If we stop at all, no one says a word. If the police find you, they will deport you to your countries, so you must be silent. We are going on a journey to London now and we will be there in two hours. Then you will be met by the people you will be working for.'

Ramon felt an unexpected and unwelcome pang of emotion as the pretty girl smiled again. She looked happier than the others, like she honestly believed she was going to be doing a proper job, like cleaning or waitressing, not being fucked for money until she burned out. Junior had always told him that he had to treat everything they did together as purely business, nothing more, and never to get squeamish about any of it. 'I know that ain't going to happen with you, though, Ramon,' he'd said. 'I can see you're a man with no feelings.'

In the old days on the estate, Ramon would have taken that as a compliment. Now he wasn't so sure.

Junior shut the van's double doors and they climbed back into the cab. Ramon put the holdall in the space behind the front seats and Junior covered it with an old blanket before looking at him carefully.

'The chances of us being stopped by the Feds are a thousand to one up here, but you know the drill if we do.'

Ramon nodded. 'Yeah, I know the drill.'

'What is it? Remind me.'

'I thought you knew it.'

'Don't fuck me about, Ramon. This is serious.'

Ramon sighed, irritated that everyone seemed to treat him like an idiot. They'd been through this a dozen times already, but Junior was going to make him go through it again. 'If we get stopped out here, and there's no one around, I pull the gun. And yeah, I've checked it. It's loaded. We cuff the Feds and nick their keys. If they get too good a look at our faces, we take them some- where quiet and finish them.'

'As a last resort.'

'Yeah, as a last resort. If we get stopped on main roads with cars around we try and blag it. If that don't work, we pull the gun again, cuff them. We get stopped in London anywhere, we abandon everything and run.'

'That's exactly it.'

Junior switched on the engine and they pulled away.

'What's in the holdall?' Ramon asked him.

'You ask a lot of questions, bruv. Too many.'

'You ask me to threaten the Feds with a gun, maybe even shoot a couple of them, you might as well tell me why.'

Junior grunted. 'What do you think's in there? Guns.'

He switched on the radio and the cab was filled with the boring Yankee rock music Junior liked to listen to.

Ramon fell silent and opened the window to let out the worst of Junior's stale breath. Jesus, he hoped they didn't get stopped. He could feel the uncomfortable bulge of the pistol – a Browning, just like the one he'd blown Terrell Wright away with – in the waistband of his jeans. Junior had said the chances were a thousand to one, but bad luck had always followed Ramon around like a stray dog. It wasn't that he didn't have it in him to threaten or even kill a Fed, but the last thing he wanted in the world was to go back to prison for the rest of his life.

When he leaned back in his seat, he could hear the girls whispering in the back. There were at least two conversations going on in different languages. The girls sounded excited, as if they were going on an adventure, and he thought of the pretty girl with her smiling face and wondered what she'd be like in a few hard years' time. Cynical, angry and lost, probably, just like the rest of us. Junior was right. It was best not to think about it.

On the radio, the rock music stopped and the news came on. The lead story was about two missing girls whose bones had been dug up somewhere out of town, followed by the double shooting of a lawyer and his client in the lawyer's home. Apparently the killers had also opened fire on a cop who was there but hadn't managed to hit him.

'Pity they were crap shots,' grunted Ramon, who hated the

Feds as much now as he had all those years ago back on the block. 'They should have killed the bastard.'

'No way,' said Junior, shaking his head angrily. 'The first rule is you never kill Feds unless you absolutely have to, especially if you've just shot two other people. Otherwise all you're on is the wrong end of a total shit storm. There's no need to shoot when they've got no guns. The boys had their faces covered so they couldn't be ID'd, so all they needed to do was mosey on out of there. That's the professional's way of doing things, Ramon, and if you want to be a pro, that's what you've got to do.'

Ramon looked at him. 'Shit, Junior. The way you're talking, it sounds like you were there.'

For a couple of seconds, Junior didn't say anything, just looked straight ahead. He didn't look happy.

'That wasn't anything to do with us, was it?'

'You know, I like you, Ramon,' Junior said eventually. 'You do what you're told, you served your time without ever snitching on anyone or going stir crazy, and you know how to kill. But there are two things you've still got to learn. One: you only kill people when it makes a profit, or it protects one. And two: don't ever ask too many fucking questions. That way you wind up back in the slammer. Or, worse, dead. You understand me?'

Ramon nodded slowly, knowing he'd struck a nerve. 'Yeah, I understand you.'

'So don't say another word about that shooting to anyone, right?'

'Right.'

Once again the van fell silent and Ramon stared straight ahead into the darkness. He was tired. It was two a.m., and it was two hours back to London.

Even so, when he got there he knew he was going to have to make a very important phone call.

Day Three
Thursday

Twenty

I forgot to set the alarm, and when I opened my eyes the bedside clock told me it was 7.50 a.m., meaning I'd overslept by close to an hour and a half. When you're working a murder inquiry the hours are long, particularly in the first few days. It's eight a.m. in the incident room at the latest, and sometimes you're not back out until midnight.

I rubbed my eyes and sat up, and it was a good couple of seconds before I remembered what had happened last night. An illegal entry into a potential witness's house; the discovery of his hanging body; a violent assault by his killers, with me on the wrong end of it; my photo taken by the same killers; and then a frantic escape during which I may or may not have been seen by a neighbour.

It hadn't exactly been my finest hour. Still, at least it had proved my theory. Bill Morris must have known something about Kitty and Dana's murders. Unfortunately, I was never going to find out what it was.

The incident had thrown up a lot of questions, none of which I'd spent much time trying to answer when I'd got home last night. Instead, I'd downed the best part of a bottle of wine in an effort to calm down – it worked – before hitting the sack and, unusually for me, sleeping a dreamless sleep.

Now, though, it was time to start thinking. I made up some coffee, and while it was brewing had a quick shower to wake me up. I had a text message from Tina Boyd telling me she was on the 10.30 a.m. flight to Bergerac in France and was hoping to be at Charlotte Curtis's current address by early afternoon. I texted back, telling her to ask Charlotte if Henry Forbes had had a tattoo of a pentacle on his underarm when she'd known him, and if so, what was the significance of it. Then I put in a call to Olaf.

As the phone rang, I wondered whether Olaf had somehow found out about my visit to Bill Morris's place the previous night, but if he had he was keeping it quiet.

'I got your message about Tina,' he said. He didn't sound massively pleased.

'I thought it was the best thing sending her down there, sir. It saves us manpower and having to wade through all the bureaucracy with the French police.'

'The problem is, she's not a police officer, Ray. And she's not exactly fucking stable either if half the stories are anything to go by.'

'She's just following up a possible lead, sir. It's not even as if it's a major one. I've already spoken to Charlotte Curtis and she didn't want to help us. It might be that Tina has more luck.'

'OK. Well, if she finds out anything, I want to be the first to know. I'm coming under a lot of pressure on this case. Have you turned up anything else?'

I thought of Bill Morris hanging in his bedroom. 'Not yet, but I'm working on a lot of leads. Don't lose me from this case, sir.'

'I'll try not to, but it's being overseen by the commander, so it may be out of my hands.'

'Then I guess I'd better turn up something fast. I thought I'd go back through the case files at home this morning rather than come in. It's quieter.'

'Good idea,' said Olaf, sounding a little too relieved for my liking.

'Can I still use Jools to help me, though?'

'For the moment,' he said, and ended the call, which didn't exactly feel like a vote of confidence.

I knew then my days on the case were numbered, so I was going to have to move fast while I still could.

Grabbing a coffee, I sat down at the dining-room table with my laptop, the case files, and my notebook.

We had two very different murders committed by the same people, if the bodies' burial in the same place was anything to go by. The first was a random abduction, and I remembered what Henry Forbes had said in my one and only interview with him: 'I know they'd killed before Kitty'. This suggested that he'd had nothing to do with Dana's murder. Kitty's, though, had required extensive planning, and Henry had been very much in on it.

Once again I was drawn back to the mystery of Kitty's disappearance. The facts as we had them simply didn't add up. Kitty travelled to Thailand with Henry at the end of July 1990. Her passport was checked on the way out from the UK at Heathrow Airport and stamped on the way into Thailand at Bangkok. She and Henry stayed in Phuket for four days and were seen together by a number of witnesses. They then travelled north to the Khao Sok National Park where they stayed for one night and were seen by further witnesses, who also testified that they saw Kitty leave the hotel alone. She was given a lift to Khao Lak on the coast by the hotel's owner. And that was it, she disappeared. And then suddenly her remains reappeared twenty-six years later six thousand miles away.

So I went through the possible explanations for how she got back to the UK.

One, Kitty leaves Thailand without getting her passport stamped and makes her way back, entering the country illegally without the authorities knowing. Afterwards, she keeps her return secret, manages not to be seen by anyone, even though there's a huge amount of publicity surrounding her disappearance, and at some point after that is murdered by persons unknown who tell Henry Forbes, who didn't return to the UK for a month after Kitty went missing, what they'd done and where they'd buried her.

I wrote all this down in the notebook and read it through twice. As a viable theory for explaining what had happened, it made no sense at all. There were at least half a dozen holes in it big enough to drive a truck through.

So what was the alternative?

I sat there staring at the notebook, turning things over in my head, again and again, oblivious to my surroundings, lost in thought.

Then it hit me. Just like that. The most obvious explanation of all.

Kitty Sinn never went to Thailand.

Of course, there were problems with this theory too. Kitty had been seen in Thailand by a number of witnesses. But had they actually seen Kitty? What if she'd been killed before she left the country and Henry had taken someone else in her place? The only way this would have worked, given the publicity surrounding the case, was if the woman he took looked a lot like her. But it was possible. And if this was the case, the theory made perfect sense. It would explain how Kitty ended up buried in the grounds of Medmenham College, and how Henry knew the location.

But who was the woman he was with? And why was Henry involved?

As far as I could see, there was no obvious motive for Henry killing Kitty. According to the background that Jools Hutchings had given me, he came from wealthy stock and didn't appear to need the money. And with that level of planning it couldn't have been a crime of passion. So, what?

I got up, poured myself a second cup of coffee, and texted Tina again, requesting that she ask Charlotte Curtis what Kitty's relationship with Henry had been like and whether they'd seemed like a loving couple. Then I went back to the files.

Henry had told me other people were involved. What could their motive have been? Could there really have been an occult aspect to both murders? But that didn't explain the level of planning involved in Kitty's disappearance and eventual death. There had to be another reason why she died. I just needed to find it.

As I drank my coffee, I went back through Sussex police's original file on Kitty, looking for something that stood out. The file contained a number of UK newspaper clippings from the time. They'd started off as small pieces on the inside pages but had grown in size as the days passed and the mystery of her disappearance grew. For a couple of weeks in August 1990 Kitty had been front-page news, her smiling photo staring out at the world.

I read carefully through each article, and it was one of the last ones that caught my attention. It was from the *Sunday Times* and dated October 1992, more than two years after Kitty had gone missing. The headline was 'A Life of Tragedy: Kitty Sinn's Mother Found Dead', and it told how Mary Sinn had been found at her home in Oxford, the victim, police believed, of suicide. Apparently bottles of pills and an empty bottle of whisky had been found next to her body and toxicology reports had revealed she'd died of a massive overdose of painkillers.

What piqued my interest was Mary Sinn's background, and the article gave a lot of detail, concentrating, as the media so often do, on the more tragic elements. And I have to admit, it had been a tragic life. Mary's father, Edgar, who was the son of the founder of the Merchant Hardware empire – the article's word, not mine – had been killed in action in World War Two when

Mary was only four years old. Her only sibling, Janet, had been killed in a car crash while on holiday in Italy in 1975, aged just thirty-six. Mary and Kitty's father had divorced after he'd begun an affair with a male family friend, and the couple had been estranged when he'd died nine years later of cancer. By 1990, all Mary had left was her elderly mother Doris, and of course her only child, Kitty.

After Kitty's disappearance, it seemed that Mary went downhill fast. She'd had a nervous breakdown that had culminated in her trying to burn down the house of her former brother-in-law Robert Sheridan – the man who'd been married to her late sister, Janet – and his family, while heavily inebriated. When Sheridan had confronted her, she'd attacked him with a knife and he and his daughter, Lola, had been forced to barricade themselves in the house until the police arrived. Mary, who must have been a feisty lady, had attacked the arresting officers as well before finally being restrained and taken into custody. Because of her mental state, Mary hadn't been charged but had been sectioned instead under the Mental Health Act, and had spent six months in a psychiatric hospital before being released. During her incarceration she'd also been diagnosed as suffering from primary progressive multiple sclerosis, the disease's most virulent form, so it wasn't a huge surprise when nine months later, and still with no word of her missing daughter, she'd decided to end it all.

No reason was given in the article for Mary Sinn's arson attack on her former brother-in-law's home but I was certain it wasn't random. That kind of thing never is. She was extremely angry with him for some reason, and I wondered what it was.

I was also interested to learn that there was money in the family. I'd heard of the Merchant Hardware Group. When I was growing up they were a big company with shops in most major towns in the UK, and I wondered how many of them the family had owned. In the end, money trumps most other motives as the most popular for murder. So who gained from Kitty's death? Her uncle, Robert Sheridan? His children?

I needed to find out more about that side of the family so I called Jools in the incident room.

She immediately asked where I was.

'Working from home.'

'Nice. Do you think the boss'll let me do that?'

'I doubt it, but then you're more popular down there than I am right now. Have we tracked down Kitty Sinn's next of kin yet?'

'I didn't know it was my job to do that.'

'She had two cousins and an uncle, a Mr Robert Sheridan. Can you find out what you can about them, then make contact and set up interviews with them individually? I'd like to talk to them about Kitty.'

'You don't want much, do you?' she grunted. 'What are you doing today?'

'Getting somewhere. I'll fill you in later.'

No sooner had I put the phone down than it rang again.

'Hello Ray,' said a deep, melodic voice I immediately recognized.

A few years earlier I'd temporarily left Counter Terrorism and joined the Serious and Organized Crime Agency, or Soca, supposedly Britain's version of the FBI, but in reality a big and slightly confused bureaucracy. I spent two years there and didn't achieve a lot, if I'm honest, but one of the more impressive people I worked with was Dan Watts. A small, immaculately mannered black man with the build of a welterweight boxer and a strong Christian faith, he had a reputation for patience and calmness under pressure, which were useful traits in the now defunct Soca.

'Hey Danny Boy,' I said. 'Long time no speak.' And it had been too, which was probably my fault. 'Where are you these days?'

'I stayed when we became the NCA.'

'Still in organized crime then. So, what can I do for you?'

'It's not a social call, Ray. I understand you're part of the investigation into Henry Forbes's murder. I have a potential lead I'd like to discuss with you. Face to face.'

'Can you give me a clue?'

'Not on the phone. But the reason I'm calling you and no one else is I know for a fact you're not corrupt. Your colleagues may not be either, but right now I don't know that, and I'm not taking any chances. I'm currently running a very sensitive operation and that's where this lead came up. You know the Hub Café in Regent's Park?'

I told him I did.

'I'll be out front at one-thirty.'

Twenty-one

Charlotte Curtis stood in her back garden, breathed in the scent of herbs, and felt the warmth of the afternoon sun on her face. It should have been a glorious day. She'd arranged to meet her friend and fellow teacher Veronique for lunch in a new restaurant that had opened in Agen, and it was her weekly art class tonight down the road in Montagu-de-quercy. In between times her plan had been to give Kado a good walk through the valley and beyond. Now Kado was dead; she'd cancelled her lunch, citing a non-existent illness; she had no stomach for attending the art class; and at some point she was going to have to call Lucien and tell him she couldn't see him tomorrow night as arranged, or for the next few days.

She went back inside and made herself a cup of coffee. The house felt too silent without Kado. He'd been her companion for the whole time since Jacques' death – always there, so that she never felt completely alone, even in her darkest moments – and she felt a remorseless stab of pain every time she thought of him now. But she wouldn't let herself cry. Not yet. Not until this terrible situation was over.

As she drank the coffee, Charlotte wondered whether even now she was being watched by her stalker. It made her skin crawl to think that there was no escape from him. She knew a lot of people would wonder why she didn't just get in her car and drive as far away as possible. But her stalker had shown what he was capable of with Kado. When you see an animal with its throat cut and realize that you could be next, it focuses the mind. Charlotte had never forgotten her brother getting mugged by a group of fourteen- and fifteen-year-old boys in south London when he was a student. Jeff was a big guy, a rugby player who could hold his own in a fight, but when he'd seen the knife one of the kids was carrying he'd frozen and handed over all his money without a fuss. 'I even asked them not to hurt me,' he'd said afterwards. 'A bunch of schoolkids who didn't even come up to my chest, yet I was absolutely terrified of them.'

And that was what Charlotte felt like now. Terrified and submissive. Even so, she was still hugely curious to find out as much as she could about Henry Forbes and what he was involved in. Her stalker had told her that she'd be asked questions about Kitty, and that was what the detective had done last night. But why was this happening now, more than a quarter of a century on? Charlotte had resisted the temptation to check the internet for more information, knowing the stalker was probably monitoring the sites she was visiting, but the curiosity was now getting too much for her. It was two o'clock, so she sat down in the lounge with her coffee and switched on the TV, keying in the code for the BBC news channel.

Immediately, Kitty's face, forever trapped in youth, filled the screen, accompanied by the newsreader telling viewers how bones found in the English countryside had now been confirmed as belonging to missing woman Katherine Sinn.

Charlotte gasped in utter shock. How could this be? She'd seen Kitty on the day she and Henry were leaving for Thailand. She'd *seen* her . . .

She composed herself and sat back, suddenly conscious that someone could be watching her, and listened intently to the remainder of story.

And as she listened, she thought back to that last time she saw Kitty, on her way to the airport to begin her great adventure to Thailand.

It took a while. Two, maybe three minutes. Maybe even longer. It was hard to tell how long she sat there for.

But when it hit her, it hit her hard. Something from that day. Something that had never felt right but that had got lost in all the years that had followed.

And in that moment Charlotte knew why the stalker had come for her after all this time.

She also knew something else: he was never going to let her live. When all this fuss had died down, he'd get rid of her. She was sure of that.

Which meant she had to make a decision. And fast.

Stay here and die eventually.

Or run.

Twenty-two

The Dark Man was in the car taking him to the airport when Laroux, his French contact, called.

'We may have a problem,' said Laroux. 'Our target is packing her bags. I think she's planning on leaving, and she looks to be in a hurry.'

The Dark Man hadn't expected this. He thought he'd cowed her into submission with the killing of her dog. In hindsight, he should have killed her instead, and made it look like an accident. He was good at that. But it wasn't his call to make.

'She can't leave,' he said. 'I need her where we can see her. Do you still have men nearby?'

'I can have two good men there within twenty minutes. We have a tracking device on her car and her phone. We can follow her wherever she goes.'

161

'I don't want her going anywhere. This is very important to me.'

'I will do everything I can.'

'Good. I'm on my way.'

The Dark Man ended the call and told the driver to turn round.

It was time to deal with Charlotte Curtis once and for all.

Twenty-three

Tina Boyd liked France. She liked the food; she liked the people – they always seemed friendly, especially when she tried her poor French on them; and she loved their roads, which were blissfully traffic-free. Commentators in the UK were always going on about the weakness of the French economy, how it was almost permanently in recession, with constant strikes and hugely powerful unions, but its infrastructure made Britain's look laughable, and the almost complete lack of traffic on her way to Roquecor had made the journey extremely quick.

She knew she was probably embarking on a wild goose chase. Charlotte Curtis hadn't wanted to talk to Ray Mason, so she was highly unlikely to say anything of note to a freelance private detective, and of course it was possible she didn't have any information to add anyway. But when he'd been in Tina's office the previous evening, Ray had been convinced that Charlotte was holding something back and that she'd sounded scared.

The murder of Henry Forbes and his lawyer, coupled with the discovery of the bones of two missing girls, was the kind of case police officers the world over dreamed of. It was that rarest of things in policework: a true mystery. When you'd spent the bulk of the past three years setting up cheating husbands or wives, tracking down errant debtors, and foiling insurance scams, as Tina had, then just the chance to get involved on the periphery of something like this was an opportunity she was happy to grab.

Before she'd left the force under circumstances she'd rather forget, Tina had been a police officer for sixteen years, and a detective for fourteen of them. She'd developed a good instinct for knowing when someone was lying to her. When Henry Forbes had come to see her the previous week, he'd been nervous as hell. He hadn't been faking it. He'd known he was a marked man, which was why he was taking steps to protect himself. His contact number was an unregistered phone and he'd paid her in untraceable cash. She remembered his exact words when he'd asked her to find Charlotte Curtis: 'It's urgent. And it's about Kitty.' He'd said something else as well, just as he was leaving her office: 'You know, for once in my life I'm doing something good.' She'd asked him what he meant by that, but his only response was to tell her once again to find Charlotte as soon as possible. And then he was gone.

So Tina was pretty certain Charlotte Curtis knew something about what had happened to Kitty, and if she did, scared or not, Tina was certain she could get the information out of her. She could be very persuasive when she needed to be.

Her mobile rang. It was Ray Mason.

'How are you doing?' he asked.

'Well, according to the satnav I'm only a few minutes away from Charlotte Curtis's current address. I got your text. I won't forget to ask her about the tattoo on Henry Forbes's underarm.'

'Thanks. I also need to know the kind of relationship Kitty had with Forbes. Was it loving, that kind of thing. And did Kitty ever talk about her cousins, Lola and Alastair Sheridan, and if so, what her attitude was to them.'

'Sure, I can do that. You know, you're a lucky man, Ray. This is exactly the kind of murder case I'd like to be involved in.'

'From what I hear, you were involved in your fair share of interesting cases.'

'I was. And I miss it.'

'Well, you're involved in this one now. I need you to convince Charlotte to come back with you to the UK so we can question her in detail.'

'What if she doesn't want to come?'

'You tell her that we'll offer any protection she needs. We just need to ask her some questions in confidence, that's all. There'll be no court case, or anything like that.'

'How do you know there won't be a court case? You can't promise her that.'

'I need her to talk, Tina. Even if I have to be a little economical with the truth. And if she still doesn't want to come over, tell her that we'll request that the French police hold her as a material witness, and then we'll force her to talk. And if she decides to run rather than face the music, make sure you don't let her out of your sight.'

'Are you paying me for any of this? Because if you're not, then don't order me around. I don't like it.'

'I'm sorry,' he said. 'I didn't mean it like that. But please do what you can. It's very important.'

He sounded like he was under pressure, a lot more so than he had been the previous night.

'How's the case coming along?'

'Way too slowly.'

'And you think Charlotte might be the key to it?'

He gave a hollow laugh down the phone. 'Jesus, I hope so.'

'I'll do what I can,' said Tina.

She ended the call and checked the satnav. The turning to Charlotte Curtis's house was just ahead, and she slowed down then turned off the main road on to a single-track road which led down between two fields to a cluster of farm buildings a hundred metres away.

Charlotte's was the first building on the right. The gates to the courtyard were open and Tina drove inside, parking behind a blue Renault and blocking its exit.

Tina got out, breathed in the fresh country air, and knocked on the front door. There was no answer so she knocked a second time, then a third. Next she tried Charlotte's mobile, figuring that she had nothing to lose now that she was here. It went straight to message.

She walked round the back of the house, and into a terraced garden with a swimming pool. Beyond the swimming pool, the garden dropped away into a valley with a forested hill on the other side. It was a beautiful view and, not for the first time, Tina wondered what she was doing wasting her time in an overpriced house located in an overpriced village that was effectively a suburb of London, with the background noise from the M25 constantly in her ears, when she could be living somewhere like this. It wasn't even as if she was a copper any more.

Feeling vaguely frustrated, she approached the back door and looked through the window, and immediately saw a woman walking into the living area, a holdall slung over one shoulder. Tina recognized her as Charlotte from the image on her primary school website. She knocked on the door again and Charlotte literally jumped in shock.

Tina opened the back door a foot but stayed outside. 'Miss Curtis? My name's Tina Boyd,' she said through the gap. 'I've come all the way from London to talk to you about an old boyfriend of yours, Henry Forbes. It'll only take a few moments.'

'I'm sorry, this isn't a good time,' said Charlotte, coming over. 'I'm just going out.'

She went to shut the door but Tina resisted.

'Please, Miss Curtis, this'll take five minutes.'

'No!' she snapped. 'Leave me alone, please.'

She pushed again on the door, but still Tina resisted, preventing her from closing it.

'Miss Curtis, I'm a private detective working in cooperation with the Metropolitan Police. Here are my credentials.' She pulled out her ID card and held it up but Charlotte didn't even look at it. 'I can tell you're scared about something. There's no need to be. We can go for a drive anywhere you like. I just need to ask you a handful of questions.'

'How many times do I have to tell you? I'm not— Oh God . . .'

Charlotte's face went white and her eyes widened as she looked over Tina's shoulder.

Tina heard footsteps on the patio, and as she turned she saw a man approaching round the side of the house, a pistol in his hand, only a few metres away. She heard more movement and saw a second man coming the other way, also holding a pistol.

Both men were unmasked, which was always bad news.

'Levez les mains,' said the older, more confident-looking of the two gunmen, gesturing with his gun.

Tina didn't speak much French but she knew what this meant and put her hands in the air as the two men moved in and the older one pushed her inside the house. Charlotte put her hands up too, and both women were hustled into the living room.

The older gunman said something else in French and spun Tina around so she and Charlotte were facing the two men. As the older one stood back, the younger one moved in, pulled Charlotte's bag off her shoulder and threw it to the floor, then patted her down with his free hand, pocketing her phone. He did the same to Tina, taking her phone as well, while the other man looked on, his gun pointed at Tina's head, a look on his face suggesting he wouldn't hesitate to use it.

'On your knees,' said the older gunman in English, 'and put your hands behind your heads.'

'Please don't do this to me,' said Charlotte, her voice shaking, but she did as she was told.

Tina followed suit, but slower, as she tried to work out what to do. This was a serious situation. She'd been in similar ones before but had always had that grim feeling that one day her luck would run out. What she hadn't expected was for it to happen here – she'd been caught off guard. Whatever these two men wanted, it wasn't good, and particularly not for Tina, as she was no obvious use to them. She was just an inconvenient witness.

From her position on the floor, she looked at the two men in turn. The older one – silver-haired, in his fifties – looked hard, and there was a coolness about him that suggested he'd done this sort of thing before. The younger one – early thirties, dark hair – appeared more nervous, as if he hadn't. But in the end, it made no real difference. She was trapped, and for the umpteenth time in her life she cursed her bad luck for turning up at the wrong time.

But at the moment she wasn't dead, so there was still some hope.

The older gunman pulled a phone from his pocket, and made a call. He had a conversation in French for about a minute, never once taking his eyes, or his gun, off Tina.

'Who are you?' he asked Tina, still keeping the phone to his ear.

She couldn't think of a lie fast enough so she told the truth. 'I'm a private detective. From England.'

The gunman repeated this information into the phone in French, and Tina felt her stomach clench. Her breaths came fast and she had to work to control them.

The gunman continued talking for another minute, his tone brusque and professional, then ended the call, turned to his colleague and gave him an order in French. The younger gunman turned and went out of the back door, leaving just the three of them in the room.

Beside her, Charlotte's trembling was getting worse and she let out a great racking sob.

'It's going to be OK,' Tina reassured her. 'Be brave.'

'It won't be. They're going to kill us. I know it.'

'Tais-toi!' snapped the gunman, taking a step towards Charlotte. 'Quiet, or I will hurt you.'

For just a couple of seconds the gunman's attention was focused on Charlotte and, with a burst of adrenalin and no thought at all, Tina leaped at him, keeping her body low. He was already swinging the gun round to shoot her but she just managed to knock his gun arm to one side as he pulled the trigger, and his bullet missed her. At the same time she launched an uppercut with her free arm that caught him directly under the chin, sending him crashing back into the dining-room table. The gun went off a second time but she couldn't hear it, having been temporarily deafened by the first shot; she saw only the muzzle flash.

Her punch had been a good one, and the gunman was lying on his back on the floor, trying to lift himself up and aim the gun. His eyes were unfocused and he looked dazed, but he wasn't going to be like that for long.

Grabbing Charlotte by her shirt, Tina yanked her to her feet, yelling at her to follow. Together the two of them ran past the gunman. Tina threw open the back door and they raced out on to the patio. She could hear the sound of a car on gravel coming from the front of the house so they couldn't get out that way. Instead, still holding on to Charlotte's arm, she ran in the direction of the swimming pool and the drop beyond, taking just the briefest glance over her shoulder. Two cars had driven into the courtyard, and she could now see three men, including the younger gunman. The men saw them running and immediately their guns appeared. Someone shouted for them to stop, but there was no way Tina was stopping now.

Letting go of Charlotte's hand, she ran along the edge of the pool, not really sure where the hell she was going. As she reached the end, she saw there was a sheer drop of ten feet down to a footpath. She didn't hesitate and jumped straight down, hoping that Charlotte would follow her. She hit the ground hard, feeling a sharp pain shoot up both legs as she rolled over in the brush, banging her shoulder on something hard. Fuelled with adrenalin, Tina was on her feet in an instant. She left the path and ran into the undergrowth that led directly down to the valley, ignoring the cuts to her face and body. The hill was steep, and as she accelerated she lost her footing, fell forward and rolled down the rest of the hill, hitting bushes and tree roots before landing on another path at the bottom with a bump.

As she clambered back to her feet, she saw Charlotte come crashing down a few feet away. Tina grabbed her arm and they pushed their way through more undergrowth, emerging into a long, overgrown field.

'This way,' panted Charlotte, hardly able to get the words out, and they ran through the field, keeping low, until they came to the shelter of a line of trees by the banks of a gently meandering stream.

Only then did Tina look back towards the house.

Three men stood in a line at the top of the hill next to the swimming pool, staring down at them. But it was the one in the middle who caught Tina's attention. He was wearing a black fedora and, although he was smaller in stature than the others, there was something cold and confident in his bearing that unnerved her, as if he knew exactly where they were going and how to catch them. Even from this distance, Tina could feel his gaze upon her.

Turning away, she started running again, knowing that whatever was going on, it wasn't over yet.

Twenty-four

Dan Watts had once been a promising amateur welterweight boxer, with a ferocious left hook dubbed the Megawatt by his local paper that had seen him win sixteen of his twenty fights by KO. He'd only narrowly missed out on making the GB team for the 1996 Olympic Games in Atlanta, and was all set to go professional. But then, in fight number twenty-one, he caught his nineteen-year-old opponent with a punch so hard that he put the guy in a coma from which he never emerged.

Dan Watts never fought again. The story went that he sank into a deep depression and only pulled himself out of it when he found God. Apparently, he was going to train as a lay preacher, but decided instead that he could do more good in the world by becoming a police officer. I wasn't sure if this part was true or not. He never talked about his past and I never asked. But I'd enjoyed working with him because, like me, he saw what he was doing as a true vocation – a righting of some of society's wrongs – not just a job with a salary.

As I crossed Regent's Park towards the Hub Café, I could see Dan standing a few yards off to the side of the café entrance, still looking as lean and wiry as ever. He was wearing a smart suit underneath an even smarter raincoat. He was also wearing a flat black cap, which he somehow managed to carry off.

The clouds had beaten back the earlier blue sky and a breeze blew across the park, leaving it quieter than usual for the time of year.

Dan and I shook hands and started walking away from the café.

'I hear Fast Eddie's running the Forbes murder case,' Dan said, using another of Olaf's nicknames, this one earned through his spectacularly slow finishing time in the Met's charity 5K run a few years earlier, in which he'd been overtaken by an eighty-two-year-old retired WPC. No one dared call him that round Ealing, even behind his back.

'That's right,' I said.

'You trust him?'

'Yeah, he's a good guy. Why? Shouldn't I?'

'No, I think you're right to trust him. He's done thirty years' unblemished service, and I'm certain he's on the money. But I don't know about the rest of your team, so what I tell you today, I don't want it going further than him.'

'I can't give you that promise, Dan. Olaf's my boss. If he wants to bring in the rest of the team, he can overrule me.'

'Then you tell him you got the information from an anonymous source. I'm serious, Ray. If what I tell you leaks to the
wrong people there are lives at stake.'

The last thing I needed was to start dropping anonymous tips
and refusing to name my sources. I was sailing close enough to
the wind as it was. But I also figured I had little choice. 'OK. Fair
enough. What have you got?'

'You worked organized crime for a while. Did you ever come
across the Kalaman outfit?'

'I've heard the name like everyone else, but I don't know a lot
about them. Wasn't the guy who runs it, Cem, supposed to have
killed his old man?'

Dan nodded. 'That's the story. Cem's father, Volkan, was one
of the first Turkish gangsters to operate in the UK. He ran
brothels and gambling dens in Soho in the late sixties. Unlike
a lot of the people operating back then, he kept on expanding
his operations in the seventies and eighties, and started making
some serious money. We're pretty sure he was involved in a
couple of murders along the way but, even so, he was considered
old school and not especially dangerous. He had two daughters and a son – Cem. Volkan didn't want Cem to go into the
business. Like a lot of immigrant parents he wanted his son to
excel and become a doctor or a lawyer, but Cem wasn't interested
in any of that. He insisted on joining the organization, and the
rumour was he was a very savvy businessman, and ruthless with
it. As Cem moved up the ranks, he tried to push his father out.
The two of them had a major falling-out, and it looked like the
organization was going to end up split in two. Then a few months

later, Volkan was assassinated along with his bodyguard, and Cem took over.

'Since then he's massively expanded the business. Annual turnover from the legitimate and illegitimate sides of the business is now estimated at over a billion a year, and that's a conservative estimate. You can buy a lot of people with that kind of money, and they have. They've also bought privacy. The names of Cem Kalaman and his associates never appear in any newspapers. No one outside law enforcement has any idea who they are. Even you don't know much about them.'

He paused.

'Three years ago, a freelance investigative journalist did some digging and wrote a pretty explosive piece about them. The Kalamans' lawyers slapped an injunction on the journalist and the newspaper that was going to print the story, effectively killing it. Three months after that, the journalist was found dead in his bath with his wrists slashed. The body of his girlfriend was in their bedroom. She'd been beaten to death with an iron. There'd never been any history of domestic violence in the relationship, and none of the neighbours reported hearing an argument or fight on the night they died. Even so, the verdict was murder suicide. Case closed.'

I sighed. 'Jesus. I never even heard about that, and I read the papers.'

'It didn't make many column inches, and no newspaper printed the connection between the journalist and the Kalamans. No one wanted to get involved, because if you cross the Kalamans, there are unpleasant consequences. These people have been around for the best part of fifty years. That's a lot of time to build up contacts, and they've got some very good ones. You remember what it was like at Soca. Go for the easier targets, leave the hard ones alone. It's the same at the NCA. I'm running the official investigation into the Kalamans, and do you know how many people I've got? Two.'

That was exactly what it was like when I'd worked organized crime. We never went after the big boys. Just the mid-rankers. It was why I'd left.

'So what have they got to do with the Forbes murder?' I asked him.

Dan took a long look round to check we weren't in earshot of anyone before continuing. 'Because it's so hard to build a case against them, our efforts have been aimed at turning someone within their organization. And now we've got someone. He's given us some good titbits of information. This morning he called telling me there's a rumour that the Kalamans were directly involved in Henry Forbes's murder.'

'What else does he know?'

'Nothing more than that.'

I didn't say anything for a few moments as I digested this new information. It made sense. Henry Forbes had been terrified of the people who'd killed Kitty Sinn, and had said that they had friends in very high places, and a long reach. Also, only an organized crime outfit like the Kalamans would have been able to pull together a three-man assassination team armed with high-quality weapons at such short notice.

'I fought with one of the gunmen,' I told Dan. 'He was about five feet ten, I think mixed race, and he had a sleeve tattoo on his left forearm and a one-inch scar on his neck, here.' I pointed to a spot just above my collarbone. 'Does he ring any bells with you?'

'Not off the top of my head,' said Dan, 'but I'll get our asset to keep an eye out.'

'I think whoever ordered Henry Forbes's killing was also involved in the murders of Dana Brennan and Kitty Sinn. How old's Cem Kalaman?'

'Forty-eight.'

'So he would have been in his early twenties when the girls died. You said his father wanted him to become a doctor or a lawyer and not go into the family business, so I'm guessing he had a decent education. Do you know where he went to school?'

Dan shook his head. 'No, but I can find out now if you want. It'll just take a phone call.'

'Please.'

We were at the edge of the park now, a long way from anyone, and it had started to rain, big heavy drops that suggested more to come. I waited patiently while Dan made the call, hoping that the gods were smiling down on me.

A minute later he came off the phone. 'Medmenham College,' he said. 'That's the place where the bodies were found, isn't it?'

I nodded, swallowing down a sudden feeling of euphoria. Finally, I was beginning to get somewhere. 'That's right. So, now we've got a connection between Cem Kalaman and the victims. What I haven't got is motive. The conventional wisdom has always been that Dana Brennan's killing had a sexual motive. Has Kalaman got any predilections that way?'

'Not that I know of,' said Dan, 'but I'm sure if he had he'd keep them quiet. He's a family man these days with a wife and three kids.'

I took out my phone and scrolled through the photos until I came to the one I was looking for, then handed him the phone. 'Forbes had a tattoo on his underarm similar to this sign I photographed at an abandoned building near the school yesterday. The killers tried to burn it off him. Have you seen anything like it before?' It was a long shot, but one worth taking now I was here.

Dan stared at it for a long time and his body seemed to bristle with tension. 'This isn't good,' he said quietly, before handing back the phone.

'What is it?'

He took a deep breath. 'I've seen this sign before. Back in my National Crime Squad days. We raided a house belonging to an Albanian people trafficker who was wanted for murder. We found the suspect and his girlfriend there. They'd both been tortured to death and the house had been ripped apart, as if the killers had been looking for something. It was a mess in there, Ray. They'd died badly, and they'd been gone a couple of days when we found them. During the search of the place, one of the SOCOs found a loose floorboard in one of the rooms, pulled it up, and found a carrier bag hidden in the space below it. There was twelve grand in cash inside. That, and a DVD. After it had been tested for prints and DNA, a couple of us played it back at the station.' He stopped and shook his head slowly, and his voice cracked when he spoke again. 'What was on it, I will never forget.'

'Tell me,' I said, even though a part of me didn't want to hear.

'It was footage of three men in a room, their faces hidden by black hoods, assaulting, raping and finally killing a young woman on a bed. The whole film lasted about ten minutes, the quality wasn't all that good, and there was no sound, but it was still one of the most horrendous things I've ever seen. And painted on the wall behind the bed was a symbol exactly like the one you've just shown me.'

Now it was my turn to take a deep breath. I'm no expert when it comes to technology, but recordable DVDs were not around in 1990, so I dispelled my initial thought, that the young woman in the film could have been either Dana or Kitty.

'Did you ever find out who killed your suspect and his girl-friend?' I asked Dan.

He shook his head. 'No. The case was a dead end. He had a lot of enemies but my guess is that he was blackmailing someone with that footage, and they came looking for it.'

'Where's the DVD now?'

'Archived, I suppose. As I said, it was a long time ago and it was never proven that the footage was real. I've always thought it was, though, and in the light of what you've shown me, I think I was right to. I'll go back and pull out the case notes from that murder, and see if there's any link between the Albanian and the Kalamans. And I'll talk to my inside man about IDing the shooter you tangled with.'

'Thanks. We need that shooter. If we get him in custody, he might talk.'

Dan put a hand on my arm and gave me a serious look. 'You've got to help me here, Ray. This op with our informant – it's not exactly official. We're running it off the books.'

'Jesus. Is that wise?'

'It's the only way we're going to get anywhere, I promise you. But the point is, I don't want anything to get out about it, or else I'm finished, and so's the whole investigation into the Kalamans. So for the moment, your info comes from an anonymous source, OK? And if I get you the shooter's name, you need to let me know before you make an arrest so I can warn my informant.' He put out a hand. 'Deal?'

There are stringent rules in place governing the police's use of informants. Sometimes they're bent a little by officers, but it's a very risky business, and a sackable offence, and I was surprised that a family man like Dan with close to twenty years' service under his belt, and who I'd always thought was straight as a die, would take that risk. He must have wanted the Kalaman outfit very badly.

'Deal,' I said, and shook his hand.

The wind had picked up, whipping the rain into us, and Dan pulled up the collar of his jacket. 'I need to go. You're digging up some good stuff on the Kalamans, Ray, and they're not going to like it. Tread carefully.'

'Sounds like we both should,' I said, and watched as he walked away, his shoulders just a little more slumped than they had been earlier, as if I'd woken memories within him he'd prefer to have kept hidden.

Twenty-five

Tina Boyd was a fit woman. She went to the gym three times a week and ran 10K every Sunday, but close to twenty-five years of smoking a pack a day had taken its toll, and her breaths were coming in painful gasps by the time she and Charlotte Curtis stopped running.

She leaned against a tree to get her breath back while Charlotte stood a few feet away, head bowed with her hands on her knees, panting like a dog. They hadn't seen a single person since they'd fled into the valley, at least a mile back now. They'd followed the stream at a hard run as it meandered through a narrow, twisting valley screened by wood-covered hills on both sides. Numerous paths and tracks disappeared off it like tree roots, every one of them a potential ambush point.

'Where are we heading?' she asked Charlotte once her

breathing was finally heading back to normal. Behind them, the countryside stretched back, green and verdant. There was no sign of pursuit. No sign of anything. They might as well have been standing there a thousand years ago.

Charlotte straightened up. Her face was red and sweaty, her eyes still alive with fear. 'I don't know. Anywhere away from here.' She looked at Tina. 'Thank you. For what you did back there.'

'That's OK. They may have wanted you alive, but I don't think they were quite so bothered about me.' Tina cleared her throat and wiped her brow, patting her jeans pockets. 'Shit.'

'What is it?'

'I left my cigarettes in the hire car.'

'And you're worried about them now?'

'I never like to be too far away from them.' She looked round. 'Where does this path lead?'

'The valley keeps going for a long way. Twenty kilometres at least, but it crosses a couple of roads eventually, and there are paths leading out at various points. The nearest village is about an hour's fast walk from here.'

'They'll expect us to go there.'

'These men definitely aren't local, they won't know the area.'

Tina wasn't convinced. 'They can read maps and they're not fools. There are also quite a few of them. I counted four altogether. They'll keep at least one back, and the others will try to cut us off at some point. We need to get off this path, and keep moving away from your house.'

Charlotte wiped her brow with the hem of her dress. She

looked like she was about to cry. 'What's going on? Look at me. I'm just an ordinary housewife. I've never done a thing wrong in my life, and now suddenly all these people are after me. They think I know something about Kitty Sinn. They've been spying on me for God knows how long, and then yesterday a masked man came into my house and—' She stopped, her face twisted with emotion.

Tina waited for her to continue.

'He killed my dog. Cut its throat, and then told me that if anyone came asking about Kitty Sinn, I was to tell them nothing or the same would happen to me.'

Tina frowned. 'Was it one of the men who held us prisoner today?'

She shook her head. 'No. I think this one was English, although he had a trace of an eastern European accent.'

'So, what do you know? Henry Forbes hired me to track you down, and he wanted to talk to you urgently about Kitty.'

Charlotte sighed and looked round. 'I've been thinking about it ever since I found out about Kitty. Do you think she even went to Thailand?'

Tina considered this. 'It seems impossible, but there were witnesses who said she did. So I guess she did.'

'Just before you turned up today, I remembered something that seemed strange at the time, but which I'd totally forgotten. Now, though, it seems relevant.'

'Go on.'

There was a pause before Charlotte continued. She wiped her brow a second time, still panting a little. 'You know, Kitty was so excited about that Thailand trip. She was an only child and her mum was very protective of her, and this was her first proper holiday on her own, probably ever. We had goodbye drinks on the Thursday night in Brighton. Just the girls.' Charlotte smiled. 'I'll always remember it. We pub-crawled all the way across Brighton and ended up losing everyone along the way, so in the end it was just me and Kitty. She was staying at my place, and on the way home we climbed some scaffolding round a church and sat up on the roof looking out over the whole of Brighton. It was a really warm night and we sat there with this amazing view, and chatted until the sun started coming up. Later that day we said our goodbyes because she was going to a party with Henry that night and then they were leaving the following day for Thailand. And I never saw her again.'

Charlotte continued to smile as she remembered that final evening, then frowned. 'Except I did. I was walking on Grand Parade on the Saturday they were leaving. It was mid-afternoon and this taxi came past and stopped at the traffic lights. I saw Henry in the back so I walked over to say hello. The thing was, it was as if he didn't want to see me. He looked away so I leaned down and banged on the window. I could see Kitty in the back with him but she was looking away as well, as if she didn't want to see me either, which wasn't like her at all. We were best friends. Eventually, Henry turned my way. I was motioning him to open the window so I could say goodbye, but he wasn't having any of it. He just gave me this little wave. So I tried to get Kitty's attention but she just gave me this little wave as well and tried not to look my way either, as if she was embarrassed. Then the lights turned green, the cab pulled away, and I was just left there staring after it.'

Charlotte shook her head, seemingly deep in thought. 'At the time I was upset, but I put it down to the fact that they must have had a big argument and just didn't feel like talking. I thought Kitty might have tried to phone me from the airport and apologize, or at least leave a message on my answering machine. But she never did, which again wasn't like her at all. She would never have got on a plane, having been that rude to me, without giving me some sort of explanation.'

Charlotte sighed. 'I really resented her for treating me like that, even after I heard she'd gone missing. And it's only today – God, what is it, twenty-six years later – that it suddenly occurs to me there was something not quite right about Kitty that day. The woman in the car looked like her – she had the same hair, the same profile – but the more I think about it now, the more I'm convinced that it wasn't her at all. It was someone else.'

Twenty-six

It had been a very late night, thanks to Junior insisting Ramon join him for a drink after they'd finished delivering their cargo, so it was after two when Ramon finally opened his eyes to begin the new day, and it took him a few minutes to summon up the energy to clamber slowly out of bed.

He chucked on some clothes and wandered into the kitchen, hunting for food to ease the growling in his stomach. The place was a mess, and apart from a Pot Noodle and a couple of blackening bananas on the sideboard, there was nothing edible. He missed the discipline of prison, of getting up in the morning, eating meals when they were served to you, going to the gym, to classes. His days had been mapped out for him then. Now, unless Junior needed him for something, he was his own boss, and he wasn't very good at it.

But this was the story of Ramon's life. He just wasn't very

good at things. When they'd released him from the pen with a little bit of money and some basic qualifications, he'd tried to go straight. But no one wanted to employ him. It wasn't just that he was a criminal, it was the fact that he was a killer too, and no one wanted to work next to a killer. It was mad really. One single moment of insanity when he'd been nothing more than a kid and he was left with something that was going to follow him around for the rest of his life.

In the end, broke, pissed off, and living alone on the tenth floor of a tower block where he knew no one, it was inevitable that Ramon would end up going back into crime. It hadn't taken long to happen. One day, a guy he knew from the old days back on the estate had approached him in the street. The guy's name was Strike and he wanted Ramon to work as his bodyguard. The pay was three hundred a week cash. Ramon was on sixty-two notes a week plus housing benefit from the social, so it took him all of three seconds to say yes.

Strike managed ten different crackhouses spread out across north-east London. He delivered them product, and collected the takings every day. Then, when he'd made sure that the takings were right, and he wasn't getting ripped off, he delivered the cash to another address. Obviously carrying this sort of money and product around was a dangerous business, not so much from the Feds but from two-bit gangbangers looking to make an easy buck by holding him up, so he needed a bodyguard. Ramon was big and scary-looking, and his murder conviction gave him street cred, so he was the perfect choice. He knew he shouldn't be getting involved, but the thought of all that money . . . In the end, it just turned his head.

The Bone Field

At first all went well. Strike was good company and Ramon had a laugh driving round with him all day. Strike was careful too in the way he operated, which Ramon appreciated, never carrying too much product or cash at any one time, and always varying the times of his pick-ups and deliveries so as not to get the Feds suspicious. It was also obvious that he worked for someone else, someone with even more street cred than Ramon, because no one ever tried ripping him off, and he was treated with respect that bordered on fear. So it was all pretty easy. Strike even paid for driving lessons for Ramon so he could be the one doing the driving. 'Then you can be like my chauffeur,' he'd said with a guffaw.

The problem was, as soon as Ramon passed his driving test, Strike started getting lazy. Most days he'd get Ramon to do the deliveries and collections while he stayed behind at home, saying he needed to get other stuff done. Since he was still paying three hundred a week and Strike never missed a payment, Ramon didn't make a fuss, though it rankled.

About this time, he met Strike's boss, Junior. Junior was impressed with Ramon, and was especially interested in knowing he was a killer who'd spent close to half his life inside. Soon Ramon was working directly for Junior and his weekly salary had doubled to six hundred notes – more money than he'd ever seen, and more than he could spend. Even his probation officer stopped leaning on him. Life, for once, was actually going well.

And then, just like it always did, everything went wrong. One night while he was at home drinking a beer, smoking a spliff and watching Spurs on the TV, there was a knock on the door. He'd had a peephole installed just in case someone tried to rob him – at the time he had more than four grand in cash hidden all over the flat – and the moment he stared through it and saw the National Crime Agency warrant card blocking his view he knew it was all over.

He was on the tenth floor and there was nowhere to run, so as soon as he'd made sure the two Feds outside his door were genuine, he let them in, fully prepared to go back to nick. In a way, he was almost relieved. At least in prison he knew where he was at and he got no nasty surprises. But it soon became clear that these Feds weren't interested in putting him back behind bars. They had a much better idea. They were going to blackmail him. The black one – a little guy in a flashy suit with a nose like a pig's snout – introduced himself as Dan, the white one called himself Frank. Dan was the boss, so he did the talking, and he told Ramon they knew all about the work he did running crack-houses. Ramon denied everything and told them to get out, which was when Dan showed him some footage he had on his mobile phone. It showed Ramon entering and leaving three different crackhouses with the holdall he used to store the drugs and money. Then, just as he was about to tell them they had nothing on him, the footage changed to inside one of the crackhouses and it clearly showed Ramon unloading a bag containing rocks of crack and handing them to another man, before taking a wad of bills from him.

'Remember, Ramon, you're out on licence,' Dan the Pig told him. 'That means we can put you back inside any time we want, just like that, and there's shit you can do about it.'

Ramon had just stood there staring down at this little black man in his nice suit wishing he could kill him, and knowing he couldn't do a fucking thing, because they had him bang to rights.

After that, Dan the Pig told him what they wanted him to do. Junior worked for the Kalamans, and so too, though he didn't know it, did Ramon. Now he was going to help bring them down by becoming Dan the Pig's snitch. It was that or return to jail.

Ramon had played out that scene in his mind a hundred times since, and every time he always told that little prick to send him back to jail if he wanted because he wasn't going to be no one's snitch.

The problem was that in real life he hadn't said that, which was why he was still free.

He poured boiling water into the Pot Noodle, gave it a stir, and walked out on to the flat's tiny balcony, ignoring the cold wind and the splashes of rain as he stared over the city beyond. It probably wouldn't have been a bad view if the two tower blocks opposite hadn't been built. In the narrow gap between them he got a view of an industrial estate and some railway tracks.

As he munched on the noodles, trying and failing to stop them burning the inside of his mouth, Ramon thought about the position he was in. It reminded him of something that had happened back when he was a kid living at his granddad's place. They'd had rats in the tiny back garden so his granddad had put out traps, and one day a real big bastard of a rat had got caught in one. When Ramon had gone out to take a closer look, it had still been alive, trying to move its head, even though it was pinned under the metal and its back looked broken. It had writhed and twitched in the trap for a long time before it died, its eyes wide open in

shock. Ramon felt like that rat now. Trapped, and with no possible way out. The Feds weren't going to stop leaning on him
until he came back with the kind of information that could really
hurt the Kalamans, even though he had a feeling someone from
the outfit would find out what he was doing and kill him long
before that happened.

His thoughts were interrupted by the sound of a phone ringing
inside his flat. It wasn't his usual phone either. It was the one Dan
the Pig had supplied him with. Ramon walked back in, shutting
the door behind him, and picked it up off the kitchen table, thinking that he was going to have to start hiding this phone better, in
case he got a surprise visit from Junior.

'Can you talk?'

The guy must have been all of five feet seven high but he
always sounded at least a foot taller and wider when he spoke.

'Yeah, I can talk,' said Ramon wearily. He'd been instructed a
hundred times only ever to carry the phone with him when he
could talk. 'What is it?'

'Take a walk. Find somewhere quiet. Then call me back in ten
minutes. Usual number.' He cut the line.

Arsehole.

Ramon hated the way Dan the Pig treated him. Like he was his
bitch. Do this. Do that. Risk your neck while I sit on my arse
writing reports.

But when he'd tried pulling out a couple of months back,
finally plucking up the courage to tell them they could sling him
back in nick if they wanted to, Dan the Pig had told him to think
twice about that, because it might get out that he'd helped the

police try to infiltrate the Kalamans, which would make him a marked man. The way he'd said it was like he was trying to help Ramon, but really he was threatening him. Pull out and we'll let everyone know you're a snitch. His life wouldn't be worth living.

They had him. The bastards had him.

Ramon flung on his coat, got the lift down to the ground floor, and walked fast for five minutes until he got to the rec near Lordship Lane. A couple of hobos were sitting on a bench next to the kids' playground drinking cans of cheap beer, but apart from them the place was empty. Ramon found a bench as far away from them as possible, under some trees and out of the rain, and called the number he had for Dan the Pig.

'You need to keep an eye out for a mixed-race man about five ten,' said Dan the Pig, getting straight down to business. 'He's got a sleeve tattoo on his left forearm and a scar about an inch long near his collarbone, at the bottom of his neck. Can you remember that? I don't want you writing it down.'

'Course I can remember. I'm not a retard, man.'

'If what you told me's right, he'll be one of Kalaman's more reliable shooters. All you need to do is give me his name. We'll do the rest.'

'But I haven't met many of the boys yet, you know that.'

'You need to start pushing to get to know people, Ramon. You've been on the fringes for six months now. That's a long time. You need to move up to the next level.'

'I'm going as fast as I can. You know how hard it is.'

'And you're doing good work. That tip this morning was a decent one. See what else you can get.'

'When are you going to let me go?' Ramon was conscious of the desperation in his voice, and hated himself for it.

'Are you going to cut out the illegal stuff?'

'Yeah, I am.' He was.

'Then the sooner you get us information we can use to make an arrest, the sooner you're free from all this.'

'And what about that film you've got? Will you get rid of that?'

'You've got my word,' said Dan the Pig.

Ramon knew his word was probably shit, but at least it gave him a glimmer of hope.

'You know I told you about the illegal run we did last night,' he said, 'up on the Norfolk coast. We picked up a bunch of girls from a dinghy, and a big, heavy holdall as well.'

'Any idea what was in it?'

'I dunno. It felt like guns.'

'So did you put the tracking device we gave you on it?'

'I didn't get a chance. Junior was with me.'

'You've got to make the chance, Ramon.'

'That's easy for you to say. You ain't the one taking the risks. If I get caught doing something like that, I'm dead.'

'Then don't get caught. You want to stay out of prison, you're going to have to take risks, brother. Where did you deliver the holdall?'

Ramon remembered the postcode and building number from the van's satnav, and he reeled it out to Dan, looking round as he did so, just to check no one was listening in on his conversation, but it had started raining properly now, and even the hobos had disappeared.

There was a pause while Dan wrote it down.

'And were there people there to take the holdall off you?'

'Yeah. But I'd never seen them before.'

'Describe them.'

Ramon couldn't remember much about either man, and it had been dark, but he gave as good a description as he could.

'Good work, Ramon,' said Dan when he'd finished writing all this down.

'Don't you want to know about the illegals we picked up? They were all young girls. Seventeen, eighteen. We took them to a real shitty-looking brothel.' Ramon thought of Brown Eyes, the girl who smiled at him, just like Keesha used to all those years ago.

'All right, give me the address. Obviously we take trafficking very seriously, but this isn't our jurisdiction, so don't expect anything to happen yet.'

Dan the Pig didn't seem interested, and when Ramon gave him the address, he had the feeling the bastard wasn't even writing it down, which was typical. That was the Feds all over. They pretended to care but they were just like everyone else. Looking after themselves.

'Some of these girls were young, really young,' Ramon added.

'And we'll look into it,' said Dan the Pig. 'Now, see if you can get me a name for the man with the sleeve tattoo and the scar.'

He ended the call, leaving Ramon sitting alone in the rain, staring through branches at a bleak grey sky and wondering if his life was always going to be like this.

Twenty-seven

I was just finishing a late lunch of fried saltimbocca with spring vegetables in a little Italian place I know in Marylebone and thinking about my meeting with Dan Watts and what it represented when I got a call from DCI Jerry Chesterman over at Thames Valley. I pushed away my nearly empty plate, took a sip of coffee and, since I was the only diner still in the place, took the call, knowing exactly what Chesterman was going to say.

I was right too.

'Bill Morris, the caretaker of the school at the time the girls went missing – the man you were interested in – was found hanging last night,' he said after the briefest hello.

The man I was interested in. I didn't like the sound of that. 'Seriously?' I said, sounding suitably surprised, and knowing I was going to have to be very careful. I have a rule. Never say more than you have to, and always take a second to think before you speak. If in doubt, take two. 'Does it look suspicious?' I asked, having taken two.

'Yes it does. The neighbour saw someone at the back door. He called the police.'

'Did the neighbour get a look at him?'

'No. All he got was that it was an IC1 male about six feet tall. I gave you Morris's details. Did you get a chance to visit him?'

One second's pause while I worked out that there was no way he could know I had. 'No, I didn't. It's a pity. I was sure he had questions to answer, and now it looks like I was right.'

I don't think Chesterman was especially pleased to hear that, but he didn't argue the point. Instead we talked about the progress of the dig. No more body parts had been found and the school was reopening the following week so he'd authorized extending the existing hole by a further five metres in both directions and, if nothing further was found, ending the operation. This seemed like a good idea, and I told him so before ending the call.

I didn't think Thames Valley would find anything in Bill Morris's house that would incriminate me. They sounded too overstretched, and I'd been careful. Sadly, I didn't think they'd find anything that incriminated or helped ID the murderer either, especially if it was the Kalamans behind it. You don't spend years creating a huge and successful criminal enterprise without being highly professional and knowing how to avoid the long arm of the law.

For the first time I felt a twinge of concern about Tina Boyd. An outfit like the Kalamans wouldn't have much difficulty in tracking down Charlotte Curtis, and if her reticence with me was anything to go by it sounded like they might have already found her. I looked at my watch. It was almost three. Getting on for two hours since I'd talked to Tina. She'd told me then she was only minutes away from Charlotte's house and she'd have called me as soon as she'd spoken to her. Tired of waiting, I'd called her just before my lunch arrived, but the phone had gone straight to voicemail and I'd left a message. There was probably a perfectly good explanation for why I couldn't get hold of her, but it still made me antsy. Charlotte Curtis knew something important and I wanted to know what it was.

I went back to my lunch, and cleaned the plate. I love my food. It's one of my few true pleasures. I cook when I can, and when I can't, I track down restaurants where they serve fresh, decent but not necessarily expensive fare like this one, and make them my regular haunts. I was tempted to knock down a quick glass of Chianti as well – red wine's another of my pleasures, especially when it's combined with good food – but I resisted, not wanting to offer my detractors another reason to kick me off the case.

Instead, I drained my coffee cup, paid the bill, and called Tina again as I walked back outside into a wet, chilly afternoon. Again it went to voicemail, and again I left a message. I tried Olaf next, wanting to let him know about the potential lead I had, but he wasn't answering either.

I'd parked my car over near Marylebone station, and I was on my way back to it, mulling my next move, when my phone rang.

It was DC Jools Hutchings from Ealing cop shop. 'You've got a problem, Ray,' she told me. There was background traffic noise and I could tell she was phoning me from outside. 'The word I'm hearing is they're moving you off the case.'

I tensed. 'Why?'

'Conflict of interest. I know DI Glenda's been briefing against you – you know how much she hates you, Ray – but I think it's pressure from above that's really counting. The problem is, there are still no leads at all on this case. No DNA from the murderers; no sign of the getaway car; no word from the street. Nothing. And there's you, the only witness to the killings, working on a case you're effectively a part of.'

'I didn't do anything wrong, Jools,' I said, wondering how long I was going to have keep saying this for.

'I know that. But it's not what I think that matters. It's all about perception. Everything's got to stand up to outside scrutiny, and to some people, your presence doesn't look right. I'm just saying, OK?'

I sighed, stepping out of the rain and into the shelter of a shop. 'Did you manage to get me that information on Kitty's next of kin?'

'I've emailed it to you.'

'Thanks.'

'We can still talk, you know. But I've got to be careful. I can't afford to lose my job.'

'I know. But I'm not off the case yet. So can you meet me at that coffee shop off the Broadway and we can run through what you've got?'

She was wise enough to spend a couple of seconds thinking about it before answering, 'Sure, I can do that.'

'I'll meet you there in half an hour.'

I was five minutes early getting to the Hot Gossip café, a three-minute walk from Ealing nick.

The place was barely a third full and Jools was already there, at a corner table well away from the window with a cup of what I knew would be green tea. Her body was very much her temple. And a nice temple it was too. She had some sheets of paper laid out on the table in front of her.

I ordered a bottle of fizzy water from the counter and joined her.

'Thanks for coming.'

'It's nice to get out of there,' she said. 'The atmosphere isn't good. It's getting very boring looking for non-existent suspects driving non-existent getaway cars.'

This was the problem these days. As a general rule, with the onset of technology and the continued stupidity of most murderers, murder investigations tended to be straightforward affairs. You checked the cameras; the DNA from the crime scene; the obvious suspects; and bingo, you usually found your killer. There was very little actual detective work involved. Consequently, when you had a case such as this where the killers were well organized, knew the police's methods, and didn't have any obvious connection with the victim, catching them was far from easy, and, put bluntly, Ealing MIT just weren't used to it.

'So, what have you got for me on Kitty Sinn's next of kin? I've only managed to find out a little bit about her background. You know, only child, dad died before she went missing, mother died afterwards.'

Jools picked up one of the sheets of paper in front of her. 'That's right. Mary Sinn committed suicide in 1992, aged fifty-four. She was suffering from advanced multiple sclerosis. The only other family Kitty had were the uncle and two cousins on her mother's side you mentioned. There was a lot of money in the family. Kitty's grandmother had an estate with a net worth of sixteen million, money that had come from her late husband's business, and when she died in 1998, apart from several small bequests to charity, all the money went to Kitty's two cousins, Alastair and Lola Sheridan, because Kitty had already been declared dead under the seven-year rule.'

Which was pretty much what I'd expected. 'Do we know anything about these cousins?'

'There's not much to know. Alastair's a very successful hedge fund manager.' Jools consulted another sheet of paper. 'He worked in the City after leaving Warwick University and set up the fund in 1996 with a handful of clients. Over the years he's grown it so that it now manages more than two hundred million of clients' money. According to his Wikipedia entry, he's worth in excess of fifty million pounds and has expressed an interest in getting into politics.'

'Wow,' I said. 'How old is he?'

'Forty-eight, and married with a five-year-old son. No criminal record. I tried to get hold of him earlier but apparently he's in China as part of a UK trade mission, along with the Chancellor of the Exchequer, so he's obviously a big cheese. And he wants to be kept in the loop on any developments to do with Kitty's case.'

'I bet he does,' I said, picking up on the fact that he was the same age as Cem Kalaman. 'He didn't go to Medmenham College, did he?' I asked, thinking that this would be too good to be true.

It was. Jools shook her head. 'He went to a private school in Newbury.'

'What can you tell me about Lola?'

'Lola Sheridan is forty-seven. Never married. Apparently she's an artist, although I couldn't find any details of any exhibitions she's ever done. She's listed on the electoral roll as living in the house she grew up in, just outside Whitchurch in Hampshire. Her father Robert lived there too until he died in 2013.'

I took a sip from my water. 'So Alastair and Lola inherited everything,' I mused.

'That's right. But I'm not sure it's a sufficient motive to kill Kitty. She went missing in 1990, so they would have known they'd have to wait for at least seven years to pass before she could be declared dead. And even then, they'd still have to wait for the grandmother to die too. In the end they didn't inherit until 1998. I mean, I've heard of forward planning, but that's taking it a bit far. If they were going to kill anyone, they'd have done a lot better to kill Grandma.'

I nodded, taking this in. 'But there was definitely bad blood in the family. Did you know that Kitty's mother, Mary, tried to burn down the Sheridan house one night in 1991 while Robert and Lola were in it? She was detained at the scene and actually tried to fight off the arresting officers.'

Jools pulled a puzzled expression. 'No, I didn't.'

'And I can't believe it was random. She targeted them, and she must have been very, very angry about something because she had no history of violence. My guess, looking at it now, knowing what we know, is that she blamed them for Kitty's death.'

'That's a big stretch, Ray.'

'She poured petrol through the letterbox and tried repeatedly to set it alight knowing there were people inside.' I thought about it some more. 'Look, I'm not saying that proves she blamed them for Kitty, but it's definitely something that warrants further investigation. You've been through the background of Henry Forbes, and Alastair and Lola Sheridan. Is there anything that links them?'

'Nothing that immediately springs to mind.'

I sat back in my chair. At the moment there was nothing at all to implicate either cousin in Kitty's disappearance, yet right now they were the only ones who had a motive, however tenuous.

'You didn't say where Lola Sheridan went to university.'

Jools consulted her notes. 'Goldsmiths. She did a degree in History.' She pulled that puzzled expression again, and then her face broke into a surprisingly infectious smile. 'Isn't that where—'

'Henry Forbes did his degree, yes. Were they there at the same time?'

'Forbes's details are on here,' she said, taking an iPad from her bag.

I waited while Jools found the file she was looking for.

'He left in 1989,' she said, 'while he was still doing his PhD, and finished it at Brighton Polytechnic. Lola Sheridan was at Goldsmiths from 1988 until 1991.'

'So Henry's doing his PhD at Goldsmiths. He'd been there since he first started at uni. Then midway through he leaves and goes to a polytechnic. I wonder why.'

Jools shrugged. 'Maybe he was bored. You've changed departments at the Met a few times, you know what it's like.'

But I didn't quite buy that. Whichever way you looked at it, Brighton Polytechnic was a bit of a career comedown from Goldsmiths. 'We need to find out whether Henry and Lola knew each other. My guess is they did.'

Jools's phone vibrated on the table, and she picked it up.

'That's interesting.'

'What is it?'

'Apparently there's been a major development. I need to get back right now.' She looked at me. 'Can you give it twenty minutes before you come back to the incident room? I don't want to make it too obvious I was with you.'

'Sure,' I said, conscious that my own phone hadn't buzzed to tell me of this important development.

She got to her feet and, as she passed me, gave my shoulder a squeeze. 'Good luck.'

I watched her go, thinking it was a pity she was married. She was pretty and kind, with a good heart and a strong backbone, and for just one fleeting second I imagined us walking off into the sunset, hand in hand, her two young sons in tow, a ready-made family for me to step into, just like before. A real life. The kind that other people have.

Then I forced myself back to reality, ordered a coffee, and tried Tina Boyd's mobile again. It was ten to four now and still no sign of her.

Where the hell was she?

Twenty-eight

They moved in silence, watching constantly for signs of an ambush. Although Charlotte led the way, Tina was the one encouraging her to keep up the pace, and it wasn't easy. The afternoon was hot, and since leaving the track next to the stream there'd been a lot of hiking uphill through woodland. Charlotte was flagging badly.

'How much further until we hit a road?' Tina asked her.

Charlotte took the opportunity to stop and answer. She was swaying a little on her feet and had the listless look of someone who wasn't going to last much longer. 'Another few hundred metres. Then it's a walk of about a kilometre into Massoules. We'll be able to get help there.'

'Is there no way of getting to Massoules without going on the road? We're going to be very exposed out there.'

'There are a couple of farms on the way. We could stop at the nearest one.'

Tina wiped sweat from her brow. She was wary of going anywhere near a road. There were four men after them, in at least two cars, and even though it felt like they'd been going for hours it was unlikely they'd covered more than a few miles, during which time they'd seen neither dwelling nor human being. This part of France was close to pure wilderness, which suited the bad guys a lot better than it did them.

For the first time, Tina could understand why they were so keen to get hold of Charlotte. After Henry had come to see her the previous week, Tina had gone through the whole Kitty Sinn case. She remembered aspects of it from when she was a young girl too, the complete mystery of her disappearance. Now it seemed that Kitty had never left England, and that someone had gone in her place. After so long it was highly unlikely that Charlotte could provide the evidence needed to ID the impostor, but someone somewhere was clearly taking no chances.

Which meant they weren't going to give up the hunt until they absolutely had to.

'OK, Charlotte, get your breath back. I'll lead the way, and when we get on the road, you do everything I say. If I tell you to jump in the nearest hedge, you jump. Understand?'

Charlotte put her hands on her hips, breathing heavily. 'I understand.'

Tina looked her in the eye. 'I'm going to get you back to safety.'

Charlotte returned her gaze. 'They're not going to stop, are they? Not until they've killed me.'

No, thought Tina, they're not. But she didn't say that. 'As soon as you've said what you need to say to the British police, there'll be no incentive for these people to touch you. And then one day you'll be able to look back on this whole experience like it was just a nightmare you once had.'

'I hope so.'

'You will. But if what you say is right, that it wasn't Kitty who went to Thailand with Henry, then we've stumbled into a major conspiracy. I know it's not easy out here, but can you think back to those days? Did Kitty ever mention anyone, anyone at all, who might have wished her harm? Because someone clearly did.'

Tina waited while Charlotte thought about it. At the same time, she looked around. The path they were on now was narrow and the trees came very close to the edges. The woods were dark and foreboding, but also largely impenetrable, and nothing moved within them.

'Kitty was an only child,' said Charlotte eventually, 'but I know she had two cousins. I only remember them ever being mentioned once. We shared a house together – me, Kitty and two other girls, Jenny Geisler and Tara . . . someone. God, I can't even remember Tara's last name. One night we all stayed in, smoked a couple of joints, and got wrecked on cheap wine. We used to do that sometimes. You know what it's like when you're a student.'

Tina knew exactly what it was like. She remembered her own times at uni. They'd been good days. Before cynicism and the real world took over.

'I remember the conversation started to get morbid,' continued

Charlotte, no longer breathing heavily. 'Someone, I think it was Jenny, started talking about the time an ex of hers tried to rape her when she was about sixteen. She got quite upset about it, but I always remember that Jenny liked to say things that got her attention, so it was hard to know whether she was making it up or not. Then someone – again, I can't remember who it was, it might even have been me – saw that Kitty was sitting there in silence with tears running down her face. We all asked her what was wrong but she wouldn't tell us. She kept saying it was nothing, but you know what it's like. People don't take no for an answer when they've had too much, and we kept hassling until eventually she just got up and went to bed.

'I was worried about her so I went into her room a few minutes later and saw that she was still crying her eyes out. I sat down on her bed and just held her in my arms while she sobbed.' Charlotte frowned. 'That's when she told me that the same thing had happened to her when she was young. She said that one time when she was about twelve, her two cousins – a boy and a girl – had held her down and molested her while they'd been in their grandma's garden, and that the boy had tried to rape her. She'd fought back but I got the feeling the assault had been pretty bad. Kitty told me that she hated them, her cousins, that they were truly awful people. I told her she should go to the police about it but she said no, she just wanted to forget about it, and she swore me to secrecy.'

'How old were these cousins?' asked Tina.

'I don't know, but I think they were roughly the same age as her, maybe a bit older.'

Tina thought about this. Her cousins might have been awful people but this still sounded like an out-of-control children's game, not something that would have led them to kill Kitty years later.

'And that's it?'

Charlotte looked at her, and something in her eyes gave Tina the idea there might be something more. But then she shrugged and said, 'That's all I can think of.'

'You had a relationship with Henry Forbes. Did he ever talk about Kitty?'

'Only when I brought her up in conversation, and he was never comfortable talking about her. Do you think he killed her? It's awful to think I might have been in a relationship with a murderer.'

'He definitely had something to do with it,' said Tina. 'When you were with him, did you ever see a tattoo on his underarm?'

Charlotte nodded. 'Yes. It was a pentacle with the letter "M" inside it. An awful thing. I asked him why he'd got it done, and he said something about it being part of a student bet. Again, it was one of those things he didn't really like to talk about.'

Tina wiped the sweat from her brow with a shirtsleeve. They had to keep going.

'Are you ready?' she asked.

Charlotte looked nervous. 'As ready as I'll ever be.' She took a deep breath. 'God, I don't want to die.'

'You won't. I've been in situations like this before.'

'Really? When?'

'More than once. I was a police officer for a long time. Do

what I say and you'll be OK.' She patted Charlotte on the arm and smiled. 'Come on, let's go.'

They continued along the path until it gave way to a quiet country road. Tina poked her head out of the trees and looked both ways. To her left the road disappeared over the brow of a hill less than fifty metres away while to her right it ran for about a hundred metres before rounding a corner. There were no cars coming from either direction and the late afternoon was still, with just the chirp of cicadas breaking the silence.

'We have to go right to get to Massoules,' said Charlotte.

Tina took a deep breath. She acted tough but she too was just as scared of death, and the fact that she'd faced it several times before didn't make her feel any better. Still, she knew from experience that hesitation was fatal, so she stepped on to the road and began jogging at a decent pace.

'I don't know if I can keep up,' said Charlotte.

'You're going to have to, I'm afraid.'

'I think there's a farm up here somewhere on the left.'

Tina could hear Charlotte's panting in her ears. She ignored it and concentrated on keeping moving. She had to get Charlotte to safety. It didn't matter that it wasn't her problem, that technically she was a civilian who had every right to turn her back on this whole thing. What mattered was that she was part of something important again. Tina felt wanted. She felt needed. Even amid the exhaustion, the thirst and the fear, it was a good feeling.

On both sides of the road the trees had disappeared now, replaced by parched-looking fields with little in the way of hiding places.

'The farm's up this track,' said Charlotte between pants, pointing at a gap in the fields just ahead. 'It's not far.'

Straight away Tina knew it was their best bet, and she ran across the road, Charlotte following. Almost immediately she heard the sound of a car coming fast, and she redoubled her pace.

'Come on – quick!'

Grabbing Charlotte by the arm she dragged her on to the track. A few yards along it, a large tangled thorn bush stuck out of the ground. Tina pulled Charlotte behind it and crouched down out of sight just as the car came driving past. Tina caught only a fleeting glimpse of it. It was black, the same colour as the cars that had pulled into Charlotte's driveway, but it didn't slow down, and after a few seconds the low rumble of the engine faded away.

Tina got to her feet and, together, she and Charlotte ran along the track. When they were out of sight of the road and they could see the farm behind a low stone wall, they slowed their pace to a walk. There was a barn and a cattle shed on either side of a courtyard and then an old stone farmhouse at the end with an ancient-looking car and tractor outside.

Charlotte stopped at a standpipe next to the cattle shed and, as the cattle watched, turned on the tap and drank out of her cupped hands. Ignoring her own thirst, Tina walked up to the front door and knocked hard.

There was no reply.

'Is no one home?' asked Charlotte as Tina knocked a third time.

'It doesn't look that way. Follow me.'

She walked round the back of the farmhouse, looking in a couple of the windows. It was clear the house was empty. It was also clear, given the fact that all the windows were shut, that whoever lived here wasn't coming back soon. Tina stopped at the dilapidated back door and tried it. The door rattled on its hinges but didn't open.

'Christ,' said Charlotte, a note of defeat in her voice. 'What are we going to do?'

Her naivety impressed Tina. 'What do you think we're going to do?' she said, finding a rock in the back yard and smashing one of the panes. She cleared out the rest of the glass with the rock then peered inside.

It always amazed Tina how many people left their keys in the lock. It was like an open invitation to burglars, and she was thankful that houseowners in France were just as slapdash. Reaching through, she unlocked the back door and stepped into the welcome coolness. Charlotte hesitated a couple of seconds, then followed.

The house's interior was old-fashioned and definitely in need of a good clean, with a smell of mothballs and lint which reminded Tina of her grandparents' house, and immediately brought back the kind of happy childhood memories that adulthood had all too infrequently produced. She went through to the kitchen, found a chipped mug in one of the cupboards, and filled it with water at the tap. She drank down three cups' worth, then splashed a load more water over her face.

Charlotte appeared in the doorway.

'See if you can find a phone somewhere,' Tina told her. 'We need to get the police up here as soon as possible. And pull out all the stops when you talk to them. Make sure they know that there are four armed men and they've been shooting at us. That way they'll take it seriously and respond in numbers. The last thing we need is the neighbourhood gendarme turning up here. It'll give away our location and they'll kill him and us.'

'Do you have any idea who they are, these people who are after me?'

Tina shook her head. 'None. But they're definitely determined, so you need to convince the cops to take this seriously.'

Charlotte nodded, and Tina watched her go. She would have killed for a cigarette right then. She checked the kitchen drawers and cupboards, hunting round not only for a smoke but car keys, in case they needed to make a quick getaway, as well as any useful weapons. There were no cigarettes, and no sign of car keys either, but Tina did find a small, surprisingly sharp filleting knife which she slipped blade-down into the back pocket of her jeans.

She walked into a musty-smelling living room where Charlotte was talking on the phone in French, sounding suitably dramatic.

'The police are on their way,' she said, putting down the phone, a relieved smile on her face.

But just as Tina was allowing herself to relax for the first time that afternoon, there was a loud knock on the front door.

Twenty-nine

A figure appeared at the back window, moving stealthily. Tina got just enough of a look to see it was the young Frenchman who'd held her hostage earlier before yanking Charlotte down behind the sofa, and ducking out of sight herself.

It was only going to take him a few seconds to realize that there'd been a break-in and then he'd know they were in here. Tina was also pretty certain that he wasn't the same person who'd knocked on the front door. He wouldn't have been able to get round the back quickly enough – which meant there were at least two of them. Potentially more. And this time they wouldn't risk taking prisoners.

Tina thought fast. She could already hear the young man at the back door, trying the handle.

She motioned for Charlotte to stay put and crawled out from behind the sofa and along the floor before slowly standing up next to the doorway, slipping the knife from her back pocket, trying to keep out of sight of the back window.

He was inside now, walking through the narrow hallway, only just the other side of the wall. Inches away.

Slowly, his feet creaking on the floorboards, he stepped into the living room. At that moment, a number of things happened. First, he spotted Charlotte crouched down behind the sofa and immediately pointed the gun at her. Second, out of the corner of his eye he saw Tina standing against the wall, and swung round towards her. Third, the older French gunman appeared at the back window, saw his colleague, as well as Tina next to him in the shadows, and shouted a warning.

Tina had a split second to react and she used it, leaping at the younger gunman, using one hand to knock his gun hand away and the other to shove the knife into his neck. Tina had killed three times in her life – always men who'd deserved it, and on whom she'd wasted no feelings of guilt – but she'd never stabbed anyone, and it was horrific seeing the blood spray from the gunman's severed artery. Even so, she hugged him close to her, leaving the knife in there and turning him so he was blocking the view of the other gunman. At the same time she pulled the gun from his hand and fired a shot through the window.

'Move!' she screamed at Charlotte, letting the mortally wounded man drop to the floor and firing a second shot at the older man as he dived out of the way and out of sight.

Charlotte didn't move. It was as if she was frozen as she stood staring at the gunman dying on the floor in a rapidly growing pool of blood.

With her finger still tensed on the trigger, Tina pulled her over to the back door. She opened it, pointed the gun round the corner so only her hand was exposed and fired two shots, one at chest height, one towards the ground, in case the gunman was lying in wait, then a shot in the other direction, before dragging Charlotte out of the door and frantically looking both ways. There was no one there so Tina thrust Charlotte forward, yelling at her to run.

Charlotte sprinted across the back yard away from the house while Tina followed, running backwards, her eyes searching for the older gunman. Almost immediately he emerged firing, getting off three wild shots before he'd even clocked her position. During her time in the police Tina had been firearms-trained, and she was a good shot. Still running, she clutched the gun two-handed to steady it and fired a single shot back. It missed, but it was close enough to encourage the gunman to jump back behind the corner of the house.

The yard ended with a low wooden fence that led into a freshly ploughed field sloping downwards to a line of trees. Charlotte was already over when Tina got to it. More shots rang out behind her as the older gunman got brave again. Tina turned and fired two more rounds back at him, noticing as she did so that a third gunman had appeared round the other side of the house and was also firing.

Adrenalin coursed through her. The strange thing about these sorts of situations was that they never felt real, and events happened so fast that there was never enough time to feel fear. Tina remembered reading somewhere that soldiers in a battle never think they're the ones who are going to be shot, and she understood that completely as she turned her gun on the newly arrived man and fired off another round, forcing him to jump behind a stone wall.

She shoved the weapon in the front of her jeans, vaulted the fence and sprinted into the field, knowing that as a moving target she was going to be hard to hit.

'Run! Run! Run!' she yelled as she gained on Charlotte, keeping a good three yards from her so as not to make it too easy for the gunmen. Tears were running down Charlotte's face as she ran at a pace she almost certainly hadn't run in a long time. But then a gun at your back does that to a person. 'Zigzag when you run!' Tina encouraged her. 'Make it hard for them!' At the same time, she turned round and saw the two gunmen at the back fence taking aim. Almost immediately they began firing but they were a good thirty metres away and not good shots either. Tina fired back, again forcing them to take cover.

And then she was pulling the trigger and nothing was happening. She threw the gun down, turned and hared off down the slope.

Even when they hit the tree line neither of them stopped. There was no path and they had to force their way through the undergrowth. Charlotte's breathing was coming in short, desperate pants but, credit to her, she kept going.

Tina looked over her shoulder. All she could see were trees but she knew their pursuers wouldn't give up. She wondered how the gunmen had been able to find them so quickly, and guessed that whoever was in the car they'd seen on the road had also seen them. As the immediacy of the danger they were in passed and her adrenalin began to fade, Tina felt the fear begin inside her gut. She'd come close to being killed back there, and once again her luck had held. But she knew, as she'd always known, that it couldn't hold for ever. That was what was keeping her running now, a fear that if she didn't run, the end might come today.

They must have gone two hundred metres through the woods when a ravine opened up directly in front of them. They stopped at the edge. The ravine stretched in both directions and there was a steep, almost vertical drop of about forty feet down to a wide stream below.

'Oh God,' panted Charlotte. 'We've got to get down there?'

'There's no other way as far as I can see. We're just going to have to climb down the slope.'

'I don't think I—'

'There's no choice, Charlotte,' Tina said, looking her in the eye. 'If we get down there, it makes us harder to follow. But we've got to move.' She squeezed Charlotte's shoulders. 'This'll all be over soon, I promise.'

Charlotte put on a brave smile. 'Thank God I've got you with me. It's my first bit of luck for a long time.'

And then, without warning, a gun went off and she staggered forward into Tina's arms, her eyes wide with shock, the smile freezing on her face.

Over her shoulder, Tina saw the man in the black fedora standing in the trees, only a few metres away, a gun pointed straight at Tina. She only got the barest glimpse of his face. He was old, in his sixties, with a heavily lined face, but what she would always remember about him was his completely calm, almost serene demeanour, as if he'd been waiting there the whole time for them to arrive.

As he fired again, Tina jumped into the ravine, pulling Charlotte with her. Suddenly she was hurtling down the near-vertical slope. She lost her grip on Charlotte, struck a bush that knocked her off course, and then she was immersed in cool water, slamming her back against a rock on the bottom.

For a couple of seconds she was too dazed to move, then she opened her eyes, saw Charlotte lying face up and motionless in the water a few feet away, and grabbed her by the shoulders, pulling her into the shelter of a narrow cut in the bank caused by the water's flow. A bullet hissed by and struck the water a couple of metres away. Tina looked up. From the angle she was at now she could no longer see the top of the ravine, which meant the gunman wouldn't be able to see her.

She looked down at Charlotte. The back of her dress was red with blood. More blood ran from her nose, and a bruise was already beginning to form on her forehead. Her eyes flickered open and tried to focus on Tina. She was whispering something, but even when she put her ear right down to her lips, Tina couldn't make out what she was trying to say.

Then her eyes closed again, and her breathing grew more shallow.

'Don't die on me,' hissed Tina, pushing her hand against the bullet wound she could see, trying to stop the bleeding as the plaintive wail of a far-away siren started up in the distance. 'Don't you dare die on me.'

Thirty

The incident room was abuzz with activity when I walked in just after 4.30. There must have been twenty people in there and the bulk of them were crowded round a single desk, including Olaf and my nemesis, DI Glenda Gardner. Jools was at her desk and she nodded when she saw me, and gave me a barely perceptible thumbs-up.

Other people turned round too, as if an apparition had just walked in. It didn't make me feel any more welcome. Glenda gave me the kind of look she usually reserved for sex offenders, but Olaf gave me a big smile, which I wasn't expecting, and peeled away from the group.

'Ah, the man himself. I was just about to call you. Where have you been?'

'I've got a potential lead for you, boss,' I said quietly. 'But I need to discuss it in private. What's going on here?' I motioned towards the group at the desk.

'We've got a lead too. Come and look at this.'

He led the way over to the desk and the rest of the group moved out of my way. Glenda glared at me as I passed but I ignored her.

A large-screen PC was on the desk, and the screen was frozen at what appeared to be a view from an upstairs window at night. The icon at the bottom of the screen showed that it was the beginning of a one-minute-eighteen-second video clip. For a single terrifying moment I thought it might be footage taken from the scene of the Bill Morris murder last night – footage that would incriminate me – but I quickly dismissed this. If they thought I'd had anything to do with Morris's murder I'd be in handcuffs right now and they wouldn't be going through this pretence. Even so, the view could easily have been into Morris's back garden and it spooked me.

Olaf leaned down beside me and pressed play. 'We got sent this an hour ago by a bloke who lives three miles away from Maurice Reedman's house.'

The footage was high-quality and clearly filmed on a hand-held camcorder from the man's bedroom as he looked down beyond his garden fence to a tree-lined track the other side of it. I could just make out a black BMW X5 and, as the camera panned into the darkness, I could see a man with his back to the camera, changing the rear number plate. At the same time another man came into view. He was no longer wearing a mask but it was impossible to see his face as he hurried past the back of the car

and into the trees, setting off the intruder light in the cameraman's garden as he did so.

'The bloke lives in a quiet area,' continued Olaf, 'and he was
upstairs when he heard a car pull up round the side of his house,
so he decided to take a look in case they were burglars. This
footage was taken nine minutes after your call to me ended, so
the timings fit for the getaway vehicle. Now watch what this dirty
bastard does.'

He pointed at the guy without the mask who, as the cameraman filmed, squatted against one of the trees, half facing towards
the house, his every action lit up by the intruder lights, and pro-
ceeded to take a remarkably rapid shit. I knew from my time in
uniform that burglars in particular like to shit in the houses they
rob. It's not so much a sign of disrespect, more a product of
adrenalin, and I guessed this was the case here. A couple of the
guys watching chuckled, including Olaf, while the women made
noises of disgust, as did the cameraman. But he kept filming,
panning in as far as he could on the guy's face. The camera
blurred as it moved towards close-up but it had got enough of
him for a possible ID. And there was something else too: the
arms of his jacket were rolled up, revealing a sleeve tattoo on his
left forearm.

I stood back from the screen as the guy pulled up his jeans and
jogged back to the car, disappearing from view. 'That's the man I
fought with,' I said to Olaf, feeling vindicated. 'And as you may
recall, DI Gardner,' I continued, addressing Glenda, 'I described
him as mixed race, with a scar near his collarbone and a sleeve
tattoo on his left forearm. And there he is.'

Glenda nodded, her mouth closed and lips pursed tight. She was breathing through her nose as if she didn't trust herself not to blow her top.

I didn't get an apology. Nor did I expect one. Instead I turned back to the film, watching as it ended with the BMW reversing down the track and out on to the road with its lights off. The cameraman tried to get the registration number but it was too dark. Not that it mattered. This was a major lead, and a real piece of luck.

'Good work, Ray,' said Olaf, clapping me on the shoulder. 'We've got a few good stills we've circulated to the super-recognizers so, if he's known, we'll have a name.'

The super-recognizers are the Met's team of some two hundred officers, spread out over the boroughs, who all share a talent for remembering faces. Set up in the wake of the 2011 riots, they regularly outperform even the most up-to-date software when it comes to IDing suspects. If anyone was going to put a name to the man who'd almost killed me, it would be one of them.

Olaf led me away from the group and into his office, closing the door behind him. He had some coffee bubbling away in his percolator and he poured us both a cup.

'I tell you, Ray,' he said with a satisfied sigh when we were sitting opposite each other, 'I don't know how he managed that.'

'How who managed what?' I said, confused.

'The suspect on the film. Taking a shit that fast. That must be a world record. And then to not fucking wipe.' He shook his head and gave me a man-to-man look. 'What sort of filthy sod does that, Ray? Eh?'

'The kind of filthy sod who gets himself caught. The kind we like.'

I smiled, and he smiled back. I could tell he was in a good mood. The pressure was off him a little, now that we were making progress.

'So what have you got for me?' he asked.

'I've heard from a source that the hit on Forbes and Reedman was the work of the Kalamans.'

'Who's the source?'

'It comes from an old colleague of mine via a source within the Kalaman outfit. You know who they are, don't you?'

Olaf shrugged, his neck momentarily disappearing into his shoulders. 'I've heard the name a few times,' he said noncommittally.

'Then you know what'll happen to the source if word gets out about him.'

'And is he an official CHIS?' Olaf asked, using the official police acronym for an informant.

'As far as I know,' I lied.

'Have you got names for the gunmen?'

'No, but my old colleague's working on it. I'll need to send him photos of our suspect. And just so you know this isn't some bullshit lead, Cem Kalaman, the leader of the gang, attended Medmenham College for seven years in the 1980s, so he had the intimate knowledge of the grounds that at least one of the killers would have needed. And that's not all.' I took a deep breath. 'I've just heard from Chesterman over at Thames Valley that the school caretaker at the time the girls went missing was found hanging at his home last night. An intruder was spotted leaving by a neighbour, so the killing looks suspicious.'

Olaf pulled a face. 'Blimey. Not another dead body. I'm assuming it's connected to this.'

I nodded. 'I'd say so. You remember I told you yesterday I thought Dana Brennan and Kitty Sinn were murdered in the grounds of Medmenham College, and that I didn't think it could have been done without the caretaker at the time knowing something about it? Well, he may not have been actively involved but I'm guessing he turned a blind eye to people coming on to the property in the summer holidays, probably for money. He was a loose end.'

Olaf sighed. 'Like Henry Forbes. These killers are good at tying up loose ends.' He took a gulp of his coffee and spilled a bit down his shirt. 'What about Tina Boyd?' he asked, moving his tie to cover the stain. 'Has she had any joy with that woman Forbes was trying to find?'

'Charlotte Curtis. I haven't heard back from her. I've left a couple of messages.' In fact I'd left three, the last one only ten minutes earlier. I wasn't panicking yet. It might be that Charlotte lived in a place with no phone reception and they were still there talking, but I was beginning to feel a little uneasy.

Olaf gave me a serious look. 'You've done good, Ray. I was coming under a lot of pressure from above to pull you off the case because of what happened the other night.'

'I hear DI Gardner wanted me off the case as well.'

'She's just doing her job.'

'She was suggesting I was corrupt in some way. I'm not.'

Olaf sighed. 'I've always known that. But let's put it behind us, eh? We're still a long way from solving this case.'

'Sure,' I said, getting to my feet and taking my coffee with me.

'Keep up the good work,' he called after me as I walked out of his office. 'And don't forget to bring back the cup.'

I went over to my desk next to Jools's and sat down. The incident room had gone quiet again, and at least half the team seemed to have disappeared, including Jools, probably taking much-needed breaks from the monotony of staring at CCTV footage. Glenda was still there, though, po-faced, banging away on her keyboard.

I took a sip from my coffee and took the photo of Dana Brennan her mum had given me out of my wallet.

I stared down at the faded image of the smiling young girl, thinking that, as far as the investigation was concerned, she was becoming forgotten in all this. But someone had abducted her on that summer afternoon in 1989, pretty much a year to the day before Kitty disappeared. Had it been a young Cem Kalaman?

One thing was for sure: it was definitely someone who knew the twisting warren of country roads around Dana's house.

I booted up my PC and went on Google Maps, using my mouse to create a map that took in the area around Medmenham College, in the top right corner, and Whitchurch, the village in Hampshire where Kitty's cousins Lola and Alastair Sheridan had been brought up, in the bottom left corner. I opened another tab and went into my inbox. The notes Jools had emailed me were right at the top, and I found the postcode for the Sheridan family address and flagged it on the map. I then looked up Dana's parents' address in my notebook and flagged that on the map too. The distance between the two properties was barely ten miles, and the Brennan home was on the way towards the school, albeit still some thirty miles away.

I didn't know what that told me. In truth, it was probably just a coincidence, and there was no reason to think that Kitty's cousins, who would have been around twenty at the time, had anything to do with Dana's abduction. Nevertheless, something about it bugged me so I printed off the map and put it on my desk, then slowly drank my coffee, pondering the case and my next move. Sometimes it's good just to sit and think. It gets the ideas flowing. Other times it just adds to the general confusion, which was what was happening now.

I was just about to give up being Sherlock Holmes for the day and start on the mountain of paperwork I had to get through when I had an idea. It was a bit of a long shot, but some deep-down instinct I couldn't quite explain told me it might come to something. And that instinct's been good to me in the past. So I went online, found the number I was looking for, and picked up the phone.

Half an hour later I had what I needed.

Thirty-one

After the phone call with Dan the Pig, Ramon had walked for a long time. He appreciated walking these days, as was often the case with men who'd spent close to half their lives hidden away in prison. He was feeling restless so he walked in a big circle, even passing close to the estate where he'd gone looking for Marlon Jones all those years ago. He'd been a scared kid then, living on his nerves as he fought to prove himself to the Youngers and the Elders in his gang, doing what had to be done to get by. And you know what? In the end, not a lot had changed. He was bigger now, harder, maybe even a bit more wise. But he was as scared as he'd ever been, maybe more so, because just like before there was no way out.

Ramon was a couple of blocks short of his flat when he felt he was being watched. A car was slowing to a crawl just behind him, and that kind of thing was never a good thing. He kept walking, pushing out his chest and keeping his head high, telling himself that so far at least he hadn't done anything wrong, so no one had any reason to hurt him.

The car was alongside him now and he heard the hiss of a window coming down. Out of the corner of his eye he could see the vehicle was black and sleek.

'Hey, Ramon,' said a deep, unfamiliar voice. 'Why not come for a ride?'

Ramon looked down, half expecting to see Dan the Pig, but the man who stared out at him from inside the back of the Merc was a whole lot scarier than any Fed, and Ramon felt his heart jump in his chest as he wondered if he'd been found out already.

The door opened and Jonas Mavalu moved aside to let Ramon in.

Ramon took a quick glimpse in the front and saw only a driver, which made him feel a little safer. The truth was, though, he knew he couldn't say no. Jonas was Junior's boss, a legend in gangland circles, even inside nick. There were all kinds of stories about him: that he'd been one of the rioters who'd hacked to death PC Keith Blakelock during the 1985 Broadwater Farms riots, when he was only fourteen years old; that he'd killed a rival gang leader with a machete in front of a pub full of witnesses when he was only sixteen years old, and got away with it because no one dared snitch on him to the Feds. Ramon didn't know how many of them were true but he did know one thing for sure: Jonas was one of Kalaman's most feared enforcers, and therefore definitely not a man to be crossed.

Reluctantly, Ramon got inside the Merc, squeezing his bulk in next to Jonas, who was also a big guy, though not as big as Ramon.

The inside of the car was silent as the driver pulled away from the kerb. Jonas just sat staring at him and Ramon felt his body tighten. He stared back, knowing from long and bitter experience that you never show you're scared. Not to anyone.

'I'm guessing you know who I am, Ramon,' said Jonas.

Ramon wasn't sure what the right answer was. Junior had told him that Jonas liked to keep a low profile so he might not like it if Ramon knew his name, but he decided to tell the truth anyway rather than risk a potentially needless lie. 'Yeah,' he said. 'I know who you are.'

'You're not wearing a wire, are you?' Jonas's face was serious, his eyes boring into Ramon's. He had an intense stare and big bug eyes that made it look like he was on the verge of launching an attack.

Ramon's expression didn't change, even though the question had caught him like a sucker punch. He knew he had to keep calm even as he wondered who it was who'd betrayed him. 'Course I'm not. Why would I do that?'

Jonas kept staring, all muscles and aggression, and Ramon had to resist squirming in his seat. What the fuck did this guy want?

Then, just as suddenly, Jonas's face broke into a big toothy grin and he punched Ramon in the arm. Hard. 'I'm just fucking with you, bruv. I know you're all right, and you can speak freely in here. This car's been swept for bugs. The Feds aren't listening in.'

'Sure,' said Ramon warily, resisting the urge to rub his arm.

'I'm going to put up the screen, Anton,' said Jonas, addressing the driver. 'I want to talk privately to my man here, you understand? You just drive around. Make sure you don't stray too far from here.'

Jonas pressed a button and a glass screen rose up from a panel behind the front seats. At the same time, Ramon glanced at the driver and immediately saw the black sleeve tattoo on his left forearm. He made a mental note of it before turning back to Jonas, who was watching him carefully with the kind of smile that would look good on a crocodile.

'So, how are you enjoying working for Junior, Ramon?'

Ramon shrugged and deliberately left it a couple of seconds before he answered. 'It's all right. The work's easy enough and I get paid on time. It's a lot better than jail.'

'Yeah, I bet it is. You know, you could go places, Ramon. You want that?'

Ramon nodded slowly, not sure where this was going, but ready to play along. 'Yeah, I want that.'

'You prepared to do what it takes? To obey orders, whatever they are?'

Ramon was getting interested now, sensing this was some kind of job interview. 'Yeah, I am. I'm not scared of getting my hands dirty either.'

'I know you're not. I heard about you popping that boy back in the day. Cost you fourteen years, right? You know why? Cos you got caught.'

Which Ramon thought was kind of stating the obvious, even though Jonas was looking at him like a muscly black Buddha who'd just imparted some great wisdom.

'Let me tell you something, Ramon,' he continued. 'When I first started out I was just like you were. I even grew up close to your ends. I made my money mugging kids, nicking their pocket money, running little bits of dope here and there. I didn't have no ambition, you get what I'm saying? I was just living day to day, trying to get respect, just like you were. I wanted to show every-one I was the best, the hardest. The one no one messed with. So one time when I held up this geezer outside the tube, and he wouldn't give me the money and tried to run, I let him have it. Put a knife in his gut. The geezer survived and I got his money, all twenty-two quid of it, but then one of my boys ratted on me, said I was the one who used the shank, and I got put away for five years.' He stared at Ramon, shaking his head. 'Five years for twenty-two quid. Do the maths, Ramon. It ain't worth it. But you know what? It did me good. Because all that jail time gives you time to think, right? It makes you realize that wasting your life doing petty little crimes, running round the street trying to scrape a few quid, just ain't the way. You've got to think big, bruv. Have a plan.' He tapped his temple with a finger. 'You know what I'm going to be doing one day? Sitting on a yacht full of hot bitches in Montego Bay counting my money. How does that sound to you? A life in the sun with all the bitches you can fuck, and all the money you can count.'

'It sounds good, man,' said Ramon. And it did. Jesus, it did.

'You can have it. You do what you're told, you act like a good soldier, and you'll be rewarded. And the sky's the limit, Ramon. You get what I'm saying, bruv? The limit.' Jonas sat back in his seat and put his hands on his head, flexing his biceps. 'You're the kind of man we're looking for. Someone who don't mind getting his hands dirty. Someone who can kill.'

Ramon stayed silent.

'How did you feel killing that boy, Ramon?'

Ramon shrugged. He'd thought about it a lot over the years, and the thoughts had been mixed. Sometimes regret. Sometimes guilt. Other times, indifference or anger. Today it was definitely anger. 'Him and his boys dissed me. He deserved it.'

Jonas laughed, a deep bass sound that rattled round the car like someone had turned the volume right up. Then he stopped and looked serious again.

'You want to join my crew, Ramon?'

Ramon hadn't expected this. A move up to Jonas's crew – a small, select group of Kalaman soldiers who wielded real power – was a major promotion. And to be honest, Jonas's words were inspiring him in a way he'd never been inspired before. He wanted what was on offer. The money, the women. The respect. And for the first time in his life, it was actually within his grasp. At that moment, even the fact that he was supposedly working for the Feds didn't bother him.

'Yeah man, I want to join your crew,' said Ramon, looking Jonas in the eye as he spoke, just so Jonas knew he was abso-lutely serious.

'Good. Junior will pick you up tomorrow night at ten outside your flats. Be ready. Right now, though, I want you to do me a favour. And I don't want you to tell Junior about it. You got a car?'

Ramon nodded. He'd bought a second-hand VW Polo as soon

as he'd passed his test. He didn't use it much but he was proud of the fact he actually owned his own car.

'You know where you and Junior dropped them girls off last night? I want you to go there at eight, pick up one of the girls, and take her to this address.' He pulled out a wallet fat with cash from inside his hoodie, found a slip of paper inside, and handed it to Ramon. 'You put her in the back of the car, you don't look at her. You don't talk to her. When you've dropped her off, you burn that piece of paper, and forget you ever went there. Understand?'

Ramon knew better than to ask questions. This was a test. He needed to pass it. 'No problem, it's sorted,' he said.

Jonas put a hand on Ramon's shoulder and fixed him with a cold smile. 'Good. I know I can rely on you. But one thing, bruv. Don't ever let me down.' The smile faded and the grip on the shoulder grew tighter. 'Cos if you do, I'll cut out your fucking eyes.' He released his grip, pressed the button, and the glass partition came back down. 'Anton, drop our man here.'

The driver pulled over. Ramon got out without a backward glance and slipped the piece of paper into his jeans pocket. As the sleek black Merc pulled away he wondered if he'd be driving one of them one day. Or whether he'd end up face down in a ditch with a bullet in the back of his head and his eyes cut out.

It said everything about his life that it could just as easily be either.

Thirty-two

It was almost eight and darkness was beginning to settle when I rang the doorbell.

Dr John Kettleborough PhD, retired lecturer and research fellow at Goldsmiths, London, lived in an attractive townhouse on a quiet north London street that, thanks to the capital's insane property prices, would have cost him a lifetime's university salary if he'd bought it today. I'd finally managed to track him down after seven different phone calls, and at least one threat of prosecution for obstruction, and had called him an hour earlier to make an appointment, so he was expecting me.

I never went to university. I joined the army instead. But I have to say when he answered the door, Dr Kettleborough looked exactly as I'd assumed a retired history and philosophy lecturer would look. He had a big head of unruly white hair, an intelligent yet slightly mischievous face, and the ruddy complexion of a man who'd enjoyed life's pleasures over the years. He was wearing a check shirt, partly covered by a burgundy waistcoat, trousers that had seen better days, and a pair of worn leather slippers that had probably been expensive once. According to his bio, he was sixty-nine, which looked about right.

I smiled and put out a hand. 'Dr Kettleborough. Thanks for agreeing to see me at such short notice.'

We shook, and he had a firm grip.

'DS Mason, please come inside.'

I followed him as he led me down a pleasantly warm hallway with an oriental carpet and paintings lining the walls, past a living room lined with books where an attractive woman about twenty years younger than him sat reading an old hardback without looking up, and into a cosy study at the back of the house, where a fire was burning in the hearth, even though it wasn't a particularly cold evening. Bookshelves lined two of the walls and the PC on the desk facing the window was open at a Word document. Next to the PC was a miniature bust of Karl Marx.

'I've been working this evening,' said Kettleborough, motioning for me to take one of the armchairs next to the fire. 'I'm writing a book. I think I'd go mad if I didn't have something to occupy my mind. Do you read, DS Mason?'

'When I can,' I told him, turning my chair away from the heat of the fire and waiting for him to take the one opposite me.

He offered me a drink but I declined. I wanted to get down to business.

'So, what can I do for you?' he asked, carefully lowering himself into the chair in a way that made me fear growing old.

'It's about one of your former students, Henry Forbes. I believe you taught him in the 1980s.'

'I thought it might be about that. I read about his passing. A horrible thing. Horrible.' He gave a little shudder as if violent death was something unheard of in his world, which I suppose it was. 'I don't know how much I can tell you,' he continued. 'I haven't seen Henry for a long, long time now, not since he left the university in 1989.'

'That's fine. I'm just trying to build up a background on him.'

'Do you suspect him of murdering Katherine Sinn? I read about her body being found in the papers, and the timing of his death seems very coincidental.'

'He is definitely a person of interest,' I said, not wanting to give too much away.

Kettleborough shook his head sadly. 'It's a pity. He was a nice enough young man. Popular with other students, a good public speaker, and a solid philosopher. But not the kind of person I would expect to commit murder, although I'm sure you'll tell me that it's always the ones you don't expect who commit murder.'

'No,' I said. 'Most of the time it's the ones you expect. Why don't you think he was the type to commit murder?'

He pondered this for so long that I thought he'd forgotten the question. But he hadn't.

'I suppose he simply didn't look like he had it in him,' he explained. 'He always struck me as a weak character. One who would never want to get his hands too dirty.'

'How long did you know him for?'

'Oh, the whole time he was at Goldsmiths. I lectured him from the very first year of his BA. And I was his mentor for his PhD.'

'Would you say you had a close relationship with him?'

For the first time Kettleborough appeared to hesitate, as if I might have hit a nerve. 'I liked him,' he said. 'He had potential, but he wasn't the kind of man who inspired people. He didn't give much of himself away and I came to the conclusion that he was actually quite shallow.'

'I know this might sound a strange question, but did Henry ever express an interest in Satanism or witchcraft?'

Kettleborough raised his eyebrows. 'Yes, that is a strange question. No, he didn't. Why do you ask?'

'He had a tattoo of an occult sign underneath his arm, here.' I pointed to the spot on my body where I'd seen Henry's pentacle. 'It looked like this.' I produced the A4 image of the sign from my pocket, unfolded it, and handed it to him.

He put on a pair of reading glasses and examined the sheet of paper before handing it back to me. 'I've never seen anything like that before. Was it a new tattoo?'

I remembered the faded ink from Henry's badly burned body. 'I don't think so. I think he'd had it a good few years.'

'He didn't have it when I knew him.'

'Really? Are you sure?'

'This is just background information you're looking for, isn't it? So I can talk to you in confidence, knowing what I say won't end up in the public domain?'

'Yes,' I said, more interested now. 'This conversation is entirely off the record.'

'I saw Henry naked on a number of occasions and he didn't have the tattoo then.'

That revelation caught me out, but I didn't show it.

'You were lovers?'

Kettleborough nodded slowly. 'Yes, I suppose we were, although it was more of a physical affair. I liked Henry. I'm not sure whether he felt the same way about me, or whether he thought it might help him do better in his PhD, but we did sleep together on a handful of occasions and obviously, under the circumstances, this is something I wouldn't want to become public.'

'I've got to say, you guys certainly live the life.'

He shrugged, and the twinkle reappeared in his eye. 'Why do a job you don't enjoy? You enjoy yours, don't you?'

'Enjoy's probably the wrong word. I think of it more as a vocation.'

He started to say something about the meaning of justice, and I got the feeling he was keen for a philosophical discussion. I wasn't.

'Henry left before he completed his PhD, didn't he?' I asked, cutting him off.

'Yes. He transferred to Brighton Polytechnic, as it was then, to complete it. I have to admit, I was disappointed. Not for personal reasons. Our physical relationship, if you can call it that, had already finished by then. I simply felt he was making the wrong move.'

'Why did he leave?'

'Thomas Mann said: it is love, not reason, that is stronger than death. Are you familiar with that quote, DS Mason?'

'Believe it or not, no.'

Kettleborough sighed. 'Well, that's what happened to Henry. He fell in love and, to my mind, he lost all reason. At the time, while he worked on his PhD, he was lecturing at Goldsmiths, and the woman he fell in love with was one of his students. They tried to keep their relationship secret but of course it became public knowledge. Henry changed. At one time I would have described him as a relatively harmless narcissist, unable to give himself to others. But he went from that to a lovesick fool in very little time. He became obsessed with this student. They once had a loud argument in the faculty building that ended with Henry on his knees begging for forgiveness. After that I had to intervene. I told him that either he ended the relationship or he kept it discreet, otherwise he'd be removed from his position in the college. He apologized and said that he would end it. I don't know if he did or not, or whether she did, but there were no more public arguments and it wasn't long afterwards that Henry requested a transfer to another establishment. I tried to persuade him to stay. He was a good lecturer, and I enjoyed mentoring him. I even suggested we could get the girl to transfer but he told me his decision was nothing to do with her, even though it was obvious it was. Anyway, I wanted him to go to Sheffield where I had a colleague who could mentor him, but he insisted on Brighton, which I thought was something of a backward step. When he came to see me the day he left to say goodbye, he'd lost weight and he looked pale and drawn. I asked him if he was all right. He said he was, we shook hands, and he left. I never saw him again.'

'Can you remember the name of the student he fell in love with?' I asked him.

'Oh yes,' he said. 'I remember it, and I remember her, although I never taught her. Her name was Lola, and she was the kind of young woman your parents warned you about. Very pretty, very demure, but also, I suspect, very manipulative.' He frowned. 'Now what was her last name? Lola . . . It was so long ago now.'

'Was it Lola Sheridan?'

He thought about it a moment, then nodded. 'Yes, I think it was. Has she come up in your investigation?'

I kept my face blank. I had to be careful here. 'Not directly, no. Should she?'

He shook his head. 'Oh no, of course not. I haven't seen her either, not since she left Goldsmiths, and that was many years ago.'

I didn't need to ask any more questions. I had what I needed: a link between Henry Forbes and Kitty Sinn's cousin, Lola Sheridan. A woman who may or may not have had a motive for killing Kitty.

It wasn't much, but I was pleased. It was another piece in the puzzle.

When I was back on the street, I checked my phone. I like to keep it on silent during interviews so it doesn't interrupt my train of thought, and during the short time I'd been in with Dr Kettleborough I'd received a voicemail from Olaf. But there was still no word from Tina. It had now been seven hours since we'd spoken, and I'd left four messages. I'd also called Charlotte Curtis's home and mobile numbers but again with no response. If I hadn't heard back from either of them by ten p.m. I was going to involve the French police.

As I walked back to the car, I called Olaf.

'Ray, where are you?' he demanded. 'You're like the fucking incredible disappearing man. We've got the name of the shooter with the sleeve tattoo. Anton Walters. One of the super-recognizers ID'd him. We've got an address for him too and we're picking him up tonight, so get back here. We need you on this.'

'When you say tonight, we're talking about tomorrow early morning, right?'

'No. We're talking tonight. In a couple of hours. The commander wants an arrest as soon as possible so we can have charges in place by the time the breakfast news starts.'

And that was the thing about collars these days. Everything had to be carefully choreographed for the media, even if it meant taking bigger risks. As every police officer the world over knows, the best time to raid a criminal's home is between four and six in the morning when he's likely to be at home, fast asleep, and not in the mood for resistance.

But, shit, what did I know? I got in the car and told Olaf I was on my way back to the station.

It was time to meet the man who'd tried to kill me forty-eight hours earlier.

Thirty-three

Ramon never knew what to say with women. Apart from a few fumbles with girls from the ends when he'd been growing up, and a couple of visits to whores since his release, he'd had virtually no experience of being in close contact with them. It didn't help that he was big and lumbering, with a rubbery-looking face and a lazy eye. Women scared him. They were like some alien species he couldn't understand, but who still gave him a tingling feeling whenever he spotted a pretty one.

They'd been driving for more than an hour now, Ramon and the girl with the brown eyes, and during that time they hadn't spoken. When he'd turned up at the brothel, he'd been surprised that she was the one Jonas had wanted him to collect, and he couldn't work out whether he was pleased about it or not. The girl had given him the same smile she'd given him the previous night when he'd helped her out of the dinghy, but the dirty-looking pimp who'd answered the door to him was watching, so Ramon had just nodded back and said nothing as he'd helped her into the back of the car.

All the way through the journey he'd wanted to talk. To ask the girl her name. To ask her if she was OK, because he could see that she looked nervous in the back, now that she'd been separated from her friends. Her plight reminded Ramon of his first day in prison, when the cell door had shut behind him for the first time and he'd realized he was truly alone in the world. That night he'd cried silently into his pillow. He wondered if the girl had cried too.

But Jonas had given him orders not to speak to her, so Ramon had turned the radio up and kept his eyes on the traffic-choked streets until the city finally gave way to suburbs, where the houses were big and well kept, where the people with real money lived.

Ramon knew he wasn't the brightest of sparks but one thing he did have going for him was his ability to survive so, as he sat there in silence, he figured out a plan. He'd join Jonas's crew, save up every penny he could until he had twenty grand, then he'd get himself a fake passport and split for good, and fuck them all. In the meantime, all he had to do was keep his head down and stay alive.

It was only when he glanced in the rear-view mirror that he saw that the girl had shifted over to the middle seat and that there were tears running down her face as she stared out of the window and into an unfamiliar night. She looked so young then, young and vulnerable, and Ramon felt something he'd been trying to avoid all day. Emotion. He could feel it overwhelming him. He suddenly wanted to protect this girl, just like he should have protected Keesha all those years ago, and he had to take a couple of deep breaths, like they'd taught him to do in the anger management classes in jail, and force the emotion back down.

But it didn't work. He kept looking at her in the mirror.

The girl saw him watching, and gave him a look that made him wince. A tear ran down each of her cheeks and he saw that those beautiful big brown eyes were red round the edges.

'Where are you taking me?' she asked in heavily accented English.

Ramon didn't have a clue. When he and Junior had been out drinking one night, Junior had slurred something about the girls the outfit smuggled in sometimes being sold off to other people, then disappearing altogether. 'Never to be seen again' were Junior's words.

'I'm not sure,' he said, turning down the radio. 'I'm just the driver.' He tried to think of something to add and finally came up with: 'I bet it'll be somewhere nice though. Nicer than that place you were in.'

'It was horrible there,' said the girl. 'They beat us and made us take our clothes off. Then they locked us in dirty rooms and didn't give us food or drink.'

'You're all right now,' said Ramon, even though he doubted she was.

'I hope so,' said the girl, her voice small in the car. 'I'm scared.'

Ramon felt another punch of emotion. 'Don't worry. You're going to be OK.'

'You seem like a good man.'

He wasn't. Had never been. And that was why no one had ever said that to him before now.

'Thanks,' he said, staring back at the road and telling himself that this girl wasn't his problem. He just had to get her to the address on the slip of paper Jonas had given him, and that was it.

The car fell silent again, but it wasn't a silence that felt right. Ramon wanted to talk. He couldn't help it. He was curious about the girl. He felt for her.

But he held back.

She didn't. 'I'm hungry.'

They were driving down a nice-looking high street and he could see a McDonald's with a drive-thru coming up on his left. Ramon knew he shouldn't stop. He'd already disobeyed orders by talking to her. Anything else was just too risky. For all he knew one of Jonas's crew was following him, checking that he was doing what he was told.

'There's a McDonald's,' the girl said excitedly. 'Please, can we stop?'

Ramon looked at her in the mirror, caught the look in her big brown eyes, and knew he was going to do what she wanted. It was that simple.

'Do you promise you won't tell anyone? If you do, I get in a lot of trouble.'

'I won't,' she said firmly. 'I promise.'

Ramon was hungry himself. He hadn't eaten a thing since the Pot Noodle at lunchtime, and he was a big guy. He turned in, stopped at the drive-thru window and ordered two Big Macs, large fries and Coke for himself, and a Big Mac, fries and Coke for her. There was a car park round the side of the restaurant and he stopped there while they both ate.

'Thank you,' she said.

'It's OK,' he said back.

'My name is Nicole.'

Ramon swallowed. It was a beautiful name.

'What's yours?' she asked.

A warning bell somewhere in his brain told him to end this conversation right now, but warning bells had been sounding all Ramon's life and he'd always done a good job of ignoring them.

'I'm Ramon,' he said, drinking from his Coke.

'That's a nice name.'

He turned round in his seat, looked at her. 'Thanks. Where are you from?'

'Serbia.'

'Where's that?' asked Ramon, whose geography wasn't too good.

'In eastern Europe, near Greece.'

'Sounds nice. Is it warm?'

'In summer.'

They fell silent, and Ramon finished his Coke. It was time to go.

'The people who brought me here said I was going to have a job as a waitress in London,' said Nicole, her face growing sad

247

again. 'I wanted to send money back to my mama at home, to help her pay for my little sister's school.'

'How old's your sister?' asked Ramon.

'Only eight. Her name's Tatia.' Nicole smiled. 'She's beautiful. I have a picture of her on my phone but they took the phone away from me.'

'How old are you, Nicole?'

'Sixteen.'

Ramon had been in prison at sixteen. Alone in the world. Just like Nicole was.

'Am I going to have a proper job?' asked Nicole. 'Because last night the girls said we were going to have to . . . to do things for money. Bad things.'

'I don't know what you're going to be doing, but it won't be what those girls are saying.' But even as he spoke the words Ramon could hear the lie in his voice. And he knew that Nicole could hear it too.

'I've never done anything like that before. Not with anyone.' She stared at him, a desperation in her expression that was ripping his heart apart. 'I just want to go home. Could you help me?'

'Come on,' he said, crumpling up the McDonald's bag and chucking it out of the window. 'We've got to go.'

They drove for another half an hour in silence and he could hear her crying softly in the back.

They were now in the kind of open countryside Ramon had never known actually existed before the last few weeks. The satnav was telling him to turn right on to a wooded road up ahead. It also told him that he was only 1.4 kilometres from his final destination. He wondered who the hell lived out here, in the middle of a wood with no one around.

Once more, Junior's words came back to him like an irritating voice in his head: 'Sometimes they get sold off to other people, and then they just disappear. You know. Never to be seen again.'

The road behind him was clear as he made the turn on to a worn-out track that looked like it was about to get swallowed by the wall of high trees on either side.

Nicole made a small moaning sound. 'Please. Why are you taking me here? You're not going to kill me, are you?'

'Course I'm not,' he said, shocked that she'd think that. He turned round in his seat. 'I'm not going to do anything to hurt you. I'm not that kind of man.'

But she'd buried her face in her hands and was sobbing.

Ramon made a decision. He pulled over to the side of the track, knowing he had to be quick.

'Look, I know you're scared, but you should be all right. If you've got any problems, you can call me. Have you got a pen?'

She nodded shakily and reached into her little suitcase of possessions, pulling out a pen and notepad.

He took it off her, wrote down the number of the phone Dan the Pig had given to him, since he knew that one off by heart and it couldn't be traced back to him by Jonas or anyone else, then ripped out the page and handed it back to her. 'Keep this safe, OK? And make sure no one finds it.'

'Thank you,' she said. She stared at the number for a few seconds and put it in the pocket of her jacket. Then, with a small smile, she reached forward and touched Ramon's face. 'Thank you so much. You are a good man.'

Ramon wanted to weep. No one had touched him like that before. No, that wasn't true. Keesha had. Sweet little Keesha. She used to touch his face and look up at him like that. But, Jesus, that was a long time ago now.

And now he was delivering this girl, someone who actually seemed to appreciate him, to an unknown place in the middle of some woods where whatever was going to happen to her was going to be bad.

Almost without realizing what he was doing, he reached into his back pocket and pulled out the miniature tracking device Dan the Pig had given him. It was a piece of black plastic smaller than a postage stamp and not much thicker. He placed it in the palm of his hand and showed it to Nicole.

'Take this,' he told her. 'It's a tracker. Keep it somewhere on you where no one can find it, and if you get scared, you turn on this little switch here and that means I can find you, wherever you are.' It didn't. It meant that Dan the Pig would know where she was. But at least it was something.

'Where am I supposed to put it?' she asked.

'I don't know. Anywhere. In your mouth if you have to. Just keep it safe.'

She stared at it for a few seconds, looking confused. 'I still don't—'

'Just do it, Nicole. We're wasting time here.'

Carefully she picked up the tracker and, as he watched, she slipped it into her mouth and pushed it up into her cheek.

With a sigh, Ramon pulled back on to the track and drove through the woods, hurrying now, not wanting to arouse any suspicion. If Jonas ever found out what he'd done, Ramon would die horribly, he knew that, but it was too late to change anything now. He just had to keep calm and hope for the best.

The wood grew darker. It looked totally empty. Ramon had never been in a place like this before. It was like being inside a game of *Call of Duty: Black Ops*, the zombie version, where the zombies suddenly appeared, staggering out of the darkness and wailing for blood. The noise and safety of the city suddenly seemed far away.

And then, just as the satnav told him he'd reached his destination, a big white house appeared behind a wall of high bushes on his right. There was a driveway up ahead and Ramon turned into it, stopping outside the front door. Inside, lights were on but there was no car around.

'Don't speak to me any more,' he hissed to Nicole. 'Not even to say goodbye. OK? Not a word.'

Nicole nodded.

He told her to stay put, then got out of the car and looked around. The air smelled different round here. Fresh, like it had on the beach last night. As he walked over to the front door, his feet crunching on the gravel, it opened a few inches and the face of an older woman with jet-black hair and eyes like stone appeared in the gap. She fixed Ramon with a stare that stopped him dead.

'Where's the girl?'

Her voice was old, but not old, and there was an unpleasantness in it that reminded Ramon of teeth scraping on metal. There was something about her too. Something that just felt evil. He couldn't describe it any other way.

Ramon suddenly felt very afraid, as if this woman could read his mind and unearth all his lies.

'She's in the car,' he said, standing taller than he felt.

'Get her.'

He returned to the car, opened the back door, and helped Nicole out, being careful not even to look at her as he took her by the arm and led her to the door.

The door opened further and Ramon saw that the woman was wearing a long black dress that reached to the floor. When she saw Nicole, the woman smiled and her eyes lit up the way a cat's do when it's found a mouse to torture.

'Come in, come in,' she said, reaching out and taking Nicole by the hand.

Ramon let go of Nicole and ignored the look she gave him over her shoulder as the door opened wider like a pair of jaws, before slamming shut as she disappeared inside.

Walking hurriedly, his mouth dry, Ramon got back in the car and drove away as fast as he could, trying not to think of what fate awaited the girl with the brown eyes.

Thirty-four

It had just turned 10.30 when our convoy of vehicles came to a halt on a side street in one of those areas of Hackney that was still a long way off gentrification. The interconnected mid-rise buildings of the estate where our suspect Anton Walters had lived all his life rose in the gloom ahead, silhouetted by the bright glow of the streetlamps.

According to Olaf's earlier briefing, this was going to be a straight in-and-out job, characterized by, in his words, 'a big chunk of shock and awe'. The first two vans in the convoy were unmarked and contained a total of sixteen heavily armed firearms officers from CO19, the Met's elite firearms unit. They would hit Walters' third-floor flat from the front, arrest him, and secure the scene. The next three cars contained detectives from Ealing MIT. One car would take Walters back to Ealing so he could be interviewed. The rest of us would go into the flat as soon as CO19 were finished and conduct a thorough search for evidence against Walters. Bringing up the rear of the convoy were two riot vans containing officers from Territorial Support, who would provide security while the search went on.

The street was quiet but I could sense a tension in the air. The Ridgeway Estate was one of the most poverty-stricken areas of one of the most poverty-stricken boroughs in London. Youth unemployment ran at close to seventy per cent, and it had been a major flashpoint during the 2011 riots. For a lot of people on the estate, the police were the enemy, and their presence was deeply unwelcome, and occasionally resisted. The distance from where we were now to the bustling wealth of the City of London, where one third of the world's money passes through every day, was barely a mile as the crow flies, but it might as well have been a different planet.

I was in the third MIT car with Jools. I could see she was nervous. It was the way she constantly shifted in her seat in a vain effort to get comfortable, and fiddled with her wedding ring, while all the time staring into the darkness, her mouth tight. We'd discussed the timing of the arrest on the way here. Like me, Jools thought we were making a big mistake going in at this time of night, when there'd still be plenty of residents up and about, most of whom almost certainly wouldn't take kindly to a heavy-handed police raid in their midst.

'What I'd do to be sitting on the sofa with Charlie right now, drinking a glass of Pinot and watching a crap movie,' she said at last.

'Yeah, me too,' I said. 'But maybe not with Charlie.'

'Ha ha. You're a funny guy, Ray.' She smiled, then looked at me with a serious expression. 'You seem very laidback sitting there. Is it an act, or are you really not bothered about going in there?' She nodded towards the tower blocks.

'Fear's a funny thing,' I said. 'You never want too much of it, otherwise you can't function, but it's always worth having a little. That way it keeps you on your toes. So, yeah, I'm nervous, but in a good way.' I smiled at her. 'Tonight'll be fine. In. Out. Just like Olaf said.' Although I wasn't entirely sure I believed it.

I don't think Jools did either because, although she nodded slowly, she didn't look entirely convinced.

'Just watch my back in there, eh?' she added.

'Course I will.'

The radio crackled into life. It was Olaf. 'Tango One to all cars, are we ready?' He sounded excited.

The calls came back that we all were, and as he shouted the words 'Go! Go! Go!', like we were on some TV show, I experienced a sudden sense of foreboding.

This was going to go wrong.

The Ridgeway Estate was built in the 1960s, a series of more than a dozen blocks of flats, each five storeys high, linked together by communal walkways and bridges, like some kind of minimalist Lego fortress. The planners must have thought they were building a village in the heart of the city, complete with green lawns and a kids' playground in the middle, but what they'd created was a criminal's paradise, with numerous places to hide, and escape routes everywhere.

There were only two roads in or out at either end, and we came in from the north, driving steadily and without sirens. As we passed a car park next to a long row of overflowing bins, a group of kids messing about on bikes turned our way, their eyes narrowing as they realized who we were. The convoy kept going as the road took us further into the bowels of the estate, the buildings looming up close to us on either side like rockfaces in a canyon, and then as we reached the block where Walters lived, the vehicles came to a halt next to the communal lawns, blocking the road.

As predicted, there were still a fair few people around. A much larger group of teenagers were over the other side of the lawns, several of them on bikes, and other residents, a mix of old and young, were beginning to appear on the balconies that ran along the front of the flats, to watch what was going on. Despite the fact that this part of the op was all about surprise, word of our arrival was already spreading like wildfire and it would only be a few minutes before everyone on the estate, including Walters, knew we were here.

CO19 poured out of their vans and split into two teams of eight. They all wore combat helmets with visors, and were heavily armed with a mixture of MP5s and assault rifles, making them look far more like special forces commandos than a Met police unit. This was deliberate and was meant to instil fear and respect in onlookers so that they wouldn't intervene in any arrest.

It worked too. As the two teams split up and jogged over to the exterior stairwells at either end of Anton Walters' building, the handful of residents within their vicinity all moved well out of their way.

Behind us, the TSG riot vans had parked side by side, blocking the road leading to the rest of the estate, and their officers, also in riot gear, spilled out of their vans but moving more slowly, on the assumption that they weren't going to be needed for anything other than guard duty.

I got out of the car too and stretched my legs, looking out across the communal lawns where the group of teenagers had already grown by a few people, and was now about a dozen strong. They stared across at me, and one of them on a bike threw me the finger. No one shouted anything. In fact, there was no noise at all. The whole estate was eerily silent. Everyone, it seemed, was just watching and waiting.

The CO19 teams were approaching Walters' door from either end of the third-floor balcony, guns outstretched in front of them. Someone opened their door a few flats down, saw the cops, and immediately shut it again.

As they reached Walters' place, one officer slipped an enforcer rapid-entry battering ram from his shoulder, took a step back, and slammed it against the door. I could hear the crack from where I was standing, it was that loud against the silence. The door shook but didn't give, so he gave it another blow, and this time it flew open with a bang, which was immediately drowned by violent shouts of 'Armed police!' as CO19 poured inside.

Thirty seconds passed. Then a minute. Olaf got out of the car in front of me holding a radio to his ear. He was talking to someone, his voice low, and I couldn't hear what he was saying. Jools got out too and stood beside me.

'What's going on up there?' she asked.

'I don't know, but I can't imagine Walters' flat being that big, so if he's there they should be bringing him out pretty soon.'

That was when I heard the sound of the bottle hitting the TSG van, sending broken glass and liquid across its roof. Instinctively I put an arm round Jools's shoulders and brought her down behind the MIT pool car. The bottle had come from the other side of the TSG vans, further down the road, but it seemed to have emboldened the group on the other edge of the lawns whose numbers had now swelled to more than twenty. One of them strode confidently towards us across the grass, a bottle down by his side, stopping about twenty-five yards away as the first of the TSG officers grabbed a riot shield from the back of one of the vans. He grabbed his crotch, sent a lively insult our way, then sent the bottle arcing towards us.

I ducked as it flew over my head and shattered against the tarmac somewhere behind us.

A dozen TSG officers immediately deployed in a line on the edge of the green, batons drawn and riot shields at the ready, putting themselves between us and the missile thrower who turned and jogged back to his friends to whoops of appreciation.

A good few minutes had now passed since CO19 had gone in and only a handful of cops had come out, and they were milling about on the balcony watching the entertainment below, with no sense of urgency in their movements.

'What's going on, boss?' I called out to Olaf, who was still standing by his car with the radio, looking irate.

Olaf glared at me. 'He's not fucking there, that's what's going on. We've missed the fucker.'

The Bone Field

I felt like telling him that Walters was always less likely to be at home at half ten at night than at five the next morning, but I guessed he wouldn't want to hear that. And anyway, I didn't get time to say anything before I heard a shout of 'Heads!' coming from one of the TSG officers over by the vans and the next second another bottle came sailing through the air and smashed on the ground a few yards from Olaf, who barely flinched but still looked extremely pissed off.

Looking round, I could see that we were now under threat from two sides. The last bottle had been flung from the area beyond the two riot vans, the route we'd come in on, while the group on the other side of the green had now grown to at least thirty strong, and were facing us down menacingly. I'd been in situations like this before. Angry mobs egg each other on, and the adrenalin starts to flow as the excitement of an impending fight takes hold, as anyone who's ever been a soldier knows. Usually a well-marshalled police line can keep them at bay, but if the mood's ugly enough, everything can turn in a second. One person charges, another follows, and suddenly you've got the whole lot of them running at you.

One of the TSG sergeants walked over towards us. 'I think it's best you get up to the flat, sir,' he shouted at Olaf. 'It's looking a bit tasty down here. We've called in reinforcements so we'll keep a lid on it but the sooner you get going, the sooner we can leave.'

Olaf banged the lead MIT car, motioning for the team to get out and follow him. 'Come on, you lot.' He strode across the courtyard towards the steps leading up to Walters' flat, ignoring the loud bang of a stone or brick hitting one of the riot vans. I had to give Olaf his dues. He wasn't overly bothered by the situation, unlike some other members of the team. Taliban Tom had gone a whiter shade of pale and was jogging alongside Olaf, presumably using his bulk as cover against the missiles that were now being chucked at a rate of one every three or four seconds. The TSG units began moving forward in both directions towards where the missiles were coming from to force those throwing them to retreat a little. The group I could see moved back towards the flats, but slowly, as if they weren't too fazed, but then they already outnumbered the TSG, so they didn't need to be.

I turned to Jools, who was still crouched beside our pool car, putting on her plastic gloves. I noticed her hands were shaking. 'Are you ready?'

She nodded. 'Let's get moving.'

As we walked across the tarmac, I stayed on the outside of her, resisting the urge to put another protective arm round her in case she took it the wrong way. The outside stairwell connecting the floors had a roof but no walls on either side so as we mounted the steps we could see down to the estate on both sides. For the first time I saw the second mob throwing missiles. There were a lot more of them. Fifty teenagers and young men at least, spread out across the road we'd come in on, hoodies up and scarves over their faces. They were better supplied with ammo than the others, having access to the overflowing communal rubbish bins we'd seen on our way in, and they were yelling and posturing at the TSG officers who were now hopelessly outnumbered, and effectively surrounded.

'How on earth are we meant to get out of here?' asked Jools, looking down as we reached the third floor.

The Bone Field

I was just about to answer when I saw something in my peripheral vision across the other side of the elevated walkway that linked Walters' building with the one next to it. A barefooted man in a wifebeater vest and tracksuit bottoms had wandered out of one of the flats, barely thirty yards from where I was standing, a cigarette or a joint in his hand. His expression was one of mild confusion as he saw the trouble that was occurring thirty feet below him. The man caught my attention because he was muscular, about five feet ten, and mixed race. With a sleeve tattoo on his left forearm.

Anton Walters might not have been at home, but it seemed he wasn't very far away either.

Thirty-five

For a couple of seconds Anton Walters didn't move. It was obvious to me that he was stoned out of his head and having difficulty processing the situation. But then he turned my way at just the moment I started running along the walkway towards him. I might have been dressed casually and not shouting at him – I figured there wasn't much point in yelling 'Stop, police!' – but there was little doubt I was a cop.

Walters immediately turned and ran away from me along the balcony but I'd already eaten up half the distance between us and now there were only fifteen yards between me and him – and he was barefoot and stoned, and I wasn't.

I was catching him. Twelve yards, ten.

Down below, some of the mob picked up what was happening above them and started yelling and shouting in our direction, but

I couldn't hear what they were saying. I was focusing entirely on taking down Walters, knowing that he was our best lead into the Kalamans. If he escaped now, I knew he'd be dead by morning because there was no way they could afford to keep him alive.

Walters looked over his shoulder and saw me gaining, and as he turned back round again he collided with a very large man who'd also stepped out of his flat to see what was going on. Walters bounced off him, hit the railings, and went down on one knee, before scrambling to his feet. The large man – white, very fat and dressed in a T-shirt several sizes too small for him – turned my way and was suddenly blocking my path.

I didn't slow down. Instead I screamed at him to get out of the way and pulled back a fist as if I was going to throw a punch. Our eyes met for only a split second but that was enough for him to know I was serious and he got out of the way surprisingly quickly as I drew level with him.

We were coming to the end of the corridor, and I knew that if Walters managed to get down the steps to where the mob was there was no way I could continue the chase. Only three yards separated us now. He stepped on something on the ground, something that must have been sharp because he instinctively slowed up, which was the moment I dived on his back, sending us both hurtling forward. I thought this would knock him to the ground but he reacted fast, grabbing the railing for support with both hands and managing to stay upright. He slammed an elbow into my face and used all his force to try to drive me against the wall. But he stumbled en route, giving me an opening. I put my back foot against the wall for support and launched a flurry of punches to his face, all of which connected. Then, as he crouched down to try to get out of the way of the blows, I drove him back hard the other way.

Too hard.

As he hit the railing, the momentum kept us both going and suddenly his whole body had gone over the top and he was hanging in the air thirty feet above the ground, desperately cling-ing to my arms, while down below the mob's shouts and yells were getting louder and more angry.

I looked Walters in the eye, remembering the way he'd looked at me from behind the ski mask two nights earlier when he'd pointed a shotgun at my head. He'd wanted to kill me then. He would have done if he'd had any ammunition left. And now he was at my mercy and he was absolutely terrified.

'Get me up,' he gasped. 'For fuck's sake.'

I'd have loved to let him drop. The bastard deserved it. Or better still, demanded to know the names of the two other men he'd been with that night, because he would have told me any-thing to get out of the position he was in. But neither was possible. I could see at least one person filming me on his mobile from down below. I was in front of witnesses here. Literally hundreds of them. And anyway, it was taking all my strength just to hang on to him, and already his hands were slipping down my forearms.

Steadying myself, I pulled him upwards.

That was when I saw it. At the top of his underarm just beneath the armpit. The same tattoo that Henry Forbes had. The pentacle with the flowing 'M' inside.

'Ray, help!'

The voice belonged to Jools. I turned and saw her further along the balcony, struggling with two guys in their early twenties. She was down on one knee on top of one of them while the other was standing above her pulling her hair and trying to drag her off. There was no sign of help coming from across the other side of the walkway. We were on our own out here.

'I'm coming!' I shouted. 'Police! Leave her alone!'

At the same time I made another huge effort to drag Walters back up.

Sensing he was nearly there, he let go of me with one hand and grabbed at the railing, trying to heave himself up. I don't know what he was thinking – maybe he was still too stoned to know what he was doing – but he then let go of my other hand before he'd got a proper grip on the railing and the next second his hands were slipping rapidly down the rails until they hit the concrete at the bottom. Before I could crouch down to grab him, he lost his grip with one hand, then the other, and suddenly he was falling backwards through the air, arms and legs flailing, his eyes wide in absolute shock.

As I stood there, mouth agape, his head hit the tarmac with a sickening crack that reverberated round the buildings, followed a microsecond later by the rest of him. He lay there utterly still. And utterly dead.

For a long moment the whole world was silent and no one moved, as if everything had been frozen in time.

And then it exploded.

With a great roar, the mob charged towards the steps at either end of the building, their faces alive with hate and bloodlust, and I knew that if I got caught now, I was dead. The two men attacking Jools seemed to get a new lease of life. The one pulling her hair dragged her to her feet and shoved her against the railings, while his friend jumped up and joined in the attack. And still there was no sign of any help.

With a roar of my own, I sprinted towards them, ignoring the pain from the blow Walters had landed. They were trying to push Jools over the edge but she was fighting back hard. As I bore down on them, one of them peeled away from her and put up his fists in a boxing stance, but I could see the doubt in his eyes, and I wasn't stopping for anyone. I charged into him, knocking his fists aside and launching a flying headbutt straight into his face, sending him sprawling. At the same time, Jools punched the second attacker while his head was turned, and he pulled himself away from her, trying to get out of the way as I came at him. I ran straight into him, punching and kicking, using my weight and adrenalin to pummel him to the ground.

There must have been thirty hooded locals charging up the steps trying to cut off our escape back over the walkway to where help was. Incredibly, Olaf and co. seemed to have no idea what was happening, and those TSG officers down below who could see it were too busy using their shields to deflect the missiles now being thrown at them in earnest to raise the alarm.

I grabbed a shaken Jools by the arm and we ran towards the footbridge. But a few of the guys coming up the steps were faster than I was expecting and the lead one – short and squat, with a scarf pulled up over his face and a kitchen knife down by his side – was taking the steps two at a time. Someone else a few yards behind him was holding a baseball bat, and others had bottles. It looked like the first guy was going to get to the top before we were past them. If that happened, we were finished.

Beside me, I heard Jools curse, her voice cracking with fear. Fear was pulsing through me too. It was like being in the middle of a nightmare, knowing that you were being pursued by an army of thugs desperate to kill you. I could hear them coming up on to the balcony behind me too. Even if help arrived now it would be too late.

There was only one way of getting out, and a moment's hesitation from me and it would fail.

At the end of the balcony the railings joined the wall that ran up the side of the stairwell, and a large brick post at the top of the steps marked the point. I knew I had to time my run just right, and it required me to finish with an all-out sprint.

'Keep running!' I hissed at Jools, letting go of her arm and breaking away from her. I heard her cry out as if she thought I was deserting her, but then the cry stopped abruptly as she saw me jump up on to the post with one foot and launch myself at the first guy in what was my best attempt at a flying kung fu kick. The guy was still three or four steps from the top so his head was at the perfect height to connect with the toe of my shoe. He never even had time to bring up the knife as the kick sent him crashing back down the steps and straight into the two guys right behind him. Unfortunately for me, I kept flying until I crashed heavily into the wall opposite me, managing to hit it shoulder first. I bounced back off it and landed painfully on my back on the steps.

Without looking back, I rolled over and jumped to my feet just as Jools came running past. She started to slow but I screamed at her to keep going, and she didn't need telling twice. I could hear the yells of the mob almost in my ear as I ran back up the steps and sprinted across the walkway towards where the rest of the cops were, not daring to look back.

And that was when the first CO19 cops appeared at the end of the walkway, weapons outstretched, levelling their shouts of 'Armed police!' at my pursuers. I ran past one, and was pushed, manhandled and pretty much flung bodily into the opposite stairwell where a puce-faced Olaf stood.

'What the fuck's going on?' he roared. 'What have you done?' I started to answer but he pushed me down the steps, shouting at Jools to follow too. 'Come on, come on, move it! We need to get you out of here before they lynch you. What happened?'

'I saw Walters and chased him,' I panted as we ran down to ground level. 'We had a struggle. He fell. I think he's dead.'

He glared at me. 'You fucking idiot! Did you push him?'

'Course I didn't,' I snapped. 'I'm not that fucking stupid.'

'Yes you fucking are. I support you through thick and thin and you kill the only suspect we've got.'

'I didn't kill him. It was an accident.'

'It was, sir,' put in Jools. 'I saw it. It wasn't Ray's fault.'

Olaf just looked disgusted. 'Save it. I'm not fucking interested.'

Below us on the green, the second mob, now some fifty strong, were throwing everything they could at the dozen or so TSG officers facing them in a long and worryingly thin line, the two sides barely twenty yards apart. When they saw us the mob suddenly surged forward with a cacophony of shouts but, credit to them, the TSG stood their ground, and two of them actually ran at the crowd, wielding their batons overhead, causing it to surge backwards just as quickly and buying us a few moments of time as Olaf ushered us across the tarmac to one of the TSG riot vans with its rear doors open.

'Right, get them out of here!' he yelled at the TSG sergeant we'd seen earlier. 'And, Ray?' he added as I clambered into the back after Jools. 'You're fucking suspended.'

He slammed one door shut. The sergeant poked his head in, told us to keep down and hold tight, and then slammed the other door shut and smacked the side of the van, which accelerated away in a screech of tyres, sending us both rolling along the floor. Missiles slammed against the windows. The van slowed, then sped up again, the sirens blaring. I caught a glimpse of a fire burning somewhere and the next second a fire extinguisher hit a side window, cracking it. I could hear the angry roars of the crowd but the van kept going, veering wildly as it tried to clear a path through the mob.

I looked at Jools, and she managed a weak smile.

'It's going to be all right,' I told her.

But as the shouting faded and the missiles stopped and we drove out of the estate and past a convoy of riot vans coming the other way in a scream of lights and noise, I knew there was no way it was going to be OK.

No way at all.

Thirty-six

It was almost midnight when The Dark Man closed his apartment door behind him, put down his overnight bag, and poured himself a small glass of Johnnie Walker Black Label. He was pleased to be home, even if he wasn't pleased with the way the day, or indeed the week, had gone.

Taking the whisky with him, he walked through the apartment and used his thumbprint to open the state-of-the-art lock to his strong room. This was the one place in his apartment, indeed anywhere, where he could talk freely. The room was like a cell. A chair and simple desk were the only furnishings. The bare walls were soundproofed, reinforced concrete. The floor was tiled marble. There were no electricity sockets. There was nowhere to hide any kind of listening device. It was as secure a space as a private citizen could create.

The Bone Field

The Dark Man sat down at the desk, unlocked the drawer and removed a mobile phone that had been bought with cash for him three years earlier. Before he'd left the previous day he'd attached a single human hair to the phone's case with spittle. If anyone had picked up the phone in the meantime, the hair would have come off. It was an old, low-tech trick of working out whether someone had been tampering with your possessions, and a very effective one. The Dark Man only ever made calls to one number from this phone, and having checked that the hair was still in place, he counted down the seconds until midnight then called it.

The man at the other end of the line had been waiting for a call in a room very similar to this one, and he picked up immediately.

'What happened over there?' he said. 'I heard on the news there had been a shooting incident involving a British national. Was that our woman?'

'It was,' confirmed The Dark Man. 'I shot her twice and she fell down a ravine, so I didn't get to see her body, but our contacts in France tell me she's dead.'

'We could have done without that kind of attention, but I trust that you made the right move.'

'There has been a complication, though,' added The Dark Man, who hated complications as much as the man at the other end did. 'Our target was visited by a private detective just before we arrived. The private detective spent some time with her and was there when the target was shot. I tried to kill her too—'

'Her?'

'Yes. We recovered her mobile phone. Her name's Tina Boyd. She survived the confrontation.'

There was a short silence as the man on the other end took in this information. 'I've heard that name before. She used to be a detective in the Met. Do you think she knows anything?'

The Dark Man had thought about this all the way home. He thought probably not. He wasn't sure that even Charlotte Curtis knew why she was being targeted. He said as much.

'Monitor the situation. If it looks like she's a potential threat, we'll have to neutralize her.' The man on the other end sighed. 'That's not the only complication. The police moved in to arrest one of the team from the Forbes hit a couple of hours ago. According to our sources there was a struggle, and our man fell to his death, so at least he can't talk any more, but I'm concerned. How did the police find him?'

So was The Dark Man. The hit team had been led by Jonas Mavalu, one of his most reliable operatives. 'I'll look into it.'

'Do you think we have a leak?'

The Dark Man thought about this. 'I will talk to our contacts in the police,' he said quietly, 'and if we have, I will sniff out the source and make the person pay very dearly.'

'Now give me some good news,' said the man on the other end. 'Do we have a new girl ready for us?'

The Dark Man smiled and took a tiny sip of the whisky, barely wetting his lips. 'Yes, she's perfect. Young. Completely untraceable. She's being groomed now.'

'Good. It will be nice to relax and enjoy her. It's been a difficult time since they discovered the bodies at the school.'

The Bone Field

'We expected that,' said The Dark Man, who'd wanted the two bodies dug up and reburied somewhere secure years ago, and whose entreaties had always been overruled. 'But we'll deal with our problems.' He thought of all the people they'd killed down the years: the innocent; the guilty; the young; the old. 'We always do.'

Thirty-seven

It was 2.30 a.m. when I walked through my front door after another long and eventful night.

In this country, you can't drop a man from a third-floor balcony in front of getting on for a hundred witnesses, most of them hostile in the extreme, and not end up undergoing some pretty serious questioning. In my case, the people doing the questioning were Hackney CID. I'd been taken to Hackney nick straight from the Ridgeway Estate and, to be fair to the cops there, they were largely sympathetic to my plight. I told them the truth. Anton Walters' fall was an accident. We'd been struggling, he'd toppled over the railings, I'd tried to save him but had been unable to. Put like that, it didn't sound like an open-and-shut case, but I was certain the estate's CCTV cameras would bear out my version of events. Although they didn't say as much, I could tell the detectives interviewing me believed my story. They'd even given me a lift home in an unmarked car, although unfortunately, in the end, it wasn't up to them whether I faced prosecution or not. That was the job of the Independent Police Complaints Authority, the IPCC, to whom the case would now be referred, and I guessed while this whole thing hung over my head there was no way I'd be allowed back on the team.

Like it or not, I was off the case – and if Olaf's words were anything to go by, probably permanently.

Well, officially, at least. Unofficially, I wasn't giving up that easily.

As soon as I'd got to Hackney nick I'd called Dan Watts and told him what had happened. The conversation hadn't gone well. At first he'd blown his top at me for not telling him about the impending arrest, but after I'd explained to him that there was no way the fallout would affect his informant, given that the lead that led to the raid had come from amateur camera footage, he'd calmed down a bit.

'It had to be you though, didn't it, Ray? The one who was having a fight with him. The one who was trying to pull him back up.'

'Look, it wasn't my fault I spotted the guy.'

'So I presume you're off the case.'

I sighed. 'Yeah, I'm off it. I still need to see your informant though.'

'That can't happen now.'

'Anton Walters had the same tattoo that Henry Forbes had, Dan. The sign I saw at the school, and you saw on that snuff film. Something major's going on here and the inquiry team aren't going to find it. They're not even looking. But me, I'm getting somewhere. I've got a lot of good information.'

'That's true, but you're also off the case. I can't be seen cooperating with someone who's suspended.'

'Then don't be seen. Come on, Dan, take a chance. You're not exactly overloaded with help. I can help you.'

He hadn't said yes, but then he hadn't exactly said no either. Instead, he'd told me he needed to talk to his informant and hung up.

I kicked off my shoes and opened a bottle of wine, my inner voice not even bothering to tell me I shouldn't be doing it. I poured myself a large glass, gulped greedily, and switched on the TV, wanting to know how they were reporting the events in the Ridgeway Estate. The story came up immediately on Sky News. They had some camera footage of the mob throwing bottles at a much bigger line of riot police, who then baton-charged them. The reporter said that there'd been a major disturbance, and a man had been killed while fleeing from police, but that it was now under control and there were no reports of further injuries.

I switched off and sat down with the wine and my laptop. I was off the case, suspended, and the subject of an IPCC investigation. I'd been warned by Hackney CID that charges could come later, including the possibility of murder. I knew I should play it safe, give up the case and keep my head down.

The problem was, I'd made a promise to Mr and Mrs Brennan that I'd bring their daughter's killer to justice. They'd believed in me. I'd seen it in their eyes. I wasn't going to let them down, even if it meant leaving the force and becoming a private detective like Tina Boyd.

Tina. In all the drama of the last few hours I'd forgotten about her. I checked my phone and saw that I'd received a message at 11.53 p.m. from an unknown foreign number.

It was her. She apologized for the delay in calling me but said that a lot had happened, and could I phone her on the number she was calling on as soon as I got the message.

I took another gulp from the wine, savouring the taste, and debated whether I should be calling her in the middle of the night, before concluding that I'd never be able to sleep without hearing what she'd found out.

Tina answered on the sixth or seventh ring. Unsurprisingly she sounded groggy as she croaked a tentative hello.

'Tina, it's Ray. I'm sorry to disturb you. I've only just picked up your message. Are you OK to talk?'

'Yeah sure,' she said, yawning, and I could hear her moving about in bed.

'Where are you?'

'In a hotel room in France with a gendarme outside my door for security.'

'Jesus Christ. What happened?'

'I've got bad news, Ray.' And straight away I knew what she was going to say before she said it. 'Charlotte Curtis is dead.'

I took a deep breath, exhaled. 'What happened?'

'We were ambushed at her place by some local gunmen. They took our phones but we managed to escape on foot across country. The problem was, there were four of them at least, Ray. They caught up with us, Charlotte got shot, and I was lucky I didn't. I got her to hospital but they told me she died on the operating table. I feel terrible about it. I let her down.'

'They would have killed her anyway. You did what you could.'

'It wasn't enough.'

'Sometimes it isn't. Are you OK, physically?'

She sighed. 'Just some bumps and bruises. I hear your day's been pretty eventful too.'

'How did you know?'

'I don't have my mobile any more so I called the Ealing MIT trying to get hold of you. They told me you were off the case but I managed to speak to a DC Hutchings.'

'Jools? Is she all right?' I hadn't seen her since we'd got to Hackney nick.

'She's fine. She told me what happened. You seem to have the same capacity for getting into trouble as I have, Ray.'

I gave an empty laugh. 'I can't deny that. I'm sorry for putting you in that situation though. I shouldn't have sent you there.'

'You didn't. I volunteered. And I'm OK. The police aren't going to prosecute me for anything.'

'What could they prosecute you for?'

'I killed one of the gunmen.'

'Jesus,' I said, taking a deep breath. 'You don't mess around, do you?'

'If I did, I'd be dead. It was self-defence.'

'Have they been able to ID him?'

'They haven't even been able to find him. The others must have taken him away. Do you have any idea who's behind this?'

'Some,' I said, not sure how much I wanted to tell her over the phone. 'Did you manage to find out from Charlotte if she knew why she was being hunted?'

I heard her moving about in bed and lighting a cigarette. 'She wasn't entirely sure, but what she did say is on the day that Kitty was going to Thailand with Henry, she saw them in a taxi in Brighton and went over to say hello. She didn't think the woman in the taxi was Kitty. She said it looked like her but it wasn't her. She was firm on that. It was only after they found Kitty's body last week that she began to have doubts.'

I sat up straight in my chair, the adrenalin starting to fizz again. 'So my theory was spot on. Someone went to Thailand in her place. Someone who looked like her.'

'That's right. And Charlotte definitely saw Kitty early the previous morning because the two of them had been out all night and seen in the dawn together.' Tina cleared her throat. 'Charlotte also told me that Kitty had two cousins, a brother and sister, whom she hated. Apparently, Kitty had been sexually assaulted by the brother when she was a teenager, but she'd never told anyone about it.'

This was high-quality information. 'The two cousins are Alastair and Lola Sheridan,' I said. 'And I'm sure they're connected to Kitty's murder. Possibly Dana Brennan's too.' I took a gulp of the wine. 'When are you coming home?'

'I'm booked on the morning flight into Heathrow. Your colleagues in Ealing MIT are meeting me for a debrief.'

I asked her if we could meet afterwards and she hesitated before answering. 'But you're off the case, Ray.'

'Officially. Unofficially I still have an interest. Will you do some work for me on a freelance basis? I'll pay whatever the going rate is.'

'What kind of work?'

'Investigating the murders of Kitty Sinn and Dana Brennan.'

'But the police have already got plenty of resources looking into it.'

'I've got a feeling they're looking in the wrong places. I think we might have more luck.'

Tina yawned. 'OK. I'll call you when your people have finished with me. Right now, I need to get back to my beauty sleep.'

'Sure.' I paused, and could hear her breathing down the phone. 'Listen, I'm glad you're OK.'

'You too,' she said, and ended the call.

I finished the wine, poured myself another glass, leaving only a third in the bottle, and walked over to the window. I felt totally alone right then, up there in my empty apartment. Me against a hostile world that seemed to keep closing in. It was why I'd wanted to see Tina again. I needed an ally. A partner. Someone who was on my side. Once I'd had my wife, Jo, but she was long gone. Then I'd had my friend and colleague Chris Leavey, and now he was gone too. Murdered in front of me barely a year ago.

I drank more of the wine, hoping to kill the pain, and told myself to calm down. At least my theory about the Kitty Sinn murder had been right. Henry Forbes had taken someone else to Thailand, presumably as an elaborate, and risky, move to cover up her murder. The motive was still unclear but I was beginning to think it was at least partly to do with a family grievance, whether it was money, a desire to cover up the alleged sexual assault Charlotte had mentioned to Tina, or something else. But that still didn't explain why Cem Kalaman was involved, and why Dana Brennan had been targeted a year earlier, though it was possible there was an occult element too. I'd seen that pentacle symbol too many times now for it to be a coincidence, and I made a mental note to try to find out what it meant tomorrow.

I put down my wine, knowing I was going to need a clear head for whatever tomorrow brought, and checked my emails on my phone.

There were two of interest. One was from Amber, my friend Chris Leavey's daughter. I still heard from her periodically. She was in her final year at university, and I'd saved her life during the op that killed her father. Although I didn't like to admit it, I avoided seeing Amber and her mum. They reminded me too much of Chris.

The other email was from Dan Watts, and it contained the file the NCA had on Cem Kalaman. It was shockingly thin, listing his directorships, his annual income according to his tax returns (about £800,000 per year), a single police mugshot, and his biography. He had no criminal convictions but had been questioned by the police on six occasions between 1992 and 2008, including once on suspicion of the murder of his own father who'd been shot to death in a restaurant alongside his bodyguard in 1999. On only one of those occasions had he been charged. That was in 2002 for conspiracy to murder after he'd been caught on a hidden microphone appearing to order the killing of a business rival. However, the tape of the conversation had somehow gone missing from the police evidence locker, no one involved in the alleged plot wished to cooperate – including the rival, who'd ended up shot to death eighteen months later – and the charges had quickly been dropped.

In all, Cem Kalaman had spent the sum total of four days of his life in police custody and yet, according to a note at the end of the file, he was suspected of being the chief executive of a billion-pound business empire that had been built on the proceeds of crime, and whose employees were suspected of carrying out a total of at least forty-five murders between 1970 and the present. Cem Kalaman was, it seemed, the British equivalent of the Teflon Don, and it was interesting to note that the police hadn't questioned him about anything for the past eight years. He'd also shown himself to be a talented operator since the business had increased in size by ten times since he'd taken over the reins. Unlike the vast majority of criminals, the guy clearly knew exactly what he was doing.

In the mugshot, dated September 2002, he didn't look particularly impressive. A young man, with black curly hair and very dark eyes, he sat staring blankly at the camera, giving nothing away. It was hard to believe he was who he was supposed to be.

It was only when I was reading the file through for a second time that I saw it. After Medmenham College, where Cem had gained three mid-grade A Levels in Maths, Psychology and Economics, he'd spent a year at Warwick University between 1987 and 1988 before dropping out. I grabbed my phone, scrolled down my inbox and found Jools's email, and skimmed through her notes until I saw what I was looking for. Alastair Sheridan, Kitty's cousin and Lola's brother, had also gone to Warwick

University. He'd been there between the years 1987 and 1990. The same time as Cem Kalaman.

Suddenly I was there. Henry Forbes knew Kitty Sinn's cousin Lola before he knew Kitty. Lola's brother, Alastair, was at the same university as Cem Kalaman. Kalaman had been a pupil at the school where Kitty was buried. It was also highly likely he had ordered Henry's murder. All, then, were linked either directly or indirectly to Kitty.

Were these people her killers?

If so, then one way or another I was going to bring each and every one of them to justice.

Day Four
Friday

Thirty-eight

Sometimes at night I dream terrible dreams. In the worst ones I'm back as a child in my burning home, hiding in the cupboard, listening as my father roams the hallway outside calling my name, knowing that he's possessed by some kind of demon and that if he finds me, he will kill me, just as I know he's killed my mother and brothers. The dreams are always vivid. They're exactly how I remember that black February night when I lost my whole family. I can even smell the acrid, choking smoke. And they always end the same way, just as that night had ended, with me forced from my hiding place, running to the bedroom window, choking on the smoke, opening it and looking down at that immense drop into the darkness, hearing my father come in the room, and jumping . . . jumping into the yawning abyss . . .

I woke with a start. The clock on the bedside table said 7.27

and the sheets were bathed in sweat. I sat up, slowing my breathing, allowing myself to come back to reality. There was a half-full glass of water on the bedside table and I picked it up and drained it before getting out of bed, already putting the dream behind me. I've had a lot of therapy over the years to try to help me come to terms with what happened that night, and thus confine it to where it belongs: in the past. But the scar runs very deep in my psyche, and I've been told by more than one expert that it will probably remain there in one form or another until I die. All I can do is attempt to control its effects, and the best way to do that is to keep busy.

The first thing I did while the coffee brewed was Google 'demonic signs', hoping to get a hit on the sign I'd been seeing so much of these past few days, but no match came up. So I Googled 'occult expert' instead. There were a number of people, mainly in the US, offering various services to do with the occult such as tarot readings, and even exorcisms, but I finally found a website run by a man called Cornell Stamoran who billed himself as the UK's foremost expert on Satanism, and who had written four books on the subject. A quick glance at the photo of the man himself on the homepage didn't inspire much confidence, but beggars can't be choosers so I gave it ten minutes while I ate some cereal, then called him.

It was still before eight so I was expecting to leave a message, but the phone was answered on the second ring by a man who sounded like a combination of Vincent Price and Graham Norton and who spun out his 'hello' for a good three seconds.

'Cornell Stamoran?'

I kid you not. He answered with a 'This is he.'

I told him who I was and about the sign that had cropped up as part of our inquiry. 'It's a pentacle with what looks like some kind of rune inside. I can't find any likeness on the internet, so I'm wondering if you might be able to identify it.'

'I know a great deal about the occult, that is true, but I would need to see this particular symbol to correctly identify it. Can you send over an image?'

'I'd rather come in person with it,' I told him. 'Whereabouts are you based?'

He gave me an address in Southwark. I wrote it down and asked him if he was free that morning. 'I can get to you for nine-thirty if that's any good. We do need to move quickly on this.'

'Er, yes, I think I can fit you in,' he said. 'Will there be any, um, remuneration? I charge sixty pounds per hour for consultations.'

'Call this community service,' I said. 'Your good deed for the day.'

'I don't do good deeds.'

'You do now,' I told him, and hung up.

I'd decided to walk to Cornell Stamoran's address. The day was sunny and cool, with the kind of chill breeze that reminds you you're in England in April, and the route took me down to the river and along the South Bank with its views across to Big Ben and the Houses of Parliament, before old merged into new and the gleaming skyscrapers of the City of London surged towards the sky.

On the way I called Tina and was more relieved than I'd like

to admit when she answered. She told me she was at the airport
and the plane was on time. Once again I told her to be careful,
and once again she told me she knew how to look after herself.

Five minutes after I put the phone down to Tina I got a call
from the Independent Police Complaints Commission. Whenever an individual dies as a result, directly or otherwise, of a
police operation, the IPCC automatically get involved. I'd last
been on the wrong side of dealings with them after shooting the
two men who'd tried to kill me outside my old apartment, and I'd
been expecting their call.

The woman on the other end of the phone wanted me to come
into their offices as soon as possible for an interview but, after a
bit of to-ing and fro-ing, I managed to put her off until nine a.m.
on Monday morning while I organized a Police Federation rep to
come in with me. I knew it wasn't going to be an easy interview,
or a short one. The circumstances of Anton Walters' death were
controversial. I'd yet to see the CCTV footage of what happened,
but I was pretty certain there'd be plenty of people out there eager
to pin the blame for his death on me.

Cornell Stamoran lived in the top-floor flat of a grimy post-war
terraced house not far from the New Kent Road that backed on to
the railway tracks running into Waterloo station. At one end of
the road was a kebab shop, the litter from the previous night still
scattered outside, while at the other was a boarded-up house with
an old fridge outside it on the pavement. To the south and north
were sleek blocks of luxury flats, yet this place seemed to have
been entirely forgotten by the gentrification going on all around,

and it made me think that maybe I should have been paying Stamoran after all, because if he lived here he clearly needed the money.

It was almost exactly 9.30 when I buzzed on his doorbell and was let into a bare hallway that smelled of wet anoraks. I negotiated two steep staircases before being greeted at the top by a very large, very out-of-shape man in a black tracksuit and slippers with an unruly beard, and much sparser yet still unruly hair that had been bunched up into a greasy ponytail that probably had its own ecosystem. I put him at about forty years old, but the kind who probably wasn't going to make it much past fifty.

'Mr Stamoran, DS Mason,' I said, flashing my warrant card and putting out a hand.

His shake was firm but slightly moist.

'Please,' he said, in that voice of his, squinting at me through a pair of cheap black glasses, 'come in.'

I followed him into a cramped living area with bookshelves lining the walls and a minute TV in one corner. Opposite the TV was a large reclining chair that looked new on which lay a very large sleeping cat, and behind the chair, next to the tiny kitchen area, was a badly chipped wooden dining table with a chair at either end. I could smell fried food and sweat.

I negotiated my way round the back of the reclining chair and sat down at the table opposite Stamoran. He offered me a drink but I said no. I took out a blown-up copy of the photo of the symbol I'd taken in the folly and placed it on the table.

'So, you're an expert on matters of the occult,' I said, quoting his website.

'That is correct,' he concurred, a suitably sombre expression on his face. 'I'm a senior member of the British Occult and Psychic Society, and the UK ambassador for the California-based Black Chapel Legion, the most important occult group in the United States.'

I didn't have a clue who any of these organizations were, and for all I knew he could have founded them himself and been the only member. But it didn't really matter. 'So can you tell me what this sign means?'

Stamoran put on a pair of reading glasses and brought the paper close to his face. 'I have seen this before,' he said as he stared at it. 'I think I know what it is, but I need to check something.' He shuffled over to one of the bookcases and scanned the shelves before finding the book he was looking for.

As he did that, I looked round. Stamoran's place was on the dishevelled side of ordinary and only a low shelf in the corner with a pack of tarot cards and two candles on it, and a tapestry of a sun just above, showed any signs of his profession, if you could call it that.

He sat back down, leafing through the book – an old hardback with a plain black cover the size of an encyclopedia – until he found what he was looking for. He held the book open and pushed it across to me. There on the page was the symbol I'd seen in the folly and on the underarms of both Anton Walters and Henry Forbes.

I nodded. 'What is it?'

'It's a rarely used symbol associated with an old Ammonite god called Moloch who was demonized in Hebrew lore. He was considered the causer of plagues and was said to be close to Satan.' He looked at my photo again. 'Where did you find this?'

I had to be careful how much I told Stamoran. Not only should I not be here, I didn't want him putting two and two together and realizing who this case was about. But at the same time I had to give him something.

'It was close to a murder scene,' I replied. 'We believe it may have been daubed there by the killers.'

Stamoran stroked his beard. 'Interesting. And was there any evidence, other than this, that it was a ritual murder?'

'Our inquiry's a cold case review which means the murder was an unsolved crime from some years ago. The remains of the victim have only recently been discovered so we don't know.'

'It's not the Kitty Sinn case, is it?' he asked, his eyes lighting up.

I shook my head. 'No. This murder happened some time before that.' I thought back to Dana Brennan, snatched from a country road on a summer's afternoon. 'The female victim was abducted and we think murdered by more than one person. Because of the proximity of the sign to where the body was found, we think it might have had some significance for her killers.'

Stamoran cleared his throat and sat back in his chair. 'You know, there are hundreds and hundreds of different demons in religious folklore. The vast majority are considered harmless.' He paused, stroking his beard again. 'But Moloch is different. He's one of the most powerful demons of all, a prince of Satan who has always been associated with human sacrifice. In ancient times he was worshipped by the Ammonites who built great bronze statues in his honour, and sacrificed women and children to him because they thought that would protect them from disaster and give them the power to destroy their enemies.'

I raised my eyebrows. 'Do you know of any groups in the present day who worship him?'

'Do you know, detective, it's a common fallacy among the general populace that Satanism is intrinsically evil, and that the worship of Satan involves all kinds of black rites. I blame it on *The Exorcist* and all the films that have followed since.' He sounded genuinely angry as he spoke. 'I'm a Satanist, yet I don't sacrifice anything to Satan, human or otherwise.'

'That's good to know,' I told him.

'Satanism is a celebration,' he continued firmly, 'of pagan, pre-Christian beliefs and individualism, and the people who practise it these days, myself included, don't wish harm to anyone. What you have here is totally different. This sounds like ritualistic murder by people who use the worship of Moloch as a cover for their own ends. And I imagine they would be very, very secretive about what they're doing, so neither myself, or any of my colleagues, would likely know who they were. And I don't think you'll find them by looking for worshippers of Moloch either.'

I thought back to the dates Dana and Kitty went missing – a year apart, but almost to the day. 'Tell me something. Is there any significance to the period of mid- to late July in Satanism?'

'Is this when your victim went missing?'

'Yes.'

He thought about it for a moment before answering.

'According to some people – and I think most of them are evangelical Christians trying to blacken the religion of Satanism – the period between July twentieth and July twenty-seventh does supposedly have a significance for Satanists. But I want to emphasize that it has nothing to do with mainstream Satanism.'

'So, what's the significance?' I asked.

He paused before answering, and when he spoke I noted his voice had lost its Vincent Price-like tone. 'It's supposedly a time for the kidnapping, holding and ceremonial preparation of a person for sacrifice. The sacrifice itself is supposed to take place on the twenty-seventh of the month in what is called the grand climax.'

Dana Brennan had gone missing on 24 July 1989, and on the phone the previous night Tina had told me that Charlotte had seen Kitty early on the Friday morning, but it wasn't her in the taxi on the Saturday afternoon when she was supposed to be flying to Thailand with Henry. I took out my notebook and checked the dates relating to Kitty's disappearance. She'd flown off to Thailand on 28 July 1990.

Which meant she'd almost certainly died on the 27th.

Thirty-nine

Slowly but surely I was building a picture of what had happened all those years ago. There were still plenty of pieces to add in, as well as the much bigger issue of gathering evidence to back up my theory, but at least I was making progress.

What concerned me was the snuff DVD that Dan Watts had found at the home of the Albanian people smuggler and his girlfriend, the one with the young woman being murdered by masked men next to a wall with the Moloch symbol painted on it. That had been years after the murders of Dana Brennan and Kitty Sinn, and it suggested that the killings themselves hadn't stopped. Yet so far no more bodies had been recovered from Medmenham College.

But they had to be somewhere.

I left Stamoran with stern words not to say anything about

what I'd been saying to anybody, and strolled back to Fulham and a café I knew on Parsons Lane that served the best all-day breakfast in the whole of west London. By the time I got there I'd worked up a good appetite. I was halfway through demolishing a full English when I got a call from a landline I didn't recognize.

It was Dan Watts. 'Is your phone secure?'

'It's the same one as last night. I'm hoping so.'

'I'm going to text you an address. If you want a meet with the contact, be there at one o'clock, and do not be late.'

Two minutes later he sent me a residential address in Hackney. I looked at my watch. It was 11.40. I ordered another coffee and thought about what I had. It wasn't a lot. I had absolutely nothing on Cem Kalaman that would even vaguely stand up in a police interview, let alone a court of law. I had theories, a possible occult motive that was outlandish and even more vague, and a lot of dead bodies. I'd messed up majorly the previous night by not taking Anton Walters alive, even though there was no guarantee he would have talked. Thankfully, the fact that Walters had been ID'd using CCTV footage meant that Dan Watts' informant wouldn't be in the frame, but even so, he was going to be jumpy. Still, it was a good time to be gathering information, because people in the Kalaman outfit were going to be talking about what had happened. The informant was going to need to be persuaded to plant listening devices or to wear a mike.

Dan was already supplying the stick. Maybe it was time to supply the carrot.

While I finished my coffee, a young couple came in and sat down a couple of tables away. They were probably mid-twenties, both student types, and dressed on the bohemian side. They held hands as they talked, and looked into each other's eyes, only tearing themselves away for a couple of seconds to order from the waitress. I watched them for a few minutes as they sat oblivious to the world around them, and remembered when I'd felt that way about someone. For just that one spell of probably no more than a year, I'd been truly happy with Jo and her girls. Sometimes, these days, I'd drive out into the countryside and just walk, piecing together all the good memories from that time. The first meal we cooked together; the week-long honeymoon in Grenada; the trip to Legoland with the girls. The good times.

But then, of course, I'd remember how it had all ended. How Jo had seen on the local news a report on the violent assault on Kevin Wallcott in his bedroom; how he'd been beaten and pistol-whipped. Unsurprisingly, the police had theorized that it was a vigilante enraged by what Wallcott had done, but they had no suspects. Nor did they ever come up with any as the weeks passed.

It didn't take Jo long to piece together what had happened. We'd talked in depth many times and she knew I had a dark side to my nature. She knew too that I had a burning sense of injustice, as well as the inside knowledge, that made it possible for me to carry out such an attack. Crucially, she'd also remembered the change in me after I'd seen the original report on the news of Wallcott's hit-and-run.

For about a month there was a tense atmosphere between us in the house. I knew what Jo was thinking but I didn't want to bring the subject up because I didn't want to have to lie to her.

Eventually, though, she confronted me one night while the girls were at their dad's.

'Was it you who attacked Kevin Wallcott?' she said, looking right at me, daring me to meet her eye. 'And tell me the truth, Ray. Please. I deserve that.'

I could have lied. And I would have probably got away with it too. I'm a good liar, and I'd been half expecting the question for weeks. But Jo was right. She deserved the truth.

'Yeah,' I said. 'It was me.'

'Why?'

'Because I couldn't face him getting away with it.'

'I can't have you round my children.'

Her words stung me like an angry slap. 'Don't say that. I'd never touch them. You know that.'

'But it's what's inside you, Ray.' She pointed to my chest. 'The darkness. I can't be with a man like that.'

I told her that I'd change. That I loved her more than anyone I'd ever known. That I loved the children like my own, and that I'd protect all three of them as long as I lived. And I meant it. I meant every word.

But it wasn't enough.

'I want you to move out, Ray. By the time the girls come back. Please. Respect my wishes.' As she spoke, tears ran down her face.

None ran down mine. I couldn't let her see my weakness. My utter vulnerability. Instead, I told her I'd go straight away.

And I did. I packed my stuff and left an hour later, collecting what I couldn't carry with me a few days afterwards when Jo and the girls were out. I couldn't face saying goodbye to Chloe and Louise. It would have broken my heart, even more than it had been broken already. I cut my ties with all three of them. Just like that.

Two months later, Jo called me. I didn't pick up and she left a message asking how I was and saying she missed me.

I didn't call back.

Funnily enough, though, sitting in the café watching this young couple, I didn't feel jealous of what they had. It made me feel good that amid all the brutality, the darkness, the pain and the loss there was still some semblance of normality in the world.

I paid the bill, smiled at them as I passed, and walked away.

Forty

The address I'd been given by Dan Watts was a vacant office building backing on to Regent's Canal not far from Hackney's Victoria Park, flanked on both sides by brand-new apartment blocks. Once this area had been dirt poor but the process of gentrification had pushed the poverty further to the north and west, into dangerous pockets like the Ridgeway Estate where I'd been last night, barely a mile away.

The main door to the building was locked and the entrance smelled of stale urine. Beyond the tinted glass, the interior looked empty but reasonably well kept, and there were no piles of mail on the floor.

My mobile rang.

'I've just seen you arrive,' said Dan Watts. 'I'm up on the roof. Take the back stairs to the top. The code to get in is 4443.'

It was four flights of stairs to the top and I was breathing more heavily than I'd have liked when I opened the last door and walked out on to the roof. Dan was standing there alone, looking down towards the street. To the south-west, the grand skyscrapers of the City of London rose majestically, while to the east, the low-rise buildings of the East End stretched like a carpet towards that second bastion of extreme wealth Canary Wharf, which stood like a huge fortress in the distance.

'Nice place you've got here,' I said, walking over.

'I need to make sure we don't get seen or heard.'

We shook hands and he gave me an exasperated look.

'So what the hell happened last night, Ray?'

'I told you, it was an accident. I was never going to drop him deliberately in front of two hundred witnesses. He was a lot more use to us alive than he was dead. It was just bad luck.'

He raised an eyebrow. 'Is that right? You know, Ray, you make your own luck sometimes, and you seem to be manufacturing some real havoc. Remind me never to have you round for dinner.'

'Well, I've known you four years and you've never invited me yet, so I think you do a pretty good job of reminding yourself. Anyway, thanks for letting me meet your informant. I wasn't sure you would.'

'I found something that makes me think you might be on the right track. Look at this.' He produced an A4-sized envelope from under his jacket and took out a high-quality black and white photo. 'This is a surveillance shot taken four months ago. The man on the right you know. The man on the left is his boss in the Kalaman outfit, Jonas Mavalu.'

I examined the picture. It was a close-up shot showing the top halves of Anton Walters and a powerfully built black man in his forties as they talked together. Walters was smiling but looking slightly nervous, as if he was afraid of the man next to him, while Jonas Mavalu himself was laughing as he held up a cigarette towards his mouth. Mavalu was wearing a basketball vest that did a good job of showing off his physique. Because of the angle of his arm as he lifted the cigarette, the same pentacle tattoo that I'd seen on Henry Forbes and Walters was just visible on his right underarm.

'How did you come across this?' I asked.

'I was going back over surveillance shots seeing if I could see any of those tattoos you were talking about. I missed it the first time round.' He paused. 'You know, Ray, Jonas Mavalu is a high-ranking Kalaman operative and a very dangerous man. He's suspected of at least five murders, one of which involved a man being dismembered with a chainsaw. We've never been able to get anything on him, and he's very surveillance aware, so even photos like this of him are rare. But if we can get my informant close to him, there's a chance we might be able to get some new information on the Forbes murders.'

I smiled, handing back the photo. 'Thanks, Dan. This is the kind of lead we need. How's the informant handling things after what happened to Walters?'

'He's jumpy. He wants out.'

'I don't blame him. So what have you got on him to keep him working for you?'

'He's a killer out on licence. We know he's been doing some bad things that could get him sent back down for years.'

'So, you're blackmailing him?'

Dan looked at me coldly, and it made me think that he might have been, that as a Christian he was a lot more Old Testament than New. 'Don't give me that shit, Ray. We're giving him an incentive.'

'I want to give him an incentive too. Something that'll keep him onside. You know I've got money, right? I want to pay him.'

'That's a dangerous game. If it ever gets out in court—'

'If *any* of this op gets out in court then you and me are both fucked. But you want these people put down, right? And so do I. Badly.'

'But you're not even on the case any more.'

'I know more about what's going on than anyone. That's why you asked me here. I'm also the only one pursuing the occult angle to the murders.' I told him what I'd found out about the pentacle sign from Cornell Stamoran. 'And Cem Kalaman's got links to one of Kitty's cousins. They were at uni together.'

'Shit, Ray, you're going to have to do a lot better than that. We need some real concrete evidence.'

'And that's why we need to keep your informant onside.'

'Well, here he is,' said Dan, motioning towards the street.

I looked down and saw a big black man in jeans and check shirt approaching the building with a lumbering gait while making far too much of a show of looking around him.

'He's not exactly acting inconspicuous, is he?'

'The Kalamans trust him, and I think he may be in line for a promotion. It's a damn good thing Anton Walters got ID'd with CCTV, otherwise he'd be in a lot of danger.'

I watched him as he disappeared from view and wondered what his prospects of survival were, and whether I should feel guilty about helping to use him this way. I decided I shouldn't. He'd made his bed. Now, like everyone else, he was going to have to fester in it.

We waited five minutes in the sunshine until the roof door opened and the contact walked out, squinting against the brightness. He had a good three inches on me and about a foot on Dan but he didn't know how to make it count. He looked nervous and out of sorts.

He approached slowly, as if expecting some kind of ambush, and stopped a few feet away. He had a lazy eye that couldn't quite focus and the kind of face that looked unfinished, with big, outsize features that didn't sit right.

'Who's this guy?' he said, staring at me with his good eye, his voice slow and deep.

'This is Ray,' said Dan. 'He's a close colleague of mine working on the Forbes murder.'

The informant grunted. 'You got anything to do with last night?' he said to me. 'That was a fuck-up.'

'He fell,' I said.

'That ain't no good for me,' said the informant. He looked at Dan. 'It's going to come back to me. You know that, right?'

'It's not going to get back to you,' I said. 'We got Walters on CCTV on the night of the Forbes murders. It'll be all over the papers tomorrow.'

'That's tomorrow. I got a meet tonight. With Jonas. Junior's picking me up later.'

'Was the arrangement made before or after Walters got killed?' asked Dan.

'Before.'

'Then you're all right. Do you know where the meeting's going to be held?'

He shook his head. 'I don't know shit about it.'

'If you're meeting Jonas, it's good news. They want to promote you, brother.'

The informant gave Dan a look of pure contempt, and I noticed he was balling his outsize hands into fists, and rubbing the thumbs against them. 'You ain't my brother. If you were you wouldn't be making me do this shit.'

Dan didn't seem fazed. 'The sooner we get evidence against the big boys the sooner you're out of there and starting a new life somewhere else. I need you to plant a recorder in Junior's car. He's obviously good at shooting his mouth off.'

'No way. He searches his car every day.'

'These things are tiny and you can't pick them up on bug finders. He won't find it.'

'If he does, I'm dead. Please, man. It's too dangerous.'

'Look, maybe I can make things a bit easier for you,' I said, knowing that this meeting with Jonas Mavalu was an opportunity we couldn't miss. I slipped on a plastic glove and pulled an envelope from my jacket pocket. I went to hand it to him but he made no move to take it. 'There's a grand in cash inside here. Another four if you give us evidence of Kalaman involvement in the Forbes murders.'

At one time, maybe even as recently as a year back, before my good friend and colleague Chris had been murdered, I would have baulked at what I was doing now. Not only was I breaking all the rules, I was also putting Dan's informant's life in potential danger. But that time had passed and, for better or worse, my moral compass had moved. I was off the case and I didn't think there was any real chance of what I was doing coming back to haunt me. Plus, I could see this guy needed some encouragement to continue gathering inside information for us.

'I've done enough,' the informant told Dan, ignoring me as well as the envelope.

'We need more,' said Dan firmly. 'You know how it is. At least wear your tracker tonight so we can see where you're going.'

'I can't. I had to give it to someone.'

Dan looked furious. 'What the fuck are you talking about? It's expensive kit. You can't just give it away. Who the hell did you give it to, for Christ's sakes?'

The informant looked sheepish. 'One of those illegals I was telling you about. The girls we picked up the other night. I had to take her to this house in the middle of nowhere. I was worried about her.'

'Why was that?' I asked, suddenly very interested.

'I didn't like the place I took her to. The woman who answered the door at this house in the woods I took her to, she looked evil, man. Like some kind of witch. And a couple of times when he's been drunk Junior's talked about girls – you know, the whores the outfit brings over – getting sold on to people and going missing. I just wanted to make sure she was OK.'

'You were taking a big risk,' said Dan. 'What if someone finds the tracker and she tells them you gave it to her? Now that would put you in real danger.'

'I'm already in real danger,' said the informant. 'And she won't. I told her not to.'

'Who told you to take her to this house?' I asked him.

'Jonas. He gave me the address on a piece of paper and told me to burn it afterwards.'

'Did you?'

'Yeah, but I remember the address.'

I took out my phone. 'Can you give me it?'

He gave me a house name and a postcode and I wrote it down.

'Have you heard anything else about those missing girls?'

'Nah, just what Junior told me.'

'Listen,' said Dan. 'I'm going to give you another tracking device to replace the old one.' He took another envelope out of his jacket and handed it over. 'It's exactly the same. There are also two more of those tape recorders. The sooner you use them to pick up people talking about stuff they shouldn't, like Junior, the sooner you're out of there. And don't give any of them away either.'

The informant took the envelope, then the other one off me, and stuffed them in the waistband of his jeans, underneath the check shirt. 'Promise me you'll keep an eye on Nicole – that's the name of the girl.' He looked at me when he said that.

'I promise,' I told him.

'You mean that?'

'Yeah, I mean that. And I'm interested in anything you hear about other girls. Anything at all. Just tell Dan, he'll tell me, and I'll follow it up.'

He nodded at me, gave Dan a glare, and turned and left us up on the roof.

'Why are you so interested in missing women?' Dan asked me a few minutes later as we watched the contact lumbering back up the street away from us.

'Because I think Cem Kalaman murdered Dana Brennan and Kitty Sinn, and this whole devil worship thing is just a front for some kind of twisted sexual thing. That DVD you found at the people smuggler's place, I bet it was Kalaman in that. It's possible the people smuggler was blackmailing him. That case needs reopening to see if there are any links between the two of them.'

'Yeah, sorry, I meant to get those case notes for you,' he said. 'I'll do it.'

'The thing is,' I said, looking out over the rooftops, 'if it's a sexual motive, Cem Kalaman and his friends won't have stopped killing women. Sexual predators like him never stop offending. It's why they're such frightening people. But it's also their chief weakness. Because one way or another, it means they always get caught.'

'You know what?' said Dan. 'Part of me really hopes you're right. But as the father of two daughters, I can't help thinking that, if it's true, it means there are a lot of dead women out there.'

Forty-one

I was driving back from my meeting with Dan and his contact when I got a call from Tina Boyd, telling me she was finished at Ealing police station and in the back of a taxi heading home.

'I've just spent two hours answering exactly the same questions as I did last night,' she said, 'asked by people who were just as sceptical that I was telling the truth. That colleague of yours, DI Glenda Gardner. She's a ball breaker, isn't she? And she really doesn't like you much.'

'There aren't many in that team that do,' I said. 'What was she saying about me?'

'She seemed to think you might have had something to do with Charlotte Curtis's killers.'

I sighed. 'Jesus. They're going to be after me for JFK next.'

'I don't think last night helped. They get a suspect for the

Forbes murders, and he dies in a struggle with you. It doesn't look good, Ray.'

This was going to be a real problem for me. Because it didn't look good. 'It was an accident. That's what'll show up on the cameras, and I don't see what motive they think I have.'

'You don't have to tell me,' she said. 'I believe you.'

'Do you still want to work for me?'

'As long as you pay, I'll do what I can. What do you need?'

I'd been thinking about this in the car. 'A photograph of Lola Sheridan circa 1990. I want to see if she could pass as Kitty Sinn. Do you think you can find something like that?'

'I'm a private detective, Ray. It's my job. I'll find something. But how are you going to go forward with this? You're off the case and, from what DI Gardner had to say, there's zero chance of you getting back on it.'

'Let me worry about that. There's something else too.' I gave her the address Dan's contact had given me, the house where he'd taken the trafficked girl the previous night, and asked her to find out who the place belonged to.

'Sure,' she said. 'But you need to fill me in on what you already know.'

'I could come over to yours and go through everything this evening,' I said. To be honest I could have gone straight over. It wasn't like I had anything better to do, but I preferred the idea of making an evening of it. 'Maybe we can grab a bite somewhere.'

She didn't say anything for a couple of seconds and I wondered if I'd overstepped the mark. But it seemed I hadn't because she then said that it sounded like a good idea, and I wondered if she was as lonely as I was.

'Come round about eight,' she said. 'I'll text you my address.'

The call from Tina put me in a good mood. I might have been suspended, I might have been public enemy number one with some people, but at least I was going to have some good female company this evening; and, who knew, we might even make some progress on the case.

The good mood lasted all of about four minutes. Then my phone rang again while I was stuck on the Embankment in the inevitable traffic you get on a sunny spring day in London.

It was Olaf, and that was never going to be good news.

'What the hell do you think you're doing?' he demanded, his voice calm but simmering nicely.

'I'm driving my car,' I told him.

'So I'm assuming you haven't been watching the TV then? Because if you had been you'd have seen an interview Sky News have just done with a fat man in dire need of a haircut in which he says that the police have come to see him because they think there's an occult link to the Kitty Sinn case. Now I know for a fact that none of my team went to see this bloke, and only one person even thinks there's an occult link, and that's you. So what the fuck do you think you're doing, Ray? You're off this case, remember? You're suspended. You're on police bail. You have literally no fucking jurisdiction.'

'I went to see him yesterday,' I lied, cursing that arsehole Stamoran for going public like this.

'Really?' continued Olaf incredulously. 'Because on the interview he said detectives had been to see him this morning.'

'Then he's lying.'

'I'm going to tell you this for free right now, Ray. If I hear one more fucking whisper that you're still sniffing round this case, just one, then I'll have you put behind bars. Do you understand?'

'Loud and clear, boss.'

'Why don't you just take a holiday or something? It's not like you're short of money. Leave the country for a few weeks and leave the rest of us in peace.'

'That's a nice idea. Maybe I'll do that. Any suggestions?'

'Yeah,' he said. 'As far away from here as possible. Now get out of my fucking hair.'

The line went dead.

I took a deep breath and shook the noise of Olaf's tirade out of my ears. It didn't change anything. It just meant I had to be extra careful going forward.

Forty-two

It was a quarter past two when I pulled into my building's under-ground car park and parked in my spot a twenty-yard walk from the main doors.

I was halfway there when two men emerged from behind a concrete pillar to my right. They were big guys in dark suits, with the blank, merciless faces of thugs. As they approached me, their pace steady, they slipped lengths of lead piping out from beneath their jacket sleeves, keeping them tucked away but ready for use.

I turned round fast, looking for a potential escape route, but two more men in suits were suddenly there, between me and the car. I looked at the door to the apartments. There was no way I could be through there before the first two caught me. Even so, it was my only option. I reached down to my belt where I kept a can of pepper spray and turned to run.

'Don't bother,' came a voice off to one side. 'No one's going to hurt you.'

I looked round and saw a fifth man in a suit, smaller than the others but still with a powerful physique, come out from behind my neighbour's car and walk towards me. He had thick black hair, a narrow, predatory face that spelled danger, and small, cunning and very black eyes like a crow's. He might have looked a lot different from the old mugshot I'd seen of him, but I recognized Cem Kalaman straight away.

I took his advice and didn't bother bolting for the door. Instead I watched him as he approached me, his four men forming a wide outer circle around the two of us as he stopped in front of me.

He was shorter than I'd been expecting, probably no more than five eight, and he looked younger than his age, but there was the kind of presence about him that made a man want to take a step back and give him a good berth.

I didn't step back. I stood in silence, waiting for him to speak.

He smiled, showing a glint of white teeth. 'Mr Mason. I've heard a lot about you.'

I didn't say anything, and he looked around.

'You have good security in this building. Very good. Technology. It's going to make all but the most determined, the most ruthless criminals redundant.'

His voice was cultured and quite soft, with only a hint of north London coming through. Again, not what I would have expected.

'You know you're being filmed, don't you?' I said. 'By an off-site company who are probably watching this right now.'

'That's right. Active S Ltd. We own them. But as I've just

pointed out, we're not interested in harming you. If we were, you'd be dead by now. These men are simply here for my security, since I know you seem to have a habit of killing people in controversial circumstances.'

'I'm not interested in talking to you.'

'Well, these men are here to make sure you hear me out, so why don't you let us into the building and we can talk more freely in your apartment?'

'That's a very kind offer, but no thank you.'

Kalaman's features darkened and he ran a tongue across his lips. 'It's not a request. Either we go to your apartment and talk, or we break your kneecaps here on the concrete, and then come back to chat another time. Your choice. You've got three seconds to make it.'

For one of those three seconds I considered pulling the pepper spray, but dismissed the thought immediately. The last thing I wanted was Cem Kalaman and his goons in my apartment, but for the moment at least it was better than the alternative.

'OK, well, if you put it like that.'

I used my fingerprints to open the security door and the six of us squeezed into the lift. On the way up to the fifth floor one of Kalaman's goons patted me down and took the spray. For a worrying second I thought he might grab my phone as well. It was bad enough that I was compromised but I didn't want to put Dan or Tina in any danger.

But right now I was the one in trouble, and as I opened the door to my apartment I knew I was making a very big mistake letting these guys inside, because there was no way they were going to want to leave without finding out how much I'd learned, and there was no way I could risk giving them that information.

I was going to have to think of something fast.

'It's a nice place you have here,' said Kalaman as they followed me inside.

I walked over to the lounge area and turned to face them as they fanned out in a rough semi-circle, with Kalaman at the centre. He licked his lips again. It was a strangely repulsive gesture.

'You know who I am, don't you?'

'I can guess.'

'Then you'll also have a good idea why I'm here. You seem to be conducting some sort of witch hunt against me even though you're suspended.'

'Well, that's the thing, I'm not. As you say, I'm suspended. It's over.'

'Don't bullshit me. I know you're still sniffing around looking for scraps. Which surprises me. You're in a very precarious position. You survived a double shooting three days ago in circumstances that raise a lot of questions. And then last night a man either fell or was pushed to his death by you in full view of well over a hundred members of the public. You're not a popular man, Mr Mason. Did you know that people of influence have been on the airwaves demanding you be charged with murder?'

'Get to the point of what you want.'

Kalaman nodded slowly. He looked like a man who held all the cards, and that was worrying me.

'I've got something with me,' he said. 'Something I think you'll be very interested in seeing.' He reached into his pocket and pulled out an iPhone, then pressed a few buttons before handing it to me. 'Go on, take a look.'

I took the phone. On the screen was the image of a man in a black ski mask entering a room. It took me a couple of seconds to realize that the man in the shot was me, and that the room I was entering was Bill Morris the caretaker's bedroom.

'Keep scrolling,' said Kalaman, his voice cold.

I flicked my finger across the screen and a second picture appeared. This one was of me sitting on the floor, my mask missing and eyes shut, rubbing my face after I'd been hit by the shot of pepper spray. It was unmistakably me. I swiped again. This time it wasn't a photo but video footage – a nine-second clip, starting with me on the floor still rubbing my face, then panning to Bill Morris's hanging body as it twitched a last time. Urine dripped down his trouser leg on to the floor. After that there were two more photos, both of me leaning out of Morris's bedroom window trying to get air, with part of his body in the background.

I finished swiping, took a breath, and handed the phone back to Kalaman. 'This doesn't prove anything.'

'It shows you at Bill Morris's house at exactly the time he was dying. It makes a suicide look like a murder.'

'But it's obvious I'm not the killer. That would have been the person photographing and filming me.'

Kalaman shrugged. 'Perhaps. Or it could have been your accomplice filming proceedings. Either way you're going to have to explain what you were doing at the house of a dying man wearing a ski mask. And don't even think about claiming that any of this is doctored, because all the police have to do is check the

ANPR cameras that night and they'll see your car was in the vicinity. If any of this is made public, the whole world will be clamouring from the rooftops to prosecute you. The DPP will have no choice. Even if you get out of the Anton Walters killing, you'll go down for this, and then this beautiful apartment of yours, in fact your whole life, will become just a distant memory.'

'Unless?'

'Unless you do the right thing, Mr Mason. You tell us what you've turned up in your investigation so far, who you've been talking to, what they know. Everything. After that, you're ours. When your suspension's lifted, you go back to work, carry on as normal, but you keep us informed of any action against us. If you get transferred elsewhere, fine. Doesn't matter. We might call in favours now and again, or we might just leave you alone. But' – he lifted a finger and pointed it at a place between my eyes – 'carry on doing what you're doing and we'll release this material in a way that causes you maximum damage. We'll destroy you.' He smiled again. 'When you look at it like that, there's not really that much of a choice, is there?'

He was right. There wasn't. Except there was no way I could do what he was demanding. I'd never give him Tina Boyd or Dan Watts' informant. Nor would I ever work for him. I'd rather die than that. And, in the end, I wasn't going to stop digging into this case either. I'd made a promise to Dana Brennan's parents, and it was a promise I was going to keep.

But I didn't say any of this. Instead I nodded slowly, letting my shoulders slump. 'All right, you win. I don't want any part of it now anyway. I don't think I even want to be a copper any more. If you leave me alone, I'll leave you alone. I promise.'

'That's a very good start, Mr Mason,' said Kalaman, putting out a hand. 'Give me the phone.'

I handed it over, and as he took it he drove a fist into my gut. I didn't see it coming and it took the wind right out of me. As I doubled over, two of the goons grabbed an arm each, forcing me upright.

Kalaman's small dark eyes narrowed, and his expression was one of pure venom. 'Now, we're going to have a little talk, and if you don't answer my questions, we're going to start breaking things from the ankle up until you do.'

He gave a barely perceptible nod to one of the goons and the next second my legs were kicked from under me and I went crashing backwards to the floor, my head hitting the sofa, which thankfully broke the worst of my fall. The two goons then grabbed a leg each and began dragging me back from the sofa towards the centre of the floor, and I saw a third goon hand over his piece of lead piping to Kalaman, who took it in his gloved hand.

I'm a paranoid man. When people have tried to kill you, especially when it's more than once, you get like that. So, to protect myself, I keep various implements in strategic places around my apartment for use in an emergency. One of those places was on the bottom of the teak coffee table, where a hunting knife with a six-inch blade was taped, along with a can of pepper spray. I was still within arm's reach of the table as they dragged me across the floor, and my arms were still free, so in one rapid movement I twisted round on my side and reached under the table, knowing that the knife was the nearest weapon.

Seeing my movement, the two goons pulled harder, and I only

just managed to grab the handle in time and yank it free. Then I sat up suddenly and swung it in a short, vicious arc, slicing the shins of both goons.

The blade was razor sharp and the cuts were deep, and they both yelped in pain and jumped backwards, giving me just enough time to turn round and leap to my feet. I ran across the coffee table, just managing to dodge the arm of one of the uninjured goons as he tried to grab my collar and yank me backwards, leaped off at the end, and then I was sprinting for the steps leading up to the bedroom.

'Get him!' I heard Kalaman yell and, to him, it must have looked like I was heading straight into a dead end. My apartment's almost completely open-plan and it ends at the bedroom on the mezzanine floor. I could hear the one who'd tried to grab me close behind as I ran up the steps, taking them two at a time. I ran past the bed, dropping the bloodied knife, and pulled out the drawer on the bedside table, grabbing the gun inside and turning it on my pursuers.

The nearest goon was almost on me, only a few feet away at the end of the bed. The other uninjured one was at the top of the steps. But they both stopped dead when they saw the gun. But then people always do, especially when the man holding it has the kind of confident expression I now had.

I'll be honest. The gun was an air pistol, but it was the perfect replica of a long-barrelled Browning and a very effective deterrent.

'Everyone back away nice and slowly,' I said.

'You wouldn't dare shoot anyone in here,' said the lead goon, but the tone of his voice suggested he wasn't going to be the one to prove that theory.

I smiled. 'You know my record. You know how many people I've killed. Do you really want to take the risk? Now, get your hands in the air and walk backwards, both of you.'

'You'll pay for this,' said the goon, but they both started retreating back down the steps just the same.

I walked over to the top of the steps and turned the gun towards Cem Kalaman, who stood staring at me, a vaguely amused expression on his face, while the two injured goons sat on my floor looking pissed off as they tried to stop the bleeding from their leg cuts.

'I'm impressed,' said Kalaman. 'I didn't think you'd do that.'

'Take the phone I just handed back to you out of your pocket, drop it on the floor, and kick it away from you.'

Still smiling, Kalaman shook his head. 'No. It doesn't work like that.'

'I'm the one with the gun, so I say how it works.'

The smile disappeared, replaced by the venomous look I'd seen earlier. 'Shoot me then.'

I kept the gun trained on him, my hand steady.

'Go on, cunt. Pull the trigger.'

The way I was feeling I probably would have done if I'd actually had any live rounds in there, but the single pellet inside wouldn't give him more than a nasty cut, even if I could hit him from where I was standing.

'See, you ain't got it in you, have you?' he sneered, the north London in his accent finally coming to the fore. 'You might talk the talk, but you're a fucking pussy when it comes down to it.'

'Why don't you come over with that piece of lead piping and

find out?' I said, unable to resist the challenge. 'Come on. Come over here. But keep that in your hand so when the police turn up the camera that's currently filming you can show I acted in self-defence when I blew your fucking head off.'

All his men were looking at him now, and for just a second I could see that the challenge had shaken him. He wasn't convinced I wouldn't fire. And, more importantly, he wasn't going to risk finding out.

For a long time we stared at each other. He didn't move. Neither did I.

But he was first to blink. With a snarl, he stormed over to my widescreen TV and used the piping to smash it with a single ferocious blow. Then he turned to his men. 'Come on, move it. Let's go.' The two injured ones slowly got to their feet, with help from their friends, leaving blood on my floor, and slowly they filed out of the door while I continued to watch them.

Kalaman was last out, and before he left, he turned to me one last time. He didn't speak, but I could see the rage pulsating out of him. All the earlier presence, the menacing authority, had disappeared, and what was left was a nasty, frustrated and vengeful child in a man's body. He opened his mouth to speak but no words came out. It was almost as if he was too angry to speak. But his eyes said it all.

And I knew then that, whatever happened going forward, I was going to have to kill this man, because otherwise he would kill me, even if it cost him the whole world.

Forty-three

It was a sunny early evening and Ramon was standing on the street just outside his block as Junior pulled up in his 4×4. The death of Anton Walters the previous night, and the meeting earlier with Dan the Pig and his friend, and the way the friend had wanted to know about missing girls, had got Ramon very jittery. Things were running completely out of his control, and he had a very bad feeling the whole situation wasn't going to end well. So he was nervous as he got into Junior's car, half expecting someone in the back seat to put a bullet in his head, like they'd done in one of his favourite all-time movies, *The Godfather*.

Junior pulled away without speaking, or looking at him, and Ramon stared at him, trying to gauge his mood.

'Are you all right, bruv?'

'I'm jumpy, bruv,' Junior replied. 'That boy that got killed last night in Hackney, he was one of ours, and everyone wants to know why the Feds went for him. Everything's just a bit hectic right now.'

Ramon bristled. 'Shit, man. Seriously? I heard they had a bit of a riot over there last night.'

'Yeah. People are fucking angry, man. Anton was a good boy.'

'Any ideas why the Feds went for him?'

Junior snorted. 'None you need to know about.'

'Why not? Don't you trust me or something?'

As soon as the words were out of his mouth, Ramon regretted them. Junior looked at him, and something in his eyes didn't seem right.

'Yeah, course I do,' he said. 'But I told you before, Ramon. You ask too many questions. Just keep quiet for a bit. I need to think.'

Ramon wanted to say something else but he decided it was probably best not to, and they drove in silence. They crossed over the North Circular heading north on the A10 towards Edmonton. It wasn't an area Ramon knew, even though he'd been brought up a couple of miles away, but then he'd never been one to travel widely.

It must have been ten minutes before Junior spoke again, which wasn't like him at all. Usually you couldn't shut the bastard up. 'Put these on,' he said, reaching down behind the driver's seat and throwing a plastic bag on to Ramon's lap.

Ramon looked inside. 'What's this all about?' he asked.

'You need to put on the blindfold and the sunglasses. Just do it, OK? I've been told you're not allowed to see where we're going.'

'Why not?'

'Because you're not a part of Jonas's crew yet. When you are, you won't have to wear them.'

Ramon didn't like this. It meant he still wasn't one of them. They were stopped at a set of lights and it occurred to him to jump out of the car and make a bolt for it.

But he didn't. He'd learned a long time ago that you never back down under pressure. You ride with it. In Ramon's world, weakness had always meant defeat.

'This is all fucked up,' he said, putting on the stuff with an angry grunt. 'Happy now?'

'Yeah,' said Junior. 'That's better.' He coughed and cleared his throat. 'Look, don't worry about nothing, all right? It's going to be fine. You're going to get introduced to the crew, and maybe if you're real lucky you'll get initiated. Then you'll be properly on the inside.'

Sitting there in the darkness caused by the blindfold, Ramon was glad he had the tracker Dan the Pig had given him tucked into his sock. At least that way if anything did happen the cops would know where he was, and would eventually send some sort of help. He hadn't brought the two recording devices they'd given him though. That would have been way too risky, and he wasn't going to be taking any more big risks any time soon. His plan had simply been to get introduced to the crew and go with the flow then report back to Dan the Pig afterwards, but now he was beginning to regret coming along with Junior at all.

The 4×4 took a few turnings, one after the other, and the sound of traffic outside grew quieter. Finally they stopped, and Junior switched off the engine.

Ramon reached for the blindfold but Junior put up a hand to stop him. 'Not yet, mate. Stay there for a second.'

Ramon stayed where he was while Junior came round the passenger side and helped him out.

'No speaking, OK? Not until the blindfold's off.'

Junior took off the shades, then led Ramon by the arm for a few yards before stopping and knocking on a door. It opened straight away and Ramon was led inside. No one was saying anything at all and Ramon could hear his heart beating in his chest. It felt like he was being led into a large room. His footsteps were making a noise on the floor and he could smell a mixture of sweat and cleaning products, which immediately reminded him of prison. And right then, Ramon wished he was back there. At least he'd been safe inside and he'd always known what was going on.

Junior brought him to a halt, and for a few seconds Ramon stood there in the darkness. He heard footfalls moving away from him, followed by silence.

'How are you doing?' came a voice a few feet away, loud in the room.

Ramon recognized it straight away as belonging to Jonas. 'I'd be a lot happier with this blindfold off.'

'You heard about last night, yeah? The guy who got killed on the Ridgeway Estate?'

Ramon could hear Jonas coming closer as he spoke. 'Yeah, I saw it on the news.'

'He was one of ours. He was also in the car with you and me yesterday.'

Ramon could feel his stomach churn and he had a sudden

vision of the scene in *Goodfellas* when Joe Pesci walks into the room thinking he's going to become a made man and gets a bullet in the back of the head instead. Ramon felt like he was going to shit his pants but he didn't show it. He knew that if he did, he was dead. It was that simple.

Instead he forced himself to speak and to stay confident. You always had to stay confident. 'Shit, man. Your driver? That's bad news.'

'Yeah, it is,' said Jonas, who was only inches away now.

'So what's that got to do with me?'

There was a silence. Ramon counted in his head. One. Two. Three.

If it was going to happen, it was going to happen now.

Four. Five.

'You ain't a snitch are you, Ramon?'

Ramon felt a desperate desire to run but he knew he wouldn't get five feet before they killed him. He was going to have to stand his ground.

'What the fuck you talking about, man?' he demanded. 'Course I'm not. I never talked to a Fed in my life and anyone says otherwise better show his face right now because I'm going to kill the fucker.'

Silence again. Ramon restarted the count. Six. Seven.

He felt someone else come in very close, could hear their breathing, knew it wasn't Junior because the breath didn't stink . . . and then, a second later, the blindfold was yanked off and he was blinking against the light.

It took a few seconds for his eyes to adjust, and then he looked around. He was in a big, bare room with concrete floors and walls. Some chains hung down from one of the walls and there was a big dark stain on the floor below them that looked a lot like blood. There were three other men in the room. One was Junior. The second was Jonas.

And, standing away from them, was the third man. He was dressed in a dark suit and hat, and he was older, maybe in his sixties, with slicked-back grey hair and pale skin. His face was ordinary enough – it was almost blank-looking and hard to describe – but straight away Ramon could tell that he was the man in charge. It was the way he held himself, and the way the other two seemed wary of him as he walked over, especially Junior, who'd gone even paler than normal and was standing off to one side, looking down at the ground.

The old man was watching Ramon like a cat watches a mouse, a slight smile on his face, like he knew all of Ramon's secrets. He stopped directly in front of Ramon, looking up into his eyes. He smelled bad, like mouldy clothes, and Ramon's nostrils twitched. Something about this man made him want to look away, but he forced himself to meet his gaze.

'My name's Mr Bone,' said the man, putting out a long, thin hand bulging with veins.

Reluctantly, Ramon took the man's hand, forcing himself to retain eye contact. The hand felt warm and slick in his, and he found himself breathing faster, his own body getting colder, as if the energy was being sucked out of it.

'I'm Ramon,' he said, conscious that he sounded like a kid talking to a grown-up.

'I know,' said the man, holding the grip for a long moment, before finally letting go and turning away. 'And you're Junior, aren't you?' he said, walking over to where Junior stood, looking terrified. 'I've heard your name before.'

Junior nodded and shook the hand that was offered to him.

'I would say it is good to meet you both,' said the man, taking a couple of steps back and looking at them both in turn, 'but the reason you're here is that we have a problem within our organization. A leak has appeared. Someone is talking to the police and telling them our secrets.' He paused, his eyes narrowing. 'And I think it's one of you two.'

Ramon and Junior both started to speak, eager to get their defences in while they still could, but the man raised a hand to stop them. At the same time, Jonas pulled a huge pistol from the back of his jeans and began screwing a silencer on to the end of it.

Ramon heard movement behind him. He turned his head and saw that two more men had appeared in the doorway. They both had guns with silencers attached too. His legs felt weak, the sweat cold on his forehead. He'd been in bad situations before, but nothing had felt as bad as this. The life he'd led had been a pretty crap one so far, but the one thing he knew for certain was that he wanted to carry on living it.

'Hold on, can I speak? Please?' said Junior. 'I thought this was about him, not me. I've been a part of the outfit for years. I've paid my dues.' He nodded towards Ramon. 'He's been here a few months. Jonas, you told me this was a set-up this morning. That we were going to do him.'

Ramon couldn't believe what he was hearing. Junior, his

so-called mate, had brought him here to be killed. Ramon started towards him, furious, wanting to rip his throat out, but Jonas pointed the gun at him.

'Stay where you are,' he ordered, his words echoing off the bare stone walls. 'Move another inch and I'll put a bullet in your gut.'

Ramon froze. Jonas looked serious.

The man in the suit, Mr Bone, stared at Ramon. 'I hear you killed someone when you were a young man,' he said.

Ramon controlled his breathing, fought the anger and the fear he felt. 'That's right.'

'How long did you serve in prison?'

'Fourteen years.'

'Did you cooperate with the authorities at all?'

'Never.'

The man nodded slowly, then walked over to Junior. 'And what about you? How many years have you spent in prison?'

'I've been in—'

The man's hand flew up from his side so fast all Ramon saw was a glint of metal, even though he was watching the two of them intently, and then Junior's whole face seemed to open up. For a second the flesh seemed to hang there in the air, leaving behind a huge, perfectly straight gash, and then the blood came pouring down.

With a wail of shock and pain, Junior grabbed at his ruined face with both hands, stumbling round like a drunk man as the blood splashed on the floor. He didn't see Jonas come striding towards him, gun outstretched, and shoot him in the foot.

Junior shrieked, hopping backwards on his good foot before falling to the floor, still clutching his face in both hands.

'You're a fucking loudmouth, Junior, you always have been,' said Jonas, standing above him. He launched a kick into Junior's back that moved him a good two feet along the floor. 'That's for Anton, you piece of shit.'

Jonas turned and strode over to Ramon, his eyes dark and wild.

Ramon had seen that look before plenty of times. The joy of violence.

'You want to be one of us?' he demanded, getting right up close, his nostrils flaring. 'Do you?'

Some deep-down instinct told Ramon the danger had passed. That he was safe tonight. 'Yeah,' he said. 'I do.'

Jonas thrust the gun into his right hand. 'Then kill this back-stabbing bitch.'

On the floor, Junior was whimpering with pain. Ramon walked over and stood over him, conscious that Jonas and Mr Bone were both watching him intently. The knife Mr Bone had used on Junior was still in his hand. Blood dripped from the blade on to the cement floor.

Ramon took a deep breath. The gun felt good in his hand. It gave him power. He pointed it down at Junior's head. Junior looked up at him from behind his bloodied hands, his eyes wide with fear.

Ramon knew that if he didn't kill him, he probably wouldn't get out of there alive himself. The two men on the door had their guns raised ready to fire and they were only a few yards away.

The Bone Field

They wouldn't miss. Out of the corner of his eye he saw Jonas take something out of his pocket and point it towards him.

It was a phone. Jonas was going to film the killing.

If he shot Junior, Jonas and his crew would have him, and it wouldn't take long for Dan the Pig and his Fed friends to find out what had happened and they'd have him back in prison like a shot.

For ever.

Whatever he did, he reckoned he was fucked. It was, he thought sadly, the story of his life.

His finger tightened on the trigger.

'Please Ramon,' whimpered Junior, his whole body shaking with fear. 'Don't do it, man.'

Ramon thought of the nights out drinking he'd had with Junior, the conversations they'd had. There'd been some good times.

The room fell silent. Even Junior's whimpering stopped, as if he knew he'd done as much as he could and now it was just a matter of finding out whether it had worked or not.

It hadn't.

Keeping his hand steady, Ramon pulled the trigger.

Forty-four

Tina Boyd lived in a village just inside the M25, and I felt myself relaxing as I passed the pub on my left and stopped just outside a row of old flint cottages. Before I'd left to come here I'd checked my car all over for tracking devices, and bought a disposable mobile phone and switched my own one off. I'd also followed some classic anti-surveillance techniques to make sure I wasn't being followed. The visit today from Cem Kalaman and his goons had got me worried. I didn't like the way my security had been compromised. It meant from now on I was going to have to be very careful – although I had a grim feeling that however careful I was, it wasn't going to be enough.

I got out of the car, breathing in the slightly less polluted air, and looked around, to check that no one was watching Tina's place, then knocked on the door.

A few seconds later, Tina answered the door. She was dressed in T-shirt and jeans. Her feet were bare, the toenails freshly painted a plum colour, and I caught a vague hint of perfume.

'I wasn't sure what to bring so I settled for this,' I said, handing her a bottle of grape juice. After the three days I'd had I could have done with a real drink but I'd heard somewhere that Tina was a recovering alcoholic, so I didn't want to throw temptation in her way. 'It's good to see you in one piece,' I told her. 'You look remarkably well.'

'So do you,' she said, 'considering you've been through the ringer too. Come in.'

I followed her into a small but quaint-looking kitchen where a laptop was open on the table.

'I've got a few things out for you,' she said, opening up the grape juice and pouring us both a glass. I caught another hint of the perfume as she gave me mine. 'You wanted to know who that address you gave me earlier was registered to,' she continued, referring to the house Dan Watts' informant had told me he'd taken the trafficked girl to the previous night.

'And what did you manage to find out?' I asked, taking a seat opposite her at the table.

'It belongs to a company based out of Bermuda called Turner Wright Holdings. When I tried to find out further details I hit an immediate dead end. We're not going to get any more that way.' She paused. 'However . . . the house is only twenty minutes from here and I had a little bit of time on my hands earlier, so I drove over there to take a look. There was one car in the driveway, a

Mercedes SLC convertible. I took down the registration and checked it out. It belongs to Lola Sheridan.'

I sat back in the chair. 'That's interesting.'

'There was something else too. Have a look at this.' She turned the laptop round so I could see it.

On the screen was an old, slightly grainy photo of a group of five young women standing in a bar, with their arms draped over each other's shoulders, laughing at the camera. They looked drunk and happy.

'The woman on the far right is Lola Sheridan. The picture was taken in 1988.'

Immediately I saw the resemblance to Kitty Sinn. Both women had long dark hair and olive skin, with the same small, almost dainty features, and big hazel eyes. They weren't a perfect match by any means but Lola would certainly have been able to pass herself off as Kitty to people who'd never seen either woman before, like holidaymakers in pre-internet Thailand.

'Where did you find this?' I asked.

'I managed to track down a woman from Lola's course at Goldsmiths who'd known her pretty well and spoke to her on the phone. Apparently, Lola wasn't very popular. Most of her fellow students, male and female, thought she was a bitch. I asked the woman if she had any old photos with Lola in them and she dug out this one from freshers week, when people hadn't yet discovered what she was really like.'

'How did you manage to get all that from a stranger?'

'I told her I was a journalist doing a new piece on the Kitty Sinn murders, and I was collecting photos of people who were close to her before she disappeared. I offered her two hundred pounds for any shot and a credit when the article was published. It was enough.'

'Jesus, you're a fast worker. How much do I owe you?'

'I'll bill you. I'm more interested in what you know about this whole thing. So what's your theory, Ray Mason? What happened? Who's involved, and why?' She sipped her drink, looking at me over the glass. 'Start from the beginning.'

I sighed. 'Look Tina, I'll be honest. It's best not to know too much about this case. I shouldn't have got you into it in the first place.'

'You didn't. Henry Forbes did. You're not responsible for me, Ray.'

'There are dangerous people involved. The kind who could easily kill you.'

'And they almost did kill me yesterday, which is all the more reason to bring them to justice. And I'm a big girl. I've dealt with dangerous people before.'

If I'm honest, I didn't know what to do. Part of me knew that the more I told Tina, the more I was putting her in danger. But right now I needed allies more than ever, and Tina was the kind of person who could dig up answers far more effectively than most of the people I've worked with. And she wanted to be involved.

And, of course, it was an excuse to keep seeing her.

'OK,' I said after a long pause. 'I've been thinking constantly about this for the last few days, so here's what I think happened, although I've got to be honest, a hell of a lot of it is guesswork.'

'That's fine,' she said. 'Go on.'

So I told her that I thought Kitty Sinn's cousin Alastair Sheridan had met Cem Kalaman at Warwick University. Kalaman was a sadist, as was Alastair, who'd already sexually assaulted Kitty as a teenager, and had probably committed other crimes as well. Together they'd abducted and murdered Dana Brennan, using Alastair's knowledge of the area. Their motive was still unclear but I suspected it was for sexual gratification masquerading as devil worship, and that Dana had been chosen because she was young and wouldn't offer much resistance. They'd killed her in the grounds of Medmenham College after Kalaman had paid the caretaker, Bill Morris, to be away from the premises. Other people might have been involved, including Lola, but I wasn't sure.

Lola, though, had definitely been involved in their second murder. Having gained confidence from killing Dana, Cem, Alastair and Lola had meticulously planned Kitty's murder, using Henry Forbes as their stooge. Their motive was still unclear but was most likely a combination of jealousy and sexual sadism, along with a desire to silence Kitty in case she made public that Alastair and Lola had sexually assaulted her some years earlier; and of course greed, since both the cousins benefited financially from her death, albeit at a much later date.

Their plan had worked almost perfectly. Kitty had been murdered just before she was supposed to go to Thailand after being lured to the grounds of Medmenham College, and Lola, who looked a lot like her, had gone in her place. The only hitch was that Kitty's friend Charlotte Curtis had seen Forbes and Lola in a taxi as they travelled to the airport together. Luckily for them both, Charlotte hadn't realized it wasn't Kitty at the time, and so they'd got away with her murder.

Tina sighed. 'So that's why Charlotte had to die. Because she could solve the mystery of the disappearance.' She shook her head slowly. 'Jesus, it seems so unfair. If that taxi hadn't stopped at the traffic lights . . . if she hadn't been walking down that street on that afternoon at that time . . . then she'd still be alive. I wish I'd saved her, Ray. I got so close. We almost made it.' She leaned forward in her seat and fixed me with an intense stare. 'That's why I want to stay involved. It's personal for me. I want to make amends.'

'I understand that,' I said, 'but these guys have got real power. Kalaman runs a huge and successful crime business; Alastair Sheridan's a well-known fund manager who hobnobs with senior politicians, and is currently on a trade mission with the Chancellor of the Exchequer. There may even be others who are part of this. It's going to be very difficult, and very dangerous, to gather evidence against them.'

She picked up her glass from the table and took a drink. 'Have you got any proof of their involvement in all this?'

'Nothing. But I have a contact in the NCA whose job it is to investigate the Kalaman outfit, and he has an informant on the inside. Last night this informant drove a young woman who'd recently been trafficked into the country to the address where you saw Lola Sheridan's car today. I think Cem Kalaman and Alastair Sheridan and whoever else is involved have continued killing young women but nowadays they use the outfit's people-smuggling contacts to source their victims.'

Tina frowned. 'So this woman's probably their next victim. Are the NCA going to raid the place? If the girl's been trafficked illegally, a criminal offence has been committed.'

It was a good point. I'd called Dan Watts on the way over here and told him all this but he'd been understandably reluctant to do anything that might put his informant in danger, and had said he'd keep an eye on things and let me know if the tracking device with the girl went on the move again.

'I don't know what their plans are,' I said to Tina, 'but they're definitely on the case.'

'That might not be enough,' she said. 'Do you think we should go over there?'

'And do what? We can't just break in. The girl might be fine. She might not want to come with us. And all we'll do is alert Lola Sheridan to the fact that we're on to her.' I sighed. 'To be honest, right now I can't afford to do anything else illegal. I'm in enough shit as it is. It's easier to leave the heavy work for the NCA and concentrate on gathering evidence quietly.'

She nodded. 'Sure. I understand.' But something in her tone suggested she was disappointed in me.

In truth, I was tired after a long and brutal week which had seen me come close to death more than once. All I wanted was to have a night away from it all, and let someone else deal with it for once.

Which, as it turned out, was to prove a very big mistake.

Forty-five

So that was it. Ramon knew there was no way back for him now he'd killed Junior.

He'd had to do it. It was kill or be killed. Dog eat dog. But he knew that Dan the Pig wouldn't see it that way. To him it would be murder, and that meant going back inside. For the rest of his life. And Jonas had filmed him doing it. Afterwards, the man in the suit, Mr Bone, had smiled then walked out without a word while Jonas had taken the gun off Ramon before grabbing him in a bear hug and saying, 'You're one of us now,' while Junior lay dead on the floor between them.

Ramon didn't feel too bad about killing Junior. Junior had tried to set him up, so he'd got what was coming to him. Even so, it hadn't felt good watching the two guys who'd been on the door emptying his pockets, then dragging his corpse out by the legs, leaving a dirty smear of blood behind them.

Jonas had given him the keys to Junior's 4×4 and told Ramon it was his if he wanted it. So here he was an hour later, sitting in it outside his block of flats and wondering what his next move was going to be. Staying put wasn't an option. If he betrayed Jonas, Jonas would show the Feds the video of him killing Junior. And if he stopped feeding Dan the Pig information, they'd throw him back inside anyway.

In the end, there was only one way out. Run. In an envelope stuffed into his jacket was six grand in cash, his savings from the work he'd done for the Kalamans, as well as the cash Dan the Pig's friend had given him today. He'd served time with an Algerian forger who still lived on Archway and the guy had promised to do Ramon a cheap deal on a high-quality fake passport if he ever needed one. All he had to do was get one sorted, then he could get across to France and lie low for a while. Figure out what to do.

It wasn't as if he was leaving anything behind. He had no family. No real friends. Junior had been the man he'd seen most of, and obviously he wasn't going to be seeing him again any time soon. He was totally alone in the world. There wasn't a single person who cared shit about him. He thought of his grandpa who would have been ashamed of what he'd become. And Keesha. His baby sister, Keesha. What would she have thought if she'd grown up and could see him now?

Ramon cursed out loud in the silence of the car, and hunted round for Junior's smokes. He found some, and a lighter, in the glove compartment, and lit one.

Nicole. The girl with the eyes like Keesha's. She'd liked him. They'd talked on the way over to that place last night and she'd actually seemed interested in what he had to say. He wondered if she was still there with that cold-eyed bitch, and what the cold-eyed bitch had planned for her. That guy today, Dan the Pig's friend, had asked him what he knew about girls going missing, and he'd seemed interested in where he'd taken Nicole.

Ramon pulled on the cigarette and blew smoke out of the half-open window. As he did so, he made a plan in his head. He was going to rescue Nicole. Take her from the cold-eyed bitch, ditch the trackers, and then the two of them could make a break for it, split the country, and leave all this shit behind.

It was a dangerous move, but then Ramon was a dangerous man. He'd killed tonight. He wasn't someone you messed about with.

Suddenly feeling good about what he planned to do, he fed the old witch's postcode into Junior's satnav, backed out of his parking spot, and drove out of the estate.

The drive to the bitch's house seemed faster than it had been the previous day and it had just gone ten p.m. when Ramon turned into the wood with its gnarly old trees looming up on either side of him that looked like something out of a scary movie.

He drove slowly, not allowing himself to feel any doubt about what he was doing. It was like that time back in the ends when he'd gone to the Clifton Estate looking for revenge and had shot dead Terrell Wright. He'd been determined to do what he had to do then, and he was determined to do it now too. And if Nicole wasn't there, he'd make the cold-eyed bitch tell him where she was. And if anything had happened to her, then Christ he'd make the bitch pay.

When he got close to the white house and saw it poke out ahead of him through the trees, he switched off his headlights and turned the car around so it was facing the way home. He cut the engine and got out, sniffing the night air. Somewhere nearby an owl hooted but otherwise the woods were silent. It made Ramon feel uncomfortable. He was used to noise.

He walked quickly along the track before cutting into the undergrowth by the side of the house. The lights were on inside and he could see a black car in the shadows on the far side of the driveway, but couldn't remember whether it had been there the previous night or not.

A high hedge blocked off access to the back of the house but there was a wooden gate about Ramon's height in the middle. It was bolted from the inside, so he hauled himself up and managed to scramble over the top, almost falling over the other side.

The back garden was a tangled mess of weeds and bushes but a narrow path led to the back door. Ramon walked up to it, telling himself that he'd got this far. Now he just wanted to get in and out as fast as possible.

The back door was locked too, but that was no problem for Ramon. You learned a lot while you were in nick, and in his last years inside, after he'd been transferred to Pentonville, he'd shared a cell with this old white guy who was a career burglar, who'd taught him all he needed to know about breaking into a house. And this one was particularly easy. The door was old, and so was the lock, and Ramon used a bump key to open each of the pins in turn, before slowly opening the door and feeling the first wave of adrenalin as he stepped inside. The old white guy, Branks, had told him there was no bigger buzz than breaking into someone's house and taking whatever you wanted. Especially when they were asleep inside. 'It's like raping them,' he'd said. 'But more fun, and a lot less trouble.' Ramon wasn't sure if this was the case or not, but he had to admit, it made him feel powerful creeping inside unannounced like this.

He was in the kitchen. Dirty plates were piled up like they were in his place, and it smelled of good food. There was a pot of something on the hob. It looked like chicken soup. He dipped his finger in. The soup was cold but he pulled out a piece of chicken anyway, munching it down in one go and wiping his hand on his trouser leg.

The kitchen led into a hallway that ran down to the front door. Ramon could hear a woman's voice coming from one of the rooms. She was talking quietly and Ramon couldn't make out what she was saying. He'd brought a large hunting knife with him because you never knew what kind of danger you were going to run into, and now he pulled it free of its sheath and walked to where the voice was coming from.

He put his ear against the door and immediately heard Nicole's voice. She sounded out of it, and again Ramon couldn't quite make out what she was saying.

Then he heard the other person speak and he recognized the voice of the cold-eyed bitch from last night.

'Stay still,' she said, her voice harsh.

'It hurts,' said Nicole.

'It won't hurt for much longer,' said the bitch. 'Stay still.'

Ramon had no idea what was going on in there but he felt a surge of anger and flung open the door.

Nicole was sitting in a big armchair, wearing a sleeveless black dress that reached down to her ankles. Her feet were bare and Ramon couldn't help noticing how pretty they looked. But it was her eyes that drew his attention. They were only half open and dazed, like she'd been on the crack, and her head was lolling to one side.

Standing behind Nicole, holding her hair in one hand and a big metal brush in the other, was the bitch from yesterday. Rather than recoil from the sight of a big black man with a knife running into her front room, she just glared at him with a face so full of hate and rage that it almost stopped him in his tracks.

'What are you doing in here?' she shouted, her voice harsh in the silence. 'Get out! This is a holy place!'

'Leave her alone!' roared Ramon, marching over to her, full of fury at the way this bitch was treating Nicole.

The bitch let go of Nicole's hair and, with a yell, threw the brush at Ramon's head. He tried to dodge it but it hit his shoulder with a hard whack, and the bitch immediately grabbed for a vase on a nearby table and went to fling that at him too.

Ramon had to hand it to her. She had some balls. But she wasn't quite quick enough. He slapped the vase out of her hands and back-handed her across the face, knocking her into a bookshelf. She lost her footing and ended up on her arse, a dazed look on her face.

Ramon looked over to Nicole, who was still half slumped in the chair. 'Come on, let's go,' he said, taking her by the arm and pulling her to her feet.

She didn't resist as he led her from the room but he had to hold her up by the arm and almost drag her. It would have been quicker to go out of the front door but something stopped Ramon from going there and they went back the way he'd come in.

'Is there anyone else in the house?' he asked quietly as they stepped out into the garden.

Nicole looked at him with eyes that just couldn't manage to focus. 'There was a man here earlier, talking to her,' she said. 'I didn't see him. Just heard him.'

'When was that?'

'Half an hour maybe . . .'

Ramon knew he couldn't rely on Nicole's timings but he didn't think the guy was still there.

He pulled back the bolt on the gate, yanked it open and led her out into the undergrowth. 'This way.'

'I'm so tired,' said Nicole.

'It's OK,' said Ramon. 'I've got you.' He lifted her into his arms and, Jesus, he had to admit it felt good to be holding a woman like this.

A peaceful smile crossed her face, and she touched his cheek. 'Thank you for coming. It's not nice here.'

'You're safe now,' Ramon told her as he carried her back to his car.

'I know,' she said, with real gratitude in her voice.

But Ramon knew that in the end you were never completely safe. There were always people out there wanting a piece of you. He'd feel a lot better when they were back in the city and booked into a hotel, somewhere where, for the moment at least, no one could get them.

He was panting when they reached the car. Nicole wasn't quite as light as she looked. He set her down by the passenger door and the two of them got inside.

'Where are we going?' she asked, her eyes closing as she made herself comfortable in the seat.

Ramon grinned at her and put the key in the ignition. 'Let me worry about that.'

He felt rather than saw the movement from the seat behind him and just had time to see the face of Mr Bone underneath his hat, his face pale and ghostly in the half-light, before a hand grabbed his forehead, pulled it back, and he felt a sharp, hot pain in the back of his neck. He choked, unable to breathe properly, as his throat suddenly became clogged with liquid and, as he looked down, he could see the tip of the same blade that had been used to slash Junior's face in two sticking out of his own throat like a bayonet. Blood dripped down from the tip on to his T-shirt, covering it in big droplets.

He heard Nicole scream but it seemed far away. He tried to look at her but his vision blurred, and he knew that he was dying. Dying fast.

And in a strange way he was pleased. It was a release. No one could hurt him again now. He was going to a place without fear. He tried to lift his hand but nothing happened. It was over. Nicole was on her own.

Ramon's last thought was of him, Grandpa and Keesha, all of them together on the back step of Grandpa's flat, when they'd still been a family way back before it had all gone so wrong.

Then his eyes closed and the darkness came.

Forty-six

The world can sometimes be a brutal place, and in my life I've seen some of the worst it's had to give; but there are moments when things fall into place, and the tunnel ahead suddenly seems brighter.

Tonight was one of those nights. Tina was easy to talk to. She understood me and I understood her. After we'd finished discussing the case, we grabbed a bite to eat in her local pub, and my tension just seemed to fade away. I didn't even have a drink, and when Tina asked if I'd like to grab a coffee before I drove home, I was always going to accept.

Home. My place didn't feel much like home right now, not after the way it had been invaded by Cem Kalaman and his people. It also meant I was going to have to watch my back for the foreseeable future, as they were sure to pay another visit. I thought about picking up an illegal handgun in case I needed it. I have an old army friend who I know has contacts in the black market; he'd be able to find me something reliable. The problem was, if I was caught with a gun by my colleagues, or God forbid if I used it in anger, I'd end up going down for years. For the moment at least it wasn't worth the risk.

Still, I didn't fancy the drive back tonight.

We sat down opposite each other in Tina's cramped little lounge with our coffees. She'd taken her shoes off and her feet were bare. She flicked her long dark hair and crossed her legs, and in that moment I thought she looked beautiful.

'Do you mind if I smoke?' she asked.

'Course I don't.' I'd never smoked. Hated the smell. But I wasn't going to complain now.

I watched as she lit up. She even managed to do that elegantly.

'You know,' she said, taking a drag and sipping her coffee, 'I was so scared yesterday when I was lying in that ravine with Charlotte. I really thought I was going to die. I've been close to being killed before, but I don't think I was as worried about it then. But that time's gone now. I don't want to die any more.'

I nodded. 'Me neither. I was scared out of my wits last night in that estate. The way the mob were acting I thought they were going to tear me apart limb from limb.'

She smiled. 'I guess it's a good thing we're both single. Our other halves would have heart attacks worrying about us.'

'That's for sure,' I said, although I remembered that when I'd been married I'd taken far fewer risks.

'Have you ever been married?' she asked, as if she'd been reading my thoughts.

'Yeah. Once.'

'What happened?'

I hesitated. I didn't know what to say. The truth was grim.

'I'm sorry,' she said. 'I didn't meant to pry.'

'No, it's OK. I think my wife found the whole police thing too difficult. It was a hard break-up though. She had two daughters, twins, who were seven when we met, and I became very close to them. Probably too close.' I sighed. 'We were happy. Really happy. Then we weren't. It hurt a lot.'

I should have stopped talking then but the words just seemed to tumble out as if they'd been waiting there all this time.

'I remember in our last year together, it was Halloween. We used to live out in Surrey in a little village near Egham and all the young kids used to dress up for trick or treat. The girls were well into it, as you can imagine. We were too. I dressed up as Count Dracula; Jo, my wife, was a witch's cat; and the girls were both witches. It was a Friday night and I'd finished work for the weekend. We went round the houses, doing the trick or treating, and it was like the whole village was out. The girls were laughing the whole time, their sweet bags were full, and we all ended up in the local pub where they were doing food for all the kids, and all the parents, myself included, were at the bar drinking and chatting, without a care in the world.' I sighed. 'You know, I remember it as one of the best nights I've ever had. I was so damn happy because I had a family I loved, and a normal life.

'We broke up in September of the following year, and I'll

never forget that next Halloween. I was living alone in a loft near King's Cross, and I was home that night, drinking on my own, and, Jesus . . .' I took a deep breath. 'It was the most lonely night I've ever had. It was like I was the only man left alive, cast adrift in this huge city where no one gave a shit about me, and where no one ever had.'

The tears stung my eyes as, for a few moments, I relived the twin memories of those two vastly different nights, and emotions that I worked so hard to keep hidden came simmering to the surface.

'I thought about killing myself then. I even had the gun in my hand.' I held up my thumb and forefinger so they were millimetres apart. 'I came this fucking close.'

Tina didn't say anything. Instead, she stubbed out her cigarette, put down her coffee, and walked over to where I was sitting.

Forcing away the tears, I got to my feet. We looked at each other for a long time. We didn't speak.

Then, with an inevitability that had been there since I'd arrived at her home, we kissed.

At first it was slow and gentle. But slow and gentle wasn't what either of us needed and within seconds we were tearing at each other's clothes as passion took hold. I don't know who dragged who up to the bedroom but that was where we ended up, and, as we fell naked into each other's arms, the world instantly became a better place.

Although I think I knew even then that it wouldn't stay like that for long.

Day Five
Saturday

Forty-seven

I was woken from a blissfully dreamless sleep by the sound of my mobile phone.

Sitting up in bed, it took me a couple of seconds to realize where I was. Sunlight streamed through the window and a clock on the wall I didn't recognize told me it was 7.40 a.m. Then I turned and saw Tina Boyd lying next to me, her dark hair splayed across the pillow, her freckled shoulders bare above the covers, and I remembered.

Tina opened one eye. 'Is that yours?'

On those occasions in recent years when I've slept with women, the next morning has always been an awkward, guilt-ridden time for me, as if I know I've somehow betrayed myself and led them on, and that's usually been followed by thoughts of how to escape as soon as possible. I didn't feel anything like that as I looked down at Tina. I felt good.

'Sorry,' I said, bending down and kissing her forehead. 'I'll sort it.'

The phone was in my jeans. I pulled it out and saw that the call was from Dan Watts.

'Hold on,' I whispered, tiptoeing out of the bedroom and down the stairs.

'Where are you?' Dan asked.

I wasn't going to tell him about Tina. 'With a friend.'

'I didn't know you had any, Ray.'

'Yeah, thanks. Good morning to you too.'

'We've got a problem,' he said.

'Give me a moment.' I went into Tina's kitchen, poured myself a glass of water and took a big gulp. 'Go on.'

'I've just got word that they've found my informant's body dumped on waste ground up near Watford. He'd had his throat cut.'

'Shit. When was the last time you heard from him?'

'When I was with you. His tracker was still on him though. It travelled with him up to Edmonton yesterday, then to an area round an isolated house near Little Chalfont in Buckinghamshire.'

'That's where he delivered the trafficked girl on Thursday night.'

'I know. And then from there it travelled directly to where they found him. So he may have died there.'

'The house belongs to an offshore company but a car belonging to Lola Sheridan, Kitty Sinn's cousin, was there yesterday.'

'How the hell do you know that?'

'I just do. Have you got enough to raid the place?'

'No,' he said, lowering his voice. 'You remember, this whole op with the informant was unofficial. I'm going to have a hard enough time trying to explain away the tracking device.'

'So what do we do?'

'The other tracker, the one my informant gave the girl, went on the move at five-thirty this morning, just over two hours ago, and it's been moving ever since, first up the M40 to Birmingham, then the M6 north. They're now on the M54 heading west towards Wales.'

'Can you get some surveillance on them?' I asked, knowing the answer to that one before I'd even asked the question.

'No way. You know the size of my team, and I haven't got a prayer of getting authority from anyone else. Right now I've got to concentrate all my resources on damage limitation.'

'So, why are you calling me?' I knew the answer to this question too.

'I want to know where that girl's going. If I keep you updated on the tracker's location, can you follow it and see where it ends up? I know you like a bit of an adventure, Ray, and you never know where this one might lead you.'

It was an unorthodox request, and frankly pretty cheeky, but I was never going to say no, despite the beautiful woman asleep in bed upstairs.

'OK, Dan, I'll do it. Can you send me the codes to the tracker so I can follow it myself?'

'No problem. And thanks, Ray. I appreciate the help. But don't go getting yourself in any trouble. It's purely a reconnaissance trip. Anything looks fishy, just report back and we'll take it from there.'

'Don't worry,' I told him. 'I've had enough trouble for one week.'

Forty-eight

'Is everything OK?' Tina asked when I walked back into the bedroom. She was propped up on her pillows, her hair falling down over her shoulders, the sunlight dappling her pale skin through the window.

The desire to jump back into bed with her was almost overwhelming.

'I've got to go,' I told her.

'Where?'

I paused for too long, not wanting to lie to her, but not wanting to tell her the truth either.

Her expression darkened. 'Don't tell me, you've got a girlfriend.'

'No, course I haven't. I've got a lead. One I need to follow up.'

'Fine. I'll come with you.' She got out of bed. 'We're in this together now.'

'Look, Tina, I almost got you killed the other day and, you know, this is hard for me to say, but I've got feelings for you.'

'Don't fucking patronize me,' she said, stopping in front of me. 'I told you before, you didn't almost get me killed, and I am not your responsibility. We're going to work together on this, and as far as I can see, right now you need all the help you can get.'

She was absolutely right, but that didn't stop me feeling protective. I'd developed strong feelings for her already, and it was such a rare thing for me to experience that I didn't want to do anything that might jeopardize that.

In the end, though, there was no way Tina was going to get fobbed off.

'It's just a reconnaissance trip,' I told her, 'and we need to make a brief stop at my place, to pick up a few things.'

'Good,' she said. 'I'll be ready in twenty minutes.'

Which made me like her even more.

By ten, Tina and I were in my car heading north on the M40 towards Birmingham when I got another call from Dan Watts.

'I don't know if you've spotted it yet,' he said, 'but the tracker's been stopped for the last half an hour at a farm in mid-Wales, a place out in the middle of nowhere.'

'Yeah, we're heading towards it now,' I said, glancing over to where Tina sat with a laptop open on her lap, 'but we're still at least a couple of hours away. Have you got any idea who the farm belongs to?'

'An offshore company called Blankford Associates. So far I haven't got anything more than that, but it's probably another Kalaman front company. If you can, just check the place out. See what might be going on there, who's in residence, take some photos and send them back to me. Then we can work out what the next move is.'

'If they've taken the trafficked girl there, and it looks like they have, she could be in real danger.'

'If things look bad, we'll call in the local police. But don't take any risks yourself, Ray. You're in enough crap as it is.'

I told him I wouldn't and we agreed to speak again when we arrived.

From the M40, we took the M42 and M6 across Birmingham before taking the A458 into Wales. The traffic became lighter as we crossed the border, and when we came off the main road, heading north, the landscape became one of rolling hills and thick patches of woodland. The traffic thinned as the roads grew narrower and more potholed, and as we crossed a bridge over a fast-flowing river, Tina told me to take an immediate left.

I turned on to a single-vehicle, heavily pitted lane that climbed upwards through thick pine forest, directly parallel to the river, for about half a mile before turning away as the woodland thinned and the pines turned to oak and beech trees.

'About fifty metres up here on our left is the track that runs directly down to the farm,' said Tina. 'The distance is about a quarter of a mile.'

So we were almost there. If this place did indeed belong to the Kalamans I knew they'd take precautions to keep out visitors, which would probably include security cameras. So I pulled off the lane, weaved between a couple of trees, and parked the car behind a large tangle of brambles and ferns so we were out of sight of anyone driving past.

'Whereabouts are we on the map?' I asked, leaning over.

'Here,' she said.

I looked at where her finger was placed on the laptop screen. A satellite map of the area showed we were on the edge of a large wood that ran down to a valley at the bottom of which was a cluster of four buildings, reached by the dead-end track. A red light was pulsing from the main building – a large stone house – as it showed the location of the tracker. Beyond the buildings more woodland rose up on the other side of the valley. There were no other buildings, houses or otherwise, in any direction, making it totally isolated.

'Right,' I said, memorizing the map. 'We need a vantage point so we can get a good look at this place. And remember, this is a recce. Nothing more. The first sign of anything suspicious, we call in the local cops. If we have to, we'll do an anonymous 999 call, say we've seen someone on the property with a gun. Agreed?'

She nodded, and brushed back hair from her eyes. 'Sure.'

We looked at each other for a moment. I wanted to kiss her. It looked like she might have felt the same way. But I didn't. We hadn't shown each other any affection on the way up either. It was as if we both knew our relationship had to wait until we'd sorted out everything else. So I got out of the car, pulled a back-pack from the boot containing the tools I like to keep for surveillance jobs, and motioned for Tina to follow me.

The Bone Field

We made our way through the trees until we were opposite the turning down to the farm. It was marked by a high wooden gate, topped with iron spikes, with security cameras facing down the track from each of the gateposts. A wire fence around ten feet high topped with a dual strip of barbed wire ran parallel to the lane on either side. I looked for additional security cameras on the fence but couldn't see any.

We continued walking until we were well past the gate and out of sight of the cameras, then followed the line of the fence as it ran away from the lane and down the hill through the trees. I stopped where the fence passed close to a large fern and took a pair of wire cutters from the backpack.

'One of the advantages of doing this unofficially is you don't have to follow the rules,' I said as I crouched down and started cutting a hole in the fence near the bottom.

Tina grunted. 'I gave up following them a long time back.'

The wire was new and strong and it took me a few minutes to cut a hole big enough for us to fit through. I threw the piece I'd removed into the ferns and crawled through on my belly with Tina following, confident that no one passing by would spot the damage we'd done.

Five minutes later we came to a break in the trees where a small rocky ridge jutted out above a much steeper drop into the valley below. I lay down on my front and pulled out a pair of binoculars from the backpack while Tina lay down next to me.

Below us, several hundred metres away in the floor of the valley, was the farm. I lifted the binoculars and took a closer look at it. The main building was an imposing-looking stone house set in a large courtyard with a barn next to it, and a smaller outbuilding opposite, next to which was a kennels. I could see two large and not particularly friendly-looking Rottweilers lying down behind the mesh wire – clearly security dogs rather than pets. Two cars were parked in the courtyard: one was a dirt-stained Land Rover Defender, the other a black, much newer-looking Range Rover. I couldn't see the plates from the angle I was looking at. Nor could I see any sign of people.

'There's no sign of the girl,' I said, handing the binoculars to Tina and waiting while she scanned the area.

She handed them back to me. 'The tracker's there, so she must be as well.'

'Have you got a signal on your phone?' I said, pulling out mine. It said two bars.

Tina nodded. 'Good enough. Three bars.'

'I'm going to get as close as I can and take a look around without taking any risks. I've got a motion-activated camera in my bag. I'll set it up so we can see who comes in and out. I have a feeling more people will be turning up.'

'And you want me just to stay here, away from all the action.' She sounded frustrated.

'There'll be no action. And I need you here in case anything goes wrong.' I looked at her. 'It's ten past one now. It's going to take me a while to get down there, but if I'm not back or you haven't heard anything from me by half two, dial 999, then get out.' I handed her my car keys. 'The same applies if you see anything while I'm gone that looks like grounds to call the police. Just do it. Remember, we're looking for any excuse to get the cavalry in.'

The Bone Field

Tina looked back at me, and there was concern in her expression. I hadn't seen someone look at me like that in a long time. 'Don't do anything stupid, Ray. I actually think I might like you, and that's a real rarity for me.'

I gave her hand a squeeze and got to my feet. 'Stay here and don't move,' I said, and turned back into the trees.

Forty-nine

A gentle breeze made the leaves rustle as The Dark Man walked alone through the trees, carrying with it the ripe, intoxicating smell of the earth and the woods. His skin tingled with anticipation at the thought of what would happen later. The girl they'd brought down here to the farm was perfect. An olive-skinned natural beauty, just like the girls he'd known as a boy back in the old country. Ripe and ready for picking. And tonight, when the others arrived – the inner circle – they would have their fill of her in the way they'd done so many times before.

The Dark Man never tired of the kill. It filled him with a joy like no other. It was the power it gave him: the knowledge that he was sucking the life out of another, absorbing their strength, stealing their soul, and then burying them beneath the soil where their families could never find them.

His was a largely joyless life. He had never loved, nor travelled; he had no children that he knew about, nor true friends. He had never liked people, even from the very beginning, and, as age began to devour him, this feeling had hardened. Now he had a cold contempt even for those he worked with and knew well, and he looked forward to the day when Cem Kalaman no longer needed him and he could retire here and live in isolation like a monk, taking what pleasure he could in his solitary walks – and, of course, the occasional kill.

Out of the corner of his eye he caught a glint of something in the dappled sunlight coming through the canopy. He turned and approached quickly as the car revealed itself behind a thick tangle of bushes. It was a new-looking Audi A6, not the kind of car you'd expect round here. He could see its tyre tracks in the dirt where it had left the lane. He leaned down and peered inside, saw nothing of any use, and took down the registration number.

No one came up this lane unless they were going to the farm. It didn't lead anywhere except back to the main road, becoming an overgrown, near-impenetrable mess on the way down. There were no footpaths around here either, nothing to attract anyone to this spot – which was the reason they'd chosen the farm as their desired location all those years ago.

So someone was here who shouldn't be.

The Dark Man felt a twinge of unease. Things had been complicated ever since the discovery of the two bodies in the grounds of the school, but he had started to get the situation back under control, and he couldn't afford anyone finding out about this place.

He slipped the gun from his jacket and looked around, sniffing the air. Whoever it was who'd come here, they weren't going to be far away.

Tina stubbed out her cigarette on the rock, made sure it was fully out and placed it carefully in the dirt. The ground was slightly damp so it had obviously rained here recently but, even so, she was paranoid about inadvertently starting a fire.

She picked up the binoculars and, almost as soon as she'd focused them again, she saw the side door to the main house open and a well-built black man in jeans and a tight-fitting T-shirt emerge. As he turned slightly away from her she thought she saw the handle of a gun sticking out of the back of his jeans, but then he leaned back against the wall, obscuring her view, and lit a cigarette.

Tina panned the binoculars, looking for Ray. He'd been gone for close to twenty minutes now. She couldn't see him down there, and for that she was thankful. She knew he knew what he was doing but, even so, he was unarmed. What had happened between them last night had really meant something to her, and she wasn't entirely sure she liked feeling that way. It made her feel too vulnerable.

The black man finished his cigarette as Tina focused in on him again, and stubbed it underfoot before going back inside the house, but this time as he turned away from Tina's view she saw quite clearly that it was the handle of a gun poking out of his waistband.

That was enough to call in the reinforcements. If there was a young woman being held in there against her will and facing death – and from what Ray had told her, Tina was pretty sure there was – the sooner the police got here the better. Putting down the binoculars, she reached for her phone and checked that she still had a signal.

The sound behind her was barely audible, a tiny scrape on the stone, but Tina still turned round fast, just in time to feel a shoe slamming down on her chest, pinning her to the ground. She looked up, her view of the man standing above her obscured by the bright sunlight, but there was no mistaking the hat he was wearing, or the gun pointing down at her face.

'So,' said the man almost playfully, 'we meet again.'

Fifty

I'd followed the woods round to the south of the farm, crossing
the track leading down to it and passing close to the river, before
slowly making my way down a steep forested hill, heavily overgrown with brambles, that led down directly behind the small
outbuilding and the kennels. I used my compass to guide me as
there were no footpaths visible, and kept my eye out for hidden
cameras. Twice on the hill I lost my footing, and the second time
I almost stepped off the edge of a hidden twenty-foot bluff that
probably would have broken my legs if I'd gone over. But eventually, exactly twenty-two minutes after I'd started, the hill gave
way to the grassy flat of a valley, and the wood turned into an
apple tree orchard through which I could see the outbuilding and
the kennels next to it up ahead.

Before that there was another fence with a Keep Out sign on

it, similar to the one I'd cut through earlier. I stopped and made a hole in this one too, unworried about my continual breaking of the rules. If I was wrong about this place then I'd only been responsible for a small amount of criminal damage for what I hoped was a good cause. But if I was right, I was helping to catch a group of serial killers who'd been operating under the noses of the authorities – and for all I knew in cahoots with them – for far too long.

I thought of Dana Brennan then, riding off to the shop to buy some ingredients for baking and disappearing into thin air on a glorious summer's day, never to be seen again. I imagined her abductors murdering her in some bizarre night-time ceremony and the terrible gut-wrenching fear she must have experienced in those final minutes as she died alone and terrified, far from the protective arms of her parents, and I felt my resolve hardening.

As I crawled through the gap and walked in a low crouch towards the buildings, using the trees and long grass as cover, and making sure I stayed well upwind of the dogs, I told myself not to let anger or recklessness get the better of me. This was a reconnaissance exercise, nothing more.

But that was my problem. It wasn't.

I had a basic plan. Set up the spy camera in a suitable spot, record anyone coming in or out of the farm, then go back to our vantage point and keep watch, even if that meant staying here all night. At the first sign of any suspicious activity I'd dial 999 on the disposable phone I'd brought with me, make some exaggerated claim of a shooting at the farm, then wait for the police to arrive and catch the bad guys in the act of whatever they were doing.

As I got close to the outbuilding, I saw that it was little more than a large shed. I went down on my front, crawling on my stomach until I was level with the front of it, and in a position where I could see across the courtyard to the main house and the barn next door. Nothing moved in either building and the dogs remained quiet. But the girl was in there somewhere.

Keeping close to the shed so I couldn't be seen, I took the replica Browning air pistol I'd threatened Cem Kalaman with out of my backpack. The pistol felt good in my hand, and a voice in my head told me just to walk across the courtyard, go straight into the house, and find the girl. I dismissed it immediately. I wouldn't get five yards without setting off the dogs, and if anyone called my bluff with the pistol, I was a dead man.

I was going to have to be patient.

I looked at my watch: 1.39. I'd been gone twenty-nine minutes. Slowly I got to my feet and poked my head round the front of the shed. There was no one around, and feeling that burst of adrenalin that always comes with the prospect of danger, I inched out of my hiding place and crept over to the shed door, knowing I was completely exposed.

I tried the handle. It opened and I stepped inside, shutting the door gently behind me. The interior smelled of cobwebs and engine oil. Tools of various sizes and shapes lined the rickety shelves, and there were three large, chest-high barrels in a row against the far wall behind a sit-on lawnmower. Hanging next to them were two biohazard suits that looked like they'd been worn a fair few times. I found a thick pair of elbow-high gloves on one of the shelves, and put them on as I went to take a closer look. The barrels were stainless steel and unmarked, and I guessed from the scratches on them that they'd been here a long time. I released the catch on the top of the middle one to break the seal and slowly pulled the lid open.

As it came free I was immediately assailed by a powerful chemical smell as vapour rose from the clear liquid inside. Turning away so that it didn't overcome me, I quickly replaced the lid. This was acid. Possibly hydrofluoric, more likely sulphuric, and in industrial quantities like this there was only one reason it would be here.

To dissolve bodies.

I took a deep breath, removed the gloves, picked up the pistol from the shelf where I'd put it and went back to the front of the shed where a small window gave a perfect view over to the main door of the house. I put down the pistol, took the spy camera out of my backpack, and made a space for it between two old cans of paint on the windowsill while I pondered what to do in the light of this new discovery.

Which was when the dogs started barking ferociously.

I froze, wondering why they'd only just caught my scent now rather than when I was outside the shed door a minute earlier. Then I saw Tina coming into view, a blindfold over her eyes, being pushed along by a man in a hat whose face I couldn't see, but who was pressing a gun into her back.

I pulled out my phone, then cursed when I saw I had no service here in the valley. I crouched down out of sight and dialled 999 hoping some other carrier had a signal here, but the call failed. I watched as the man walked Tina over to the door of the main house. Twenty yards separated us, no more, but there was no way I could take him out before he turned his gun on me, and even as I was trying to work out what to do, the door opened and a black man I immediately recognized from Dan Watts' surveillance photo as Jonas Mavalu emerged. Mavalu had a short conversation with the man in the hat before shoving his head back inside the door and shouting to someone inside.

Tina turned and ran, trying to take advantage of the distraction, but she got no more than a yard before the man in the hat yanked her back by her hair and drove a knee into her coccyx, sending her crashing to her knees. Before she could get up, Mavalu strode over and kicked her in the ribs. Tina squirmed in the dirt and the pain on her face made me feel sick.

The next second, two more men, both white and dressed in farm overalls, came out of the house. One of them was holding a double-barrelled shotgun. The other helped Mavalu haul Tina to her feet, and I saw that Mavalu had a gun pushed down in the back of his jeans. The two of them frogmarched Tina over to the barn before manhandling her inside. Meanwhile the man in the hat said something to the one with the shotgun – an older, grizzled-looking guy who looked like he'd worked outside his whole life – but I couldn't hear what above the sound of the dogs barking. They talked for a good minute and then the guy with the shotgun started walking purposefully in the direction of the kennels, pulling a couple of shells from a pouch attached to his belt and loading the weapon, while the man in the hat hurried back inside the main house.

I took stock of the situation. Tina was unarmed and currently helpless, so it was four of them against one of me, and at least three of the four had guns. If I went back the way I'd come and called the police when I got a signal again, the chances are they wouldn't be here for half an hour, maybe longer. By which time Tina could be dead. And if they let the dogs out, I'd be caught before I even made the call. Then we'd both be dead.

In the end, it was self-preservation rather than bravery that propelled me to act. I counted to five to give the guy with the shotgun time to walk past the shed en route to the kennels, picked up the air pistol and opened the shed door. I couldn't see the man in the hat anywhere so, moving as quickly and quietly as possible, I walked out of the shed in the direction of the kennels. Ten yards ahead of me, I could see that the guy had propped up the shotgun against the kennel fencing and was leaning down to open up the mesh gate where the two Rottweilers waited eagerly. Since Tina had disappeared they'd calmed down, but as soon as they saw me they started barking again.

I couldn't afford to have the guy open the gate and let the dogs out so I broke into a run, turning the pistol in my hand so I was holding it like a club.

He heard me and swung round, his mouth open in shock, then lurched for the shotgun.

He never made it. I charged into him, slamming the butt of the pistol into the side of his head and sending him backwards into the kennel fencing as the dogs went wild. The blow had dazed him but I struck him three more times, twice in the forehead and once just below his eye. The pistol broke on the last blow and half the handle fell off, but the guy was already unconscious as he slid from my grasp and dropped to the ground.

I wasn't sure how badly I'd hurt him but I'd worry about that later. As long as he was incapacitated for a while, that was all that mattered.

This was all about speed now. With the dogs still barking, I picked up the shotgun, grabbed a couple of spare shells from the guy's pouch, stuffing them in my pocket, and ran towards the barn where Mavalu and the other guy had taken Tina, half expecting to see the man in the hat aiming a gun at me. But I couldn't see him anywhere, although with the noise the dogs were making he was going to realize something was wrong very soon.

As I reached the barn door, I heard it. The unmistakable rattle of a chainsaw being fired up. Coming from inside. And I remembered what Dan Watts had told me about Jonas Mavalu, how he'd once supposedly dismembered a man with a chainsaw.

I tried the door. It was open. Taking a deep breath as my heart beat loudly in my chest, I pushed it open the rest of the way and, with the shotgun raised in front of me, went inside.

The room was large and gloomy, two skylights in the roof and a single bulb hanging down providing the only light. Tina was in the middle of the room. She was sitting with her back to me in a steel chair that had been bolted to the floor, a thick leather strap round her midriff holding her in place. Off to one side of her stood the man who'd helped Mavalu bring her in here. He was holding a dirty rag in one hand and a bucket in the other, and he was watching intently as Mavalu stood directly in front of Tina with the chainsaw raised in both hands, an unpleasant smile on his face which vanished the moment he saw me.

I stood back against the door, propping the shotgun beneath my arm and searching for the lock with my free hand, all the time watching both men. I found the bolt, pulled it across, and stepped away from the door, aiming the shotgun at Mavalu, who seemed to be the only one who was armed.

'Move back and put down the chainsaw,' I shouted, taking another step forward.

'It don't work like that,' he shouted back over the noise, moving the blade so it was only a few inches from Tina's neck. The slightest movement and it would rip through her flesh, severing her jugular and killing her in a matter of seconds. 'Put the gun down or I'll kill her. Right now.' He moved the blade even closer, until it was almost touching the skin. 'Do you think I won't do it? The only reason she's alive is because I needed to find out who else was with her. Now I know. Which means she's no use to me.'

'Touch her and you die,' I called out. 'Put the chainsaw down and you live. The police are on the way.'

Mavalu hung his head low and glared at me like a bull surveying a rival, the veins on his neck standing out. He shook his head, his huge hands steady on the handle. 'You've got five seconds or I take off her head,' he roared. 'And I've had plenty of practice.'

The thumping in my chest grew louder and I felt lightheaded. I could see the other guy inching towards me. He was young and looked determined. I had only seconds to resolve this situation but I didn't know how I was going to do it without risking Tina's life. I couldn't even imagine what she was thinking right now, and I was thankful I couldn't see her face, because I suspected her fear would have been infectious.

If I put the gun down I was dead. We both were.

'Four!' yelled Mavalu. 'Three!'

I knew then I wasn't going to lower the weapon, that I was almost certainly going to lose the only woman I'd had feelings for in the last five years. But I had no choice. If I died, the investigation was finished, and I couldn't have that. I'd made a promise.

'Two!'

I kept the gun pointed at Mavalu's chest, making calculations in my head. If I hit him in his right shoulder I might knock him and the chainsaw backwards and when it dropped it might just miss Tina. But I hadn't fired a shotgun in years. I almost certainly wouldn't get it right.

Somewhere deep down I felt the panic building. Tina was going to die. I was going to be responsible.

'Last chance, boy!' roared Mavalu, his eyes alive with the thrill of violence.

My finger tensed on the trigger and I moved the shotgun ever so slightly upwards. The man with the bucket inched further towards me. The chainsaw roared in my ears.

In one movement I swung the gun sideways and shot the guy with the bucket in the chest, the blast echoing round the room as he went down like a lead weight, sending the bucket clattering. Then I swung the shotgun back towards Mavalu, who'd already thrown down the chainsaw and was pulling the pistol from the back of his jeans as instinct took over, just as I'd hoped. I didn't have time to see if Tina was unhurt. I fired again, just as Mavalu cracked off a shot at me.

Surprisingly, at least to me, I hit his right shoulder, taking out a big hunk of flesh, while his round missed me. The gun flew out of his hand, clattering across the floor, as he staggered backwards, staring at the injury in shock.

His hesitation gave me a valuable headstart and I sprinted over towards the gun, swinging the shotgun round my head one-handed and flinging it at him.

Mavalu ducked as it flew past his head then he too ran for the gun.

He was closer but I was faster, and I literally dived the last few feet, acting on instinct rather than judgement, knowing that if I got this wrong I was probably dead. I hit the ground chest-first with a jarring thud, reached out, my fingers finding the trigger guard, and rolled round as he loomed above me, launching a ferocious kick into my ribs that knocked me bodily along the floor. I felt the wind come flying out of me but I had the wherewithal to keep my grip on the gun and start firing.

Mavalu still had momentum from his charge and he veered away from me and ran back towards the chainsaw, which was vibrating loudly on the floor a couple of yards from Tina's feet.

I aimed the gun at his back and fired in rapid succession, hitting him at least three times, and he fell to his knees. Even then he still had the strength and purpose to reach over and grab the chainsaw. I saw Tina's face, frozen in panic as she struggled vainly in the metal seat.

With a roar louder than the noise of the saw, and still on his knees, Mavalu lifted it one-handed above his head even as I shot him a fourth and a fifth time.

Tina screamed and I fired again, the sixth bullet taking off the top of Mavalu's head in a fine cloud of brain and bone just as he threw the chainsaw at Tina.

It seemed to arc through the air in slow motion, passing millimetres from her leg before bouncing across the floor towards the far wall; but then I saw the expression on Tina's face change to one of pain, and I realized it had made contact.

I was on my feet in an instant as Mavalu toppled forward, dead. As soon as I got to Tina I could see the cut on the top of her thigh leaking blood through the ripped fabric of her jeans and I prayed that it hadn't severed an artery. 'Don't move,' I said, forcing myself to stay calm as I removed the leather strap round her midriff and wrapped it as tightly as I could round her thigh.

'I'm all right,' she said quietly as I did up the strap. 'I think it only just caught me.'

I looked up at her and was relieved to see that she didn't seem to be going into shock. 'You need medical help and fast. Have you got a signal here?'

She reached into her jeans pocket and pulled out her phone. 'No.'

'Can you stand?'

She nodded, and I helped her to her feet.

I released the clip on Mavalu's handgun and checked the number of rounds I had left as Tina limped over to the chainsaw and switched it off. I handed her the gun. 'There are three rounds left in here. Take it, and as soon as you get a signal dial 999.'

Tina shook her head. 'There's still at least one of them left. It's the same man who killed Charlotte in France.'

'Leave him to me.'

I took out the two spare shells I'd grabbed from the guy at the kennels and fed them into the shotgun.

'You take the pistol,' she said, limping back over. 'You'll need it against him. I'll take the shotgun.'

I thought about arguing but decided against it, and we exchanged weapons.

'The guy in the house must have heard the gunfire, so he might be waiting for us out there. Follow me, OK?'

Tina nodded, and we approached the door on either side. Tightening my grip on the handgun, I unbolted it and flung it open, moving quickly out of the way.

No shots came, and after a few seconds I peered slowly round the doorframe. The courtyard was empty and I couldn't see anyone in the windows of the main house. I moved my head out further, looking round.

'What can you see?' Tina whispered.

'Nothing.'

'Be careful. This bastard's good. And he's cool with it.'

I continued looking and listening but everything was silent bar the occasional birdcall. 'OK,' I said after a few seconds, 'follow me out.' I stepped out on to the gravel, checking the windows of the house again, and heard Tina come out behind me.

A sudden flash of movement on the second floor caught my eye. I looked up just in time to see the flash of a gun muzzle through the half-open window.

Shots flew past my head and I immediately fired a round back as the figure in the window disappeared from view.

'Are you OK?' I shouted over my shoulder.

'I'm fine,' Tina called back.

'Then go. Round the side of the barn, away from the house. I'll cover you.'

I stood in front of her acting as a shield, my eyes shifting from window to window as I waited for him to reappear. I took a rapid glance over my shoulder and saw Tina limping along the side of the barn, the shotgun in her hands, her progress faster than I'd been expecting. From the angle she was at, she couldn't be seen from the house.

As I turned back round I saw movement behind the door to the main house, and the next second the glass exploded as more shots rang out in my direction. I dived to the ground, and as I looked back up I saw a face behind the broken glass staring at me, and I swear he was smiling.

Fifty-one

Jumping to my feet, I yelled at Tina to keep moving and ran towards the house, gun outstretched in both hands. I crouched down beside the door and shoved it open, staying out of sight, then peered in.

The door led into a large traditional kitchen with a wooden dining table on which there were half-eaten plates of food. The room was empty. I took a tentative step inside, then another, feeling myself being swallowed by the silence within.

I kept moving, one slow step at a time, conscious that I was breathing far too heavily. A single bead of sweat ran down my forehead and into my eye. I blinked it away and continued through the kitchen and into a large hallway where a wide staircase zig-zagged up to the next floor. I looked up but the balcony that ran round the top of it was empty. There were doors to my left and doors to my right, all half open. Strangely, even though I was putting every ounce of my concentration into trying to spot an ambush, I noticed that there were no pictures on the walls, or ornaments anywhere. The place was as empty as a show home.

I stopped in the middle of the floor, the carpet soft beneath my feet. And that was when I heard it. A thin rasping sound, like someone trying to clear their throat, but harsher. More urgent.

I walked slowly in the direction of the sound, my finger tense on the trigger, and saw that a door was open directly underneath the staircase leading down to the basement. The sound was coming from there.

It stopped for a couple of seconds then started again, but this time it was the sound of someone choking and gasping for air. I moved closer, conscious that I had my back to one of the half-open doors, and that this could be a trap.

Then I heard something else coming from down in the basement. A man's voice, soft, and with the faintest foreign inflection, calling up to me. 'Come down here, my friend,' he said, his tone strangely welcoming.

I stopped at the door and looked down into the darkness. At first I could see nothing; then, as my eyes adapted, I made out a steep flight of steps leading down to a room with an uneven cement floor. A feeling of claustrophobia swept through me as long-ago memories of a night trapped in a cupboard while my father tried to find me came racing to the fore.

'I'm here, my friend,' came the voice again. 'Waiting for you.'

And then, as I watched, a teenage girl, probably no more than seventeen, staggered into view. Her feet were bare and she was wearing a black dress. A steel collar, attached to a thick, rattling chain, had been placed round her neck, and when she looked up at me I saw that her mouth was open and full of blood. She was trying desperately to say something but no words would come out, and it took me a couple of seconds to realize that her tongue had been cut out.

She spat out a mouthful of blood and tried to climb the steps but the chain only let her go as far as the second. There was such pain and pleading in her dark eyes that it made my stomach turn over. Instinctively I turned round to check that no one was coming up behind me, but the hallway remained empty.

I knew it was a trap. It had to be. The guy was inviting me into the cellar. But I couldn't just stand where I was, watching this girl, now on her knees as the blood poured down her chin, desperately trying to take the collar off her neck.

I had to go down there.

Into the blackness. Into a small dark space with no light. And if the door shut behind me, I'd be trapped down there for ever.

My legs felt like lead; the fear crawled up my spine like cold fingers; but I confronted it and forced it back down, as I'd always had to do, and began descending into the darkness.

The girl looked at me. The blood was everywhere now and I knew that there was no way she could survive this. That my coming down here was pointless.

I mouthed the words 'Is he there?' and she took a quick glance and shook her head wildly, motioning for me to get the collar off her.

I raced down the last of the steps and she grabbed me in her arms as I stepped into the basement, looking round in both directions. The room was big, the size of my apartment, and straight away my eyes focused on the huge bed with chains attached to it against the far wall. Even in the gloom I could make out the pentacle above it with the flowing 'M' inside – the symbol of the killers of Dana Brennan and Kitty Sinn. Beside it a doorway led through into another, even darker room.

The girl was wriggling in my arms, making frightened, gurgling noises, and I could feel her blood soaking into my shirt. Knowing I only had a very short time to save her, I felt round her collar looking for a release but could only find a heavy lock that was going to be too hard to break. I needed a rag or something to stop the bleeding.

That was when I smelled it. Petrol. The girl's dress was wet with it.

In that same moment the room beyond the doorway was lit up by a single flame from a lighter, and in the shadows the flame threw up I saw a pale, ghostlike face smiling at me from beneath the brim of a hat.

I fired a shot, the noise almost deafening in the confines of the room, but the face had already been swallowed up by the darkness, while the flame seemed to sail through the air before hitting the floor and becoming a line of fire racing towards me as the fuel was ignited.

Instinct took over. I threw myself free of the girl as she burst into flames, making a sound from deep inside her that I will hear in my nightmares for ever, then raced up the stairs as the entire basement became a wall of fire and heat.

And then, as I reached the top step, an explosion shook the building and I was thrown headfirst across the floor with such force that I ended up smashing through one of the half-open doors and into another room.

Rolling on to my back, I turned and saw a ball of flame like a dragon's breath erupting from the basement door and scorching the wall opposite. I was out of range of the flames but I knew I had to get out fast.

Still dazed by the blast, I realized that I'd lost the gun, and there was still one bullet left in it. I got to my feet and looked around, saw the gun a few feet away, and picked it up. There must be another exit from the basement, which meant that the man in the hat had to be close by and like me, he was going to want to get as far away from this house as he could.

I ran out into the hallway, reeling against the heat, through the kitchen and back out of the door.

The man in the hat was over by the kennels, putting a bullet into the prone body of the man I'd knocked unconscious earlier.

I ran towards him, holding the gun two-handed, knowing I had to get a perfect shot, but he'd already opened the kennel door and suddenly the two Rottweilers were out and running at me, barking ferociously.

The man in the hat lifted his gun, fired two shots my way with a casual nonchalance that suggested he didn't really care if he hit me or not, and then I was forced to concentrate all my attention on the dogs. The first one was already leaping at my throat as I pulled the trigger, taking it somewhere in the chest. Momentum still drove it into me, knocking me to the ground, and the next moment the second dog was on me, its jaws only inches from my face as I put both hands round its huge neck in a desperate bid to hold it off.

My arms quivered, began to give . . . and then another shot rang out. The dog let out a pitiful yelp and fell off me.

Still lying where I'd fallen, I looked up and saw Tina limping towards me, the shotgun in her hand.

'The police are on their way,' she said, stopping in front of me.

Slowly I clambered to my feet and looked over to the kennels and the orchard beyond. There was no sign of the man in the hat.

'He got away,' I said, panting from the shock and exertion of the last few minutes. 'And the girl's dead. I failed.'

Tina shook her head. 'We're alive, Ray, and I'd call that success. They'll find the guy, especially if he's taken off on foot.'

'I hope so,' I said, but I wasn't sure I believed it.

She took my arm and together we half walked, half staggered up the driveway as behind us explosions ripped through the farm buildings, destroying the evidence of what had gone on there.

For the moment at least, the battle was over.

Two Weeks Later

Fifty-two

The last of the evening sunshine was glinting through her kitchen window as Tina Boyd put the finishing touches to the Moroccan lamb and chickpea stew she was cooking. She wasn't much of a chef but she'd found this recipe in an old Gary Rhodes cookbook at her parents' place and had added her own improvisations, making it something of a signature dish.

She looked at her watch again, but only ten minutes had elapsed since the last time she'd looked, and it was still twenty minutes before he was due to arrive. She smiled to herself as she realized how much like a teenage girl she was acting. But the truth was, she was falling for Ray Mason. They'd seen each other four times since that day at the farm in Wales, and this would be the first time they'd seen each other two nights in a row. Tina had had false dawns before where relationships were concerned, and had lost the man she'd long considered the love of her life eleven years ago. But she was allowing herself just to go with the flow with Ray and see where it took them.

She leaned over to empty some chopped coriander into the pot and felt the itch of the scar where the chainsaw had cut her that day. The wound had required fourteen stitches and would leave a permanent mark, but of course it could have been so much worse, and she shuddered as she recalled the way Jonas Mavalu had held the chainsaw just inches from her neck, and how she'd come within seconds of dying.

Both she and Ray had survived the interrogations of the investigating officers afterwards, who'd wanted to know how they'd ended up amid a pile of burning ruins containing four dead bodies in the middle of a national park two hundred miles from home. To protect Ray's contact Dan Watts, and the unofficial undercover operation he'd been running, they'd concocted a story about how they'd been carrying out an unofficial surveillance op on Jonas Mavalu and had followed his car down to the farm. It wasn't particularly plausible, and it was clear the police didn't believe them, but the discovery of partially dissolved bone fragments belonging to at least six different people buried in the grounds, two of whom were women who'd been missing for years, had served to deflect attention away from them both, and just about kept Olaf off Ray's back.

The investigation into who'd murdered the girls was ongoing but so far, according to the newspapers, no one had been arrested, nor was it known who exactly owned the property, given that the offshore company listed was owned by another offshore company, and so on. So far, too, the Kalaman name hadn't made it into the newspapers. Jonas Mavalu might have had ties to Cem Kalaman but they were loose. The trafficked girl who'd died had not been identified; nor had the man in the hat, who'd almost killed Tina in France. He'd disappeared into thin air. As for Lola Sheridan, because Dan Watts' use of the tracker devices that connected her to both his informant and the trafficked girl was unofficial and therefore illegal, and Tina's sighting of her car at the house in Little Chalfont was inadmissible, there was no evidence against her for anything. As far as Tina knew, Lola's name hadn't even come up in the investigation. Nor had her brother Alastair's.

So the Welsh farm case remained open, as did the Dana Brennan/Kitty Sinn case, and for the moment Tina and Ray were planning their next move. He was still suspended and had been threatened with arrest for obstruction of justice if he was caught again interfering with police investigations, but there was no way they were going to give this one up. They owed it to the dead.

But tonight they wouldn't talk about that. Tonight they'd eat, relax and talk. They both deserved that.

The sound of her mobile ringing interrupted Tina's thoughts and she immediately hoped it wasn't Ray saying he was going to be late.

She picked up the phone from the kitchen table and saw that it was from an unknown caller. She never liked to answer calls when she couldn't see the number, but for some reason she made an exception this time.

'Tina?' said a familiar-sounding woman's voice down the other end of the line.

Tina frowned. 'Who's this?'

'It's Charlotte Curtis.'

FIND OUT MORE ABOUT
SIMON AND HIS BOOKS ONLINE AT

www.simonkernick.com

 /SimonKernick

@simonkernick